French Toast

Glynis Astie

Happy Reading!

To my mother, Joann, for always reminding me that anything worth doing will be challenging.

And to my father, Alfred, for helping me to laugh through it.

Chapter One

I closed my eyes and took a deep breath. She couldn't possibly be serious. Could she? I opened my eyes, looked over at Louis and tried to smile. I can only imagine the look which registered on my face, but I highly doubt it was anything remotely positive. Louis had just finished telling me about his mother's latest plans for our wedding. I took another deep breath and reminded myself, yet again, *I* had agreed to let her plan the wedding in its entirety (with the exception of choosing my wedding dress). Why would I agree to something so *completely* insane? It might have had something to do with the fact that this would be our third wedding.

Indeed, I said THIRD wedding and no, I don't have an Elizabeth Taylor complex. And I can prove it! Allow me to give you the short version. After a disastrous romantic history dating back to college, I, Sydney Bennett, was swept off my feet by the incredible Frenchman, Louis Durand. Louis was in California on business, but following our first week together, he accepted a transfer from his company's Paris office to the San Jose office.

To the great shock of our families and friends, we became engaged a few weeks later. We began planning a beautiful wedding in Monterey for the following September, only to be thwarted by Louis' unexpected job loss in January. In order to avoid his deportation, we were married shortly thereafter in my home town of Haverstraw, New York. So my dreams of a beautiful wedding wouldn't be crushed, we elected to have the originally planned event in Monterey as well. Everyone needs gorgeous wedding photos! The first wedding was definitely more practical than gorgeous.

One would think two weddings would be more than enough for one couple in love, but due to Louis' status as an only child with an extremely large extended family and his mother's dream of a wedding which his whole town (population: four hundred) would attend, we simply *had* to have one more wedding. Besides, a wedding in the beautiful French countryside sounded amazing, right?

This way my family and I would have the opportunity to experience the wedding customs of Louis' country as he and his family would experience the customs of ours at the wedding in Monterey. (The first wedding was kind of light on customs as it was predominantly a vehicle to keep Louis in the country.) My mother and siblings were thrilled at the prospect of a trip to France, while my father bemoaned his need to set foot in traitorous territory. He is German and likes to complain. Although I *knew* he was practically drooling at the prospect of the gastronomic experiences in his future.

While three weddings did afford a certain amount of stress, in the end, I think it helped me. My mother had planned the first wedding (in the span of one week), I was planning the second wedding (in the span of one year) and Louis' mother was planning the third (in the span of Louis' lifetime). This allowed for all parties to end up with a wedding they were happy with.

I must admit, the idea of having three different wedding dresses is kind of fun. Hey, now! There's no need to judge! The three events are *very* different levels of formality. The first was an informal town hall wedding, the second would be a formal evening wedding and the third would be an afternoon wedding in the French countryside. If you really think about it, you'll realize having three wedding dresses is an absolute necessity.

Now that my seemingly ludicrous statement of three weddings has been explained, we can return to the problem at hand. Louis has informed me of his mother's purchase of an ensemble for me to wear to the rehearsal dinner. (Honestly, this is becoming comical. This will be our THIRD rehearsal dinner.)

Let me remind you of Simone's very...particular fashion sense. All the garments she wears are short, tight, brightly colored and/or bedazzled. Given she is now sixty years old, my hat goes off to her. I hope I have the guts to wear miniskirts into my sixties. Having said that, I have never been one to dress quite so....um...how do I put this? My taste is *slightly* more conservative than hers.

Louis was nearly in tears from laughing so boisterously while he described the dress to me. Simone had chosen a gold sequined halter mini dress with red satin roses on the straps and red satin ruffles along the bottom of the skirt. She also saw fit to purchase red satin stilettos with matching red satin roses on the toes. I resisted the urge to strangle my husband and began to pace the room.

Clearly I made a serious error in judgment when I allowed Simone to make all decisions for the wedding except for my wedding dress. In my defense, I really didn't think her purview extended to my wardrobe choices for pre-wedding events. It was becoming quite obvious I had a lot to learn about her.

I attempted to slow my heart rate and let my mind wander. Everyone seemed to be enjoying the planning of our third wedding but me. This was mostly likely because I was the only one who would have to go through a number of humiliating experiences. Not to mention my complete focus on planning MY perfect wedding.

I know it sounds horrible, but I was invested in the second wedding, my *real* wedding, while I was merely a participant in our third and final, French wedding. I had yet to meet my mother-in-law and had no way to communicate with her since she doesn't speak English and I don't speak French. I kept meaning to sign up for lessons, but never seemed to find the time. Planning a wedding is very time consuming! I can barely fit in going to work.

Every day seemed to bring a new tale of woe for me and Louis was enjoying himself far too much for my taste. I was absolutely convinced he was making secret phone calls to my dad during the day, so they could enjoy my impending mortification together. My dad may have put Louis through the ringer when he first met him (as any father would upon finding out a "shifty French yokel" was going to marry his daughter after only knowing her for a few weeks), but now they were thick as thieves.

The more details I hear about the French wedding, the more scared I become. I realize when you think of a wedding in the south of France, scary is not the word that comes to mind. I think the more details which come to light will lead you to understand just how scary it can be.

The first hint of apprehension came when Louis informed me there would be four days' worth of activities leading up to the wedding, two of which would take place without the support of my family. (Apparently, some traditional French events were not meant for Americans, except the one who was seeking passage into the family.) I didn't think to ask any questions at this point, since we had just returned from our *first* wedding. My head was still trying to adjust to the idea of Louis as my HUSBAND and I had a million details to nail down for our Monterey wedding. (Yes, this is wedding number two; try to keep up!)

As I felt the familiar descent into anxiety, I closed my eyes and tried to calm down. My French was terrible and I was going to be surrounded by literally hundreds of people I didn't know, who had ridiculously high expectations of the woman who had captured Louis' heart. How could I possibly keep from embarrassing myself while being on display for FOUR days? Especially when I barely spoke the language and there would be so much wine involved???

I decided to let it go since I knew there were many French customs surrounding a wedding and it was my responsibility as Louis' wife to indulge his mother's desire for each and every one of them. I knew all too well I had to make epic concessions to her since she wasn't able to be there for our first (and legal) wedding. She had settled for viewing the ceremony via web cam and it simply wasn't the same as being there in person.

Especially when we are talking about the wedding of her only son to a woman whom she had yet to meet. A woman who had caused him to move to another country - far, far away from her. She had also generously allowed for the French wedding to take place last, thereby reducing my stress level as much as possible. At that point, I would have had my dream wedding and would just be acting out someone else's.

A couple of days later, Louis told me a few of his former girlfriends would be attending not only the wedding in France, but also a number of the pre-wedding events. He explained how close his mother had remained to them, since she had known them for so long and the town was so small. I took yet another deep breath (I really should practice meditation with all of the deep breaths I take) and resolved not to be insecure, knowing Louis loved me *and* he was already my husband. This was the mature choice, wasn't it?

Well, I also resolved to look as good as I possibly could. I had seen photos of his former girlfriends and they were all incredibly beautiful. I was smart enough to know I was going to have to try twice as hard to impress everyone due to my status as an American. At the very least, I was going look gorgeous while I was doing it!

While my mother and my sister, Kate, were sympathetic to what I was going to have to go through, my friend Maya thought it was HILARIOUS. Big surprise. She has always enjoyed laughing at my expense. In fact, she enjoys it so much she's going to attend the French wedding as well so she can take pictures of my humiliation to cherish for posterity. And maybe share with a few friends. Possibly a few strangers, just for fun. (Don't laugh! It actually happened once.) I think she plans to blow up the photo of me in the gold sequined dress to hang in her office. I already get strange looks from her coworkers due to photos from an unfortunate night in New York City. I still don't know how I ended up in the river, but I'm sure she had something to do with it.

In direct contrast to my discomfort, Louis has been completely content throughout the French wedding planning process. He would be able to have a wedding surrounded by his family and friends, in his language, with his beloved cuisine. (Though he loved some American food, he felt we were light years behind France in terms of culinary skills.)

The entirety of our relationship thus far had taken place in the context of my country, my family, my friends and my culture. He had picked up his entire life and moved it thousands of miles for me, married me before anyone in his family had met me and had agreed to have my dream wedding before his own. The time had come for some of the focus to be on what he wanted.

It was for this reason, I kept my own discomfiture from him at the mention of the gold sequined dress. This third and FINAL wedding was really all about him and his family and if I had to endure a few fashion faux pas to keep everything running smoothly, then so be it. He had certainly gone through enough for me. Though we can have a discussion of my budding neuroses later. Right now, we have a wedding to finish planning...

Chapter Two

My first month as Madame Durand was absolute bliss. Louis had still not found a job and was therefore devoting all his time to pampering his new wife, including orchestrating an unforgettably romantic Valentine's Day. Thankfully, I earned enough from my job as a Human Resources Representative to cover our rent and basic expenses. Until he found a new job as a computer programmer, we would have to be very careful with our extraneous expenses and our entertainment budget was nonexistent. I guess it was a good thing we were newlyweds and wanted to spend most of our time alone in our apartment.

Kate was a little less than understanding when it came to the amount of time I spent with Louis. She had not been a newlywed for quite a few years and had little patience for not only my lack of presence, but also for my dreamy state when she managed to pin me down. Kate was seven and a half months pregnant and took the expression "raging hormones" to a whole new level. Her poor husband, Nick, was beside himself, since he had never encountered such a beast in the form of his wife. Kate was by definition perfect and this new iteration of her personality was not welcome. I kept reminding him, her transformation was only temporary and his loving wife would be back before he knew it.

Unfortunately for me, he seemed to need constant reassurance of this fact as well as consultation on a multitude of female "needs" which Kate had assigned him. I sighed when I saw his cell phone number pop up on my work phone for the fifth time that day.

"Hi, Nick! Did she not like the slippers we picked out?" My sister's revolving footwear desires were really starting to irk me.

"Slippers are fine. Moving on to item twelve on the list." Ah yes, the infamous list. The contents changed every day, with Nick receiving email updates from Kate on an hourly basis. She had been placed on bed rest two weeks ago and Nick was slowly losing his mind. I took a small sense of satisfaction in finally seeing a few signs of normalcy from this seemingly flawless couple.

"What's item twelve?" I rolled my eyes. What could she possibly need now? She had everything under the sun already.

Nick hesitated. "Um…" I heard papers shuffling in the background. Was he still trying to locate item twelve?

"Nick? Are you OK?" I was trying to imagine what heinously embarrassing thing she had asked him to procure this time.

He cleared his throat. "I really don't want to say this."

I suppressed a giggle. Nick had had to describe many feminine products to me over the last few weeks in a bid to arrive home with the correct item. "Just get it over with, Nick. You'll feel better." How bad could it be?

A muffled sound came over the line. "She wants….cream." His voice was barely above a whisper.

"OK. What kind?" Kate was really particular about her creams. Only certain ingredients, certain brands from certain stores; you get the idea.

"Well...it's cream for your...um....your....feminine parts." He sounded completely mortified.

I thought for a moment. "Which feminine parts are we talking about?"

"How many are there?" He choked out.

"Did her doctor prescribe it for her?" I was totally confused. He really needed to man up and tell me what it was. Especially since he couldn't deal with purchasing it himself!

"No! She wants cream for her...for her..." He started to cough.

I had reached my limit. "Nick! *Say* it!"

"Nipple cream! She needs nipple cream!" A huge chorus of laughter erupted from Nick's end of the line.

I couldn't help cackling, but quickly tried to cover my slip by clearing my throat. I don't blame Nick's coworkers for busting a gut over such a gem. "So, do you know what kind?" A few more giggles escaped before I could stop them.

I could only imagine the look of humiliation on Nick's face. "No idea. Maybe you could call her?"

I frowned. As a most unfortunate side effect of her pregnancy, my perfect sister had become a perfect *bitch*. It was all too bizarre. Speaking to her at this point in time was along the lines of trying to charm a dragon.

The laughter eventually died down on Nick's end of the line. He sighed. "Please, Syd? I don't think I can call now after the razzing coming my way. Talking to her will make it so much worse. You have *no* idea what she asks me to say to her."

I thought it over. He did have it way worse than I did. At least I had an office door I could close. Working in Human Resources afforded a few niceties which didn't befall most computer programmers, as important as they may be. "OK. I'll call her, but it'll have to be later in the day. I have to get to a meeting in about ten minutes."

There was silence at the other end of the phone.

I brought out my stern voice. "Nick, I'll call her as soon as I can. I'm running the meeting I mentioned, so I can't be late."

"OK." He sounded resigned. "*Please* don't forget."

After I promised him five more times I wouldn't forget, I hung up the phone. Imagine my surprise when it rang as soon as I put the receiver back in its cradle.

I lunged for the phone, nostrils flaring. He really had to get a grip. "Nick! I told you I would call her as soon as I could! I can't think about my sister's nipples right now!"

A slightly feminine guffaw emanated from the other end of the line. "Honey, if you're ever thinking about your sister's nipples, then we have a serious problem."

I slapped my hand against my forehead in exasperation. Thank God I had remembered to close my office door before my conversation with Nick. "Hey, Maya."

She scoffed. "Well, it's nice to chat with you too, Syd."

I exhaled loudly. "I'm sorry! Nick's driving me nuts."

"Hey, you gotta hand it to him. He's really dealing with a lot now and he hasn't run screaming. Your sister has lost it. She's like....Pregnantzilla. Seriously, you should sell tickets."

I laughed. While I'm sure my sister would slap Maya silly for such a statement, hearing her say it made me feel a little better. Between having the sole responsibility as breadwinner, planning my perfect wedding, hearing almost daily of new ways I would be embarrassed at our French wedding AND dealing with the downfall of my perfect sister, my nerves were fried.

"Thanks, Maya. I needed to laugh." I sighed.

"No kidding, Syd! Where have you been lately? Have you had ANY fun?"

"What about you? I haven't seen you in over a week! How is Mr. Wonderful?" Maya had been dating one of her coworkers for two months now. I was thrilled since the majority of her "relationships" lasted less than a week. The only frustrating thing was her stinginess with the details of her new amour, Devon. Considering she had made it her goal to extract every last bit of information during my courtship with Louis, I felt her lack of information was ridiculously unfair. Especially since I could really use some free entertainment...

"He's fine." Really Maya? That's it?

"Hell no, Maya. Not today!" I paused. "Need I remind you, my last conversation involved the discussion of my sister's nipples? I need this!"

She sighed. "Fine, Syd. He is a gorgeous, brilliant and funny man. He has gotten to know me better than anyone has before and he accepts me just as I am. Oh...and his talents in the bedroom are unparalleled. Happy now?"

Wow. Maya was the pickiest person I knew when it came to men. And I'm pretty picky! She had at long last met her match. I was beginning to think this day would never come.

"Syd? Are you there?" Irritation permeated her words.

I shook my head to snap myself out of my trance. "I'm sorry! I was at a loss for words. I...am thrilled for you."

She laughed. "Yeah, you really sound like it."

"I *am*! Maybe I would be able to show you this if you'd let me meet him."

Silence.

"Maya? I'm your closest friend. I'll have to meet him at some point."

"I'll think about. Gotta go! Love you, hon!"

Click.

I stuck my tongue out at the phone and hung it up. Really mature, I know. Even twenty-eight year old women have moments of juvenile behavior which must be expressed. I did feel a little better afterwards.

I glanced at my watch and jumped up from my desk. I was five minutes late for my meeting. I grabbed my laptop and ran, hoping everyone else was as behind as they normally were. The Human Resources team was meeting to go over a new benefit plan and I was leading the discussion. I felt sorry for my coworkers since my brain was not functioning as well as it normally did. I was simply not able to keep up my usual image of perfection. This was definitely one of those times when it would have to be good enough.

⌒

Thankfully, I managed to look like I knew what I was doing and we settled on a new dental insurance plan. This meant a butt load of informational meetings to be given for the employees and countless phone calls and emails for further explanation. I sighed at the prospect of how much time I would lose and resigned myself to bringing work home again tonight. This wouldn't go over well with my husband.

Husband! I was still trying to get used to this term. I had only known Louis for seven months and he was already my husband! Though I was absolutely thrilled to have found and married the love of my life, such a quick turn of events had left me a little breathless. The first year of marriage is supposed to be really hard. We were still getting to know each other and were under severe financial strain to boot. Everything seemed to be fine; so why did I have such a feeling of dread? Was I waiting for the proverbial other shoe to drop? What does that even mean?

I shook my head and turned off my computer. As I packed up my work bag, I thought about how much easier it would be if Kate were actually Kate instead of Kate the Dragon Lady. My sister had always helped me to keep a hold of my sanity. (It had a nasty habit of running away.) She was the one reminding me, along with my ever patient mother, "good enough is not nearly as wonderful as perfect, but it is good enough." When would I stop thinking everything in life had to be perfect?

I shut off the lights to my office and walked to the parking lot, talking to myself the entire way. You need to get it together, woman! Men like Louis are hard to come by. Don't blow it by succumbing to your freaky alter ego. I sighed as I got into the car and put my head on the steering wheel. Everyone expects this marriage to fail. In my heart, I believed Louis and I had what it took to make our marriage work. But the truth is, my brain was beginning to wonder if we had gotten married way too fast.

Chapter Three

My second month as Madame Durand was decidedly less blissful. The initial newlywed harmony was starting to wear with Louis' increasing stress level at not being able to find a job. He was also just plain bored. (There are only so many hours a day he could devote to a *productive* job search.) When he had been laid off from his job, he was forced to return the company rental car and we couldn't afford to buy a new one on my income alone.

Since he had yet to find the desire to get up early enough to drive me to work, this left him with nothing but a bicycle to make his way around town. This meant I still had to run the majority of our errands, including grocery shopping, on my way home from work. Adding this responsibility to my increasing workload was causing my precariously balanced sanity to slip. To my great dismay, I began to realize Louis was perched right next to me on the edge.

Bizarrely enough, I was alerted to the cracks in his calm façade by the state of his dreams. In our first few months together, Louis would wake me in the middle of the night by caressing my body and speaking to me in French. The overall effect was very romantic, though I imagine my lack of knowledge of French contributed to this assertion. He could've been telling me I needed to shave my legs and I would have had *no* idea. The funny thing was when I commented on his behavior the next morning, he had no memory of the interaction. As many of these nocturnal adventures ended with very satisfying sex which he also had no memory of, I felt a little guilty for the added spring in my step…

I knew trouble was brewing when I was awakened one evening to a loud banging sound. I opened my eyes to find Louis standing next the window in our bedroom. Was I crazy or was he trying to rip the blinds off the wall? Completely bewildered, and not entirely awake, I asked Louis what he was doing. After receiving no response, I walked over to him and touched his arm. He flinched, turned back to me and told me to get back in the boat. I'm sorry, did he just say the *boat*??? He continued to try to remove the blinds from the wall, insisting this would help us to keep the boat afloat. After ten minutes, I was able to coax him back to bed. He had absolutely no knowledge of this incident the next morning and firmly believed I had made it all up to give him a good laugh.

Over the next week, Louis woke three times with his heart racing, screaming in French that there was danger. (After the first night of his yelling, "*Aidez-moi!*" I had to find out what he was saying.) During one of these evenings, he even lifted me out of the bed and ran into the living room for protection.

I was having a hard time staying awake at the office due to my nightly rousings. Louis never woke up so he didn't suffer from fatigue during the day, but it was very difficult for me to go back to bed after all of the excitement. I had started drinking far more coffee than I could handle. Let us not forget I was also planning a wedding and dealing with an extremely pregnant sister. My fragile psyche was teetering on the edge of destruction. Something had to be done!

The next morning, I decided I had to bring the subject up with my husband soon or I was going to come apart at the seams. I had planned to discuss it with Louis at dinner, but he surprised me by getting up early. I had just finished drying my hair when Louis came into the bathroom to shower. I wondered if he had forgotten to tell me he had a job interview today. Some good news would be really welcome right about now.

"You look beautiful, *mon coeur*. Do you have to go to work today? You could play hooky…" He began to kiss my neck.

I smiled. "I would love to, Bluey, but I have a mountain of work waiting for me." Simply the thought of it made me want to crawl back into bed.

He wrapped his arms around my waist and chuckled. "I have not heard you call me Bluey in a long time. I missed it."

I thought about it. I guess I hadn't used this endearment in quite a while. You may be wondering where on earth it came from. You will be astonished to hear it was the result of one of my legendary slips of the tongue. Early on in our relationship (a whole six months ago), I had tried to pull off calling him "Boo", but chickened out and tacked his name onto the end. The end result was "Bluey" which stuck due to his incredibly beautiful blue eyes. I still found them to be completely mesmerizing.

I turned to face him and put my arms around his neck. "I love you, Bluey." I kissed him tenderly and attempted to finish getting ready for work. Louis, it would seem, had other plans for me.

He began unbuttoning my blouse and whispering to me in French. For a couple of minutes I was completely distracted, but a sudden jolt of reality crept in as I thought of the stack of paper on my desk. I tried to pull back so I could tell him I really had to go, but he was persistent.

Ultimately, I had to swat him forcefully on the behind to get his attention.

"*Mon coeur*! I did not know you had such spunk in you!" He quickly returned to undressing me.

"Bluey! I have to go to work!" I removed his hands and began to redress myself in a hurry.

"You *could* stay home with me today, you don't *want* to." His eyes flashed angrily. Uh oh. Louis pretty much always maintains a calm demeanor. This job search must be hitting him a lot harder than I thought.

I sighed. "I'd much rather be here with you." I walked over to him and held his face in my hands. "I'm really sorry, but I have to go. Someone has to pay our bills." Oh shit!

He removed my hands from his face and stormed out of the room. Crap. I had insulted his masculinity to the umpteenth degree. I would have to take the time to fix this and be late to work. Otherwise, I may not have a husband to come home to.

I took a moment to collect myself before going after him. He must be absolutely seething after my thoughtless comment. I was incredibly lucky that Louis had been sensible enough to walk out instead of exploding at me. He had been bottling up his emotions for the past two months and he could no longer contain them. In my haste to make it to work on time, I had pushed him too far.

After I had mentally prepared myself for facing Louis' wrath, I walked out to the living room to find him. I frowned at the empty room. Where did he go? My eyes frantically darted around the apartment, looking for traces of an angry Frenchman. Then I noticed the door to the balcony was open. I ran over and found him leaning on the railing, looking extremely pissed off.

I slowly walked onto the balcony and stood next to him. "Bluey….I'm so sorry. I didn't mean to say what I said. It just came out all wrong." I had been so tired lately, it was a miracle I was forming coherent sentences.

He glared at me. "It is exactly what you meant. I am not fulfilling my responsibility as your husband. I am supposed to support YOU. My unemployment is …shameful."

I closed my eyes. This is going to take longer than I thought. I realize the average American man feels such a responsibility towards his wife, but Louis was not only French, but also from an extremely traditional family. Many of his aunts were housewives and even those female relatives who worked made considerably less money than their husbands. Louis' current difficulty in finding a job was challenging his French sense of self-worth. Being supported by his new American wife was nearly the most emasculating thing he could imagine.

I tentatively put my hand on his back. "Louis, you have no reason to be ashamed."

He scoffed. "I decide to differ." I tried not to smile. We still had some work to do on his American expressions.

"Bluey, look at me." He reluctantly turned my way. "This is just a rough patch for you. The economy has tanked and finding a job has gotten harder."

He frowned at me. "It shouldn't be this hard for *me*." I really had to stifle a laugh this time. While I was always reminding myself that *I* wasn't perfect (and this was OK), Louis really believed *he* was perfect. In some ways we were a completely bizarre match.

"You have to keep in mind, while you're great at your job, there are very few opportunities out there right now. Many people get jobs because they know someone, not because they are necessarily the best for the job. You need to get out there and network."

He regarded me quizzically. "How will setting up a network help me find a job?" Ah, the miscommunication which occurs when you live with a computer programmer who speaks English as a second language.

I grinned. "Not a computer network, a people network." He appeared even more confused. "You join organizations for computer professionals, attend continuing education seminars relevant to your field and conduct information interviews with computer professionals in the area. The more people you meet, the larger your network becomes, opening you up to many more job opportunities."

Louis watched me for a moment. Then he broke out into a huge grin. "You Americans are crazy! You have a detailed plan for everything."

I laughed. "Don't knock it until you try it, Frenchie!"

He scooped me into his arms and laughed until tears came out of his eyes. Thank God! The tension had been broken and my Bluey was back.

I stroked the back of his neck. "The combination of your amazing intellect and kick-ass charm will definitely land you a job. Networking is exactly what you need!" And it was exactly what *I* needed to get him out of the house and in a better mood. Being around the house all day had made Louis into a very cranky version of himself which I didn't recognize.

Louis sighed. "What would I do without you, *mon coeur*?"

I gazed up at him and smiled. "You'll never have to find out."

I kissed Louis good-bye and left for work in a much better mood than I had anticipated. I was still completely exhausted, but I felt like I had gotten through to Louis and he was on the upswing. I knew I had chickened out on broaching the subject of his unhappiness, but my pep talk had gotten him to where he needed to be, so I decided it was a win. With my brain functioning at such a low level, I had to keep everything as simple as possible.

One thing which continued to be far from simple was handling my sister, Kate. She was now two weeks away from her due date and had reached her limit with bed rest. Since she was bored out of her mind, she put her speed dial to use and called every member of our family until one of us was brave enough to pick up the phone. She had no qualms whatsoever about calling repeatedly until she got an answer. In her mind, her needs were more important than the status of anyone's employment.

I had been successful in dodging her calls three times that day, but knew my luck was running out. I decided to call my mom to see if she had spoken to Kate yet, and more importantly to find out if I needed to be concerned. I was the only family member in the vicinity, while the rest of those ungrateful bastards were in the safe cocoon of New York.

I rested my head on my hand as I dialed my mom's store and hoped the news would be good. I hadn't been to Kate and Nick's house in two days and was afraid for my life at this point in time. Kate may have been too large to cause any real damage, but Nick was absolutely mobile and had tension he needed to release. As I waited for my mom to answer I thought about the many ways in which he could try to come after me.

"Paintables, may I help you?" How odd. My mom has caller ID, which means she usually greets me by name.

"Hi, Mom!"

Silence.

"Mom, are you OK?" This was really, really strange. My mom ALWAYS gushed over me when I called.

She breathed a sigh of relief. "Syd, it's you. I thought it was Kate."

Crap. This can't be good. "Did something happen? Is Kate alright?"

My mom chuckled nervously. "She's fine, honey. She was rather...*animated*...during our last conversation."

Interesting. "When did this happen?"

"Oh...about ten minutes ago...." She trailed off quietly.

Something was definitely wrong. "Mom, what's going on? You sound weird."

"Weird? Why do you say that?" There was the freaky laugh again. My mom had a rich, guttural laugh which came out often. There was no hesitation to it whatsoever.

I was too tired for this bullshit. "Enough, Mom. Out with it! What happened?"

She exhaled loudly. "Your sister is simply tired, Syd. The hormones are taking over her body."

I enunciated my words very clearly. "What did she say, Mom?"

"Well, she…she said…um…" My mom was clearly at a loss for words. What did my hormone-addled sister come up with this time?

"Mom, I have aged about three years while I've been waiting for you to get this out. Please, for the love of God, just tell me." When I'm tired, my manners have the tendency to take a back seat. I managed to say, "Please!"

"She told me I was a 'fucking lunatic' because I wanted to be in the room with her when she gave birth."

I was momentarily stunned into silence, but my recovery was surprisingly quick for someone with my level of fatigue. "Well, being a 'fucking lunatic' runs in the family, Mom." And then I burst out laughing. I took a page out of Louis' book and laughed until tears were spilling down my face.

"Sydney Ben..Durand! It is not funny! Your poor sister isn't quite herself!" I could hear her making all of her "I'm so disgusted with you" noises. (I decided not to bring up her difficulty in remembering my new last name. This was simply not the time.)

I felt bad for embarrassing my mom, but I couldn't help it. I think I had heard my sister swear a total of five times in my entire life. Her pregnancy had kicked up her attitude something fierce!

After a few minutes, my mom succumbed and she and I laughed like idiots together. My father then picked up the extension in the back of the store and joined the conversation.

"Duck! What are you doing to your poor mother? All the customers are staring at her." He was feigning embarrassment, but I could tell he, too, was laughing his ass off. My dad had a wicked sense of humor, which included giving me the nickname "Duck" from his interpretation of my seven year old face when I pouted.

We really were quite a pair, my dad and I. I often forgot we didn't actually share any genes. He had adopted me and my siblings when he married my mother. I was seven years old when this had happened, so he had been the only father I had ever really known and I was truly grateful for his presence in my life. My biological father was more interested in his mistress than his children.

I slowly began the descent from my crazy spell. "Come on, Dad. They're only painting pottery. They could use a little entertainment!" This comment launched the three of us into a laughing fit which lasted another five minutes.

My dad eventually hung up to receive a delivery of bisque and my mom and I were left to recover together.

"So, Syd, you haven't told me how YOU are doing."

I thought it over. How much should I tell her? My mom was used to my boat load of crazy, but she was so worried about Kate at this point, I didn't want to spread her too thin. I decided to keep it simple.

"Everything is fine, Mom. Don't worry." Shit! Why did I say that? Telling her not to worry *always* makes her worry! I must be too tired to keep my usual cover in place.

She sighed. "Sydney Julia…Durand." This wasn't going to be good. But she *had* gotten the name right this time. "Now it's my turn to say this to you. Out with it!"

Damn it! I really sucked at pretending to be OK. "Well, Mom, I'm tired. Both physically and emotionally. I'm still learning about my new husband, work is killing me and I'm trying to help Kate and Nick as much as possible. Louis is really stressed, I don't get much sleep and I'm even more insane than I normally am."

She chuckled. "Is that all?"

What? Am I being mocked by my MOTHER?

"Sydney! Relax. I'm not making fun of you." Phew. I didn't think I could take it if she were. It was just too…weird. My mom ALWAYS has my back. Always.

She stifled another giggle by clearing her throat. "It's going to be OK, sweetheart."

See what I mean? Always.

"I want to believe you, Mom, but I'm rather overwhelmed right now."

"Sweetheart, of course you are, but you need to remember you're showing a lot of strength right now. You're taking care of your husband, your sister AND your brother-in-law, as well as all your employees. I'm really very proud of you. You're handling it all beautifully."

See that? Right there. I don't care how old you are, you always need your mother. I found myself smiling and could feel the tension draining from my shoulders. It was all going to be alright. Eventually.

"Thanks, Mom. I needed to hear your words of reason."

"I'm always here for you. *Stop* carrying the weight of the world on your shoulders."

I laughed. "Well, things do feel a bit heavy right now…" I could definitely give Atlas a run for his money. (Shout out to my fellow Greek myth nerds!)

"It will all work out. You'll see." I could hear the smile in her voice.

I glanced up and noticed Paul, my most persistent employee, waiting for me outside my office door. Clearly, I had another fun afternoon ahead of me. I wonder what issue he's come up with now. His last dental claim was almost the end of me. I never want to have to see those before and after photographs again. Ever.

"Mom, I have to run. Paul is waiting."

She caught her breath. "Good luck." I had shared more than a few of my "spirited" employee stories with my mom. (Minus the confidential details, of course.) Paul was one for the record books.

"Kiss Dad for me. I love you!"

"We love you too! Give Louis a big hug from us."

I hung up the phone and waved Paul into my office. After the day I had experienced thus far, I hoped just once he would bring me a question which was easy to answer.

⌒

After a thirty minute discussion with Paul about the benefit of life insurance for a single man, including the pros and cons of making his dog his primary beneficiary, I sent him on his way with a wide array of reading material. It suddenly occurred to me, Louis and I hadn't discussed making changes to our current life insurance selections. We were now two months into our marriage and I hadn't completed any change of beneficiary forms.

What was wrong with me? I lectured my employees often about the vital importance of keeping beneficiary information up to date. Did I secretly believe this marriage wasn't going to succeed? Did I not want Louis to have the money if I met an untimely death? Would it really matter at that point?

As I sat at my desk planning my next move, I wondered if I were really cracking up this time. The lack of sleep and crushing amount of stress both at work and home were threatening the minimal brain functioning I had retained. At the forefront of my mind was my relationship with Louis. I had been able to pull him out of his funk this time, but with the mounting tension at every turn, how long would we be able to avert disaster?

The pressure on the success of our relationship was becoming almost unbearable to me. I knew I loved him with all my heart, but was still unsure this would be enough to make our marriage last. There's a reason one in three marriages end in divorce! (Thank you, Mark Darcy, for this helpful statistic. Can you rely on a fictional character's accuracy with information like this?) Tired of trying to analyze every possible angle, I stood up and dusted the remains of my lunch from my sweater.

As I set off in search of my eighth cup of coffee for the day, I realized my lack of clairvoyant abilities meant I couldn't discern the fate of my marriage in my head. I would simply have to go about this the old-fashioned way. Hard work and a healthy dose of panic.

Chapter Four

At the start of the third month of my marriage, I concluded it might be important to finish planning my dream wedding. While the venue, photographer, flowers, dj, invitations, favors, bridesmaids dresses and most importantly, my dress, had been selected, I still had a lot of work to do. I had repeatedly pushed back our tasting session with the hotel, since I had not been able to narrow down my choices for possible *hors d'oeuvres* and entrées, had not made any progress with the cake selection (other than it would be chocolate) and had not been able to get Louis to commit to a decision on where we would go on our honeymoon. If we could afford to go on a honeymoon...

It suddenly dawned on me, our wedding was in six months and the number of important details which were still up in the air was astronomical. I had to make hotel reservations for out-of-town guests, plan the rehearsal dinner and the post-wedding brunch, select bridesmaid and groomsmen gifts....um....choose the tuxedos for my dad and brother....OK, I'm starting to hyperventilate. The list goes on and on and *on*. How would I ever be able to manage this on my own? Kate was no longer in her right mind and Maya was off with the man of her dreams. I was totally screwed. What a fun way to spend a Saturday morning!

Just breathe, Sydney. This is not a matter of life and death. NO, it really, isn't. No one is doing to die if you're not perfectly satisfied with the entrée selections or if you choose the wrong style bow tie for the father of the bride. You have found your dream dress, selected exquisite flowers for your bouquet, found a beautiful location for the wedding and booked an awesome dj for the reception.

I slowly began to calm down and decided it was time to visit my favorite wedding planning website. After I entered my login information, I rolled my shoulders and stretched my neck. It was time to get some serious work done.

As the screen was loading, I thought about consulting Louis on some of the wedding details. Maybe it would help him feel a little better if he had something else to concentrate on other than his job search. Yeah....and maybe I would enjoy going with him to his Thai boxing training! Louis enjoyed talking about wedding details about as much as I would enjoy donning protective pads and kicking other people.

At least he had found an outlet for his frustration at not being able to find a job. During the course of his networking adventures, he had come into contact with a man who owned a martial arts studio. Bastiaan was impressed with Louis' status as a five time national Thai boxing champion in France and asked him if he would be interested in teaching at his studio. Louis jumped at the chance for activity and spent much of his time there. Thankfully, this also brought us a small amount of money, since our bills were mounting.

After a very long two minutes, the screen with this week's wedding planning activities popped up. There were eighteen items on it. Wait...I'm getting married in six months, how do I have eighteen things to do this week???

I quickly perused the list. I didn't even know what half of the items were

How many events did people have leading up to their weddings? Create a video montage for the cocktail hour...I haven't even selected the food for the cocktail hour! Proper wording for the wedding invitations, speech structure for the wedding toast, necessary pre-wedding outings, selecting a theme for the rehearsal dinner, choosing the right confetti, coordinating escort cards with your invitations??? What the hell is an escort card? It was like a train wreck...but I *had* to keep reading. The importance of setting the tone for the bridal shower and bachelorette party....What??? Wasn't someone else supposed to plan those? Shouldn't Kate and/or Maya take care of these things?

I felt like someone had poured a bucket of ice water down my back. Kate and Maya were MIA, my mother was three thousand miles away *and* running her own business and my friend, Maggie, who moonlighted as a wedding planner was so overbooked she barely knew her own name. There was no way I could ask her for help without feeling like a giant ass. Things were getting desperate. I was heading towards a full-fledged Sydney freak out – which is something you NEVER want to see. There was only one thing to do. It was time to call in the big guns. The long-distance big guns.

I dialed my sister-in-law, Zoe's, cell phone, tapping my pencil on my wedding notebook as I waited for her to answer. Please pick up, please pick up, *please pick up*! While Zoe was not as familiar with my psychotic breaks as Kate, her no-nonsense attitude made her incredibly capable of handling me. The three hour time difference between New York and California and our opposing schedules made it difficult for us to chat often, but I was still very close to her. Although, I hated to expose her to my inner lunatic since she had joined our family voluntarily. Kate had no choice but to handle me; we were related by blood.

Zoe picked up on the third ring. "Hey, Syd! How are you, pretty lady?"

I sighed with relief. Thank God for Zoe. "Fine. How are you?"

She laughed. "Really? You're fine? Because it sounds like you're juggling enough to make anyone lose their shit."

I cackled. "OK, you got me. I'm dying!!!! I have a *ginormous* list of wedding things to deal with. Louis couldn't care less about anything and Kate and Maya have abandoned me. I wish you were here."

She sighed. "Kate hasn't abandoned you. She's almost nine months pregnant. I know she's…not quite herself, but she's really having a hard time right now. Be good to your poor sister."

That's easy to say for someone who's THREE THOUSAND miles away from her. But she was right. Kate had always taken care of me. And here I was being a total selfish bitch in her hour of need.

"You're right, Zoe. I'm a bad person." I paused. "I'm *really* stressed. I've stretched myself way too thin."

"Syd! You're not a bad person; you're just under a ton of pressure. Take a deep breath and try to relax."

"Are you high? I haven't been able to relax in over two months." Now, Sydney, there's no need to snap. You don't want to piss off one of your only functioning allies. "I'm sorry, Zoe. I'm….struggling." I felt tears forming in my eyes.

"Don't worry! We'll figure this out. Get out your crazy-ass list and let's go through it." Zoe knew I loved this website for its order and precision, but had told me *repeatedly*, it was also undoubtedly propaganda to get excited young brides to buy a whole lot of stuff they didn't need to create their "perfect weddings." She felt it was her job to help me cut through all the bullshit. Especially since Louis and I were on a tight budget. My parents had pledged to give us the same amount of money they had given to my siblings for their weddings (in installments), but even with our conservative choices, the wedding was shaping up to be pretty expensive, so we still had to kick in a decent amount ourselves.

Thirty minutes later, Zoe had helped me to whittle down the scary list to a much shorter, doable list, filled with things which were actually necessary. I breathed a sigh of relief.

"Thank you, Zoe. You have saved my sanity."

Zoe chuckled. "For the moment."

I shook my head. "Sadly, you're absolutely correct. Let's hope this bout of sanity lasts longer than the last one."

"Syd, you've got to learn to take things less seriously. You've already married a man whom you love very much. Now you're just planning a party." She paused. "A very important party, but a party nonetheless. OK?"

She was right. I wanted it to be beautiful, but it didn't have to be perfect. When would I ever get this through my head?

Zoe snapped me back to reality. "Alright, hon. I have to go. Your brother and I are going car shopping." She sighed dramatically.

I laughed. My brother, Charlie, was a huge car enthusiast. Zoe was in need of a new car and he took this need as an opportunity to explore a myriad of possibilities. She had a clear idea of what she wanted, but Charlie was like a kid in a candy store. He had to try out ALL the options. I felt sorry for Zoe as I thought of the conversations she would have to listen to about engine size, horsepower, torque and turbo chargers. Charlie really knew his stuff. His favorite thing to do since he was a teenager was to buy an old car and fix it up himself. Zoe; however, was not looking for another project.

"May the Force be with you." I said a silent prayer for her afternoon to be as painless as possible. "Thanks again for all your help. I really appreciate it."

"Any time, Syd. We're sisters, remember?"

Though she couldn't see me, I nodded my head. "Indeed we are. And I'm grateful. I love you, Zoe." I sniffled. Good God, woman! Get it together!

Zoe laughed. "I love you too. And don't worry! You're going to be fine. Say hi to Kate and Nick for us, OK?"

I shook my head to wake myself up. "Will do. Have a good time!"

After I hung up with Zoe, I thought about Kate. I was really pissed at myself for not being there for her in her time of need. She was going absolutely bonkers after over two months of bed rest and I was too wrapped up in my perfect wedding details to help her. I officially sucked. It was time I stopped being an idiot and took care of my perfect sister. Well, I hoped she would return to being my perfect sister after the baby was born.

⌒

After a quick phone call with Nick, I was on my way to their house to pick up Kate. She was going stark raving mad and had badgered her doctor until she agreed to let Kate go out for a quick duration. She had chosen her favorite vice, so my job was to take her to the Prolific Oven for their famous chocolate on chocolate cake. Not a bad choice for me at all. She could have wanted to do more shopping for the baby's room (Even though *literally* nothing more would fit in it.) Chocolate cake always made things look better. This was going to be good.

I hummed to myself as I walked up the path to her front door. I was about two feet away when the door swung open and Kate came waddling out. Wow! She seemed even bigger than she had when I saw her two days ago, during our rather unsuccessful attempt to stock the baby's dresser with clean clothes. Apparently I have no skill in folding onesies, those little footy pajamas or anything else for that matter...

I quickly plastered a smile on my face. "Hi, Kate! You look great!" Oooh, I might have gone a *little* too far.

She barely glanced at me. "Let's go. I'm hungry."

OK! Off we go. I helped Kate into the car and had a particularly hard time getting the seat belt around her in a safe yet comfortable way. It was no wonder Nick had been lamenting his need for a padded cell.

We quickly arrived at the Prolific Oven and I settled Kate at a table while I went to the counter to order the much-needed cake. After I had secured two servings of the most decadent chocolate concoction in existence and two decaf lattes, I sat down and peered tentatively at her.

"How are you feeling?" I cringed inwardly as I waited for the answer. Her moods were rather unpredictable.

She leveled her gaze at me and sighed. "Fat. Tired. Ugly. Evil." She chuckled. Is that my Kate in there? I think I can see her!

I smiled genuinely at her. "You're NOT fat. You're pregnant, Kate. And I don't care if you tell me I'm being cheesy, but I think you're beautiful."

Tears formed in her eyes. Oh crap! What have I done? No matter what I said, I upset her. Nick was going to kill me!

I grabbed her hand. "I'm so sorry! I didn't mean to make you cry."

She smirked. "Don't be silly, Syd. These hormones are killing me." She paused. "And everything hurts – my back, my legs, my ankles, my head… I'm always worried about the baby. And I'm *always* tired."

I felt a pang of sympathy. How could I have been such a jackass? My poor sister was going through so much and all I could think about was how she wasn't helping me. I had some serious growing up to do.

"Try not to worry, Kate." This sounded bizarre coming out of my mouth, but it was the truth. "You're almost there. Everything will be fine. Remember, Nick and I are here to take care of you." Though Nick had really been bearing the brunt of it lately. I had let him down too. That changes right now.

Kate blew her nose. "Ugh. I have to go to the bathroom again. Will you please help me up?"

I got up from my chair and gently brought her up to a standing position. She winced in pain for a second and almost immediately her features smoothed out. "It's getting harder and harder to stand up, Syd. This sucks!"

I was about to say something supportive to her when an expletive burst from her mouth. It seems Pregnant Kate swears like a sailor. Regular Kate would definitely not approve.

"Shit! I leaked again. I swear, pregnancy is a bitch on your body. I'm going to have to do a massive amount of kegel exercises to be able to stop from peeing myself after the baby is born."

Oh, man. "I'm sorry, Kate. Do you want me to take you home?" Pregnancy really is a bitch, *not* my sister.

She exhaled loudly. "No need. I carry an extra change of clothes in my bag." She hefted her enormous pregnancy tote. "This isn't the first time."

"Do you want me to carry your bag? Help you change?"

She laughed. "No, I got it, Syd. I'll be right back. Oh, would you please ask the waitress to have someone wipe down my chair? I'll have to leave an extra big tip…"

I was about to flag down the waitress when I turned my head to look at Kate walking away. Something wasn't right. She was leaving a trail of liquid behind her as she was walking to the bathroom. How could she not notice?

I quickly walked after her, being careful not to slip in her backwash. I gently tapped her on the shoulder. "Um….Kate?"

She jumped and turned to me. "Syd! I told you I don't need any help."

"Um…." I stammered. "I *think* your water just broke."

She glared at me incredulously. "Don't you think I'd know if it did?"

I breathed deeply. "Humor me and look behind you, towards our table."

She carefully turned her head and suddenly became very pale. I held out my arms for her before she fainted. "Don't worry, Kate. You're officially in labor. No big deal." I shook my head. "I'm going to take you to the hospital, OK?"

She beheld me with her deer-caught-in-headlights face and nodded almost imperceptibly. I took her tote bag, steered her back to the table slowly and grabbed my purse. I emptied the entire contents of my wallet onto the table (because can you really leave TOO much money as a thank you for cleaning up amniotic fluid?) and moved Kate towards the door.

Ten minutes later, we were in the car on the way to the hospital. Kate was wrapped in the emergency blanket I kept in my trunk and Nick and Kate's doctor were going to meet us in the labor and delivery unit. Kate and I were practicing her breathing rather than talking. "Hee hee, hoo. Hee, hoo." It was pretty catchy! Kate's contractions were ten minutes apart, so she wasn't in any danger of giving birth in the car, but we were both very anxious to get to the hospital. Neither one of us had any first-hand experience with the birth of a baby and we wanted the experts on the case as soon as possible. Sooner.

As we pulled up to the emergency room, I spotted Nick pacing back and forth while wringing his hands. When he caught sight of my car, he ran over and starting opening the door before I had come to a complete stop. This didn't bode well for the rest of the birthing experience. I really thought Nick was going to be the calm one in this situation. It would seem this role had fallen on me. I resolved not to fail this time. I would keep it together for the two of them. Somebody had to, right?

After Nick had safely transferred Kate from the car to the awaiting wheel chair, she looked at me with fear in her eyes. I got out of the car, despite the dirty look from the security guard, ran to her and hugged her gently.

"Don't worry." I whispered. "You can do this." I kissed her gently on the forehead.

She smiled weakly. "Please call Mom and Dad. Oh and Charlie and Zoe. And then get your ass up to the labor and delivery suite ASAP. I need you to hold my hand."

Nick regarded me with a nervous smile. "Relax, Kate. Syd is about to be an aunt. She wouldn't miss this for the world." Then he gave me a hug and whispered, "She's probably going to break your hand, so be sure to give her your left…"

With a smile frozen on my face, I waved good-bye to them and jumped back into my car. I quickly drove over to the visitor's parking lot, found a space and turned off the car. I took a quick minute to collect myself. I inhaled and exhaled deeply five times and then counted to ten. You can do this, Sydney!

I yanked my cell phone out of my purse and quickly made my phone calls. My parents were the definition of excited (particularly my mom, who hung up on me so she could call the airline to move her flight up since the baby was a few days early) and Charlie and Zoe gave me a quick pep talk for the delivery room. All four of them had made me promise to call the moment the baby was born.

As I rode up in the elevator, it occurred to me I had forgotten to call Louis. Shit! When was I going to start thinking like a wife? Your husband is pretty high on the priority list for matters like these. Concerned I had already taken too long to get to my anxious sister, I quickly texted Louis the details and promptly turned my phone off. Kate needed my complete focus right now.

However, despite my best efforts, I couldn't shake the concern from my mind about forgetting to tell Louis. I knew I was legitimately under pressure in getting Kate to the hospital, but I had honestly almost forgotten to call him. Where was the strong bond we had? We had barely seen each other over the past couple of weeks. Was this the direction our marriage was heading in? Or was this just a rough patch? With all these questions and more, I exited the elevator and went in search of Kate. I pushed my thoughts aside, fully aware that my marital concerns were simply not relevant right now. There was a baby on the way and I couldn't wait to meet her. Or him!

Chapter Five

At two thirteen the next morning, Kate, Nick and I were introduced to Samantha Erin Wilson. I was so tired, I thought I was going to die, so I could only imagine how Kate felt since she had done all the work. The only pain I had was radiating from what used to be my left hand. (Thanks for the tip, Nick!) Even though Kate had been given an epidural, the medication had run out in the height of labor and it wasn't possible to give her anything else. I'm now officially petrified of giving birth. Maybe Louis and I can adopt...

On the positive side, I've never seen Kate and Nick so happy and they are pretty much happiness personified. Samantha, hereafter known as Sam, was absolutely perfect. Even her little cries were perfect. Not that I was biased or anything. Aunts are known to be very objective, you know. We're much more clearheaded and impartial than say, parents or grandparents. I would really be able to serve as an incredible resource for Kate and Nick along the journey of raising this flawless angel.

I was very proud to have remembered to text Louis about the birth of our niece as soon as I was able to get my hands on a phone. He must have been sleeping (an odd idea for four in the morning, right?), since I didn't hear back from him until three hours later. By then I had heard from my mom, who made me promise to remember to pick her up from the airport the following afternoon, from Maya who requested a picture and from Charlie and Zoe who were already planning to visit next month with my dad tagging along. It clearly took a very important event to get these die-hard New Yorkers to venture to the west coast. The next time we would see them on this coast would be for my perfect wedding. If I could pull it off.

It was late in the afternoon by the time Louis arrived at the hospital. We had spoken briefly that morning, when he informed me he had to teach through the early afternoon, but would head to the hospital as soon as he could. I found myself rather resentful of his inability to find someone to cover for him during such an important time for my family; I mean OUR family. He had married me, after all, and now had a significant role to play. Being an uncle for the first time was a pivotal event in a man's life and I didn't feel he was taking his responsibilities very seriously. Why did everything have to feel so hard?

As I stood in front of the main entrance of the hospital, I wondered what it would take for me to feel connected to Louis again. I missed the closeness we had experienced from early on in our relationship. He was always so calm and supportive of me. He broke down my walls and got me to trust him, in record time no less. (Note: I proposed to HIM after six short weeks…following his suggestion of a trip to Vegas.) He was the first man who accepted me exactly as I was. And this is no small feat, let me tell you. You have only heard a *modicum* of the crazy which exists in my head.

For the last few months, Louis had become very introspective and well…cranky. I was trying to be understanding because I knew he was going through a difficult time, but my patience was wearing very thin. Now that I was an aunt, and the only relative Kate and Nick had in the immediate area, demands on my time and ever shrinking brain functioning were only going to get worse. How was I going to handle everything when I didn't have Louis to rely on? It was an incredibly selfish thought to have when he was going through such a hard time, but there it is. He married a selfish woman.

I sat down on a bench and put my head in my hands. As I prayed for some kind of miracle to ease my mounting sense of anxiety, and let's face it, despair, I heard Louis' voice.

"*Mon coeur!*"

I peeked up and tried to smile. There was no question I was deliriously happy about the birth of my niece, but it was easy to be distracted by all the difficulties I had been facing shortly before this joyous event.

Louis seemed concerned. "Are you alright?"

I sighed heavily. "I'm exhausted."

He pulled me to my feet and hugged me. "I have missed you."

"You have?" Oh my God! I was so tired, I actually said that out loud. Crap! Is it terrible to have had such a thought? He hasn't been himself lately. I wondered if he had changed his mind about me. Though the joke was on him if he had, since he had already married me….

Louis pulled out of the hug and put his hands on my shoulders. He gazed so deeply into my eyes, for such a long time, I began to feel uncomfortable. "Why would you say such a thing, Sydney?"

My eyes darted around the hospital entrance. "Um, I'm sorry. I'm exhausted…"

He regarded me sternly. "You have not given me enough of an explanation. What is going on?"

Shit. I really didn't want to have this conversation, oh EVER. But now is simply not a good time since I can't form coherent thoughts. Sleep deprivation does nasty things to people.

I closed my eyes and slumped my shoulders. "Louis, I... can't think right now. I'm *really* worn-out." Tears spilled down my cheeks before I could stop them.

Louis lifted my chin up and waited for me to open my eyes. This is a nasty trick he pulls to keep me from avoiding answering one of his questions. I fall for it every time. His gaze is so intense, I have to tell the truth.

Resigned to my fate, I opened my eyes and met his gaze. The expression on his face was not at all what I had expected. He seemed more vulnerable and dejected than I had ever seen him. Seeing him like this caused even more tears to flow. I threw my arms around him and hugged him as tightly as I could.

"I love you so much, Bluey. I'm sorry I haven't been there for you. I've been so caught up in my job and wedding planning and Kate and Nick...the list is endless. I'm so sorry that I've let you down. I'm an awful wife."

Ever to catch me by surprise, Louis cracked up. I freed him from my embrace and peered at him with my tearstained face. The look on my face pretty much said, "What the fuck?"

He bit his lip to curb his laughter, while studying me cautiously. "No, *I* am sorry, *mon coeur.*"

I looked at him quizzically. "Why would you be sorry?" Seriously, what had he done? Oh my God! Did he cheat on me? I'm going to kill him!

Louis laughed. "Syd! Stop letting your mind run wild." He sighed. "I am sorry for letting *you* down. I have not provided for you as a husband should. I have...spent too much time feeling sorry for myself and have taken out my frustration at not being able to find a job on you. I haven't been fair to you."

I was shocked. I had been a complete bitch and here was my husband apologizing to me? This feeling sorry for myself bullshit had to stop now. I had to start taking care of my husband.

I put my hand on the side of his face. "Please stop. You haven't done anything wrong. I've been very selfish. I haven't been taking care of you." Louis shook his head. "Just listen. I know you come from a very traditional family and you think it's your job to take care of me, but you must understand that you married an American woman, my friend. In my family, husbands and wives take care of *each other*. Whether or not you realize it, you need for *me* to take care of *you*."

He smiled at me. "You will have to be patient with me. I am not good at accepting help from other people. Especially someone I love as much as I love you."

I grinned at him. "I've really missed you." Suddenly I remembered I had told Kate I would be back upstairs in twenty minutes, which was at least forty-five minutes ago. "Crap! I have to get back to Kate!"

Louis took my hand and led me into the hospital lobby. "You go up to see Kate. I want to go by the gift shop and buy her some flowers. I hope they have tulips!"

White tulips were Kate's favorite flowers, a detail which had stayed in Louis's mind since he first met her six months ago. His capacity for important details was amazing. I reminded him of Kate's room number, kissed him quickly on the lips and ran for the elevator. Nick had gone home to grab a few things for Kate, so she had no one to take care of her other than the overworked nursing staff. She had been a mother for less than twenty-four hours and needed intensive TLC.

I arrived at her room in two minutes flat to find her softly snoring. Baby Sam was sleeping next to Kate's bed in her little hospital bassinette. What a beautiful picture they made. I found myself tearing up again and started to chuckle. Not fifteen minutes ago I was in tears because I felt my life had become almost unbearable. Right in front of my face were two very important reasons for me to feel incredibly lucky, not to mention the reason which had just come up behind me.

"Are they both asleep?" Louis whispered.

I turned to face him and beamed. "Aren't they gorgeous?"

His face lit up in wonder. "Indeed they are. Not as gorgeous as you, but don't tell Nick I said that." He kissed me tenderly and rubbed my back.

"What shouldn't she tell Nick?" We were both startled to find Nick bustling into the room with three large duffel bags.

As I wondered what he could possibly have packed in these three enormous bags, I heard a voice behind me.

"Hey, everybody." Kate smiled sleepily from her bed.

Nick seemed petrified. "Did we wake you?"

"No, Pookie, you didn't." She continued to smile. I took this as a good sign. Motherhood was agreeing with her so far. I hoped Perfect Kate (also known as Regular Kate) was on already her way back to us.

While Nick and Kate caught up, Louis found a vase for the beautiful floral arrangement he had brought for her. He had selected white tulips, blue irises (a nod to his wife's favorite flower) and eucalyptus leaves. When he brought them into the room, Kate brightened and held out her arms.

"Oooh, those are gorgeous. Are they for me?"

I rolled my eyes at her. "Silly woman, who else would they be for?"

She squealed quietly with delight. "My first hospital flowers! I love them! Thank you, Louis!"

Louis cleared his throat. "You are too kind, Kate, but the flowers are from your husband. He asked me to find a vase for him while he brought up your bags." He had quickly assessed poor Nick had not had time to buy flowers for his wife and had generously covered for him.

It took me a moment to catch up since due to the lack of sleep. Once my active thought process had engaged, I piped in. "Don't worry, Kate. We'll bring you your second flower arrangement."

Nick glanced back and forth between me and Louis with gratitude in his eyes. It's a wonder he had survived the last few months of Kate's pregnancy and this was the very least we could do to help him.

Since Nick seemed to be at a loss for words, I decided to bring up the matter of most concern to me at that moment. "Is anyone hungry?"

Louis laughed. "I imagine it has been more than two hours since you last ate?" He always joked I had to be fed every two hours or my mood was intolerable. In direct opposition to my pride, I would have to agree with his assessment.

I cocked my head to the side. "I have no idea when I ate last. The only thing I remember is stale saltines." I wrinkled my nose.

Kate put her hand to her head dramatically. "*How* have you survived?"

I smirked. "I honestly have no idea. I've never gone this long without eating. You must be pretty important to me."

She threw back her head and laughed quietly. "You kill me, Syd."

Louis came over and put his arms around my waist. "Why don't we go get something for everyone to eat?" He eyed Nick. "I am sure you must be pretty hungry at this point, man."

Nick ran his hands through his disheveled hair. "I'd kill for a burger."

I squeezed Louis' hand. "OK. We're on it. The usual?"

Nick smiled. After all the years of knowing him, I had learned his detailed food preferences. "Please." He thought for a moment. "Extra fries would be great."

Simply the mention of fries made my stomach growl. Everyone looked at each other and tried not to laugh. We were all well aware of the age-old adage, "Never wake a sleeping baby."

I walked over to Kate and kissed her gently on the forehead. "You're amazing! What a beautiful daughter you have."

She took my hand and we both stole a glimpse of Sam. "She really *is* beautiful, isn't she?"

I nodded as the tears threatened to come back to my eyes. Lack of sleep not only made me stupid, but also really weepy. I had to get some sleep soon. Life was not going to make any sense until I did and I needed my brain firing on all pistons to handle the craziness going on right now. Maybe I should send Louis to the airport tomorrow to pick up my mom. They hadn't had a proper chat in quite some time.

⌒

After Louis and I ensured Kate and Nick had been properly fed (following my incredibly satisfying French fries on the car ride over), we bid them goodnight and headed back to our apartment. I had called my boss earlier in the day to let her know Kate had given birth and asked if I could take a few days off to help out. We had already discussed my taking some time off, but the time frame had been up in the air. Babies are rather unpredictable!

Thankfully, Vivian gave me her blessing and requested I pass on her best wishes to Kate. I absolutely loved working for a company in general, and a boss in particular, who was so attuned to the importance of work-life balance. It was a concept lost on many an employer in Silicon Valley at present.

On the short drive to our apartment, Louis and I held hands contentedly. I was completely out of my mind with exhaustion, but I somehow felt more in my right mind than ever since Louis and I had talked. I marveled at how easy it had been to feel out of touch with him and vowed to keep our lines of communication open. I was bound and determined to prove to myself once and for all I had made the right choice in marrying him. As far as his choice in marrying me, well, that was all on him.

Chapter Six

The last two weeks had been a whirlwind of new baby activities. Once again, and rightfully so in this case, my wedding planning had taken the back seat on my list of priorities. My mom had been staying with Kate to help ease her transition into motherhood, so she and I had spent countless hours washing baby clothes, cooking meals, navigating the use of a breast pump (I'm still scared of those suction cups) and running to the store for whatever Kate needed. Time had quickly run out and my mom was due to return to New York and my non self-sufficient father tomorrow. Luckily, I was able to steal her away for a hasty lunch while Baby Sam and Kate took their afternoon naps.

As we pulled up to her new favorite lunch spot in Palo Alto, The Grapevine, my mom began to chuckle. I knew she hadn't been sleeping much and had noticed she had become a little slaphappy of late. Though she was nearly brokenhearted at the idea of leaving Sam, the stress of caring for a newborn on her sixty-something (I will not put my life in jeopardy by listing her exact age!) year old body was becoming too much for her.

I smiled. "What are you laughing about?"

A few more giggles escaped her before she could answer. "It's just nice watching your sister become a mother."

I scrutinized her with raised eyebrows. "And this is funny *how*?"

She examined her hands. "This is going to sound bad."

Now she had my attention. "What do you mean?"

My mom shrank in embarrassment. "Well…everything has come rather easily to your sister."

I was at a loss for where this was going. "And?"

She sighed. "Being a mother is wonderful; it's rewarding…it's life changing. But it's also undeniably hard."

I was still confused. "And what, you don't think she'll be able to handle it?" Because the Kate I knew could handle ANYTHING. Including her bat shit crazy sister.

My mom shook her head. "No, she can handle it; your sister is very strong. But it won't be pretty. At least not in the beginning."

"And…this is funny?" It was really not like my mother to laugh at someone else's difficulty, particularly one of her children's.

She rolled her eyes at me. "No, I don't think it's funny. It's good to see her in a more…human way." She started to giggle again. "I had to help her this morning…" The giggling took over until her whole body was shaking uncontrollably. This wasn't like my mother. She was clearly taking a page out of Louis' book. What had he implanted in her when he picked her up at the airport?

"Uh…Mom…you're starting to worry me." This comment only drove her into further laughter, because, well, this is a ridiculous statement coming from me. But it doesn't change the truth of the statement.

After a good five minutes, my mom stopped laughing and brought her gaze to meet mine. "I know your sister has always been the epitome of perfection to you. And she's undoubtedly the most self-sufficient of my children. It's new for her be a little vulnerable. She's in completely unchartered territory, but she's handling it."

I narrowed my eyes at her. "Still failing to understand the big-ass giggling fit you just had."

"Sydney Durand! I've always told you, profanity should be saved for a special occasion."

I raised my eyebrows. Wondering if your mother was losing control of her faculties was an occasion for the use of profanity if I've ever heard one. It seems she didn't agree.

"Can't control it sometimes, Mom. My apologies. Please, get to the point."

She exhaled slowly. "I found your sister nodding off this morning in her rocking chair."

"Ha! Ha! What a laugh riot." Was my mother really starting to lose her mind? Or maybe it was merely the lack of sleep at her age. Either way, it was quite troublesome.

She scowled at me. "Let me finish."

I slowly rolled my eyes at her. "Be my guest."

"She had been using the breast pump. The cup had detached from her breast and latched on to her stomach. I tried to extract it, but forgot to turn the pump off first. She woke up suddenly, screaming that her stomach was being eaten by aliens. The noise woke Sam up and they screamed together."

I stared at my mother in horror. "This? This is what was making you laugh so hard?"

My mom had the grace to look ashamed of herself. "You should've seen the look on her face."

I pondered her description for a moment and felt the corners of my mouth turn up. Picturing my perfect sister in such a ridiculous situation *was* kind of funny. I started to cackle and my mom joined in. As the tears of laughter streamed down my face, I thought about what terrible, awful people we were. Truly hateful, awful people. But we were also two people who'd just laughed their asses off. I made a mental note to bring my sister flowers. I felt I owed her for my current state of levity.

Over dinner that evening, Kate threw a curveball I was not expecting. (I suppose I deserved it for laughing so heartily at her expense earlier in the day.) I had just sat down with my second plate of Nick's delicious chicken cutlets and was debating adding more pasta when my mom asked me how the wedding plans were shaping up.

"Well, thanks to you, we have the tuxedos taken care of. I've scheduled a tasting session at the hotel, which will include cakes, and have booked a block of rooms for out-of-town guests. I still have to plan the rehearsal dinner and the post-wedding brunch, find the wedding party gifts and book our honeymoon." I smiled at Louis. He had told me we both really needed a honeymoon, even if all we could afford was a weekend in San Francisco. We simply needed time alone away from everything and everyone.

Kate cleared her throat. "There's one more item you need to add to your list."

I thought it over. "You're right! I'd forgotten about the place cards." Kate never forgot the details - even when she was barely getting any sleep. She really was impressive.

She shook her head. "No, I meant something else."

I wracked my brain for details. "What else is there?" What on earth had I forgotten?

She seemed a little embarrassed. "Well, you didn't forget anything. It's…"

Nick put his hand on hers. "Kate, *tell* her. It's not a big deal."

She shook her head. "You're a guy. You don't know the amount of work involved. It *is* a big deal."

What the hell were they talking about? It sounded pretty serious. "Um…Kate, is everything alright?" I felt my heart starting to race as I imagined the possibilities. Was there some kind of post pregnancy complication no one has told me about? Is Kate going to die? Or is it Sam? What is wrong with my perfect niece?

My eyes must have been huge as the door of crazy swung open and lit my brain up with outrageous possibilities. Kate immediately put her hand on my shoulder.

"Syd! Relax. Everyone is fine." She cleared her throat. "I merely need a wardrobe adjustment for your wedding."

I cocked my head to the side. I wasn't expecting that. "I thought you liked the dress." She had been very excited about the plum, off-the-shoulder dress I had chosen for my six bridesmaids. (Yes, I said six. We don't have time for your skepticism right now. I'll have to fill you in later on why I needed to have six bridesmaids.)

"I love the dress, Syd. It's gorgeous. It's…well…I don't think I'll be able to wear it."

I wondered if my confusion registered in my face. "Did something happen, because you look great!" Kate had already dropped half of her baby weight and the wedding was still more than five months away. (It sounds insane, I know, since it had only been two weeks, but with Kate's level of perfection, I was surprised she hadn't left the hospital at her original weight.)

Kate stammered. "Well, I think the top will be a little tight…" She was starting to turn pink.

Louis leaned into me and whispered, "Her chest has expanded greatly due to the breastfeeding."

Upon hearing this, I blushed what I'm sure was a deep shade of crimson. "Oh, Kate! I'm so sorry! I didn't even think about your…*endowment* when we chose the dresses." Kate had been a generous D cup pre-pregnancy; now she must be an E or an F…if such a size even existed. No wonder she was concerned. The bodice was very close fitting.

She shook her head. "Neither did I! We were planning so feverishly, and then you two ended up getting married early and my pregnancy took over…" She sighed. "I'm sorry. I know what it took to choose this dress."

Well, I couldn't deny her assessment. It had been a gigantic pain in the ass, since I was dealing with six different body types and skin tones and one very opinionated Maya. I cringed inwardly as I thought of starting back at square one. (Not that Maya would have much to say as I could never get her on the phone. I couldn't even remember the last time I had set eyes on her.)

As I pondered where to start, the baby monitor Kate had next to her plate came to life with flashing lights and the sound of Sam's cries. Nick got up from the table and kissed her on the head. "I'll go check on her. You strategize with Syd."

I met her eyes. "Don't worry! We'll figure it out. If we can't find a dress to fit your chest *and* work for the other girls, we'll keep them in the existing dress and give you a different style in a similar color."

She grinned. "I *am* the matron of honor."

I nodded. "Exactly! And that means you deserve a special dress."

Kate seemed relieved. I felt a lot better knowing she could relax. She was barely getting four hours of sleep a night and needed as much of her brain as possible to figure out how to be a mother. She should leave the worrying about mundane wedding things to me. (I also had every intention of keeping her happy. Regular Kate was far more preferable to Pregnant Kate, otherwise known as the Dragon Lady.)

My mom helped herself to another cutlet and turned to Louis. "Since we've settled this matter of importance, tell us, Louis, how are your mother's wedding plans going?"

Louis squinted. "I'm afraid I have been working at the martial arts studio so much that I have not been able to speak with her in a week." The nine hour time difference and his lack of interest in wedding details helped to ensure they didn't speak often. To his mother's great dismay...*she* wanted to share every single detail with him.

Kate smiled at Louis. "Well, what do we know so far? The wedding will be outside, with the entire town in attendance."

Louis laughed. "Not the entire town…well, not at the wedding ceremony. The entire town will be invited to the reception."

My mom whistled. "I can't even imagine how you prepare enough food for four hundred people."

It was my turn to laugh. "Don't forget our family. Dad and Charlie eat enough for, like, eight people."

I had succeeded in shocking my mom. "Sydney Bennett! They certainly don't eat *that* much! There's no need to scare Louis." When was she going to remember my last name had changed? Never mind, now is not the time. I have other points to make.

I shook my head. "Mom, you forget that a) Louis has met Dad and Charlie and b) very, very little scares him."

Louis burst into laughter. "Your daughter knows me very well, Mrs….Lyn." She had insisted he call her by her first name from the moment we were married. He was still having trouble adjusting. The need to respect his elders had been drilled into him from an early age.

My mom regarded me with disdain. "You would do well to show respect to your father, Sydney." Apparently it was OK to mock my brother as much as I wanted. In all fairness, my father did join our family voluntarily when he married my mother. At the age of seven, I gained not only a father, but three grown stepsisters. Though he was my stepfather in reality, he was my real father in my heart. (I thought this earned me the right to mock him occasionally.)

Louis turned on the charm in an attempt to distract her. "You know, Lyn, one of the pre-wedding events will be a trip to one of our family's vineyards. You absolutely have to try the newest Saint Chinian…"

I let out a small sigh of relief. My new husband certainly had the knack for charming my mother out of difficult situations. This ability will come in *very* handy over the course of our life together. I was pleased to notice for the first time in the past few weeks, I had a very positive outlook on the fate of my marriage. Whether or not everything had happened too quickly and whether or not we were under way too much pressure right now, I believed we were going to succeed. Ours would *not* be one of the marriages to end in divorce. Not if I had anything to do with it.

Chapter Seven

One of the scary things I was learning about marriage was even though things were going really well at one moment in time, this didn't prevent them from raging out of control, barrel-assing down a huge hill and into a ditch in the next moment. (Yes, this is definitely an occasion for profanity. Besides, that particular profane word ALWAYS makes me laugh.) I was absolutely flabbergasted at the ease with which this happened.

One moment, Louis and I were comfortably enjoying our life as man and wife and the next we were snapping at each other for the smallest things. Try as I might, I couldn't figure out what was happening. I kept thinking there had to be some sort of pattern and if I could just figure it out, I would be able to stop the insanity. (Thank you, Susan Powter, for this memorable expression from the early nineties.)

A month had passed since my mom returned to New York and it was almost the end of May. This meant Louis had been without gainful employment as a computer programmer for four months. While he enjoyed teaching

Thai boxing classes, he wasn't receiving the necessary intellectual stimulation and the level of compensation he required to satisfy himself. He was simply spinning his wheels until he could find the right opportunity.

It certainly didn't help that our money concerns were growing by the day. I had done my best to keep our wedding expenses under control, but even the least expensive options cost a decent amount of money. As the days went by, I could see Louis' carefully controlled personality begin to disintegrate before my very eyes. I felt helpless as there seemed to be no way for me to make him feel better without damaging his pride. He absolutely hated having to worry about every penny we spent and I had the very uncomfortable job of reminding him we could not afford the very expensive cheese he loved on a weekly basis. (Seriously, twenty dollars an ounce?!?)

I was hoping Louis' job at the martial arts studio would, at a minimum, bring in enough to support his cheese habit, but several things happened at once to make this a moot point. The cost of our renter's insurance went up substantially, the next portion of our deposit on the hotel was due and my parents had experienced a difficult few months with their store, leaving them with little ability to help with the wedding expenses. They had sunk a sizeable chunk of their retirement savings into the shop, believing the popularity of pottery painting studios would allow them to make it back (and more) within the first couple of years. Apparently, the good people of Rockland County were not willing to jump on the bandwagon of painting your own dishes and figurines. Because Rockland is really the height of sophistication…

I knew things were getting bad when I came home one evening to find Louis drinking a coffin. This is a particularly nasty cocktail composed of one shot of gin, one shot of vodka and one shot of tequila, served over ice. Yes, it's as gross as it sounds and yes, it's considered to be deadly by my standards. Louis hadn't had one of these since the night we met. He told me he only drank this concoction when he was nervous or upset. As he poured himself another round of shots, I tried to prepare myself for what event had occurred to drive him to drink. Louis rarely drank, and if he did, he would choose a beer or a rum and coke, so something pretty bad must have happened to warrant this trip to the liquor cabinet.

I put my purse on the kitchen counter and carefully approached him. I slowly sat down opposite him at the dining room table and tried to smile.

I cleared my throat nervously. "How was your day, Bluey?"

He stared up at me with a degree of misery I had never seen in his eyes. I wanted to jump across the table and hug him, but forced myself to stay where I was since I had learned he didn't like to be "coddled" when he was this upset.

We sat in silence for a few moments while I thought over my options. A) I could ask him what was wrong. Though this method didn't usually yield positive results because he didn't want to admit he ever had problems. B) I could try to distract him. An impromptu strip tease might bring him out of his funk. Except I had gotten dressed in a hurry this morning and wasn't sure what quality of undergarments I had put on. Certain articles might put him in a worse mood if he were to see them. C) I could act like nothing was wrong.

As I dithered back and forth, Louis made the decision for me.

"My interview fell through today."

Shit. This was the one opportunity he had been excited about in the last four months. He had found a small startup in South San Francisco searching for programmers to develop a new line of video games. Louis enjoyed playing a wide variety of video games, as evidenced by the four game systems we owned, but he especially loved the ones rated "M for mature" the best. He had been around guns all his life and had even spent time as a sniper for the French Military. Since he no longer had access to active firearms, playing adult-themed target practice games filled the void of his former activities. This job would have married two of his favorite things – programming and creating gun-laden video games.

I walked over and slid my arms around his neck. "I'm so sorry, my love. Is there anything I can do to make you feel better?" Double shit. Do *not* make him think you feel sorry for him! That is the kiss of death! I stammered, "I mean…maybe I could cook you a nice dinner and we can just relax?"

Nice save, dumbass. I'm sure you really fooled him. I was pretty close to reaching around him to pour a coffin for myself. I needed something to calm my ever-fraying nerves. It's a bad thing if you feel the need to drink in order to get through conversations with your spouse, right?

Louis closed his eyes. "You have worked all day. I do not want you to have to cook now."

I kissed the top of his head. "Don't worry. I'll be happy to cook dinner."

I went into the bedroom to change my clothes. Putting on my sweats was one of my favorite things to do. Especially since things had gotten so tense at home. At least I felt like my clothes were giving me a warm hug. My husband hadn't been so interested in touching me lately. I'm sure the scarcity of sex wasn't helping either one of our moods.

When I returned to the living room, Louis had poured himself another drink. Seeing this made me start to panic. I had no idea how many drinks he had consumed before I got home, but I *did* know he was on his third drink (composed of three shots) in ten minutes. I had never seen him like this before. I felt completely out of my element. Louis had always been the one to knock some sense in to me. I hadn't the slightest idea what to do for him.

He grinned. "Why don't we go out to dinner, *mon coeur*?"

I sighed. The last thing I wanted to do was change my clothes again and go out. Besides, we couldn't afford it. I would have to try to distract him. Bringing up the subject of money when he was already in such a delicate state could have disastrous consequences.

I smiled at him. "Bluey, I was going to make you a western omelet." Louis had fallen in love with this omelet when I dragged him to IHOP last month. We both needed a break and it was a cheap place to eat. Besides, I love eating breakfast any time of day. When is bacon *not* a welcome addition to a meal?

A ghost of a smile appeared on his lips. "You have convinced me. Don't be shy with the cheese, Syd."

Phew. One crisis averted. Hopefully we'll be able to avoid all other hot-button topics for the night. The only difficult part was I didn't always know what those were. Louis' moods were becoming startlingly similar to Kate's during her pregnancy. Was it possible for men to spontaneously generate estrogen? Dear God, I hope not. The shoes of the crazy woman of the house have already been filled, quite successfully thank you very much, by me.

While I gathered all the necessary ingredients for tonight's meal, I was relieved to see Louis pour himself a glass of orange juice (with no secret ingredients.) I wasn't prepared for the "I think you've had too much to drink" discussion. Having confrontational discussions with Louis was something I knew nothing about and was desperately hoping the reality of such a discussion would never come to light.

Reminding him to put the toilet seat down was something I could handle. Rolling my eyes as I told him he had left his trimmed beard hair all over the bathroom floor was something I was very familiar with. Telling him I was concerned he was drinking too much was much too far out of my comfort zone. And since he wasn't showing any signs that the alcohol was affecting him, I decided to let it slide for now.

Unfortunately, I still had a rather large problem facing me which I couldn't ignore. My husband was missing. My sweet, funny and incredibly romantic husband had officially left the island. I closed my eyes and attempted to keep the tears from falling down my cheeks. I *had* to find a way to bring my Bluey back, even if it killed me. I simply had no idea how to go about it. This problem felt like the pinnacle of the avalanche which was threatening to fall and crush the life out of me at any moment.

Louis cleared his throat. "I went down to Micro Center today and applied for a job." He laughed bitterly. "They said they would call me."

Oh my God. The avalanche was rumbling. Louis had completely swallowed his pride and applied for a job in a computer store. I knew him too well not to understand this had been a completely humiliating experience for him. I had no doubt they'd taken one look at his resume and known he was only searching for something to do during his job search. They probably didn't want to waste the time getting him up to speed (which would have taken about five seconds) and have him leave as soon as he found a real job.

I was well and truly stuck. What could I say which wouldn't sound patronizing? I hoped for a miracle and took a leap of faith. Here goes nothing!

I scoffed. "You can't waste your talents in a place like that! Before you know it, you'll find something worth your time." Survey says?

Louis regarded me skeptically. "Are you trying to cheer me up?"

"Is it working?" I asked playfully.

He shook his head. "Not as well as it used to, but I appreciate the effort."

With a lack of something better to say, I gestured to the frying pan and said, "Let's eat!"

As I plated Louis' omelet, I noticed the answering machine light was flashing. Hmm. Louis usually checks the machine hourly to ensure he hasn't missed a call from a recruiter. Unless he was screening calls from his mom again…

I put our plates on the table and grabbed a selection of condiments from the fridge. Louis waited for me to sit down and then dug into his coveted western omelet. After a few bites, I decided the subject had to be broached.

"So, I was surprised to see we have messages on the machine. Do you want me to go check them?"

Louis didn't even look up from his omelet. "Don't worry, it's just my mom again."

I knew it! He was screening her calls. This wouldn't end well for either one of us. His mother called him once a day when she was able to get him on the phone. When she wasn't, she called him three or four times a day. The more she called, the angrier he got, which made him even more determined to ignore her calls. It was a vicious cycle which was threatening to drive both of us completely insane – though for different reasons.

I still had immense guilt over the fact Louis had married a woman whom his mother had never met. Louis had been fully accepted into my country, my family and my lifestyle. His assimilation had been fairly easy, minus the interminable job search and resulting loss of pride. Not only had I never met his parents or any other member of his family, but also I didn't speak their language or have much knowledge of their culture. I felt like, for all intents and purposes, I had stolen him.

I thought he could do his part in making her feel better by talking over a few harmless wedding details. Never mind how he hated planning parties. (And weddings were like the mother of all parties. My apologies, when I'm in one of my crazy rants I tend to make *really* bad puns.) Never mind how he had a difficult time talking to his mother for long periods of time because the level of detail she brought into each conversation about the most trivial matters made Louis want to rip the hair out of his head. Never mind how she was still trying to control his life from thousands of miles away. Oh, Sydney. You're asking too much of your poor husband.

Despite this conclusion, I decided to push forward. The only excuse I can give you is I was not in my right mind. The amount of pressure I felt at this moment in time was astronomical. Some of it had to be relieved.

"When is the last time you spoke with her?"

He speared the last bite of his omelet. "I don't know. Sometime last week?"

I stopped myself from rolling my eyes at him. This would only serve to incense him. Why were men so dumb when it came to women and weddings? A week was a long time to go without a conversation. I had to proceed delicately.

I picked at my plate. "Maybe she has something important to ask you."

He laughed. "What could she possibly need to ask me? What color napkins to use? What kind of dessert wine to serve? I really couldn't care less."

Ouch. I knew we were already married, but this was going to be the wedding his whole family and all his friends would see. He didn't care what it was like?

I took a deep breath. Stop being so sensitive, Sydney. He's going through a rough time. And he's probably more than a bit tipsy.

I put down my fork. "Maybe you could call her tomorrow?"

He glared at me. "Maybe *you* could."

What? Oh…he was giving me shit for not learning French. He really didn't want to go down that road right now.

"And how would I communicate with her, Louis?" I asked quietly.

The look on his face was thunderous. "Perhaps if you spent a little less time, and a lot less money, planning this ridiculous wedding and a little more time learning French, you would be able to communicate with my family." He threw his hands up in the air. "We are already married! We don't need all this bullshit."

I closed my eyes. For the past few weeks, Louis and I had gone through a lot of ups and downs. The pain of the constant uncertainty was seeping through my body and I wasn't sure if I could take it anymore. I had spent the last three months telling myself I hadn't made a mistake in marrying Louis. I had convinced myself I hadn't made a mistake in throwing caution to the wind and believing in love (almost) at first sight. I kept telling myself I hadn't made a mistake by throwing my meticulously careful personality to the side and charging ahead with reckless abandon.

And where had it gotten me? At the current moment, I was buried under an avalanche of a preposterous scale. I knew the first year of marriage was supposed to be the hardest, but I doubted all couples had to endure this level of stress. The average woman would have known her husband better before she married him. The average woman would not only have met, but also would have been able to communicate with her in-laws rather easily - or at least would have spoken the same language. The average woman would *not* have had to support her husband for the first however many months of marriage. The average woman would *not* have been planning the wedding of her dreams during her first year of marriage while worrying what level of humiliation she would be exposed to during her THIRD wedding in a foreign country. The average woman also would *not* have been trying to help her sister through her first year of motherhood AND be the best aunt ever to the sweetest little girl in the world. No, the average woman certainly would *not* have been going through all this at the same time.

I had no idea what to say to Louis. I believed he was lashing out at me because he felt so helpless, but I didn't have any understanding left in my poor, stress ransacked psyche. I wanted to scream at him how I didn't have time to learn French because I was working like a dog to support us. I wanted to scream at him how tired I was of trying to take care of everyone in my life and I was a terrible wife because I had nothing left for him. I simply didn't have it in me to open such a dangerous can of worms. I knew if these words escaped my lips, irreparable damage would have been done to our relationship.

As the barrage of possible scenarios swirled around in my mind, I noticed I was starting to have difficulty breathing. I had to get out of the apartment before I chose to lock *myself* in a padded cell for a very, very long time. I got up from the table, went into the bedroom and threw my toothbrush, toiletry bag and pajamas in a bag. I swung the bag over my shoulder, walked out of the bedroom and picked up my purse.

I turned to Louis. "I need some air. I'm going to Kate's."

He didn't look up from the table. He only shook his head and said, "Do what you do best, Sydney. Run."

I quickly grabbed my keys and fled. What was I expecting? For him to stop me? As the tears spilled down my cheeks, I realized the old Louis would have stopped me. The old Louis would have apologized, held me in his arms and told me we were going to be fine. The old Louis and I would have sat down on the couch, snuggled into each other and worked out a plan to clean up the big mess we had in front of us. The new Louis had no interest in moving forward. The new Louis simply wanted to mire in melancholy. I really, *really* missed the man I married.

Due to the late hour, by the time I arrived at Kate's house, Sam was already in bed. I was disappointed not to see her, but knew since I would be sacked out on the couch tonight, I would be able to see her promptly at five in the morning. I winced a little at the idea of such an early start to the day, but knew her little face would do wonders to heal my soul from its current state of wretchedness.

Kate tucked me in to my comfy bed on the couch and made me promise to tell her everything in the morning. She could see I was in no mood to talk about whatever was bothering me and eagerly made her way to her bed for some much-needed sleep. I lay awake for hours thinking about my disastrous marriage. This was the first night I had consciously chosen to spend apart from my husband. How did things get so bad? When would they get easier? Would we be able to fix the massive amount of damage we had inflicted on each other? Suddenly, Sam's cries interrupted my seemingly endless spiral of painful questions. I cried right along with her since I had absolutely no idea what I was going to do.

Chapter Eight

Regrettably, nothing appeared any better to me the next morning. I was greatly cheered by the exuberant gurgles from the cutest baby on the planet, but even holding her to my chest while she slept did nothing to cure my anxious state. I was no closer to figuring out how to reach Louis. And the scariest part was, I wasn't sure I had any desire to try. I had utterly no idea what was going to happen next. For someone who carefully plans every aspect of her life, this was about the most terrifying thing possible.

Luckily for me, I had not one, not two, but three sources of advice from the east coast in the form of Charlie, Zoe and my father, waiting for me at the breakfast table. They had made good on their promise to visit the newest member of the Bennett-Wilson family and as a side benefit, they were able to provide counseling to me in person for the first time in a very long time. My saint of a brother, Charlie, had gone to check on Louis last night, since I was worried about the amount of alcohol he had consumed while I was with him and feared he had gone on a major drinking binge once I had left.

Charlie returned later in the evening and confirmed that Louis was fine. He had stayed with Louis for a couple of hours, cut off his access to alcohol and put him to bed. Thankfully, the only car we owned was currently in my possession. I sincerely doubted he would have decided to go for a late night joyride on his bicycle…

After I had called in sick to work (there was no way I was going to be of any use today), I decided it was time to face the music. As I sat down at the dining room table, I was greeted by Sam's adorable face and five very different facial expressions from my family. Kate was doing her best to pretend everything was fine (probably hoping she and I would be able to discuss what happened in private.) Charlie was grinning like an idiot, a sure sign he was really uncomfortable. Zoe looked like she was cautiously waiting for me to bring up the painfully obvious topic. Nick was busying himself with feeding Sam, but I could tell he was nervous. And finally, my father was staring me dead in the eyes with an expression I believed to mean, "Start talking."

I sighed. "Good morning, everyone."

My father scrutinized me. "Is it, Duck?"

My eyes fell to my lap. "Dad, I don't really know if anything is good right now."

He put his arm around me. "Tell us what's going on. Something must have happened for you to stay here last night."

I looked around the dining room table. I felt…confused. Part of me was ashamed of the state of my marriage. I felt like I had definitely broken my relationship curse when I met Louis and here I was, nearly a year later, back in a very painful place. Another part of me was so tired of everything being so difficult. I wanted all the problems to just go away. And at this point, I was so hurt and angry, I wasn't sure if I wanted Louis to be part of the disappearing act or not. Suffice it to say, I was more than a little conflicted. I guess it couldn't hurt to seek advice from the awaiting panel of judges…

I took a deep breath. "I don't know where to begin."

Zoe put her hand on mine. "Why don't you start by telling us what happened last night?"

I tried to smile. "OK." I cleared my throat. "I came home from work to find Louis drinking."

My father frowned. "He isn't much of a drinker."

I nodded. "I know. That's why it really worried me to find him with three bottles of alcohol on the table." Granted it didn't take much for me to start worrying. With my current state of stress, someone could simply look at me funny and I would need to be talked down from the ledge.

Charlie met my eyes. "You know, when I got there last night, he didn't seem drunk. I only put the bottles away as a precaution."

I held his gaze. "It's really strange. The couple of times I've seen him have a few drinks, he didn't act any differently than he normally does. Either he can really hold his liquor or he's a very controlled drunk." I played with my wedding ring while wondering which of these options was worse.

Kate put a cup of tea in front of me. "Have you spoken with him this morning?"

"No." I rubbed my temples. "I'm being a total chicken."

My father cleared his throat. "Duck, you and Louis are facing a lot of difficulty right now."

Charlie laughed. "Tell her something she doesn't know, Dad."

Zoe swiftly wacked Charlie in the stomach and told him to be quiet. I stifled a chuckle which was threatening to come out since it seemed rather inappropriate to laugh during the lecture I was about to get from my father.

My father tried again. "Listen, marriage isn't an easy thing. Plus, you set the odds against you when you married Louis so quickly after meeting him."

I hung my head and tried not to cry. I thought my father liked Louis. Now he was telling me I had made a mistake in marrying him.

"Duck!"

I snapped my head back up and stared at my father.

He winked at me. "I'm not telling you that you made a mistake."

My eyes widened. When did he become a mind reader?

He put his hand on the side of my face. "I'm just saying you have a lot of hurdles to get over."

Kate spoke to me gently. "We think you can do it, Syd. Marriage takes a lot of work."

I felt my eyes stinging with tears and tried my best to hold them in. Big shock, Sydney! Once again, you're showing yourself to be the weakest link in the family.

My father took my hand. "Syd, I've no doubt Louis is struggling as much as you are." He sighed. "He's a French man who grew up in a very traditional household. Being supported by you is hard for him to deal with."

A few tears rolled down my cheeks. "I know, Dad, but I'm having a difficult time being understanding when he's acting like such a…."

Charlie volunteered. "An asshole?"

Zoe wrinkled her nose. "A jerk?"

Kate chimed in. "A dumbass?"

My dad settled it for all of us. "A fucking prick."

We all erupted into peals of laughter. My father has such a way with words. His comment was exactly what we needed to ease the tension of the conversation.

"Listen, Duck. We all love Louis. None of us envy what you're going through right now, but we all have faith you two kids can work it out." He leaned closer to me. "Right now you're coming to terms with the fact that he's showing signs of being human."

What? I know he's human! I used to think he was perfect, but that ship sailed once I started living with him. But if I really thought about it, until the last couple of months, he had been perfect in all the important ways. He had never let me down when I really needed him. He had talked me down from the ledge on a number of occasions. He had taken really good care of me.

Suddenly, I felt like *I* was the fucking prick. That's right, Syd! As your mother always says, save profanity for a special occasion. Like letting yourself know how much you'd let your husband down. Again. When was I going to learn?

I exhaled loudly and decided to share my revelation with my family. "I think *I'm* the fucking prick."

Five pairs of eyes turned my way quickly, but no one said a word.

I shrugged my shoulders. "What, no comments? No questions?"

Zoe glanced around the room. "I'll ask the question. Why?"

I put my head against the back of the chair. "Because you all know what a complete nut I am." Five heads bobbed up and down. "And Louis has put up with all my craziness since the very beginning. He hasn't complained." Uh oh…here come the tears. "He has only told me how much he loves me. And here *I* am…crumbling when he's having such a hard time."

Kate came over to me. "Syd, you have a lot on your plate right now. It's totally understandable you're having…um…a little bit of trouble."

I shook my head. "No, it's not. A wife is supposed to take care of her husband. I have to stop being so selfish."

My dad wiped my tears away with his handkerchief. (I tried really hard not to wonder when he washed it last. My mom was in New York running the store and Kate had a baby to take care of…)

"Duck, stop putting so much pressure on yourself. Take one day at a time and TALK to your husband. Be honest with him. You two can figure this out together."

Kate kissed the top of my head. "Listen, Sam is starting to sleep for a few hours at a time, which means I can help you finish the last few wedding details."

Nick tore himself away from his daughter to grin at me. "And as much as we love having you here, you can certainly spend more time at home with Louis."

Kate nodded. "We'll be fine."

I bristled. "Are you trying to get rid of me? I don't want Sam to forget about her Aunt Syd."

Zoe rolled her eyes. "Syd! She won't forget about you."

Charlie laughed and wacked Zoe in the stomach. "And remember, Sydie, you can always call us. We know a thing or two about solving marital problems."

I chuckled, hearing Zoe tell him they would have much fewer problems if he would just listen to her. As I watched them bicker quietly, I wished for the hundredth time we didn't live on opposite sides of the country.

I bit my lip. "Well, my boss *did* tell me that things should slow down at work in a couple of weeks, so maybe the rest of my life will become more manageable." Was that a glimmering of hope in my future?

Kate grinned. "It's all falling into place, Syd. One day at a time." She started humming the tune to the seventies sitcom. Suddenly, everyone but my dad joined in and we had a spontaneous sing-along. We *may* have made up most of the words, but there was a great time had by all.

My dad eyed each of us curiously. "You young people are a little nuts."

The four of us cracked up while my dad filed away another piece of evidence to share with my mom as to why we should all be committed to an insane asylum.

I let out a few last cackles and decided to delve into a serious question. "Why does life have to feel like such a roller coaster?"

My dad laughed. "That's marriage, Duck. You feel giddy, sick and terrified all at the same time. And if you get off, you might feel safe, but it would be far too boring."

We all turned to stare at my father. Every now and then, he had these moments of absolute clarity. There was no sarcasm, no judgment. Just real, honest to goodness advice

- like the endearing grandmother in the 1989 classic, *Parenthood*.

He looked back at us with his clear blue eyes. "But if you want to throw in the towel, you can always have Louis deported."

Did I fail to mention these moments of clarity were usually followed by some kind of zinger? After all, my dad did have a reputation as a smart-ass to uphold.

I closed my eyes and smiled as laughter exploded around me. Once again my family had shown me the way back to my sanity. Would I ever be able to find the path myself? Or would this job always belong to someone else? It seemed like an awful lot to ask of anyone. Was it really fair to continue to inflict this loathsome task on Louis? Especially in his current state of unease?

Following a relatively relaxed breakfast with my family, I packed up my things and prepared myself for tearful good-byes. Charlie and Zoe were leaving for Napa today and had an early flight to New York the following morning. My father was leaving for the airport this afternoon and already had his suitcases waiting by the door. I really hated saying good-bye to them and once again cursed the conflict I felt about living on the west coast.

I hugged each of them as tightly as I could and told them how much I loved them. They each left me with words of wisdom.

"Cut him a little slack, Syd. The guy is down on his luck." Charlie kissed the top of my head.

Zoe held my hands. "It's important to be understanding, but don't let him walk all over you. Stay strong!"

My dad pulled me close and whispered, "If that doesn't work, hit him where it hurts. A good kick in the nuts will make you feel much better."

I really love my dad. He was able to make me laugh instead of cry as I left the three of them standing on Kate and Nick's doorstep. I got into my car and drove away with a somewhat lighter heart. My family had reminded me both Louis and I were human. And being human sometimes involved making bad choices. As I pulled up to our apartment complex, I resolved to be the person I was meant to be. To be the wife Louis deserved. To finally harness the crazy once and for all. Don't believe I can do it? Just watch me.

Chapter Nine

Over the next two weeks, Louis and I slowly began our journey back to each other. We had talked at length following that harrowing breakfast with my family. Louis confessed to me his immense difficulty with my earning the majority of the money to pay our bills. I told him I was resentful of his comments about my spending habits for our wedding. (There is only so much one can economize when it comes to the perfect wedding day.) I also told him I was really nervous about meeting his family and I *might* have taken out some of this stress on him. We agreed we would be more supportive of each other and would make a conscious effort to spend more time together.

Mercifully, my workload lightened, allowing me more time to spend with Louis. However, in an attempt to bring in as much money as he could, Louis picked up more hours at the martial arts studio. I had the growing desire to tell him all the hours he spent toiling away didn't bring in much money and his time would be better spent repairing his marriage. (Isn't this in direct opposition to our commitment to spending more time together? Was I the only one listening?) However, in order to stick to *my* promise of being more supportive of him, I kept my mouth shut and searched for new ways to spend my free time.

Maya was still pretty much MIA. I would get the occasional text message filling me in on her latest escapades with Devon, or if I were really lucky, she would send me an email complete with photos of the adorable couple. I hate to admit it, but I found myself jealous of her. The joyous looks on their faces reminded me of how I felt in the early days of my relationship with Louis. While things had gotten much better between us, there was always a hint of tension in the background, just waiting to spoil our hard won progress. Every day felt like a fight against feeling depressed and overwhelmed. Despite the obstacles, I kept telling myself we were going to win this fight together.

A very happy consequence of my newfound free time was dinner with my good friends Nigel and Grace. Long before the days of Louis, Nigel was one of my roommates in a hastily found rental following the discovery of my boyfriend in a *menage a trois* (which didn't include me). There were seven of us in total and while I tried to tell myself I was living in an episode of *The Real World, San Francisco*, it was really more like *Big Brother* gone very, very bad.

The house was extremely old and desperately in need of remodeling and I was sharing one bathroom with FOUR boys. The house was also jokingly referred to as "The High House" since it was located on High Street, but there were definitely other reasons to call it as such. When I first moved in, I felt like I had jumped from one nightmare to the next.

The silver lining of this questionable living situation was meeting my good friend, Nigel. British to the core, he had the most wonderful accent and the sunniest disposition of anyone I had ever met. These traits coupled with his slightly short stature and fair hair resulted in everyone in the house calling him "Pip." Thankfully, he was an avid fan of *South Park* and possessed a wicked sense of humor, so the nickname was well received. Nigel's company enabled me to face each day of my uncertain future. He made me laugh and accompanied me to more coffeehouses, bookstores and restaurants than I can remember.

Shortly before I moved out of the High House, Nigel was asked out by a very attractive coworker of his named Grace. She was from Hong Kong, spoke Mandarin and was off the charts intelligent. Nigel was shocked at his good fortune, but I knew the depths of his delightful personality and felt Grace was every bit as lucky as he. Their romance moved fairly quickly and Nigel began staying over at Grace's studio apartment on a regular basis. I didn't blame him; I would have jumped at the chance to stay somewhere else too. (Especially given the incredibly gorgeous and charming company he was keeping.)

Nigel and Grace moved in together a few months later and ended up getting married the following year. Though they felt it was a little fast, Nigel was being sponsored by his company for a green card and since Grace was from Hong Kong, she stood a better shot of getting a green card as his spouse than on her own from the same company. (I know, I know, immigration is confusing. Don't let yourself get bogged down in the details.) They tied the knot at the city courthouse and I threw a wedding celebration dinner for them at my new apartment. My roommates, Jess and Maggie, were kind enough to help me construct a three tiered cake complete with accents of fresh flowers. Only the best for Pip and his lovely bride!

Now that we have gotten through all of the preamble, we can get back to dinner. Nigel and Grace had asked me to meet them at one of our favorite bistros in downtown Palo Alto. After parking my car, I started walking to the restaurant, trying to remember if I had told them Louis wasn't coming. I hoped they didn't ask too many questions. I wasn't in the mood for any serious topics tonight.

As I approached the door, I caught sight of Nigel. He beamed at me and came over to give me a hug. I smiled and gave him a big squeeze. I desperately wished his good nature would transfer to me by osmosis.

"Where is your useless husband?"

I laughed. Louis and Nigel had an artificial rivalry going due to the natural dislike which existed between their two countries. Naively, I had thought they would instantly bond over being European, but was quickly educated to the contrary. In truth, they were good friends, but enjoyed mocking each other senseless. Crazy European men.

"Louis had to work tonight." I tried to keep a bright expression on my face, but wasn't sure I could fool my friend.

He kept his opinion to himself. "Well, then Grace and I will have the pleasure of monopolizing your company this evening."

Right on cue, Grace came up behind Nigel and smiled. "Syd! How are you?"

I gave Grace a huge hug and told her how much I had missed her. She hooked her arm through mine and walked me into the restaurant leaving Nigel to bring up the rear. I felt a weight lift off my chest and breathed a sigh of relief that I would be able to relax for a while.

Following a glass of wine and some amazing stuffed mushrooms, Grace asked me how the wedding plans were going.

I took a sip of my merlot and pondered the answer. "Well, Kate has been amazing. She helped me choose the menu items for the cocktail hour, the reception and the post-wedding brunch. We also chose the cake, finalized the rehearsal dinner, selected invitations and found an affordable option for a honeymoon." I was forgetting something. "Oh, and she helped me fix the whole bridesmaid dress debacle."

Grace appeared confused. "Dress debacle?"

I giggled. "Kate's chest is absolutely enormous from breastfeeding and she couldn't fit into the dress we'd originally chosen."

Nigel almost choked on his beer. Grace and I had a good laugh as he mopped up the stray drops which escaped into his lap.

Grace helped Nigel right himself and turned to me. "So, how did you fix it?"

I finished chewing the bread I had grabbed during the great beer clean up. "We chose a new dress for her in the same color as the other girls' dresses."

Grace nodded. "That works."

Nigel cleared his throat. It must be time for an important question. "You will be having an open bar, right?"

I laughed. "No, Mr. Frugal. You'll have to get drunk on your own dime. We can barely afford the wedding as it is."

He regarded me with feigned horror as Grace slapped him in the back of the head.

I laughed even harder. "Relax. You can drink as much wine and beer as you want on us." I was exceedingly glad Nigel hadn't mentioned that Kate was making all the final decisions with me instead of Louis. Nigel was one of my favorite people in the entire world, but he had very little tact. Grace did her best to prep him ahead of time in terms of items *not* to discuss, but he didn't always follow her advice.

Grace clapped her hands quietly. "Great job, Syd! You are in excellent shape with a little over three months to go."

I cocked my head to one side. Three months to go? Was it really so soon? It was mid-June and the wedding would be at the end of September, so Grace was absolutely right.

Nigel grinned at the waitress when she set a large plate of pasta in front of him. I could see the anticipation in his eyes as he waited for her to finish serving Grace and me. I almost laughed out loud at his childlike enthusiasm for his favorite meal. His love of food made him incredibly easy to please..

He took a huge bite of pasta and grinned at me. Once he swallowed, he asked me a question which struck terror into my heart. "So, who's going to officiate the ceremony?"

Apparently, I hadn't thought of everything. Since Louis and I were already married, we didn't need anyone to officiate, but we certainly couldn't just stand there. What was I going to do? Tap dance for everyone? Have my father sing an aria? He was German, so he should know one….there were operas in Germany, right?

"Um…" I stammered. "What an excellent question!"

I could see the look of panic cross Grace's face. I had kept as much as I could from them, but they weren't stupid; they knew something had happened between Louis and me. I recognized her desire to provide a stress-free evening for me and I could see her mentally cursing her husband for finding the one detail I had missed.

I shook my head. "Don't worry, Grace. I'm fine." I turned to Nigel. "Thank you for finding this huge, and rather embarrassing, deficiency, Pip. I still have time to fix it."

Grace narrowed her eyes at him and then turned a happy face back to me. "So, how are the dress fittings going?"

Nigel began to babble nervously. "Yes, yes, tell us about your gorgeous dress! What color is it? Does it have any beading or…perhaps some lace?"

I grinned. The best way to cheer up a bride was to have her describe her wedding dress. I tried to be as brief as possible, so as not to bore Nigel to death. (Despite his questions, I knew he didn't give a crap what my dress looked like.) "It is a white spaghetti strap ball gown with a satin beaded bodice and a full tulle skirt. The skirt is my favorite part! It is so totally poofy, has beading patterned into the tulle and has a hint of a train. The dress really is gorgeous!"

Nigel breathed a sigh of relief. "I'm sure you will look stunning in it. And will you be wearing a tiara? A veil? Or perhaps a tiara and a veil?"

I giggled. He was really trying to make up for almost freaking me out a couple of minutes ago. And then I realized something absolutely horrific…I hadn't chosen ANYTHING to wear on my head. Shit! What was I going to do? Would I be able to get a veil that matched my dress so close to the wedding? Did they have to be custom made with the same fabric? Maybe my mom, the master seamstress could make one? Unlikely, as she lives THREE THOUSAND MILES away from the dress. Oooh, maybe Maya could bedazzle something for me to wear on my head. A headband? A jaunty cap? Maybe a dunce hat???

I felt the color drain from my face. "I…uh…" Poor Nigel! He had the knack for finding all my deficiencies.

Grace was absolutely mortified. For a moment, she didn't know what to say. Then she turned to her husband and began whispering furiously. Poor Nigel looked like he wanted to die. I felt so stupid! What had I done to my amazing friends? No one was to blame here but me. I should stop this before it gets any worse. I didn't want to draw anyone else into my nightmare.

"Guys!" They were far too involved in their fast-paced discussion to hear me.

I cleared my throat and tried again. "Guys!" I yelled a little louder than I had intended. "Oooh…sorry." I smiled sheepishly. "Please calm down. I'm fine."

Grace still gave the impression of wanting to hurt her husband. "Is there anything we can do to help?"

I needed to think about something, anything other than my wedding plans. I was becoming sick of them. Or at least I was sick (and tired!) of making mistakes with them.

I massaged my neck. "Yes, there is! Please tell me about YOUR French wedding."

Did I fail to mention they too would be having a wedding in France? It seems Louis and I had not cornered the market on having a civil ceremony first and a story book wedding at a later date. Nigel and Grace's wedding would take place at the end of next summer in a big, beautiful castle in the Loire Valley. It sounded incredibly romantic. For the next hour, I was regaled with stories of the history of the castle, the details of the ceremony and most importantly for Pip, the rich bounty of food which would be served.

As I sat on the other side of the table listening to them tell each of these stories in tandem, I thought about how good they were for each other. They didn't seem to struggle the way Louis and I did. Were they simply better suited for each other? It was true they'd not been under the same degree of stress we were currently under, but who's to say they wouldn't have handled it just as well as they seem to handle everything else? I'm not saying they never disagreed, as evidenced by their lively sidebar earlier this evening, but it was never about any big issues. Any quarrel they had seemed to be minor and was forgotten about before the end of the conversation. They made everything look so easy.

For the rest of the evening, I made sure to smile as much as possible regardless of the nonsense floating around in my head. Nigel and Grace had made every attempt to keep me in good spirits and I didn't want to disappoint them by showing them any evidence of my confusion. I kept wondering if Louis and I were in a better place now. It was certainly true we were getting along better, but we were also keeping our conversations on a more superficial level. I still felt like we were walking on eggshells and it made me unbelievably sad. I sincerely hoped by the time we were standing in front of each other, three short months from now, sharing our vows of love and fidelity (again) that we would mean every word. It couldn't be just for show.

Chapter Ten

Invigorated by my evening with Nigel and Grace, I set off to correct the two crucial omissions from my perfect wedding. Way to drop the ball, Sydney! After a quick conversation with Zoe, I was granted permission to borrow the veil she had worn when she married Charlie. The color was a bit off from my dress, but it was gorgeous and it would be my something borrowed. (I'm ahead of the game! My last something borrowed was discovered ten minutes before the wedding ceremony.) Much to my delight, my amazing boss, Vivian, came to rescue and agreed to "officiate" our ceremony. She had seen everything unfold between the two of us and I felt honored she wanted to tell our story through her eyes to all our loved ones.

With those gaping holes plugged, I felt infinitely better. Though I was still unsure of what to buy for our wedding party. I was tempted to go with Louis' idea that being in the wedding party was a gift in itself, but knew I would hate myself later for such an idiotic choice. While he was keeping his comments on the final stages of our wedding plans to a minimum, I could see he still believed the innumerable details were ridiculous. I decided for the sake of my marriage, it wouldn't be a good idea to bring up that his mother's wedding related activities were far more complicated and costly than ours. (Thankfully, she was footing the bill for her own shenanigans!)

I surveyed my final list, which had fallen below five items, and glanced at Louis. It was Saturday morning and he was sitting on the floor in front of the TV playing one of his favorite games, *Manhunt*. Whenever he got a new video game, he would sit in the living room in his underwear for the entire weekend trying to beat the game as soon as possible. Normally, cabin fever took over and I would do my best to get him out of the apartment for a couple of hours. (He would always get really twitchy and stare at the clock, so we never lasted very long.) Every so often he would grin at me and then immediately scowl in concentration as he resumed his game. I smiled, knowing we were getting closer to the happiness we once shared.

For the past three weeks, Louis and I have been spending a minimum four nights a week together and it has been AWESOME! Though Louis had yet to find a job, he had gone on a number of promising interviews and was hopeful one would turn into gainful employment. We didn't discuss wedding plans, American or French, focusing only on enjoying each other's company. I'm deliriously happy to note this included a lot of time in the bedroom. Louis is an incredible lover and the many lazy afternoons and evenings we spent in bed did wonders for both of us. We slept better, laughed more and had a much more positive outlook on life.

I closed my eyes and thought of a particularly satisfying evening involving massage oil when I was jolted out of my reverie by the phone ringing. I quickly glanced at the caller ID. Uh oh…here it comes.

"Bluey! Your mom is calling."

He peered up at me. "I'll call her back later."

He must be kidding. It was eleven in the morning! There was a nine hour time difference and his parents went to bed by eight. Come to think of it, she should be in bed. A knot formed in my stomach. Louis's mom did *not* make phone calls from her bedroom. She always sat in her favorite chair in the living room. So if she were calling when she would normally be in bed...

I shook my head at him. "Something is wrong. You need to speak with her."

He rolled his eyes. "Do I have to?"

I picked up the phone and walked over to him. "Trust me. Something is very, very wrong."

He sighed and pushed the talk button. "*Maman?*"

The yelling from the other end of the phone was deafening. Seriously, she just put my dad to shame.

Louis' faced morphed quickly, settling in a resemblance to a deer caught in headlights. For the millionth time I wished I spoke French. Granted his mom has a thick southern accent, and she uses a lot of slang and local language, but I would be able to catch every fifth word or so. I might have been able to make sense of something!

After five minutes of yelling, Louis joined in. He began to yell at the top of his lungs – again, no clue what he was saying – and the cacophony in the apartment was almost comical. The only thing that made me feel better was I knew no one had died. There wouldn't be this much yelling if someone were in danger. This could only mean there was a serious French wedding issue. Shit.

I began to pace the living room. What could have happened? Was someone important not coming? Had one of the vineyards had a break in? (What was a wedding in France without wine?) Were they not able to locate enough tables for four hundred and fifty people? Did a bunch of farm animals get into Simone's secret stash of wedding flowers? Did something happen to one of my wardrobe items? I crossed my fingers and hoped it was the last one.

Louis screamed a string of expletives (he taught me those early on) and slammed the phone down.

I stood there looking at him, at a total loss for anything to say. His whole body was shaking with rage. I was barely breathing as I waited for him to react.

He surprised me by sitting down on the couch and putting his head in his hands. I thought he would have thrown something. I would have wanted to if I were in his shoes. More power to him for his degree of self-control.

I knelt on the floor next to him and rubbed his back. "Are you OK, Bluey?"

He shook his head. "I...I don't know what to say."

"Um...why don't you tell me what all the yelling was about?" I tried to smile.

He sighed. "My mother had a tantrum."

Oh. A tantrum. I knew she was rather...excitable...but I didn't realize there were tantrums.

I stroked the back of his neck. "Did something happen?"

"You could say that."

OK. And what could I say happened? How about we get to the point? The suspense is killing me!!! Whoa, calm down, Sydney. Dial down the sarcasm. I took a deep breath. "Is everything alright?"

He brought his eyes up to meet mine. "No, it is not. My mother is very upset."

I bit back another snarky comment. "I gathered from the massive amount of yelling."

He cracked a smile. "I guess this was a sign." He cleared his throat. "She had lunch with one of her friends today who whipped her up into a frenzy about the French wedding coming last."

I furrowed my brow. "But, she said it was fine. She has extra time to plan..." And more importantly, she would have a less stressed bride to deal with.

"Well, my mother is very easily swayed by other's opinions. Her friend told her she was being treated very poorly by her American daughter-in-law and she needed to stand up for herself."

WHAT??? I've never even met her! What have *I* done? Besides appropriate her only son…

It was my turn to put my head in my hands. She hasn't met me and she already hates me. What could I do to fix this?

Louis pulled me close to him. "Syd, relax. My mom cares way too much about what other people think. Her pride was wounded; that's all."

I put my head on his shoulder. "But why did her friend say I mistreated her?"

He sighed. "Because we will have had two American weddings before the French wedding."

I studied him. "And they think I'm the only one making decisions?"

He chuckled. "No, they know I would defer to you, since you are my beautiful bride."

I snuggled closer into Louis. I had to come up with a plan. I couldn't let my mother-in-law hate me. We were barely going to have a relationship as it is because we don't speak the same language. I had to do something for her. And it had to be big.

I exhaled slowly. "I have a plan. It scares me, but it's doable."

Louis raised his eyebrows at me. "*Mon coeur…*"

Did I really want to suggest this? Well, no, I didn't, but I had to. Shit.

I cleared my throat. "We can't move the American wedding given all of the deposits we've made and the travel plans, etc. But we *can* talk to your mother about moving the French wedding up."

Louis' eyes widened. "What are you saying?"

My hands started shaking. "I'm saying if your mother is willing to do it, we can have the French wedding before our Monterey wedding."

He stared at me like I was crazy. Which, of course, I was, but this needed to be done. Louis had made a very long list of concessions for me and it was time for me to pony up for the sake of his family.

Louis took my hands. "Syd, we have finally gotten back to a place where we are happy. I am afraid of what this change will do to you."

"Bluey, we're going to be fine. Think about it from your mom's perspective." I paused, momentarily lost in thought. "Because of me, you moved thousands of miles away, speak a different language more often than you speak French and have absorbed another culture. You live in a different world now."

He grimaced. "And I did marry an American."

I swatted him in the back of the head. "Whom she has yet to meet."

He squeezed my hand. "And cannot communicate with."

I gazed into the most beautiful blue eyes in the world. "We have to do something big for her to make up for all that. And I think this is it."

He thought for a moment. "Do you promise I will not lose *my* Sydney?"

I grinned at him. "You may have to get me a padded cell, but you won't lose me!"

He kissed me tenderly. "Thank you, *mon coeur*. This will mean a lot to her."

I tapped his nose playfully. "You mean a lot to me. It's definitely worth it."

Louis grabbed the phone and called his mom. I was grateful she gave him the opportunity to speak instead of immediately yelling. My idea did the trick and we were both back in her good graces. The wedding was set for the end of August, one full month before our wedding in California. I would have enough time to recover, right? What could possibly go wrong?

I closed my eyes and thought about what I had done. Fuck. That's right, I said FUCK!!! This is definitely an occasion for some serious profanity. In fact, if I weren't afraid of shocking you, I would bring out my father's favorite string of profanity. It consisted of ten very colorful words. And I must admit I always felt much better after uttering them.

There was only one thing to do. It was time to bring Maya out of hiding...

After Louis left for his afternoon shift at the martial arts studio, I called Maya. Surprise, surprise, I got her voicemail. I left a message detailing what I would do to her if she didn't show up at my apartment within one hour. This was not a drill.

My next call was to Kate. I was lucky Sam was sleeping and Nick didn't have too many weekend projects to catch up on. (In all fairness, it had been quite some time since Crazy Sydney had been in residence, so Kate was due a small amount of time to "defreak" her sister.) Kate told me she would be there, with a bottle of wine, in ten minutes.

An hour later, Kate, Maya and I were sitting around the table. Maya and I had polished off the bottle of wine Kate had brought, but I was still very high upon the ledge. Poor Kate had to endure this discussion stone-cold sober. Breastfeeding kept her from drinking in the middle of the afternoon like the other two lushes at the table.

Maya leveled her gaze at me. "Syd, what's the big deal?" Her lips twitched as though she were trying not to smile.

This coming from the woman who was keeping a list of the mortifying activities coming my way once I flew over the Atlantic. I think she was planning on creating quite a photo album...possibly to auction on eBay.

Kate frowned at Maya. "You need to stop getting so much enjoyment at my sister's expense."

Ha! I told you my perfect sister had come back to me.

Maya rolled her eyes at Kate. "She's going to be fine. SHE is the one who decided to move the French wedding up. YOU need to stop coddling her." Then she stared at me. "Grow a pair."

I stood up and got another bottle of wine. I slammed it down on the table and pointed my finger at Maya. "Listen, just because you're suddenly blissfully happy doesn't mean no one else has any problems. I mean, where the hell have you been for the past few months??? My marriage was crumbling!!!"

Maya was taken aback. "Excuse me for having a life for once."

Tears started spilling down my face. "You *always* had a life. You used to share a little of it with me." I sank down into my chair. "Everything got so hard and…it felt like you had abandoned me. And now you're giving me shit when I have a legitimate problem."

Kate had a murderous look on her face. Nobody messed with her little sister. Especially not some sassy little girl she could snap like a twig. Not that she ever would, of course, because she was a lady.

Maya took my hand. "I'm sorry, Syd. I didn't realize how bad things had gotten."

I shook my head as the tears continued to fall. "I kept trying to tell you, but I couldn't get you on the phone."

Maya opened the bottle of wine and poured me a fresh glass. I nodded my thanks and took a big sip.

Kate refilled her seltzer and sat back down at the table. She rifled through the candy bowl until she found a Kit Kat bar and promptly threw it at me. "Eat! It'll help you think."

I gobbled the chocolate and chased it with some more wine. Though it was probably a stupid idea, I was trying to eat and drink my way into serenity. Why was I making such a big deal out of this? I mean, I was only going to France, right? There would be delicious food, copious amounts of wine and many, many happy people. So what if I didn't speak the language? I could pantomime with the best of them. So what if I knew nothing about life on a farm in a small town? I would learn how to milk a cow! So what if tongues were already wagging because I'm a spoiled American? I…would…win…them…over…

Oh, who am I kidding? I gave up and drank straight out of the bottle. Kate's jaw dropped to the floor. "Sydney Julia Durand!"

Maya laughed so hard she had wine coming out of her nose. A most disgusting, yet satisfying sight. I would have something to mock her with for at least a week. I giggled uncontrollably while Maya grabbed a stash of napkins.

Kate was truly appalled at the pair of us. "Alright, ladies, let's break this down."

Maya finished mopping the wine from her chin. "Break what down? Do you want to place odds on how long it will take Syd to lose her mind?"

Kate shot death rays at Maya. "No, as fun as such a bet might be, we have more important things to discuss." She pulled a notebook and pencil out of her purse. After checking off a few items, she turned her gaze to me. "Syd, you have everything but the wedding party gifts taken care of. You can easily shop for those before you leave."

Maya cleared her throat. "I have a few ideas. Maybe I could help you?"

I eyed her cautiously. "None of your ideas involve replicas of genetalia, do they?"

She regarded me with a straight face. "Absolutely not. Tasteful, traditional ideas. I promise."

I peered over at Kate who nodded. In my current state of mind, I needed a second opinion on Maya's ability to define "tasteful" appropriately.

I held up my glass to her for a refill. "Thanks, Maya. I would really appreciate the help."

Kate beamed. "When you get back from the wedding, the *French* wedding, you'll only need to make your final phone calls to all the vendors confirming your orders. See? No big deal."

I was starting to feel a little tipsy, but was clearheaded enough to know Kate was right. One way or the other, I was going to have to go to France to meet the Durand family. I could pull the usual Crazy Sydney fare and freak out all over the place *or* I could make a serious attempt to change my perspective. It was time I saw the positive side of things. I was so tired of living on the dark side. (Even if Darth Vader is undeniably awesome.)

I looked back and forth between Maya and Kate. "I can do this."

Kate laughed. "Silly girl, of course you can!" She kicked Maya under the table.

Maya sprang into action. "What are you worried about, Syd? They'll adore you! They'll be thrilled to have you as a part of their family." A bit much for Maya, but I appreciated the sentiment. The girl was really trying.

I nodded. "Piece of cake." I was totally full of it, but I had to put on a brave face for the two of them. I took comfort in knowing they would both be with me for the majority of the trip. They would protect me from the scary French contingency if things got ugly. Kate can talk her way out of anything (*And* she speaks French!) and Maya is quite scrappy.

Maya winked at me. "And besides, you're already married to Louis. So if they have a problem with you, they can suck it!"

I really love her.

After Kate and Maya left, I snuggled down on the couch to watch *Sense & Sensibility*. While the opening credits played, I reminded myself I would do my best to make a good impression on Louis' family, starting with learning a few basic French phrases. My accent was absolutely heinous, but the effort had to be worth something. My mom had given me a lesson in French food and my dad had given me a lesson in French history (Though I'm pretty sure his view is skewed, since he kept referring to Louis' countrymen as "those crazy French bastards.") But the bottom line is some knowledge is better than none. Kate and Maya were helping me plan my wardrobe, along with hair and makeup, for all the wedding events. It was of vital importance to me that I look as good as possible. There HAD to be one area in which I wouldn't be judged harshly.

I closed my eyes, hoping as hard as I could this trip would go well. At least Louis and I had repaired most of the damage to our crippled marriage. I felt much better knowing he would hold my hand if things got rough, because come hell or high water, Sydney Durand was going to France.

Chapter Eleven

The following week marked a very important event in the Durand household. (We are a now an established household!) The one year anniversary of the day I met my incredible husband. I smiled, remembering we were also four days away from our six month wedding anniversary. The whole thing seemed so completely bizarre. A year ago I thought I was going to be alone for the rest of my life. And only a few hours later, everything changed dramatically. My life would never be the same again.

It was a beautiful Sunday morning and I lay in bed for a few moments contemplating what Louis and I would do to celebrate this momentous occasion. Perhaps some of Louis' delicious crepes? Maybe he even splurged on a bouquet of flowers! It would be really nice to have a small amount of indulgence today, since we had been living so carefully for the past few months. I felt giddy as I practically jumped out of bed in search of my husband. I couldn't wait to tackle him and remind him why he married such a frisky American.

After a quick detour to the bathroom to brush my teeth, I wandered into the kitchen expecting to find Louis. Hmmm. Maybe he ran out for some brunch ingredients? While I fervently hoped he wouldn't go overboard (money was still pretty tight), I noticed a note on the counter. Crap. It seemed Louis would be at the martial arts studio all day. I had forgotten Bastiaan was leaving for Holland for a month tomorrow and the studio would be closed for the duration.

I guess it made sense that Louis would want to get in as much time as he could before his departure. Thai boxing with Bastiaan was one of the only activities he had enjoyed since his job search began. I begrudgingly decided to be understanding of his absence, but was still disturbed by the lack of mention of our very important anniversary.

With no Louis to pamper me, I took matters into my own hands. I made myself French toast, eggs and bacon for breakfast and sat down in front of Breakfast at Tiffany's. Audrey Hepburn was the model of grace and elegance. Maybe some of her style and poise would rub off on me before my trip to France.

This thought caused me to guffaw in a most unladylike manner. Watching this movie *millions* of times wouldn't enable me to have even a microscopic portion of Audrey's sophistication. My French relatives were simply going to have to deal with the neurotic, klutzy, paranoid mess that I was. I was starting to feel sorry for them.

As I pondered the pros and cons of implanting a microchip in my brain to control my outbursts, the phone rang. Thank God! Louis remembered our anniversary! I grinned and ran for the phone, forgetting to check the caller ID first.

"Hi, handsome!"

There was nothing but silence at the other end of the line. How odd! Louis always enjoyed my compliments.

"Thanks, Duck! A father needs to hear that sometimes."

Oops! I giggled. "Sorry, Dad, I thought you were Louis."

He pretended to sniffle. "You mean you don't think your poor father is handsome?"

I sighed. "Of course I think you're handsome, Dad. I was expecting a call from Louis."

"To wish you a happy anniversary?"

I paused. My dad didn't have a good memory for dates. "Did Mom remind you?"

"Duck, I do have the capacity to remember things. I'm not *that* old."

Uh huh. Not buying it. "Dad, you have a great memory for things which are important to you. Anniversary dates do *not* fall on this list." He could; however, tell you the price of his favorite Cadbury bar every year since nineteen fifty-two. Because knowledge of this sort comes in really handy in today's day and age.

He cleared his throat. "She *may* have said something about it."

I chuckled. "I thought so."

Just then my mom joined the conversation. "Happy Anniversary, Syd!"

"Thanks, Mom!"

My dad chimed in. "Yes, Happy Anniversary, Duck! It is really ironic you two met on Bastille Day."

Here it comes.

He took on his instructional tone. "Since, as you know, Bastille Day is the French version of Independence Day."

This never gets old, Dad. Please tell me more.

"And the day he met you was the day he lost his independence." My dad laughed. I had no doubt my mom and I were rolling our eyes in unison.

My mom sighed. "What are you and the fabulous *Monsieur* Durand up to today?" My mom loved to hear the details of Louis' romantic plans. I didn't have the heart to tell her there was a very good chance he had forgotten.

Quick, Sydney, make something up! "Um, well, he's at the martial arts studio for the day, since Bastiaan is leaving for Holland tomorrow and will be gone for a month. So, we're going to have a romantic dinner at home tonight."

My dad scoffed. "At home? You kids should be going to a nice restaurant."

My mom must have taken her extension to the back where my dad was sitting because I heard him say, "Ow!" His comment must have earned him a good smack upside the head.

"Ted, you know they're watching their pennies."

"Going out once in while won't break the bank; besides the Olive Garden has a very good early bird special." My dad fell in love with the Olive Garden on his last trip out here. Endless supplies of bread he could slather with butter was his idea of paradise.

I heard them bickering quietly in the background and started to chuckle. I really missed them. Even in these moments of conflict.

"Mom! Dad! Don't worry. I'm going to make Louis an amazing dinner tonight. I've planned all his favorites."

My mom whispered something with emphasis to my father and then turned her attention back to me. "I'm sure dinner will be lovely, Sydney. Please pass on our anniversary wishes to Louis as well."

"Yes, Duck, please remind our son-in-law how lucky he is."

I laughed. "To be married to me or to be part of our family?"

My dad thought for a moment. "Both."

OK, it was time to go. "I love you both! I'll speak to you tomorrow."

"We love you too." They spoke in unison. I hoped one day Louis and I would exhibit such glorious synchronicity.

A few hours later, I had prepared a delicious meal and had dolled myself up for what I hoped would be a deliciously satisfying evening. I wasn't sure exactly when Louis was coming home, so I had the chicken francese, roasted potatoes and asparagus warming in the oven. The smell was heavenly and I was doing my best not to pick too much at the Tuscan chick pea dip I had prepared. Keeping dinner in the oven was a deliberate deterrent for me to sample the main dishes, since my klutzy nature would have led to a few nasty burns. Spending the night in the emergency room was not part of the plan for our romantic evening. I sipped on my second glass of wine and wondered if it was time to hit the chocolate.

Once eight o'clock rolled around, I became nervous. I had tried calling Louis' cell phone a few times during the day, but only reached his voicemail. My heart sank as I wondered if he had decided to go out for dinner with the guys from the martial arts studio. He would have called me to tell me he was going to be late, right? We were in such a good place; please, please, please let him have remembered what today is. Please let him have concocted an awesomely romantic plan. Please! I *need* this.

I breathed a sigh of relief when I heard Louis' key turn in the lock. I stood up and smiled only to be greeted by a very sweaty Louis followed by Bastiaan. What the hell was HE doing here?

My face froze in a forced smile as Louis took in the atmosphere. While he surveyed the dim lights, romantic music, candles and the mouthwatering aroma from the kitchen, his face morphed into a state of confusion.

"What is all this, *mon coeur*?"

I walked over to the light switch and returned the room to its usual level of brightness. Poor Bastiaan seemed like he wanted to flee. As I blew out all the candles, I locked eyes with Louis and said, "Happy Anniversary!"

Louis' face fell. "Today is July fourteenth, isn't it?"

I nodded. "That it is." I was more resigned than shocked. Louis and I had made great strides in our relationship, but this didn't mean he wasn't feeling the pressure of his job search. He was still not quite himself.

Bastiaan began to back towards the door. "Listen, man, I don't want to interrupt anything…"

I suddenly felt terrible about the awkwardness in the room; it certainly wasn't Bastiaan's fault Louis forgot. "Please stay, Bastiaan. I made a really delicious dinner. I'm sure you're quite hungry."

Louis snapped to attention. "I am so sorry, *mon coeur*, I was so focused on today being Bastiaan's last day; I completely forgot."

I sighed. "Don't worry, Bluey. Why don't you jump in the shower? I'm ravenous."

Louis turned to Bastiaan. "Why don't you take the first shower? There are towels in the cabinet next to the sink."

Bastiaan nodded and left the room as fast as he could. He had to be feeling pretty damn uncomfortable right now.

Louis came over to me and put his hands on my face. "I can't apologize enough. The showers broke at the studio and I didn't want Bastiaan to have to drive back to San Francisco after working the whole day without getting clean, so I offered the use of our bathroom."

I gazed into his beautiful blue eyes. "It's OK. I made too much food anyway." I was making an effort, but I couldn't help being a little pissed.

He shook his head. "I have been so distracted lately. My job search has hit a wall…"

I rubbed my temples. "It's fine. I've been wanting to get to know Bastiaan better anyway. He seems really nice." Louis spends a good portion of his time at the studio now and Bastiaan has been able to help him in ways I couldn't. I should show the man some gratitude.

I tilted my head towards Louis. "I'm going to change." Suddenly the short black mini dress I had chosen seemed inappropriate.

After my wardrobe had been corrected to a more appropriate ensemble of a black V-neck sweater and jeans, I set another place at the table and pulled out my secret stash of chocolate. After the turn of events this evening, I deserved a little sugar. Who knew how long it would be before I got my sought after dessert?

Bastiaan turned out to be a really great guy. He had lived a very full and interesting life in his thirty two years. Over dinner, he regaled us with stories of his life growing up in Holland and the years he spent traveling around the globe during his time as a professional fighter. The truth was he reminded me a lot of Louis. I could easily see why my husband spent so much of his time at Bastiaan's studio.

They were both very independent in nature, highly intelligent, well-traveled and very good-looking (Not that this last item made a bit of difference in their friendship; I was only making an observation.) It was too bad Maya was so in love with Devon. Bastiaan was a huge catch *and* he was looking for a woman to brighten his life. Maya would most definitely light it on fire.

I smiled genuinely as I said good-bye to Bastiaan. He thanked me profusely for dinner and promised to bring me back a huge stash of European chocolate. (It didn't take him long to figure out how to get into my good graces.)

Louis kissed me on the top of my head. "I am going to walk Bastiaan out to the car."

I knew Bastiaan could handle himself since we lived in a pretty safe neighborhood AND he made a living out of beating people up. This meant something was going on. I wondered what it was they needed to discuss out of my earshot.

Five minutes later, Louis called me to tell me Bastiaan's battery had died and he needed to give him a jump. Funny, I thought I was his next customer.

Slightly annoyed, I went into the bathroom to take a shower. As the steaming water beat down on my back, I remembered Louis had not come back to the apartment for the car keys, which meant he had taken them when he went to walk Bastiaan out. Which is odd, because he didn't keep car keys on his key ring, just the house keys. I was the main driver of the car. Something is definitely up.

Once I had steamed most of the tension out of my muscles, I dried off and put on my favorite cotton pajamas. They had blue skies and clouds all over them, which was exactly what I needed. Blue skies and sunny days…

I walked out to the living room, trying to dream up an excuse to avoid the dreaded task of cleaning up the kitchen. Wait. It's awfully dark in here. Didn't I leave the lights on?

"Happy Anniversary, *mon coeur*." Louis' sexy voice permeated the room.

As I took in the candles, flowers and CHOCOLATE CAKE on the table, my shoulders relaxed for the first time that day.

I beamed at him. "What did you do?"

He put his arms around me. "I put together an anniversary more worthy of you."

I kissed him tenderly. "This is wonderful. Thank you."

He looked into my eyes. "No, thank you. You were so incredibly gracious with Bastiaan and with your…dumbass husband." He sighed. "I am sorry I let you down."

I shook my head. "Don't give it another thought. I love you so much, Bluey."

He smiled. "And I love you, *mon coeur*. More than you can ever imagine."

After Louis pulled out my chair for me, he removed a bottle of champagne from the refrigerator.

I gasped. "Where did you get that?" We couldn't afford champagne!

He grinned. "It was a gift from Bastiaan."

"I see. So the whole thing with the battery was…"

"Bullshit. Bastiaan and I were on our phones researching stores which were still open whenever you went into the kitchen."

It was all falling into place. "So the two of you kept asking for different condiments to buy more time."

He had the grace to look ashamed. "And why I pretended not to know where anything was in the kitchen."

I giggled. "I really wanted to kill you after the tenth time you asked me for something. I was *so* hungry!"

"And I was desperate."

For the next hour, we happily fed each other cake and drank the expensive bottle of champagne Bastiaan had given us. We then made our way to the bedroom for the dessert I had been waiting for all day. With each touch, I reveled jubilantly in the sweetness I had been craving.

What an amazing night it had turned out to be. It was really strange to go from wanting to kill your husband to feeling incredibly cherished by him. After the last few months of unpredictability, I was grateful for an evening that ended in bliss. The more I thought about it, the evening was an analogy of our relationship thus far. Despite a few bumps in the road, we were at long last getting it right. Hallelujah!

Chapter Twelve

A week into Bastiaan's absence, Louis' nerves were starting to fray. He was in a holding pattern with three different jobs and was at a standstill with the rest of his employment search. (With the limited job market, new listings were extremely rare and there were only so many times a day you could call recruiters before they assigned you stalker status.) Since I was saving all of my vacation time for our trip to France, I was not able to take any time off to help distract him.

This meant my day was peppered with phone calls from my patently bored husband reaching out for a lifeline during his long hours in the apartment. I kept trying to get him to go out for a little fresh air, for both our sakes, but he was too paranoid he would miss a call from a recruiter. Never mind that they ALL had his cell phone number. There was simply no reasoning with him. Apparently Crazy Louis was now in residence. I found myself counting the days until Bastiaan came back to the states.

With the French wedding just over a month away, Louis' mom was going into overdrive. Let me impress upon you the incredibly frightening reality of Simone Durand in overdrive. When the wedding was months away she called one to four times a day, depending on how busy she was gossiping with her friends. She was now calling at least TWENTY times per day. AT LEAST TWENTY TIMES PER DAY. Keep in mind these conversations were never short. EVER. On top of this, she now had no regard for the time difference and would sometimes call in the wee hours of the morning, claiming the matter was absolutely crucial. Louis kept reminding her she had all the decision making power, but she insisted his input was really important to her. Personally, I think she was simply enjoying fucking with us.

It was in light of this desperate situation, I chose to splurge for Louis' birthday and booked a night at a hotel in San Francisco. I knew we couldn't afford it, but I also knew if Louis didn't get out of the apartment for an extended period of time and I didn't get away from his mother's crazy late night phone calls, someone was going to get hurt. I found a great midweek deal at the Hyatt and was graciously granted permission by my boss to come in at noon the next day. I think she was hoping this night away would help to return Normal Sydney to the building. Crazy Sydney had been showing up at the office a little too regularly over the past couple of weeks…

I left work that night with a spring in my step. Louis and I were going to have some time alone together with NO distractions. (Read: NO Simone.) We chatted happily in the car on the way up to San Francisco and had just settled into our room when his cell phone rang. He looked at me and winced.

I rolled my eyes. "Is it your mother?"

He nodded. "Who else would it be?" He regarded me with sad eyes. He knew I would expect him to answer it because not answering only multiplied the number of calls.

I thought about it. "OK, as a special birthday present – to both of us – you don't have to answer any of your mother's calls for the rest of our stay in this hotel." His mother had gone completely rogue with both the number and the timing of her calls. She deserved to go without communication from her son for a day or two.

He grinned from ear to ear. "I love you so much, *mon coeur.*"

I laughed. "You're a grown man, you know. You don't have to do what I ask you to do. You could have refused her calls even when I asked you to take them."

He turned off his phone and pulled me into his arms. "I know. · But if you are fine with my not taking her calls then she has gone too far and needs a cooling off period. You, my beautiful wife, are far more patient than I am."

I put my forehead against his. "I see. I'm your barometer."

He chuckled softly and began kissing my neck. "Something like that. Now let's see what we can do about all of this pesky clothing…"

⌒

The night Louis and I spent in San Francisco was miraculous. With no interruptions, we were able to focus solely on each other and savor the passion which had ignited our relationship last year. We took long, luxurious showers and spent hours making love by the fire. (Yes, our circumstances had become so dire to warrant such a crazy expense.) I was so enraptured with my husband, the thought of food didn't even cross my mind until eleven o'clock at night. This was a new record for me, since I come with feeding instructions which dictate snacks every two hours. Apparently, my need for my husband far outweighed my need for food.

To my great surprise, we were awakened at six o'clock the next morning by MY cell phone. I recognized Kate's ring tone immediately and lunged for my purse. Before I even said hello, I heard Kate's voice echoing in my ear.

"Make it stop! Make it stop! Make it stop!" She shrieked.

I was bewildered. "Make what stop?"

"The phone calls! Make them stop!"

Phone calls? Had my sister lost her mind? "Kate! Who is calling you?"

She was on the verge of hyperventilating. "Simone! Simone! Simone! Your insane mother-in-law won't stop calling me!"

What the fuck? Why would she call Kate? "I don't understand. Is everything alright?"

Louis came up behind me. "What is going on?"

I shrugged my shoulders at him as Kate started shrieking again. "She wants his opinion on the ring bearer! She keeps calling!"

I turned to Louis. "How did your mom get Kate's number?"

The color drained from his face. "My cell phone wasn't working for a couple of weeks, so I gave her the number in case we were visiting with Kate and Nick. I told her it was only for emergencies."

Clearly his mother had a very different definition of emergencies than most people. What the hell had I gotten myself into? I was very grateful there were thousands of miles between us and his mother AND that I could not speak French. I wanted no part of this mess. (I was also grateful Louis had never given his mother *my* cell phone number. I'm thinking this might have had something to do with a teeny-weeny threat on his life if he ever decided to do so…)

Louis took the phone from me. "Kate, I am so sorry for my mother's behavior. I turned off my phone for a few hours…I had no idea this would happen. What can I do to make it up to you?"

I held my breath while we waited for an answer. God knows what she would ask for. God knows what she had been through in the last few hours. Kate needed whatever precious sleep she could get and Simone had no doubt taken most, if not all, of that from her. Simone was VERY lucky to be out of Kate's reach at the moment.

Louis smiled. "Done. I will be there in one hour." He hung up the phone and handed it back to me.

I regarded him cautiously. "How are you going to pay the piper?" Seriously, he owed her big time for her exposure to his mother's shenanigans.

He raised his eyebrows at me. "Who is the piper?"

Damn these stupid American expressions. "What are you going to do to help Kate?"

He grinned. "Got it. I am going to take care of Sam so she can rest and get some things done. I think I promised myself to her for the day."

So much for the romantic morning we had planned. If he had promised Kate he would be there in an hour that meant we had to leave...right now. Crap. Not even time for a quickie in the shower.

Louis and I raced around the room gathering our belongings and were on our way to Kate's house in ten minutes flat. My appearance was borderline horrific, but I doubted anyone in the Wilson household would care. My suspicion was no one slept very well last night.

Extremely Grumpy Kate answered the door. She didn't speak, she only scowled and handed Sam to Louis. A minute later she was gone, leaving no direction for Louis. This was highly unusual for Kate. There were typically lists and diagrams and perhaps even a few instructional videos.

A quick look around told me Nick was not in residence. It was now seven-thirty and I knew he didn't leave for work until eight. He rarely ever left the house before he absolutely had to. Where was he? Was he driven from the house by the endless phone calls? I felt like I was forgetting something...

The note taped to the fridge reminded me in an instant. Nick was out of town! Shit! Having no husband made last night even worse for Kate. I sank down at the kitchen table opposite Louis and a very happy Sam. She was staring up at Louis with wonder in her eyes and would coo and smile at him every couple of minutes.

I already felt better. Sam's smile could cure anyone's woes. Even the great Louis Durand. Why didn't I think of this before? Suddenly, Bastiaan's absence was not such a bad thing. With more time on his hands, Louis could come here and smile rather than go to the martial arts studio and engage in combat with grown men. Sure the combat option was helpful in getting out all of his aggression, but Sam could give him something even better. Pure happiness! The end results of his visits with Sam would be good for all of us.

There was only one small problem. Louis knew absolutely nothing about babies. He was an only child and the youngest of all his cousins. There had been no babies in his social circle when he was growing up, so he hadn't been exposed to how to care for them. I had just enough time to give him a crash course before I had to go to work. This would leave no margin for error.

I ran to the study and grabbed *What to Expect the First Year* and *The Girlfriends' Guide to Surviving the 1st Year*. Both provided excellent sources of information, but the latter title also made you laugh. This was always a good thing when you felt like you were going to cry because you couldn't figure out what the hell your cute little baby wanted.

In the span of three and a half hours, Louis and I went over feeding, changing, sleeping and intellectual stimulation. (Yes, even babies enjoy lively conversation now and then. Louis could educate Sam on the wonders of the Ultimate Fighting Championship!) I showed him where to find all of the important items – diapers, wipes, onesies, pajamas, Kate's stored breast milk and most importantly, Piggy. Piggy had been given to Sam on the day she was born. He was a beautiful, cuddly, newborn-safe little slice of pink heaven. Sam absolutely adored her Piggy and wouldn't sleep without him.

I stared Louis straight in the eye. "Do *not* lose Piggy."

He saluted me. "Don't worry. I won't lose the pig." Sam peered up at him from her bouncy seat and gurgled. "See, Syd? She knows she can trust her Uncle Bluey."

The poor bastard had no idea what he was in for. "Don't joke. If she *doesn't* have Piggy, she *doesn't* sleep." And if she *doesn't* sleep, you will *not* survive.

He was doing his best not to roll his eyes at me. "Syd, we will be fine."

I tried not to worry. "Bluey, she has a sixth sense when it comes to Piggy. If something happens to him, your life will be hell."

He sighed. "Syd, relax. Go to work. We will be fine."

I knelt down to say good-bye to Sam and whispered, "Go easy on him, sweetie. He's not as tough as he looks."

I kissed Louis and crossed my fingers everyone would make it through the afternoon in one piece. The last thing I saw was Louis shaking his head at me as I walked to my car.

$\backsim$

The first hour of Louis' shift passed without incident. It was during hour two that the phone calls began. First Louis had trouble with the breast milk. He somehow managed to burn the first batch while heating it up in the microwave, which was not the Kate Wilson required method, but he had waited too long to feed her and using the sanctioned stovetop method would have taken too long. Strike one.

Then, he somehow managed to drop a full diaper onto the floor, causing Sam's room to reek of poop despite his repeated attempts to clean the rug. Nap time was in serious danger. Who could relax enough to sleep in a room smelling of poop? Strike two. Finally, he forgot to turn on the vibrating mechanism on the bouncy chair, denying Sam her afternoon massage. This put her in quite a wicked mood. A massive strike three, Louis. You're out.

However, all this was nothing in comparison to his last mistake. During the diaper incident, a small amount of poop splattered onto Piggy. Louis decided it would be a good idea to put Piggy in the washing machine to remove not only the odor but also the vast array of germs which now inhabited Sam's coveted companion. Thirty minutes later, Kate and Nick's washing machine held the remains of poor Piggy. It would seem even the gentle cycle was too much for him to survive.

When Louis called me to relay all of the above, I let myself have a small laugh (covering the phone the entire time, of course.) Despite my best efforts, I was unable to calm him down. Though I imagined Sam's indignant cries had made it an impossible task. There *had* to be a solution. Think, Sydney! Think!

I hung up and quickly called Kate. She had gone out to run a few errands and I didn't want Louis to call her in his current state of hysteria, sending her running home once she heard both his distress and her distraught daughter in the background.

She picked up right away. "Syd? Is everything alright?"

Shit. She already knows something is wrong. Be very careful, Sydney. Be very, very careful. "Everything is fine, Kate. No cause for alarm."

She was silent. I wonder if she bought my bravado. I was pretty convincing, right? Right? Oh, who am I kidding? She always knows when I'm hiding something! I'm *so* dead!

I cleared my throat. "I have a quick question. Um…do you by any chance…have….um another animal Sam likes?

"Sydney Julia Durand. What has happened to Piggy?" Uh oh. Her voice was almost unrecognizable. She didn't even speak, it was more of a growl.

"Um…Louis tried to wash him, because there was poop on him…"

She cut me off in a second. "Poop on Piggy?"

Yikes! She was going to kill my husband. I texted Nick frantically to see if he had a solution. He was probably in a meeting, but it was worth a shot.

I could hear her car starting in the background. She switched me over to her speakerphone. Kate was nothing if not a responsible driver. Although, she was most likely racing home to commit murder...

As I wracked my brain for something to say to her to calm her down, I received a text from Nick. Thank God! Piggy has a twin!

"Kate!" OK, I need to calm down too. I lowered my voice. "Kate, I can call Louis and tell him where Piggy, the second is."

"Piggy the second is only for emergencies, Sydney." Ouch. She's still really pissed.

"Um...I think this is the *definition* of an emergency, Kate. Piggy is in pieces."

The string of expletives which came out of Kate's mouth was both frightening and hysterical. For the moment, fear won out and I simply quaked in my boots.

After a minute or two, Kate said, "You make sure your husband finds the replacement pig. Or it's his ass." Damn! Perfect Kate may be back, but she sure has an attitude.

Click.

I quickly called Louis and told him the location of the backup Piggy. I decided not to share Kate's last words with him until his current crisis was over. He and I would scour the internet this evening for Piggy the third. The important thing was Sam would now take her nap. And Louis was safe from my sister, as least for the moment.

After I put Louis to bed that evening (Sam had sapped every last ounce of energy out of him), I thought about the eye opening experience he had been through. When I tucked him in, he had profusely apologized to me for *ever* doubting how much energy and attention child rearing took. He looked deeply into my eyes and whispered that he didn't want to consider children for a few years. With a hint of fear still lingering in his eyes, he told me he would need to build up much more stamina in order to have a chance of surviving being a father. I heartily agreed with him. Life was complicated enough without introducing a mini Louis into the fray. And a mini Sydney would probably kill us both.

Chapter Thirteen

After last week's phone stalking disaster, Louis made sure to keep regular contact with his mother. With less than four weeks until the wedding, his mother was spinning faster than the Tasmanian devil in a last ditch attempt to ensure every single detail was perfect. (Maybe we had more in common than I originally thought.) Unfortunately, this massive burst of French energy coincided with Louis' final round of interviews for a job he desperately wanted.

He had been through three rounds of interviews for this company over the last three weeks and his nerves were shot. He was having trouble sleeping and had begun twitching spontaneously during the day. I knew he was so close to getting a job he could taste it, but he was afraid to hope this phase of uncertainty would truly be over. I crossed my fingers he would have some relief soon.

Amidst the pressure of Louis' job search and the strain of the final stages of both weddings, Simone Durand did something so egregious, she sent her son over the edge. (As if the CONSTANT phone calls weren't enough to kill us both.) What could she possibly have done to cause the final blow? While she had accepted that we wouldn't get married in a church, due to Louis' status as an atheist, she had not accepted Louis' request to not invite the town priest to the wedding. I had NEVER seen him so irate. It really freaked me out to see him this way, but I had no choice but to keep it together, because we couldn't afford to have both of us locked up in a mental institution. Although given his current state of mind, I think Louis might end up in prison…most likely a French prison.

But let us get back to the religious issue. It's not like Louis worships the devil and participates in crazy satanic rituals. The explanation is much more banal than that. What it boils down to is, Louis is an engineer and operates solely by logic and reason. During his education in Catholicism as a boy, he was full of questions regarding elements of the Bible. When the town priest was unable to answer his questions in a factual manner, Louis became concerned about religion in general.

After he refused to stay quiet following the priest's lectures regarding the superiority of faith over scientific reasoning, he was summarily kicked out of Catholic school. Louis was extremely relieved, but his mother was humiliated and the topic of religion has remained contentious between them ever since. By inviting the priest, the very same priest from his childhood, Louis felt his mother had purposely humiliated him.

I must admit I was pretty pissed at her given the ENORMOUS concession I had made to her by suggesting we move up the French wedding. Louis and I were both at the end of our ropes and her latest stunt threatened our very existence. Louis jumped every time the phone rang, hoping for news about a job and I was dealing with one last wedding issue. Yes, I mean for the third and final wedding, MY REAL WEDDING, the one which *used* to be the second wedding. The one I wish were still the second wedding!!! Wow. Please excuse my outburst. The stress is starting to eat away at my soul. Where were we? Oh yes, I was about to say Louis and I were leaving for France in two and a half weeks and I was still having difficulty finding gifts for the bridal party. None of the options I had come up with so far had been agreeable to both Maya and Kate. If I didn't figure out a solution soon, I was going to lose my mind.

After Louis slammed the phone down on his mother, we stared at each other in silence for a moment. I had to think fast. Our circumstances were becoming desperate. I glanced at the clock and did a quick calculation. It was six-thirty, so we should be able to make it. I grabbed the phone and dialed Kate. Ten minutes later, Louis and I were in the car on the way to Kate and Nick's house. I had found the key to our salvation. Samantha Erin Wilson was about to save the day.

Over the last week, Louis had spent a number of days with Kate and Sam. He still felt terrible about the demise of Piggy the first and wanted to do something to make up for this egregious offense. He took Sam out for walks, read her books and began giving her French lessons. Kate was delighted for the company, not to mention the opportunity to nap, and begrudgingly forgave him for the aforementioned slaughter.

I knew a visit with our favorite niece was exactly what we needed to pull our heads out of our asses. She was a living reminder of the possibilities we had ahead of us. The joy, the wonder and yes, the chaos, but I was choosing to focus on the positive at this point in time. I needed to be able to function through the next four weeks with more than a small amount of intelligence and grace. The only way I could think of to accomplish this in my current state was to infuse myself with a little of Sam's magic.

I peeked at Louis. "You're humming, aren't you?"

He grinned. "I am! I need to warm up for my performance."

I laughed. "I thought I recognized the melody as *Old MacDonald Had a Farm.*"

He winked at me. "Be prepared to provide the animal noises."

"Quack! Quack!" I dissolved into a fit of giggles.

Louis laughed until tears spilled down his face. "I am only trying to get you in on the act."

Once I had regained the power of speech, I turned to Louis. "You've been teaching Sam the names of the animals in French, right?"

"*Mais oui.*" He smiled. "This is very important in light of her upcoming trip to an authentic French farm." The change in his mood was staggering. And we hadn't even set eyes on our little miracle yet!

I decided it would be a good idea if I had a basic farm vocabulary as well.

I cleared my throat. "OK, I think it's time you educate your wife as well." I had been asking Louis to work with me on my French for months now, but with everything going on, this request had fallen to the bottom of the priority list.

His eyes lit up. "What would you like to know?"

I snorted. "Well, right now the only words I know besides *bonjour, s'il vous plait* and *merci* are profane, so anything would be helpful. But, why don't we start with farm animals? I have a feeling this knowledge will come in handy during the visit."

He chuckled. "This is true. Let's start with duck." His face became serious. "*Le canard.*"

I did my best approximation. "*Le canard.*"

He had me say it a few more times until he was satisfied with the result. One of the hardest things about learning French is the pronunciation. Even if you master the verb tenses and vocabulary, if you don't pronounce the words just so, those meticulous Frenchies might not understand you. No wonder they had the reputation for being so smug...

For the remainder of the ride, we covered the full gamut of farm animals. Louis taught me the last one as we pulled into the driveway. Little did I know this word would end up being the bane of my existence.

"OK, Syd, we will end our lesson with the word for chicken." He paused. "*La poule.*"

I concentrated. "*La poule.*"

He shook his head. "*La poule.*"

I tried again. "*La poule.*"

He mulled it over. "That will do, but you need to be careful. If you put too much of the 'ooh' sound in it, you will end up saying the French word for sweater – *le pull.*"

I frowned. "*Le pull?*" They sounded exactly the same to me.

He smirked at me. "You just said chicken again."

I exhaled. "OK. *Le pull.*"

"OK, Miss Chicken."

Aaaaaah! This pronunciation is going to kill me! God knows what I'm going to end up saying to his relatives. Maybe it would be best for me to keep my mouth shut.

As we walked up the path to the front door, I kept trying to say the difference between *la poule* and *le pull*, but I simply couldn't get it. Louis was attempting to be supportive (by not laughing his ass off), but he was on the edge of losing it. I did my best not to get annoyed with him, especially once I remembered a fit of laughter I had in the middle of Hagen Daas when he ordered two "balls" of chocolate ice cream. In all fairness, he had been in the country for two months at the time, but the moment was priceless.

Kate opened the door just as I was giving it one last attempt. She burst out laughing. "Syd, what the hell are you trying to say?"

Her reaction was all it took for Louis. His laughter echoed throughout the entranceway to their home. Sam's little eyes searched for the source of the joy from the comfort of her bouncy seat in the living room.

As I was about to explain my pronunciation exercises to Kate, Louis found the power of speech. He put his arm around Kate and grinned down at her.

"I am trying to teach your sister how to pronounce the difference between *la poule* and *le pull*."

Kate grinned. "A pretty important distinction."

"I know!" He was barely holding it together.

Kate turned to me. "You'd better be careful when you get to France and you try to buy a sweater, Syd. You will most likely end up with a live chicken!"

Kate and Louis become completely hysterical, causing such a ruckus Nick came to investigate.

"What's going on out here?"

Since neither one of them had regained the ability to speak, I rolled my eyes and offered Nick an explanation.

"They're mocking my poor pronunciation of the French language."

Nick cracked a smile. "It can't be that bad, Syd."

I sighed. "I think those two beg to differ, my friend. Why don't you ask them to tell you the story? It'll make your night."

Smirking briefly, I walked past them and sat next to my little angel. She wouldn't willingly participate in the boisterous mocking of her aunt.

Ten minutes later, the three traitors decided to join us in the living room. Kate was still wiping tears of laughter from her face and Nick and Louis both had red faces from the exertion of mirth.

Instead of hating them for ridiculing me, I chose to be happy Kate and Nick had kept Louis laughing for such a long period of time. At least that *was* the case until my sister wouldn't let the subject die.

"Syd, are you telling me you really can't hear the difference between *la poule* and *le pull*?"

Sydney, keep your temper in check. Louis is feeling so much better. Do *not* take away his good mood by getting angry.

I took a deep breath. "I can hear the difference, Kate. Apparently, I'm not able to *say* the difference."

She scoffed. "I'm sure you can. Let's give it another shot."

She then proceeded to show me how to purse my lips in order to produce the proper "oooh" sound necessary to convey I was speaking of a sweater and not a chicken.

As I thought about the best way to punch her in the nose without scaring Sam, Nick came to my rescue. I think he could see I was staring daggers at my sister and didn't like to think about what I was capable of under this level of stress.

He put his arm around his wife protectively. "Kate! Why don't you tell Syd what you found?"

She studied him quizzically. "Oh! That's right!" She turned to me. "Syd, I found the BEST earrings for the girls." She bounced up excitedly and pulled me by the hand toward the study. I heard Nick breathe a sigh of relief and smirked at him before I left the room.

Kate brought up a website quickly. "Look at these! Aren't they gorgeous?"

I leaned over her and saw the most beautiful pair of Givenchy chandelier earrings. They were simple, elegant and had just enough sparkle to impress, yet not overwhelm. They were in a word, perfect.

I gasped. "Kate! These are awesome! Thank you so much!"

She jumped up and we started bouncing and squealing at the same time. Then we heard Nick yelling at us from down the hall.

"You are disturbing the sanctity of bath time, ladies! Lower the volume!"

D'oh! Kate and I both knew if bath time didn't go well, then bed time wouldn't go well. None of us wanted such an outcome.

Kate lowered her voice to a whisper. "I knew you'd like them, so I took the liberty of ordering six pairs."

Yes, I've already told you that I have chosen six bridesmaids. I know it might seem a little tacky, but each one of them is important to me. I actually wanted to have two or three more, because I wanted to include all of my closest friends, but my wedding party would have been truly pretentious. And an ounce of pretention is worth a pound of manure! (I really love *Steel Magnolias*.)

I sighed with happiness. "Kate, you didn't have to! But I'm so glad you did! Tell me how much I owe you and I'll write you a check." I started walking towards the living room to get my purse.

She grabbed my hand. "Don't be silly! Consider them a gift."

I stared at her with wide eyes. "Kate, I appreciate your generosity, but those earrings were not cheap."

She tapped my nose. "Only the best for my sister."

I threw my arms around her. "Thank you! That's a very generous wedding gift!"

She laughed. "The earrings are not your wedding gift! They're 'a life has been very hard for you and I love you to pieces and want you to feel better' gift."

Damn it, Kate. I had tears in my eyes. I hugged her even tighter and felt myself relax for the first time in a few days. My perfect sister had checked the last item off my list for me. And she had done it in a most Katelike fashion; with generosity, elegance and kindness. I had no choice but to forgive her for the degree of heckling she delivered to me over what would come to be known as the great chicken sweater fiasco, but it was close. EXTREMELY close. (I spared you from the worst of her comments, because I, too, am a lady.)

While Kate and I shared our sisterly moment, Louis had been in heaven during bath and story time with Sam. He generously allowed me to join him for a duet during song time. Luckily for me, Sam really loved our rendition of *The Wheels on the Bus* and I was asked to join for an encore performance.

After Sam went to bed, we thanked Nick and Kate profusely for bringing us out of our doldrums. We had been infused with enough of Sam's magic to keep us going through the next few days. They promised us we were more than welcome to come by as often as we needed to before our departure to France. We all had a feeling the intensity was only going to get worse the closer we got to the wedding and a hit of Sam's baby dust would vastly increase our chances of survival.

As we drove home, I held Louis' hand and smiled. He smiled back at me and we breathed a collective sigh of relief. While I was a little jealous that Sam was able to relieve her Uncle Bluey's tension when I couldn't, I was ultimately grateful someone had the capacity to make him feel better. I was even more grateful this particular someone had the capacity to make us BOTH feel better. In the end, it took the entire Wilson family to pull us out of our funk. Having perfect people as a part of your family certainly has its benefits.

Chapter Fourteen

With only two weeks to go before our departure to France, Louis brought up a topic which was, well, rather strange. He expressed concern regarding the delicate fabric of my wedding dress. There's no need to be shocked. Of course I showed it to him! It's the third wedding, wait, I mean the second wedding. Damn it! I can't even keep it straight anymore. I don't think we need to be concerned about bad luck at this point. Besides, I *had* to show him the dress because I needed to make sure I wouldn't be committing any sort of French wedding *faux pas*. Who knew if there were any type of wedding dress offenses we commit in America on a daily basis? This was the one choice I had been able to make for our French wedding. It had to be just right.

Intrigued by Louis' concern, I asked why this, of all things, would trouble him. He then said he didn't want my dress to rip when we sat on the hay bales in the back of the horse drawn carriage. This information stopped me in my tracks. Apparently, we would tour the town following the ceremony, accepting congratulations from the townsfolk and all visiting relatives. From the back of a carriage. Whilst sitting on hay bales. Totally didn't see *that* coming.

As I was attempting to control the anxiety threatening to overwhelm my system, Louis requested I obtain a longer veil to keep the bugs off my face during said ride in the carriage. Let me point out, this conversation took place *after* I had been told I would be learning how to make Louis' favorite cheese (without the use of a gas mask). I had no choice but to put all of it out of my mind or I would have had a complete mental breakdown. And possibly have killed my husband, which might have put a damper on our second and third weddings.

In the midst of the chaos of the final French wedding preparations, Louis was waiting for an extremely important phone call. He had been through SEVEN rounds of interviews with a financial software company in San Francisco, and had been told by his recruiter he should be hearing directly from the company any day now. So, this would of course be the time when his mother would start to call once an hour with a matter of dire importance. (What time is your flight arriving? What are you planning to wear to the rehearsal dinner? Do you want me to invite any more of your old girlfriends to the wedding? Wait, what time did you say your flight was arriving?) If he hadn't been waiting for a job offer, he would have changed all his phone numbers and dropped out of his mother's world for a long, long time.

I came home from work one day to find Louis sitting at the dining room table staring at the phone. In fact, he was staring at both his cell phone and our home phone. He was looking back and forth between them with an exasperated expression on his face. It was almost comical. I didn't dare laugh though; his mood had been exceptionally unpredictable over the last twenty-four hours. I wondered how long this company would take to put him out of his misery. Were they going to hire him or not?

I put down my purse and approached him carefully. "Hi, Bluey."

He glanced up at me, apparently just noticing I had entered the apartment. His level of concentration was insane. He was able to shut out all background noise and focus solely on the content of his thoughts. It must be the intense military training. Or possibly growing up with an extremely loquacious mother.

He had yet to say anything, so I was becoming concerned. I tried again.

"How was your day, my love?"

His hand twitched as he picked up his cell phone. "I have been waiting for hours for these assholes to call."

I chanced a smile. "If they're assholes, maybe you don't want to work for them."

He smiled sheepishly. "Why do they make you wait so long? It is inhuman."

I sighed. I had found myself on the other side of this equation often with my job. On many occasions, I had obtained all necessary approvals, completed all background checks, had all the I's dotted and T's crossed, but was still forced to hold an offer for an incredible candidate for some idiotic reason. Corporate bureaucracy can be a real bitch.

I walked over and put my arms around his neck. "Don't worry, Bluey. It won't be much longer." I decided now was not the time to ask him how the other jobs were faring in his search, because it was never a good idea to put all your eggs in one basket. I think he would have been quite tempted to sock me in the nose if I had said those words to him. And I wouldn't have blamed him one bit. He had been through so much in the last seven months; he was entitled to his own mental breakdown.

It was unlikely he would receive a call with a job offer this late in the day, but I didn't say a word for the next hour as he sat and stared at the phones. I changed my clothes, checked my email, had a snack and began to prepare dinner. As I put the pasta to boil, the phone rang, causing Louis to jump about six feet in the air. Apparently if you stare at a phone long enough, it will ring. Though this practice never worked for me in my long days of dating.

To Louis' great disappointment, the call was from my father. I picked up the kitchen extension quickly and told him I would call him back on my cell phone in two minutes.

I grabbed my phone out of my purse and dialed the store.

"Duck! What's going on? Why can't you use your home phone?" My dad didn't see the sense in using a cell phone when you had a perfectly good landline available. For someone who refused to wear a hearing aid, cell phones were a mixed blessing. He loved the convenience they offered, but hated the inevitable attack of poor connections.

"Everything is fine, Dad. Louis has been waiting for a call with a job offer for two days now. He's getting a little antsy. I don't want to stress him out by tying up the landline."

"But don't you have call waiting?" He sounded confused.

I sighed. "Yes, Dad, but using the land line would cause my husband unnecessary stress. So I chose to use my cell phone."

"You young people and your bizarre reasoning." Pot, kettle, old man. What was the point in saying it?

I changed the subject. "So, how have you been, Dad? I've missed you!"

"No kidding, Duck! Where've you been?"

I leaned my head against my hand. "Wrapped up in final wedding arrangements."

"I thought you had everything tied up. Did something fall through?"

"Everything is set for the California wedding." I paused as I debated the nicest way to put this. "Louis' mom has been making, um…a few last minute changes to the French wedding."

My dad pretended to choke. It was one of his favorite party tricks when he was trying to be funny. "What exactly does she have planned now?"

I closed my eyes and tried not to feel sick. There had been seven outfit changes, three venue changes, two complete event overhauls and one wedding party replacement. One of Louis' cousins had made Simone incredibly angry by insulting one of her culinary masterpieces at a pre-wedding tasting event. I silently wondered if she hoped for a last minute bride change, even though Louis and I were already legally married. I did not doubt she had a backup in mind.

My dad coughed. "Are you still there, Duck?"

I laughed. "I'm sorry, Dad. I was reliving some of the happenings of the last week. I would rather spare you the details. I wish I could've escaped it."

"I can't wait to meet Simone. She's starting to make *you* look normal!" My dad's guttural laugh burst across the phone line.

At that moment, our landline rang. I peeked at Louis and held my breath. Could it be?

Louis answered the phone with a cautious expression on his face. He gave me the thumbs up sign to indicate it was indeed the company in question. Now we had wait to find out if the recruiter was telling the truth. It was doubtful the company would call directly to reject him, but you never knew.

I was so wrapped up in the fate of Louis' phone call, I forgot I had my Dad on the line.

"Duck! Did I lose you? Damn cell phones…"

I quickly surmised my dad was about to hang up and call me on our land line since this was the number he had memorized. I didn't want Louis to have to deal with the constant beeping in his ear, because my dad wouldn't give up until he got either a person or an answering machine.

"Dad! Wait!" I yelled a little louder than I had meant to. I whispered a frantic apology to Louis and returned to my Dad. "Louis is on the phone right now about a job. I was momentarily distracted."

"So, did he get it?" My dad was unavoidably blunt.

"I don't know yet."

"Well, how long has he been on the phone with them?"

I thought about it. "Maybe four or five minutes?"

He snorted. "How long does it take to offer someone a job? What is it with you kids these days and all of your preamble? Just get to the point!"

I had to stifle a laugh since my father is one of the most long-winded people I know. But it would simply not do for Louis to have his hysterical wife in the background of his important phone call.

I watched Louis to see if he had received any indication of the status of an offer of employment. Nothing was clear from the expression on his face. He just kept nodding and saying, "Yes" and "I understand."

I heard my dad's voice again. "What's going on now?"

This was exasperating. "I have no idea. He isn't saying much."

"Well, poke him in the ribs and ask him."

"Dad! I can't do that. He's on the phone. I can't disturb him."

"Oy vey! You can't disturb him. Like he's negotiating world peace or something…"

I wanted to throttle my father. Are these kind of statements payback for when I tortured him as a snotty eight year old? Is this his thanks for my many tantrums and cries of unfairness? Something told me this type of behavior would only get worse as he aged.

Eventually, Louis turned to me and nodded his head. He directed his attention back the phone and said, "Thank you very much. I accept your offer."

I grinned from ear to ear. I gave my ecstatic husband a quick hug and he walked over to the dining room table to write a few things down.

I spoke in a low voice to my dad. "He got it!"

"What did you say, Duck? I can't hear you. Stop mumbling."

I raised my voice a little. "He got the job, Dad!"

"I think I lost you. All I'm hearing is static." He paused for a second and then yelled in my ear. "Lyn! Bring me the other extension; this one is out of battery again. I need to call Syd back on her home phone. This cell phone business sucks."

No, no, no! "Dad!" Shit. He hung up on me. I dialed the store on my cell phone as quickly as I could and was thrilled when my mom picked up.

"Syd? Your dad was about to call you back. He said he lost you."

I practically bit her head off. "He didn't lose me! I was talking to him, but he couldn't hear me because he won't put in his damn hearing aid!"

Calm down, Sydney. It wasn't your mother's fault.

I exhaled slowly. "I'm sorry, Mom. Louis is on the landline getting a job offer, which is what I was *trying* to tell Dad." I sighed. "I don't want anything to ruin this moment for him."

She laughed. "Especially not your father's incessant beeping." We had all fallen victim to his impatient need to speak with us whenever he felt like it. He could be a total phone stalker.

I allowed myself a small smile. "I'm so thankful, Mom. He's been working so hard."

"Yes, he has. And so have you, Syd. It's wonderful! You'll both be able to relax – even if it's just a little."

My mom knew only too well Louis would throw himself into his new job full force and her daughter was incapable of relaxing completely. Especially with two weddings on the immediate horizon.

I laughed. "True enough. But it'll be nice not to have to worry quite so much about money." Another salary coming in meant I could afford to buy a new pair of sneakers. My old pair was in tatters from the exorbitant number of times I had used our apartment complex's gym in an attempt to calm my frazzled nerves. All the exercise had done nothing to relax me, but I had inadvertently lost ten pounds!

More money coming in also meant I could afford to buy a few new outfits to take with me to France instead of making do with what was in my closet and pilfering from both Kate and Maya. I was hoping Louis would help broker a few wardrobe changes for me with his mother so there wouldn't be quite as many photos of me in scary ensembles. (Though we wouldn't state this as the reason for the requested changes.) I honestly wasn't sure if Simone was trying to embarrass me into not wanting to be part of her family anymore or making a desperate attempt to infuse me with an acceptable sense of style. She seemed to think my current fashion choices were exceedingly boring, so it really could be either option.

My mom broke into my daydream. "You're imagining the possibilities, aren't you?"

I grinned. "You know me too well, Mom."

Suddenly I heard my Dad in the background. "Did he get it or what?"

My mom chuckled. "I love you, Syd. Pass on our congratulations to Louis. I'm going to give you back to your father. He'd love to finish his conversation with you."

"Duck! What's the good word?" This expression always cracked me up. Isn't the word "good?" Why is it a question? Though this time, I couldn't wait to tell him the good word was good news! And he would hear me this time since the connection seemed to be solid. Something else to celebrate!

"He got it, Dad!"

"Good-o! That kid is really smart. I knew he would get it."

I guess my dad was busting out all his peculiar expressions involving the word "good", but as this last expression was only used when he was really happy, I decided not to mock him. I was in too GOOD of a mood!

⌒

After I hung up with my father, I went to the refrigerator and pulled out a bottle of champagne I had hidden for this very special day. It was made in the Champagne region of France, as any French person would expect from something which is referred to as champagne, and was decidedly not merely a sparkling wine made pretty much anywhere else. (I learned this courtesy of an hour long lecture from my new husband regarding the sparkling wine, mistakenly billed as champagne, which was served at our first wedding reception. French people take their champagne VERY seriously.)

As I pulled out the glasses, Louis hung up the phone in triumph. I ran across the living room to him and engulfed him in a huge hug.

"Congratulations, Bluey! You must be so excited!"

He twirled me around a few times. "I AM excited! I have a job!"

I giggled and squeezed him tightly. "When do you start?"

His grin was enormous. "Monday."

I stared at him with wide eyes. Tomorrow was Friday. "That's amazing! Will your background check have cleared in time?" Yes, these are the things I think of. It's an occupational hazard of the Human Resources profession.

He was too excited to stand still. "They are going to expedite my paperwork tomorrow. I will be able to work for a week and a half before we leave for France."

We grinned at each other for a few minutes. We had been under so much financial pressure for so long, we were positively giddy at the prospect of it coming to an end. Sure, we still had wedding expenses to deal with, but now we would have a lot more breathing room.

I handed Louis the bottle of perfectly chilled champagne. "Will you do the honors, *Monsieur Durand?*"

He sighed with contentment. "*Absolument, Madame Durand.*"

Louis laughed as he popped the cork and filled our glasses until they were brimming with bubbly. We silently toasted our good fortune. Then we ripped each other's clothes off and celebrated in a manner which would make me blush if I were to tell you the particulars.

I fell asleep in Louis' arms that night with nothing but happy thoughts swirling through my mind. We had finally overcome our many obstacles, we were hopelessly in love and had bright prospects ahead of us. Who knows? Maybe we would even be able to enjoy our painstakingly-planned weddings! I felt more relaxed and had a much more positive outlook on life than I had in a very long time. Things were looking up for *Monsieur & Madame Durand*. Little did I know, it would be quite a while before there was any peace in our future...

Chapter Fifteen

The following day, Louis snatched back my sense of relief by announcing his intention to purchase a motorcycle rather than a car as his mode of transportation to his new job. He reasoned it was less expensive and would allow him a faster commute, since he could legally ride in-between cars on the highway. Thank you, California, for your great concern for the safety of motorcyclists. I informed him, my mental health was worth the extra money for a car. Unfortunately, I didn't win this battle since my husband is a self-proclaimed adrenaline junkie.

It became apparent rather quickly that Louis had been planning this purchase for quite some time. Shortly after he dropped the motorcycle bomb on me, he casually mentioned how he had spent a great deal of time researching the exact model he wanted during the downtime of his job search. That evening, he brought me directly to a Yamaha dealership and asked for an R1. For those of you who are not familiar with motorcycles, this isn't a bike which is used for leisurely rides down the highway. This is what is known as a RACING bike. Why would he possibly need a racing bike to get to work? The answer is rather simple: so he can reach his destination as quickly as possible AND can perform wheelies without fear of injury. As if this were not the most ridiculous statement EVER.

While I tried to imagine not having a heart attack on a daily basis as a result of this "beautiful piece of machinery" (I choose to refer to it as a DEATH TRAP!), Louis informed me he was going to modify the engine in order to make it louder, thereby announcing his presence with authority to those suckers on the road who drove cars. He insisted it was a safety feature and I should appreciate this additional measure for my concern. He also bought a high quality helmet, protective jacket and gloves.

I hadn't seen such a huge grin on Louis' face in many, many months. Not since our wedding day. This glaring similarity made it very clear to me the level of love he feels for motorcycles. I suppose it makes perfect sense; he has been riding some form of motorcycle since he was three years old. I guess I was hoping he would grow out of that phase of his life, because I wasn't sure *I* would survive the massive amount of worry each time he got on his "crotch rocket."

In the end, the motorcycle cost just as much as a car (between the necessary protective gear, engine modifications and wicked expensive insurance), but Louis was so euphoric I had to keep quiet. I did *not*; however, keep quiet when he asked me if I would like to purchase protective equipment as well. I told him while I understood his great love for the rush he received with risking *his* life, I had no intention of ever getting on the back of his donor cycle. He simply smirked at me and told me I could always change my mind later.

Once we returned to the apartment, Louis dove back into the reference material he was given when he signed his offer paperwork the day before. He had been able to have a short meeting with his new boss and had come back laden with textbooks. Louis has never been much for novels, but extremely tedious technical books about computer programming really get his blood going. He planted himself on the couch and immersed himself in the wonders of Java.

After twenty-four hours of this nonsense (I'm honestly not sure if he slept), I had to get out of the apartment. Thankfully, I had been able to con Maya into going shopping with me for the afternoon. Not only did I need a few new outfits for our trip to France, but also, I needed someone to give me a slap upside the head. Of the verbal variety, of course. I once witnessed Maya literally bitch slap some nasty girl in a bar and it took the poor girl a good five minutes to get up. Maya may be petite, but she evidently packs quite a wallop.

As an afternoon shopping with Maya never comes without a price, I met her at the Peninsula Creamery with the promise of paying for lunch. Since we had serious shopping to do, I insisted on going to the one in the Stanford Shopping Center. The easier the access to stores, the better. We had no time to waste!

I arrived first and was perusing the menu, when I heard a familiar voice.

"Why do you bother looking at the menu? You always get the same thing, Syd."

I peered up to find none other than Nigel grinning at me. I broke out into a grin of my own and jumped up to hug him.

"What are you doing here, Pip?"

He laughed and patted his stomach. "You've gotten me hooked on this place! And Grace hates you for it."

I smiled sheepishly at him. "Where is your delightful wife?"

"Off at the shops. I have to meet her in Blooming-dale's in an hour. Are you on your own?"

Right as I was about to answer, Maya came up behind Nigel and poked him in the ribs.

"Pip! How are you?"

Nigel brightened at the sight of Maya and gave her a big squeeze. I have yet to meet a man who doesn't brighten at the sight of this woman. It has become rather aggravating. Especially since she can be such a bitch.

"Maya, you gorgeous girl, it is so wonderful to see you!"

Maya and I took advantage of our happy coincidence of running into Nigel and asked him to join us for lunch. The two of them proceeded to talk for the next ten minutes without involving me in the conversation in even the smallest capacity. I had suddenly become obsolete. Not really the best feeling for someone in my mental state. I had introduced them, after all. They were supposed to be MY friends!

Shit. Sensitive Sydney has joined the party. She's a HUGE downer. She's not as high maintenance as Crazy Sydney, but she sits in the corner and cries a lot. Not too much fun for anyone to be around.

"Earth to Sydney!" Maya was tapping me on the shoulder.

I shook my head and focused on her. "I'm sorry, what did you say?"

She rolled her eyes. "Pip asked you how Louis is doing."

I wanted to smack her across the face for giving me such attitude considering she had been monopolizing my friend for the better part of the meal. In order to distract myself from such an inclination, I turned to Nigel and smiled.

"I'm sorry, Pip. I'm afraid I was lost in my thoughts. Maya really knows how to take over a conversation." I ignored Maya's dirty look and focused on Nigel. "Louis is doing really well. He's *really* excited about his new job."

Maya coughed. "And his new motorcycle…"

Nigel's eyes widened. "He bought a motorcycle???"

Maya laughed. "He did! And he calls it a 'crotch rocket'!"

I kicked her under the table and turned my attention back to Nigel.

"You know how much Louis loves motorcycles. He's been building them for years. And with the crazy traffic on his commute and the lack of parking in the city, he thought this would be the best way to meet all his needs." The need for speed being the most important one.

Nigel grinned widely. "Bloody awesome!"

I raised my eyebrows. "Don't get any ideas, Pip! Grace will KILL me if you do anything to put yourself in danger." His lack of coordination didn't help matters. (He and I were kindred spirits in this regard.) His mind had grandiose ideas of activities which his body simply couldn't carry out without causing severe damage.

Maya scoffed. "Will you relax, Syd? What's the big deal? Motorcycles aren't definitive health hazards. You need to get a grip."

I narrowed my eyes at her. "Really? Have YOU ever been on one?"

"Of course I have. I'm not a scaredy-cat like you. I've lived *outside* the bubble."

Ouch. That was harsh - even for her. She hasn't been this bitchy in a long time. (Yes, I know I *just* said she could be very bitchy, but this was bad even for her.) I wonder if something had happened between her and Devon. Now is definitely not the time to ask though. Maya wouldn't want Pip to know her business. Or more likely, she wouldn't want him to know she had any problems. She preferred to keep her image perfectly intact.

Nigel regarded her appraisingly. "How was it?"

Maya smiled wickedly. "Amazing!"

Nigel seemed wistful. "I have *always* wanted to ride one. Just never have the opportunity." And now that he had married Grace, he never would. She would NEVER allow such a blatant risk to his safety.

Nigel's excitement got me thinking. Was I a total wuss? He was desperate to get on a motorcycle while I was completely petrified. Was I missing something? Or was I simply not part of the "eager to die" club?

Nigel shoved me playfully by the shoulder. "Come on, Syd! You should give it a go!" He kept nodding his head at me with encouragement.

Maya simply shook her head at me. "She'd never do it in a million years. Even though it would be the most exhilarating experience of her life."

Hearing the two of them telling me not to be such a chicken gave me pause. It's unquestionably true that Sydney Bennett would *never* get on the back of a motorcycle. But maybe, just maybe, Sydney Durand would. Hmmm...

We had a very successful shopping trip that afternoon, which, to our great delight, ended up including Grace. Pip ended up holding all of our bags while we hit fitting rooms in stores from one end of the Stanford Shopping Center to the other. Most men would have been pretty annoyed, but he was happy as a clam since Grace had had the wherewithal to bring him a selection of pastries from his favorite French bakery.

At least now I had a selection of beautiful clothes to bring with me to meet my new family. Maya, Grace and I put together several different options to fit any occasion. We also chose shoes, accessories, makeup and perfume. Maya even insisted on some new lingerie. Personally, I think she merely wanted to mess with me one more time before I left for my trip. Making fun of me is her favorite pastime and since I would be leaving a full week before she was, she would be experiencing some serious withdrawal. (Her renewed presence in my life clearly indicated her need to mock me outweighed her exclusive need for Devon.)

⌒

Three days into Louis' new job found me very unhappy. You would think after months of wishing for this very thing,

I would be on cloud nine, right? We didn't have to worry about money anymore! Louis had enough activity to keep his overpowered brain engaged! He was finally earning the majority of the money for our household. He was *finally* happy!

So, why wasn't *I* happy? For starters, I NEVER saw my husband. One of the only pieces of evidence I had of his existence was the Louis-shaped imprint I found in the bed when I woke up in the morning. He left for work before the crack of dawn and didn't arrive home until long after I went to bed. To add insult to injury, he somehow wasn't able to find time to speak to me during the day. The only communication I had from him were the texts I demanded announcing his safe arrival at the office. This was certainly not what I had been expecting with the advent of Louis' new job.

What HAD I been expecting? I had been expecting the return of my happy husband. I had been expecting the return of my sex life. I had been expecting plenty of blissful alone time with my husband once he returned home from the office. And yes, if you must know, I was expecting a little pre-France coddling. (I was still scared shitless!) All these things would require the actual presence of my husband.

Upon waking for the third morning in the row *sans* Louis, I snapped. I sent him a text which read, "Do you still exist?" No emoticon included. I wanted it to be very clear I was in no way joking. Sydney Durand was *done*. New job or not, he WOULD find five minutes to talk to me.

Following a less than satisfying shower in which I washed my hair far too vigorously, I checked my cell phone. Still no message from Louis. I was seething with anger. Was he really so focused on his new job, he hadn't noticed no words had been exchanged OUT LOUD between us since very early Monday morning? Had he forgotten about me completely? Didn't he miss me? Didn't he realize we were seven days away from the impending doom of our trip to France?

Over the next hour, I changed my clothes three times, slammed every cabinet in our kitchen and threw four pairs of shoes across the room. Not the most mature of responses, but I wasn't in a mature mood. I was tired of being overlooked by my husband and in light of everything I had ahead of me, I fully expected him to show me the courtesy of a five minute phone conversation.

I also have yet to tell you that his mother has been leaving more than twenty messages a day as he is evidently avoiding her calls as well. This has done nothing to reduce my stress level. Every night I come home and listen to the messages, hoping they're from my husband and all I hear is HER voice. I then listen to her messages obsessively, trying to discern what evil she has plotted for me in her home territory. No, I'm absolutely not paranoid. She mentions my name a lot in her messages, and my name is always followed by laughter. It sounds very much like derisive laughter…

Just as I was about to admit defeat and leave for work, the phone rang with a San Francisco area code. Could it be Louis? He still hadn't given me his work number, so I would have to assume it was.

Here goes nothing. "Hello?"

"Good morning, *mon coeur.*"

"So you do exist." Yes, that was passive-aggressive. It was the kind of mood I was in. Go ahead and bite me.

He chuckled. "Yes, indeed, I do."

I was so angry I decided it was better not to say anything than to say something bitchy.

"Syd? Are you still there?" He sounded exasperated. Quick turnaround, Bluey!

"Yes, I'm still here." I paused. "How's your new job?"

"Good. Busy." He cleared his throat. "I have to run to a meeting. I'm sorry…"

Sure you are. I sighed. "Fine. Have a good day."

"What is the matter?" He had a definite edge to his voice.

Really? You're going to be pissed at me? After forgetting for THREE DAYS that you have a wife?

"I haven't seen or spoken to you in three days." My voice was barely above a whisper. I was trying very hard to stay calm.

"Sydney…" He exhaled loudly. "I am really busy. We are leaving for France in less than a week and I have so much to do. I don't have time for this."

Wow. After everything we've been through over the past few months. After my extremely stressful concession of moving up the French wedding. And after the magnanimous amount of insanity I agreed to let his mother put me through in front of hundreds of people…he acts like I'm simply an annoyance he needs to extract.

I felt the pain hit me almost immediately. The last thing I wanted to do was cry on the phone with him during his first week at work, so I did my best to swallow it for just long enough to say good-bye and hang up.

I cleared my throat. Shit! The lump was still stuck there and my eyes were starting to water. How am I going to be able to speak to him without indicating the tears have come? I felt so humiliated.

"I'm sorry, Louis. I didn't mean to bother you at work. I have to get going." My voice was barely above a whisper.

"Good-bye, Syd. I'll speak with you later." Not likely.

As I hung up the phone, my thoughts turned unexpectedly to poor Bastiaan, who would now need to replace Louis with another instructor in his Thai boxing studio. Certain Louis had been so excited about his new job he had forgotten to call Bastiaan, I made a mental note to call him later in the day. I was in no shape to talk to anyone right now. Suddenly, I found myself in the depths of despair. I was pretty pissed off since I thought I had finally escaped that hellhole.

I kept telling myself I was overreacting; it was only pre-French wedding anxiety seeping through my system. I had to believe Louis needed time to adjust to his new job and he would be back to his old self soon enough.

That was believable, right? I wasn't deluding myself, was I?

Damn it! How the hell did we get back on the freakin' roller coaster? I know my dad said life would be too boring if you got off it, but so help me I wanted to! I was tired of the highs and lows, the peaks and valleys, blah, blah, blah! Because frankly, I had experienced predominantly valleys lately. I longed for stability. Like the merry-go-round. Now there's a great ride! There are no huge drops and no uncertain turns, just a smooth journey along a preordained path. Plus, there were twinkling lights, beautiful mirrors, intricately carved designs and pretty animals to ride on.

My mind instantly flashed back to the movie *Parenthood*. (Yes, it is one of my favorite movies. It is a veritable gold mine of insightful quotations.) The grandmother would definitely not approve of my preference for the merry-go-round. She was all about the thrill of the gigantic roller coaster. Well, screw that! No matter how much you sugar coat it, Grandma, the roller coaster will only end up causing you heartache. You have no idea what you're talking about, you crazy old bat!

OK, Sydney. You're really losing it this time. You have sunk to a new low, even for you, in ranting to fictional movie characters.

Take a breath. Everything will work out. No, no, no. Don't doubt your inner monologue. Everything will be fine. Say it with me. Everything will be fine. Louis will come back to you and you will live happily ever after. This is what you have been working towards for the past year. You will *not* lose sight of it now.

I took another deep breath and hoped with all of my heart I wasn't lying to myself. We were leaving for France in six days and I had never felt less connected to Louis…

Chapter Sixteen

Friday night rolled around and you guessed it! Louis was still at work. He eventually called me at ten o'clock to tell me it would be another late night. I was so miserable, I almost didn't answer the phone. Our conversation lasted less than thirty seconds and ended without an "I love you" before he hung up. There hadn't been a declaration of love from Louis since he started this new job. I guess there simply wasn't time for love anymore.

When I awoke Saturday morning to find the bed empty again, I nearly screamed with rage. I got up and went to the bathroom to brush my teeth, slamming the door soundly to express my extreme irritation. To myself. Yes, I know, I needed to get a life. I almost jumped out of my skin when Louis opened the door to investigate the reason for the loud noise.

"Are you ok, Syd?" He appeared to be coming out of some kind of trance. I guess computer programming languages were kind of trippy. I must admit, looking at the code in his textbooks for even a few minutes made me quite dizzy.

"I'm sorry. I didn't think you were here." I turned on the shower and began brushing my teeth. (OK, environmentalists, pipe down. It took a good five minutes for the water to get hot. I had plenty of time to brush my teeth.)

Louis took a quick glance around the bathroom and left. I can only guess he was heading back to the hole he had crawled out of.

A hot shower helped to raise my spirits a little, but I had no idea what to expect once I left the safety of the bedroom. Was Louis still going to be upset with me for my phone call on Thursday? Did he even remember our call on Thursday? I had no idea how much sleep he had been getting since all his nighttime rest had taken place when I was asleep.

After giving myself a quick pep talk, I ventured out to the living room. I found Louis in his office nook, tapping away on his laptop. He appeared to be in serious concentration mode, so I passed by him and began to make myself a cup of tea.

I decided breakfast together might be a good way to bridge the cavernous gap to my husband. I began to take out the ingredients for his favorite omelet, hoping food would put him in a friendlier mood.

"How about a western omelet, Bluey?" I did my best impression of a smile.

Silence. Does this mean he's mad at me or he's not paying attention? Let's give this another try.

I raised my voice a little. "Bluey?"

It took a minute, but I did get a response this time. "Hmmm?" He didn't look my way, but at least he spoke. Progress.

"Would you like an omelet?" I tried smiling again. I was giving it my best effort. I knew he was exhausted and stressed. Didn't change the fact that I was pissed at him, but I was trying to be the bigger person.

He shook his head. "Not hungry."

OK! Not hungry. I decided to try another tactic. I walked over to him and put my arms around his neck, resting my chin on his shoulder.

He sighed. "What is it, Syd? I have a ton of work to do."

I quickly retracted my arms. "Sorry."

He stopped for a moment and looked at me. "I have to work all weekend to help finish a big project before we leave for France."

I nodded and did my best to blink back the tears threatening to come out.

He turned his focus back to his computer with a vengeance. "I'm going to have to bring my laptop with me on our trip. Please do *not* give me a lecture about work-life balance. Someone has to pay our bills."

I had cringed inwardly when he mentioned taking his laptop on our trip, but the comment about paying our bills was like a sucker punch to the gut. How long had *I* had this responsibility? Then I remembered saying the same thing to Louis during a period of extreme stress, so I decided not to say anything. Unfortunately, this enlightening revelation did nothing to change the hollow feeling in my stomach.

Once I was sure the lecture was over, I searched for an easy exit. I grabbed my tea and fled to the bedroom before tears started spilling down my face. We were leaving for France in four days. FOUR DAYS! And now he has basically told me he has to abandon me, in a foreign country where I don't speak the language; where people are lying in wait to judge me AND to dissect all my faults (and that could take a while).

As if I weren't going through enough crap already, Louis informed me yesterday of his mother's plan to host a bridal shower for me involving ballroom dancing. This was Simone's true passion and she attended dances once a week to hone her skills. Unfortunately for her, her new daughter-in-law was born without any sense of coordination. No amount of lessons had been able to cure me. Sadly, it was a trait which ran in my family, so my mother and Kate weren't going to be able to do anything to save the already damaged opinion of American women in the Durand circle. Our only hope was Zoe; however, based on what I've seen so far in my life, she wouldn't evince better than average skill. Though it *is* possible she could become sufficiently drunk to cultivate a new talent. Crap! How was I going to get through all this?

I put my tea on the nightstand and cried quietly. I certainly didn't want to attract any attention to myself. I didn't need to further darken Louis' mood. With tears pouring down my face, I considered my options. I could stay here and hope he would eventually mellow out or I could get out and try to distract myself from both his black temper and my impending tribunal. I wholeheartedly went for option two.

After washing my face, I applied some makeup and put a change of clothes and a toothbrush in my biggest purse. I had no idea how long it would take for me to feel better (and actually want to set foot back in my apartment), so I decided to be prepared to stay at Kate's tonight. It's not like Louis would miss me. No doubt he would be able to take out all of the resentment lurking inside him on his mother, if he chose to accept her phone calls. He had twenty-something opportunities ahead of him today!

I cleaned up the mess I had left in the kitchen as fast as I could and then told Louis I was going to visit Kate. He gave me a small grunt and returned his full focus to his work.

As I was about to start the car, my cell phone rang. Did Louis realize what an asshole he had been? Was he calling to beg me to come back to the apartment? Was he going to tell me everything was going to be alright?

No such luck. It was Maya. Wait. What was she doing up before noon on a Saturday?

I picked up the call. "What are you doing up before noon on a Saturday?"

"Devon had an early squash game. I couldn't go back to sleep." She yawned loudly. It was probably a long night of passion. I *really* hated her right now.

"What can I do for you?" Though I wasn't sure I could do anything for anybody right now but cry.

She laughed. "No, the question is, what can *I* do for you?"

Uh oh. This type of comment from Maya usually meant she had some sort of asinine idea resulting in more ludicrous Sydney pictures for her collection.

I sighed. "Really? What did you have in mind?" At this point, what did I have to lose?

"You, my friend, are desperately in need of a good time. And I, given the great person I am, plan to provide such an evening for you."

I was intrigued. "You've captured my interest. What are we doing?"

Maya's evil laugh came over the line. "You'll just have to wait and see."

I was torn between feeling giddy at the prospect of going out and having fun and dreading the distinct possibility that Maya was going to either embarrass me within an inch of my life or scare the crap out of me. Then I thought about it a bit more and concluded there was a good chance she would do both.

What the hell! "OK, I'm in."

"Of course you are. Be at my place in an hour."

Click.

Why did Maya rarely feel the need to say good-bye? Once she had said what she needed to say, the conversation was over. There was never the requirement of niceties. Wait a minute! Why did she want me to be at her apartment in an hour? Following those instructions, I would arrive by eleven am. What was she planning for tonight? And what lengthy process did we have to go through to prepare for it?

Maya's plan turned out to be a masquerade ball in San Francisco. She had booked massages, facials, manicures, pedicures, blowouts and um…waxing…for both of us. (Yes, I know, I got tired simply telling you about it. Imagine what it was like to go through it all.) She also had a rack of dresses for me to choose from.

If I stopped to think about it, I would seriously wonder why she had a rack of size four dresses when she's a size zero, but I honestly didn't care. I had been beautified in every possible way and I planned to go out and have fun if it *killed* me. I was bound and determined to forget about my desolation. I did have the presence of mind to text my husband to let him know I would be out late with Maya. I didn't think he would miss me, but the last thing I needed was for him to ultimately notice I was gone and freak out over my whereabouts.

Now, back to the dresses. I selected a black strapless floor length ball gown. It was the epitome of elegance and it lifted my spirits immeasurably. Maya vetoed it, stating it resembled a black version of my wedding gown which was too *existential* for her taste. I didn't think existential was the word she was going for, but decided to forgo the argument. She had gone through a lot of trouble to cheer me up, so I was going to keep my mouth shut.

Maya then selected a dark blue dress with spaghetti straps and a long skirt with a generous slit up the side. The fabric had a hint of sparkle and the overall effect of the dress was magnificent. She added silver strappy HIGH-heeled sandals and a few jeweled bangles.

My jaw dropped at the sight of the sandals. "You do know I need to be able to *walk* in these, right?"

She rolled her eyes. "Spend a few minutes practicing and you'll be fine."

I peered over at her cautiously. "Thank you, Maya."

She sighed. "I was worried about you, Syd."

I nodded. I knew I wasn't allowed to cry, for two very important reasons. One, Maya had done my makeup to perfection, as usual. And two, Maya didn't like women who cried. Kind of makes you wonder why she's such a good friend of mine, doesn't it?

She put her hand on my shoulder. "Are you alright?"

Wow. She must be really worried to ask me to open up my can of crazy. I'll have to take it easy on her. She may pack a wallop, but I could decimate her in a few seconds with my level of psychosis.

I shook my head. "Not really. I thought Louis would be happy once he got a new job; that he would feel fulfilled and we wouldn't have money stresses anymore. But now, I rarely see him and when I do, he's distracted and cranky. Right before you called this morning, he told me he has to work every minute until we leave *and* he has to bring his laptop with him…" I felt the tears threatening, but boldly pushed on. "We'd already been through so much during the first six months of our marriage. I thought we'd fixed most of our issues and now it's like we've totally regressed. And I have to meet his gigantic family…and they're going to hate me…"

Perhaps I went a little too far. Maya really doesn't do well with this much emotion.

Maya brought me over to her sofa and sat me down. "Listen, Syd, I'm sure Louis is happy about his new job. He's probably also nervous about seeing his entire family and introducing them to you. It's also likely he's feeling a lot of pressure, now that he has the status of someone who has 'made it in America.' He has a lot on his plate too."

I think I've mentioned before how every once in a while, Maya shows such insight and such depth of feeling, I'm literally shocked into silence. I gawked at her helplessly, trying to formulate a response.

She giggled. "I know, I stunned you with one of my lucid moments. You don't have to say anything." She made a shooing motion with her hands. "Go get dressed. Devon will be here any minute."

WHAT??? All this AND I get to meet Devon? SHUT UP!

I grabbed the dress and accessories from her and ran into her bathroom. I put myself together in record time and returned to her in the living room grinning like an idiot.

She smirked. "I'm only going to say this once, Sydney."

I stared at her with rapt attention.

"DO NOT embarrass me."

I feigned innocence. How could I possibly embarrass her? I paused for a moment to think over if she were more concerned about stories I might tell once I had imbibed a little or things I might do once I had imbibed a little. I'm thinking option one would be off limits. At least she would get a good laugh out of option two. And she could add to her photo collection.

The doorbell rang. Here it comes….the moment of truth!

Holy crap! He's GORGEOUS. Not like, run-of-the-mill gorgeous, but stop-you-in-your-tracks-gawking-like-an-idiot gorgeous. He was about six feet tall, with short, jet black hair and the most striking green eyes. His face looked as though it had been chiseled out of the finest marble and it was clear, even through his tuxedo, that his body was perfectly sculpted. I had seen a photo of him a couple of months ago (after A LOT of begging), but it didn't do him justice.

It was not lost on me how the two of them made a breathtaking pair. I wondered what it was like for them to walk down the street together. I bet they could stop traffic. In fact, I bet they could cause accidents. I would most likely find out for sure soon enough.

When Maya introduced us, I politely shook his hand and told him how happy I was to finally meet him. I kept my attitude friendly, but reserved. It was hard work though; I don't think I've ever been in the presence of such a magnificent man. No, I haven't forgotten about my husband during our time of trouble. Louis is undoubtedly an extremely attractive man, but Devon is the reason 'drop dead gorgeous' became an expression. Simply looking at him could easily give you heart palpitations. Though I must admit, gazing at such a ridiculously handsome man was a welcome distraction from the anxiety riddled saga my life had become.

The night out with Maya and Devon was exactly what I needed to regain a slight hold on my sanity. I made sure to drink enough to keep me happy, but nowhere near enough to get me into trouble.

It spoke volumes that Maya was more concerned about maintaining a proper image for Devon than in finding new and interesting ways to embarrass me. Though I'm sure this was due, in part, to the company they both worked for being a major donor for the event. It would cause too much damage to Maya's reputation for her to bring someone who would behave in a drunk and disorderly way on such an important occasion.

Maya tucked me into bed that night and promised me French toast from the Peninsula Creamery the next morning. I texted Louis just before I fell asleep, informing him I would stay at Maya's for the night. I didn't receive a response.

The next morning, I woke to Maya and Devon canoodling over coffee and takeout containers filled with breakfast wonders from the Creamery. While I had enjoyed the time spent with Devon, and was unequivocally thrilled for Maya, I felt a sense of misery in witnessing the love and passion which was missing from my own relationship. After a delightful meal with these two lovebirds, it was time for me to return to deal with the disaster known as my love life.

As I put my key in the door, I determined while I may have been sensible enough *not* to get completely drunk and embarrass myself, it would seem I did drink enough to have a persistent headache. What I really needed was my dad's

scary tar remedy. (It tasted like it contained tar to me.)
Hmmm. I wonder if he would give me the ingredients for
it over the phone. You know what? It's simply not worth
the humiliation resulting result from my asking him,
especially with two wedding toasts in his immediate future.
The last thing I needed to do was to give him more material.
Sadly, he had way too much at his fingertips already.

I walked into the living room and noticed it was strangely
devoid of Louis. His laptop was sitting on his desk spewing
random characters. I sighed. He must have set up a build
and run to the bathroom. I hoped he was in a better mood
than yesterday.

With each step I took towards the bedroom, my heart
felt a little heavier. He hadn't told me he loved me since he
started this job; what's worse, he hadn't called me *mon coeur*.
It may sound stupid to you, but this absence of tenderness
really broke my heart. Hearing those words gave me
strength. They helped me to calm down. They helped put
Crazy Sydney back behind the curtain.

I entered the bedroom and put my purse on the dresser.
Just then the bathroom door opened and Louis came out
with a towel wrapped around his waist. Have I mentioned
there has been no physical tenderness for quite some time?
I felt completely disconnected from him, which he must
have seen as I stared listlessly in his direction.

Louis smiled sadly.

I returned his sad smile and sat down on the bed.

He dressed quickly and came to sit next to me. "I am so
sorry, *mon coeur*."

I turned to comfort him when he handed me a small
velvet box. I gasped in surprise, delight flooding my face.
What girl doesn't love getting a velvet box?

"What's this, Bluey?"

He grinned. "Something to remind you of how much I
love you." He paused. "Even when I behave like a jackass."

I burst out laughing and threw my arms around him.
"You haven't been a jackass. You've been stressed about

your new job…about our trip…about your family meeting your, um, eccentric wife."

He nuzzled into my hair. "I have missed you so much."

I sighed contentedly. "I've missed you more."

He pulled out of our embrace and pointed to the box in my hand. "Please open it."

I didn't have to be asked twice.

As the lid creaked open, I saw a small diamond heart on a delicate white gold chain. It was so beautiful, and it meant so much to me I didn't know what to say. *Mon coeur.* My heart.

I gazed up at him with tears in my eyes. "It's perfect," I whispered.

He smiled tenderly. "Just like my wife. And in a few days, my entire family will know this as well as I do."

I looked deeply into his eyes and marveled at how quickly I could go from feeling so separated from my husband to falling right back in sync. Rather than trying to dissect every possible reason for this and question how long this feeling of closeness would last, I opted to focus on the fair amount of misery we had muddled our way through in the last few months. Instead of throwing in the towel at the first sign of trouble, we kept working and working and working. Over the last seven months, I had learned marriage is without a doubt one of the hardest things in this world, but it's also one of the sweetest.

Speaking of sweet, my husband's remark about my being perfect was an incredibly kind thing for him to say to his crazy wife at such a stressful time. Regrettably, the reality of the journey we were about to take still struck fear into the deepest regions of my heart. It may seem dramatic, but I kept thinking – only three more days until the trial commences. Three more days until I'll be cross examined, assessed and possibly even tested in my capacity as Louis' wife. Only time would tell if I had a chance of making it out alive.

Chapter Seventeen

The night before our flight to France, all hell broke loose. I suppose I should qualify this ruckus took place in my head. Louis was still at work and I was trying to finish packing for our trip. As I thought about all the people I was going to meet and all the events I was expected to be the star of, I began to shake. I sat down and put my head between my knees, but no amount of deep breathing was going to help me to calm down.

There was only one person who could save me now. I reached for the phone and dialed Kate. Fortunately, the phone was picked up instantly. Unfortunately, instead of hearing Kate's voice, I heard Sam's blood curdling screams emanating from the receiver. What was happening? Had something happened to Piggy the second? If so, Piggy the third and fourth were waiting in the wings. (One hundred dollars and four hours of my life later...)

"Kate? Are you OK?" My heartbeat sped up even more. If I kept up this level of anxiety, I was going to pass out in about two seconds.

I heard clattering sounds and then an exasperated Kate saying, "Oh, crap!"

I instantly felt better, knowing Kate uses profanity (well, her watered down version of it) when annoyed, not in danger.

"Hello?" An exhausted Kate managed to pick up the phone.

"Kate? It's me, Syd. Are you alright?"

"Syd!" She sighed. "I think so. Sam is *really* irritable. I'm at the end of my rope."

Sam? Irritable? Is something wrong with my perfect angel? I took it as a very bad sign if Sam were in a bad mood. She had the sunniest disposition ever. Maybe she knew something about our trip to France that I didn't. After all, babies are particularly intuitive.

"Syd? Are you there?"

I cleared my throat. "Sorry, Kate. I'm a little…um.." How to describe my current state of mind? Nervous? Apprehensive? Just plain crazy? Insert your favorite Sydney adjective here…

She sighed. "You're a little insane?" Another good one.

I chuckled nervously. "Always. But let's get back to Sam. Is something wrong? She's normally such a happy girl." I couldn't possibly bother my sister with my idiotic bullshit considering everything she had going on. And since my husband was also occupied elsewhere, I was going to have to learn to be more self-reliant. What a concept!

"Well, her doctor thinks she may be teething, which totally sucks. I thought we had more time before that train wreck began, since she's only four months old, but it happens."

Poor Sam! "Is there anything you can do for the pain?"

Suddenly, Nick picked up the phone, with Sam screaming uncontrollably in the background. "Kate?" He sounded categorically desperate.

"Gotta go, Syd. When Sam gets really upset, she wants Mommy."

Click. At the absence of a dial tone, I stayed on the phone in case Nick needed a friendly ear.

"Hello?" I could still hear some faint screams in the background, so I wondered if he had left the phone off the hook in his frantic state.

"Syd? Are you still there?" He didn't seem like himself in the least. He sounded…lost.

"Hey, Nick. I'm here. Are you OK?"

He sighed. "We're both exhausted. Sam's been taking a lot out of us lately."

"I can only imagine. Do you need anything?" Maybe helping them would help me to forget my impending doom across the Atlantic.

"Thanks for asking, but we'll just have to take whatever comes at us." He paused to yawn. "Sorry to cut your conversation with Kate short. Is there any message I should pass on to her? Or are you merely freaking out as usual?"

As usual? The kind of stress I was going through right now was anything but usual. This kind of stress was astronomical….it was immense…maybe enormous was a better word. Suffice to say it was REALLY, REALLY BIG. The kind of stress that would knock you on your ass if you weren't hypervigilant. The kind of stress you might feel when you were about to meet a very large number of French people who expected you to be perfectly amazing in every way despite your status as ugly American. Who doesn't speak their language. Or know a great deal about their culture. Or their particular regional customs. And who is completely without any type of composure or physical coordination. Or intellect…or fashion sense…oh shit.

I scoffed. "Hey, now! This isn't *usual*. Even *you* would experience stress if you were in my shoes right now, mister. Cut me a little slack."

He chuckled. "Agreed. I was only trying to get you to laugh." He went into the big brother mode he enjoyed when Kate was otherwise engaged. "Remember, you're *already* married, you two love each other and his family will accept you no matter what."

I nodded grimly and felt tears forming in my eyes. "It doesn't mean they have to like me." Right now I was somewhat unsure of how much my husband liked me.

"Syd! Stop looking for trouble. *Try* to relax and remember you're going to France tomorrow with your husband. He's really excited for you to see where he grew up and to finally meet his family. Just do your best. They're going to love you."

I let out a shaky breath. "Thanks, Nick." Maybe he was right. Maybe Louis would be less stressed once we were on the plane and would be better able to help me through my panic spiral.

"I'll have Kate call you tomorrow and give you the pep talk you need before your flight, alright?"

"That would be great." I paused to wipe a few stray tears. "I love you both."

"We love you too."

I hung up the phone and inspected my suitcase. I had packed the trendy new outfits Maya and I bought for the trip, but I was having second thoughts. She was infinitely more daring than I was when it came to fashion and she looked amazing in everything. I sighed as I rearranged my clothes yet again. Who was I kidding? I was *never* going to pull this off. I was trying to impersonate a sophisticated woman; someone who was filled with confidence, poise and glamour. Louis kept telling me I was perfect exactly as I was, but I didn't believe him. I knew he would say anything to make me feel better. Or to get me to shut up.

I picked up the phone again, hoping this time my sanity would be saved. I dialed my mother's store, praying she had a free moment. Since it was minutes past closing time, I might be able to catch her before she began cashing out the register.

Just when I thought I was going to get the answering machine, I heard my father's voice.

"Duck!"

I smiled at the sound of his voice. "Hey, Dad!" I tried to feign levity, but my lie couldn't pass the massive lump in my throat.

"What's wrong? And don't tell me 'nothing.' I know you."

I searched for the right words. "I...."

"You're worried about what Louis' family is going to think of you."

I nodded, clearly oblivious that he couldn't see me, while tears streamed down my face. Then came the hiccups. Way to be sophisticated, Sydney.

"Duck." His voice was very gentle. "You've always been such an anxious person. But, it's OK; it's part of your charm." He chuckled softly.

"Thanks, Dad." Maybe this had been a bad idea...

"Listen to your father." He paused. "You're a wonderful person. I've had the pleasure of watching you grow into an intelligent, funny and even, at times, confident young woman. Try not to worry so much about what they'll think. Louis loves you; they will too. Or he'll tell them where they can go."

I laughed through my tears. My dad had it right there. Even in his current state of stress, Louis wouldn't tolerate rude comments of any kind when it came to me or any member of my family. He could become quite ill-tempered if he felt someone was mocking one of his "peeps" as he called them. I had observed this often enough during phone conversations when his father or one of his uncles told him an anti-American joke.

"I know you're right, Dad." I sighed. "I can't help feeling like I'm under a lot of pressure."

"From whom?" He asked.

I thought about it. If I were really being honest...

"From myself." More tears spilled down my face. "I want to make Louis proud. I want his family to like me."

"Listen to me, Duck. They will LOVE you. Even if they can't understand your horrible French accent. In fact, it might be a *good* thing they can't understand you. Just stand there and look pretty."

I bit my lip. I knew exactly what he was doing. My dad was a master at making outrageous comments to snap me out of my craziness. Ninety-five percent of the time it worked. The other five percent, I went completely nuclear. Thankfully, this was part of the ninety-five percent. I still had my head in my hands, but had laughed myself silly.

My father let out a sigh of relief. "There's my girl."

Suddenly, I heard the front door of the apartment open. Crap! Louis was home and there was no way I would be able to put myself together before he saw me. He had been so on edge these days, I was afraid of how he might react if he saw me in this state of disarray.

I cleared my throat. "Thanks, Dad. I needed a dose of sanity."

"That's what fathers are for."

"I have to run. Louis just got home and I'm going to have some explaining to do about my current condition." I took a deep breath. "Will you please tell Mom I love her and I'll call her in the morning?"

"Will do, Duck. I love you."

"I love you too, Dad. Oh, and please don't tell Mom about my latest...episode. I don't want her to worry."

"It'll be our secret."

"Thanks, Dad. You're the best."

"Don't I know it!" My dad was always one to toot his own horn. It was one of his most annoying, yet endearing qualities.

As I hung up, Louis opened the door to the bedroom. "*Mon coeur*, are you ready to...." He stopped dead in his tracks when he saw me. His face fell and he walked over to me.

Damn. I was hoping he would stop to go through the mail before he came into the bedroom. I didn't even have the chance to fix the damage to my blotchy face. I smiled as convincingly as I could. "How was your day?"

He held my face in his hands. "Forget about me. What is going on? Why are you so sad?" Thank God he was in a decent mood today. He must be finding his rhythm at work. On a bad day, he could have just as easily left the apartment in a huff.

I sighed. I could only imagine what I looked like right now. My makeup must have been smeared all over my puffy, tear-stained face.

"I'm fine, Bluey. Only the usual dose of crazy."

He swept me into his arms and held me tightly. "Why do you do this to yourself?"

As I inhaled his familiar scent, I felt like I could breathe for the first time in days. "Because I'm crazy. Duh."

He pulled out of the hug and gazed into my eyes. "Syd, I LOVE you. My parents are going to love you. The rest of my family is going to love you. Will you please stop worrying?"

I rolled my eyes. "You may as well ask me to stop breathing." Truth be told, I worried less since Louis had entered my life, but the current situation was much too stressful for me to keep my anxiety at bay. Crazy Sydney could not be kept dormant.

Louis gave me a stern glare. "Seriously, *mon coeur*, you can't put this much pressure on yourself. It is not healthy."

I let out a long breath. "You're right. I...I really want to impress your family, the way you impressed mine."

Louis laughed. "Oh yes, they were so impressed with me, they thought I was marrying you for a green card."

I swatted the back of his head. "That wasn't about you! It was about getting engaged after knowing each other for six weeks!"

"My point is, their regard for me was not immediate. Please do your best to enjoy the visit." He put his finger underneath my chin, smiling slightly. "You know, many women would be thrilled with a two week trip to France."

True, but many people wouldn't be put through the wringer by his family in general and his mother in particular. Given his good mood, I decided to keep that thought to myself.

I grinned at him. "I am looking forward to it." Well, most of it. At least the parts where I would be alone with him…and eat pastries…ooh, and French chocolates…and drink wine.

He tapped the tip of my nose. "Really? You are so convincing…"

"Bluey! I really *am* looking forward to it! Especially to our time alone in Paris." Louis had surprised me with a night in Paris, staying at the Georges V no less, on our way back to California. I figured he knew things wouldn't be as easy for me as he was saying and he wanted a chance to calm me down before bringing me back home. But this was only a theory…

Louis got up and began to take off his work clothes. "So, I talked to my mother today."

This explained his calming nature with me just now. He knew there was even more pain coming my way. I needed to sit down for this.

I flopped down onto the bed. "Really? Has she added any other activities to our schedule?" Try as I might, I was not able to keep the sarcasm out of my voice.

His face gave nothing away. "Not any particular events; she only mentioned she would like you to spend some time with her in the kitchen."

I was suspicious of Louis' decision not to block this request as he had often told me his mother wasn't a very good cook. Was this simply more of the American daughter-in-law hazing process?

I eyed him doubtfully. "OK. Does she want to cook anything in particular?"

He smiled at me. "Well, she wants you to teach her how to bake chocolate chip cookies…"

I instantly relaxed. Louis' father had decided chocolate chip cookies were the epitome of American cooking and was eager to try them. Louis raved to his parents about how well I baked and it was time to put my money where my mouth was. I only hoped he hadn't set them up for a big disappointment.

"And...she wanted to show you how to cook a few traditional French dishes," he added casually.

Damn. I knew that was too easy. I had studied my French books as much as possible during all the wedding planning, but I have to admit, I wasn't able to focus as much as I would have liked. Aside from the vocabulary, the endless verb tenses and pronunciation issues, it was virtually impossible for me to master the exact accent of Louis' region, which seemed to be necessary for his family's comprehension. This appeared to be the case from my several botched phone conversations with his parents. Louis' dad still asks if I enjoy wearing chickens for warmth in the winter. I'll *never* live such a monumental pronunciation error down.

Add to this the complete lack of knowledge of how to say anything relevant to this task in French other than fork and butter (and chicken/sweater); how was I going to deal with being alone with his mother in the kitchen? As these thoughts raced through my mind, I noticed Louis approaching me with concern.

I stared back at him blankly. "What? Is something wrong?"

He eyed me carefully. "Have you ever plucked a chicken?"

I gaped at him and caught my breath. And then everything went black.

Chapter Eighteen

The following morning, Louis admitted his whole chicken joke was perhaps in poor taste. Instead of knocking me out of my bout of the crazies (his affectionate term for my insanity), it literally knocked me out. It took him five minutes to revive me from my fainting spell. That taught him a lesson about how to deal with Crazy Sydney. Joking is not an option...Crazy Sydney takes everything *way* too seriously. Unlike Normal Sydney who only takes everything *moderately* too seriously.

When Louis and I left for work that morning, I resolved to relax and let everything go. It was unlikely I would succeed, but I had to try. We were leaving for the airport as soon as we got home from work and at this point, there was nothing else I could do to prepare. Louis had banned me from reading any French books on the plane and ordered me to look at nothing but trashy magazines - my favorite airplane fodder. It was a thirteen hour flight from San Francisco to Paris (not to mention the four hour layover, an additional two hour flight from Paris to Montpellier and an hour car ride to Louis' hometown of *Le Caylar*), so I was looking forward to catching up on some actual reading as well. I had two new Chick Lit books from Kate I couldn't wait to read. In case you haven't noticed, I'm a sucker for a romantic comedy.

Why was I planning on so much activity? Wouldn't sleep be a better way to avoid thinking about the impending French doom? This wasn't really an option for me. Even though the flight left at seven, I knew I wouldn't sleep much. I could never sleep on planes. It had nothing to do with fear (imagine that?), only discomfort. There was no leg room, the person in front of me ALWAYS put his/her seat back into my lap and I was simply unable to fall asleep in a barely reclined position.

Louis, on the other hand, could sleep anywhere at any time of the day or night. A year in the French military had forced him to learn this ability quickly. This meant it would be a long and lonely trip for me, filled with opportunities to imagine the possibilities of the days ahead of me...in the clutches of my new family. Good times!

The day passed quickly, and I suddenly found myself sending a few final emails to cover my workload while on vacation. As I was about to leave the office, my phone rang. I debated letting it go to voicemail, but worried it might be a question which needed to be answered before my long absence. I sighed heavily and reached for the phone.

"Sydney Durand, how may I help you?"

"It's been seven months and I'm still not used to your new last name. I keep expecting you to say, 'Sydney Bennett.'" My mom chuckled.

I decided to gloss over how amusing it was that she couldn't remember my new last name. She probably wouldn't appreciate my sense of humor, since I was essentially laughing at her expense.

"Mom! I'm so happy to hear your voice." I sat down in my chair with a thud and felt an instant sense of relief. A few minutes with her would do a massive amount of good to my overwhelmed psyche.

"I told you, Mom! You're exactly what she needed."
Kate? Where did she come from?

"Um...how is it you guys are both on the phone with me at the same time?" Had Kate gone to New York for a stopover before flying to France next week and forgotten to tell me? She was working on very little sleep, so anything was possible.

Kate laughed. "Syd, haven't you heard of conference calls?"

"Of course, I have." Duh. I always mess them up, since no one can write a phone manual which makes sense, but I know what they are! "I didn't know either one of you had the technology."

My mom interjected. "The store has been so busy that we put in a second line. Your father thought it would be a good idea to include the conference feature."

I giggled. "I'm sure this is exactly what he had in mind."

Right on cue, my dad picked up another extension in the store and promptly started dialing. He always had the volume on the phone turned up really high (he still won't wear his hearing aid) and the sound of the deafening beeps while he dialed the numbers was excruciating. Kate and I screamed, "Dad!" while my mom screamed, "Teddy!" He was notorious for picking up the phone and punching in numbers without checking for a dial tone first.

"Hello?" My father queried.

Kate jumped in, "Dad! We're having a conversation here."

"Oh, hi, Katie. What are you and your mother talking about?"

My mom sighed. "We're trying to prepare Sydney for her flight to France."

"Duck is on the line? Duck! We covered this yesterday. You're going to be fine."

Damn it, Dad! It was supposed to be our secret! You sold me out!

My mom was becoming exasperated. "Teddy, your concern is appreciated, but this conversation is for the girls."

My dad did his usual mock whimpering routine. "Well, if you don't need me." He sniffled.

I rolled my eyes, quite happy he couldn't see me. "Dad, I love you. I heard you yesterday. And thank you very much for sharing our secret." I sighed. "I know I'll be fine, but it can't hurt to have another pep talk, right? Every little bit helps."

"You girls have fun. I love you all. You're nuts, but I love you." After his gem of a comment, he quickly hung up the phone.

My mom scoffed. "Well if that isn't the pot calling the kettle black..."

Kate and I burst into giggles. Our family really was peculiar, but in a good way. I guess I should just embrace my genes of insanity and move on.

Kate was the first to recover. "Syd, seriously, are you OK? *Anyone* would be stressed in this situation. You know that, right?"

I thought about it for a moment. "For the time being, I'm holding it together. I'm trying to take things one day at a time. If I think about all the people and the events and the expectations, I start to have trouble breathing. I mean, what if I screw up?"

My mom chuckled. "So what if you do? It's highly unlikely you will, because you are, after all, Sydney Ben - I mean - Durand. But it won't be the end of the world if you make a mistake. From what Louis has told me, his family is far from perfect. I doubt their expectations of you are anywhere near as high as the expectations you have for yourself. Please, give yourself a break, my darling."

Kate jumped in. "Mom's right, Syd. You put far too much pressure on yourself. You have a wonderful husband who loves you. I know it's been a rough few months, but you guys are on the right track now. This trip has the potential to be amazing. Give his family a chance to get to know you. They'll absolutely adore you! And I bet you'll adore them too."

Damn it, Kate. Why do you have to be right all the time? It was beyond annoying. I hadn't realized in the process of my massive freak out, I was judging Louis' family too harshly. I had assumed they would be waiting for me to fail, rather than helping me to succeed. It was high time I changed my perspective.

I sighed. "I hope you're right, Kate."

"I always am." She was pretty smug for someone who threatened to kill my husband over the accidental destruction of a stuffed pig. But that was beside the point.

I glanced at the clock and discovered I would have to rush to get home on time. I had a few last minute items to pack before the car came to pick us up.

I quickly gathered my belongings and said, "I love you both so very much, but I have to go. I didn't realize it was so late."

"Have a good flight! We love you!" Kate yelled.

My mom quickly interrupted. "Call us when you get in, please! I'll worry until I know you're safe."

I laughed. "I wonder where I got my anxious personality from? Thanks, Mom! I'll call you when we get to Louis' parents' house."

I hung up the phone and ran for the door. The last thing I needed was to leave for the airport without doing a final luggage check. So what if I had already checked five times? I needed to make sure I hadn't forgotten anything important, like my intellect or my sanity. If only I could pack an extra set of each...

⌒

Thankfully, I made it home with plenty of time to do my luggage check. Our car arrived on time and Louis and I had an easy time checking in at the airport. Just breathe, Sydney. So far, so good. To my surprise, I found myself starting to feel excited. All the wedding details had been taken care of. I had mentally prepared myself (as much as you can), for the pre-wedding activities and had resigned myself to the fact that I would most likely make a fool of myself once. OK, probably twice. Three times, tops. No big deal, right? It's not like I haven't humiliated myself before! At least I wouldn't really understand the comments being made at my expense. Everything sounds good in French, doesn't it?

As we settled into our seats, I found myself smiling and humming to myself. Maybe Sydney Durand had finally learned to take herself less seriously. MAYBE Sydney Durand was going to have a great time in France.

Louis turned to me suddenly. "Syd, I don't want you to panic, but there is something I need to tell you about the ceremony. There is something my mother would like you to do for her..."

Then again, maybe not.

I fixed Louis with my death stare. He should know by now, prefacing a statement with "I don't want you to panic" will absolutely cause me to panic. Honestly, I don't know where I had gone wrong in his Sydney-handling education.

He sighed. "Please don't worry. It is not a big deal. It is just..."

My eyes widened. "What? What now? What else do I have to do? What *possible* other hoop is there for me to jump through for your family?"

Yikes. Way to be harsh, Sydney. I guess I was tired of the requests for this wedding and all the activities which went along with it. Beyond all the stress for this trip and this wedding, I still had a feeling of dread that something would go wrong with MY dream wedding while we were out of the country. There were way too many scenarios I could run through in my mind to cover the potential disasters for the weddings in both locations. I really do have such talent. But there's no need to be jealous...

I closed my eyes and let out a deep breath. "I'm sorry, Bluey. I've been doing my best to relax, but it seems like every time I turn around, there's something else I need to do. I want to please everyone, but I'm starting to feel like a performing seal."

Lest you think I had morphed into Bridezilla, allow me to apprise you of the list of activities coming my way before the wedding: I was to be a special guest at his mother's weekly church group, one aunt's garden group, another aunt's bridge club, one uncle's hunting group and another uncle's fishing group. I was also to be recognized at a special town hall meeting in our honor, attend several dinners with Louis' childhood friends and accompany his mother to two dances - all during the week before the wedding.

Each event involved some type of special task due to my status as Louis' bride. Lucky Louis wouldn't even be attending most of these events, since he had his own list of activities with the male side of the family. (Most of which involved guns and motorcycles. At least HE would be having fun.) I had no idea how in the world I was going to survive on my own with a serious lack of knowledge of both the culture and the language. I haven't even started on the pre-wedding events, which would mercifully include my family as well. I don't want to overwhelm you, so we'll have to discuss that later. Now we must return to my conversation with my husband...

Louis regarded me with chagrin. "I know this is a lot for you, *mon coeur*. And I really appreciate how hard you are trying."

I stared at the ceiling, taking as many deep breaths as I could without hyperventilating. "What is it that you would like me to do?"

He smiled tentatively at me. "Well....there is this poem she would like you to read right before we say our vows."

I opened my eyes and glared at him. "And?"

"And since the ceremony is in French..."

I sighed. "I'll need to read the poem in French."

"Syd, your French is nowhere near as bad as you think it is." He was desperately trying not to laugh. The bastard was really enjoying all the lengths to which I had to go to please his family.

I narrowed my eyes at him. "Do I get cue cards?"

He hesitated. "My mother would really love it if you could do it from memory."

That's it. I need a drink. In fact, it's a good thing Louis' family owns a vineyard, because I'm going to need to drink A LOT of wine in order to get through all this. Take a deep breath, Sydney. This is important to Louis, so you must grin and bear it.

However, I would like to state for the record, I'm the one who has to do all the outrageous shit. His part sounds pretty easy; in fact, it actually sounds like quite a bit of fun. I wondered if these events weren't actual French customs and his family was simply messing with me because I'm American. I closed my eyes and laid my head against the seat. His family had missed out on a lot, so if I had to be hazed to be accepted, then so be it. It's not like I haven't embarrassed myself before. It was just unfortunate, in this case, every horrific experience was going to be recorded for posterity.

Louis very wisely selected this time to go to sleep. I decided to ignore my concerns for a while by employing wine and magazines. In order to avert the disaster that was our last flight to New York (waking in the airport infirmary in an alcohol fueled state), I decided to get some food in my stomach quickly. Since the food on most airlines is pretty heinous, I busted out my snack regimen of cashews, crackers and chocolate. (No, I'm not restricted to foods which begin with the letter "c." I find these particular items make a tasty snack mix.) After two more glasses of wine, and the bread and cookies from my otherwise questionable dinner, I managed to fall asleep.

Louis woke me right after the fasten seatbelt sign had been turned off. We were in Paris and it was time to get off the plane. Thankfully, I only had a slight headache (and a moderate case of the stumbles) due to my wine adventure. Once we cleared customs, Louis took me to an airport cafe and ordered an assortment of fresh pastries. The smells wafting from the cafe were heavenly. Did I detect a hint of CHOCOLATE?

Our waiter brought over coffee, tea and a basket of croissants, pain au chocolat and a few other pastries I had never seen in my life. Color me excited! I bit into a pain au chocolat and let out a small moan. It was really tasty.

Louis threw back his head and laughed. "You are so easy, *mon coeur*! This isn't even the good stuff."

I looked at him with wonder (and a mouthful of pastry.) "It's not?"

He wrinkled his nose. "It's frozen. Wait until we get to *Le Caylar* and I take you to the village bakery. It will blow your mind!"

This trip was suddenly looking a lot better. I then remembered all the events I would be attending prior to the wedding would have food. Really good French food, with lots of bread and pastries. This would help me. A LOT. So what if I put on a few pounds? In fact, that might not be such a bad idea...maybe then I wouldn't be able to fit into the costumes his mother had purchased for me. (It started out as one dress, but they kept multiplying. I know, I know, I didn't tell you. I was trying to shield you from my horror.) Both of my wedding dresses were a bit loose from the stress of the last few months...hmm....this could work. As long as I didn't overdo it. I grinned and grabbed another pastry from the basket. Sydney Durand had formulated a plan.

Following a very satisfying breakfast, we boarded our plane for Montpellier. This time I fell asleep (no doubt due to the mountain of carbohydrates I had inhaled) and Louis stayed awake. What felt like only a few minutes later, he was gently shaking me awake.

He stroked my face and whispered, "*Mon coeur*, it is time to wake up. We are here."

I opened my eyes and yawned. "I'm ready." I smiled and held out my hand.

He returned my smile and helped me up. We both grabbed our carry-on bags and exited the plane. As we walked down the corridor towards the airport, Louis took my hand and squeezed it.

"Are you ready for this, Syd?"

I took a deep breath and felt my knees start to wobble. "As I ever will be, Bluey."

We had to retrieve our luggage from baggage claim before we could enter the portion of the airport open to the general public. I was grateful to have a few final moments to collect my thoughts before we joined his parents. Within minutes, our suitcases came out and it was time to face the music. The unfamiliar French music.

When we reached the threshold of the door into the main concourse, I inhaled sharply. There were roughly thirty people standing there holding signs bearing the name, "Durand." I recognized Louis' parents and his two favorite cousins, was iffy about five or six of the other people (I knew I had seen them in photographs) and was completely clueless about the identity of the remaining crowd.

Louis took in my wide eyes and laughed. "Welcome to the Durand family, *mon coeur.*"

Chapter Nineteen

I stood with my mouth hanging open for a small eternity. All I could think was, "Holy crap! Who ARE all these people?" What a beautiful picture I must have made for Louis' extended family! Not exactly the image I was hoping to project. Once this thought occurred to me, I quickly closed my mouth and did my best approximation of a smile. I had done the best I could with my hair and makeup, but nearly twenty hours of traveling and fitful sleep had taken its toll. I *had* to get my facial expressions to behave.

Suddenly, everything seemed to speed up. Louis was swarmed by a group of people and I was summarily pushed to the side. There was a flurry of activity and hordes of people were calling his name and patting him on the back. It was sweet to see how much his family had missed him, but I felt like an extraneous accessory. I then heard Louis saying my name and gesturing to me. I gazed up at the sound of his voice and found the horde advancing towards me.

In an instant, I was completely engulfed in a stream of people whom I had never met. Each one beamed at me and said something in French so fast my head spun. It was then the official greetings began. Initially, I had felt prepared for this. Louis had always kissed my family twice - once on each cheek - so this is what I intended to do with his family. I could've killed him for not warning me that traditionally, his family kissed THREE times, starting with the left cheek. The lack of this knowledge, landed me in a few embarrassing situations. One of his uncles ended up with a kiss on the lips. I was mortified, but he seemed to be quite pleased, so I guess it wasn't a total loss.

Throughout the greeting process, I kept reminding myself not to hug anyone. Hugging is an American thing and considered to be yet another *faux pas* to the French. I was exhausted and completely overwhelmed, so it was a constant mantra in my head....Don't hug anyone, don't hug anyone, don't hug anyone! What I found hilarious was while hugging was considered inappropriate, his aunts (Cousins? Friends?) had no problem with touching my face, smoothing my hair, pinching my waist and rubbing my back. I find these gestures to be far more intimate than hugging, but what do I know? I'm just an uncouth American.

With each person I met, I tried my best to commit his or her face and name to memory. Unfortunately, I have a hard enough time remembering people's names when my brain is functioning at full capacity. I was at a distinct disadvantage given my current state of fatigue induced anxiety. I had no idea how I was going to keep everyone's name and relationship to Louis straight. He really should have thought ahead and made me some kind of chart to study. Yet again, his task was far easier than mine. My family is so small; he only had to remember six names, well, seven now that Sam has joined us. Seven names versus seventy. (Apparently, there were another forty family members who couldn't make it to the airport.) My sanity was in serious danger.

On top of the whole name conundrum was the language barrier. For some reason, each of his relatives were speaking to me as though I were fluent in French. Admittedly, I had put a lot of effort forth in studying this beautiful yet complicated language, but the results were not what I would have hoped. To complicate things further, they were all talking over each other with their thick Southern accents.

That's right, thick FRENCH Southern accents!!! Just take a moment to imagine what this would sound like. To say I was a deer caught in headlights would have been a severe understatement. I was a deer caught in headlights with my hind legs dangling off a precipice. Over a pit of lava. With poisonous gas rising towards me. Nope. It still sounds too tame.

I desperately searched the room for Louis and found him laughing with a group of men. I recognized one as his uncle, Luc, with whom he shared an extremely close bond, so I simply continued to smile and nod at people, hoping he might remember he had a wife at some point. I suddenly felt a hand on my shoulder and turned to find Louis' mother, Simone, smiling at me. She and I had spent many an hour trying to communicate over Skype. I didn't understand most of what she said, but she smiled a lot and kept telling me how beautiful I was. At least, I think that's what she was saying...

After the requisite three kisses on the cheek, she held my face in her hands and started to speak to the women standing next to her. I only understood every other word - hair, pretty, tall, eyes, pants? My vocabulary was crumbling, clearly indicating my urgent need to sleep. Right now I was the embodiment of stupid tired.

I craned my neck to search for Louis, only to find Simone taking my left hand and holding it painfully close to another woman's face. (And I do mean painful. She had nearly pulled my arm out of the socket.) The two of them appeared to be examining my engagement ring and wedding band. There were a lot of "oohs" and "ahs" and a bunch of other words I couldn't understand. For the next ten minutes I was led around by my hand so EACH and

EVERY woman, including some outside of the Durand entourage, could see what beautiful rings I had been given by her generous son. While I appreciated the beauty of my rings more than anyone, this madness had to stop. I didn't know how much longer I would be able to maintain a vertical position.

At that moment, Louis' favorite cousin, Monique, came to my rescue. She smiled at her Aunt Simone and gently removed me from her grasp. She took me over to the nearest cafe, ordered me a cup of tea and began to speak to me in Spanish. I laughed heartily. I took Spanish in high school and college and was infinitely more comfortable speaking Spanish than French. I was so relieved, I forgot my manners and hugged her. (Oops!) Monique didn't seem to mind in the least. She hugged me back and told me in Spanish she thought I was doing really well.

Ten minutes later, Louis came to find me. He seemed worried until he noticed I was sitting with Monique.

"*Mon coeur*! I am so sorry. I got caught up in seeing everyone. I didn't mean to leave you alone for so long." He kissed me on the forehead and rubbed my back.

I gazed up at him. "Relax, Bluey. I met a lot of really nice people." I furrowed my brow. "I don't think I understood most of what they said, but I smiled and nodded. They seemed happy."

He laughed. "They are all exceedingly pleased to meet you." He kissed Monique on the cheeks, three times, of course and she rubbed his head affectionately.

He and Monique then spoke in French for a couple of minutes. They both laughed a lot, but I was so tired I couldn't follow the conversation. When Louis glanced over at me, his smile faded and he put his hand under my chin.

"You are exhausted, Syd."

I took his hand and squeezed it. "I really need some sleep."

He said something quickly to Monique and took my hand. "Let us go get our rental car and start the drive to *Le*

Caylar. I cannot wait for you to take a tour of the farm."
He was grinning from ear to ear.

I smiled weakly at him and hoped he meant AFTER I
had slept for several hours. And had eaten several more
croissants.

You will be happy to know the *entire* Durand entourage
escorted us to the rental car counter, waited for the
transaction to be completed and then escorted us to our
rental car. As we said good-bye to everyone (thirty people
at three kisses a pop takes a lot of time), I thought about
how nice it would be to have Louis to myself for the hour
long drive to his parent's house. Unfortunately for me,
Louis' mother happily installed herself in the rear passenger
seat (Louis had addressed the issue of the front passenger
seat belonging to his wife on the walk to the car) and
proceeded to talk for the ENTIRE car ride. I closed my
eyes, took a deep breath and prayed to God we could have
a little peace when we arrived at his parents' home.

An hour later, we exited the highway. The first thing I
saw was a huge metal statue of an elephant. Was the circus
in town? I wondered if I were hallucinating from fatigue. I
shook my head and peered out the window again. It was
still there. As I imagined what could have prompted the
erection of this massive pachyderm at the entrance to a
town of less than four hundred people, Simone tapped my
shoulder.

I turned to face her, making my eyes as bright as I could
in my current state of fatigue. She pointed frantically and
rattled on in French at about a million miles an hour. Since
I had absolutely no chance of understanding what she was
saying, I trotted out the smiling and nodding, and it seemed
to make her happy. Louis sat next to me and laughed. I
had a feeling he was going do this quite often during our
stay in France. I really hoped I made it back to America
without making a complete ass of myself. Though the odds
were decidedly not in my favor.

A few minutes later, we exited the main road and traveled down a long gravel drive with no dwellings in sight.

Louis turned to me and grinned. "This is it."

I looked around and saw nothing but land for many, many miles. "Wow! I had no idea the farm was so huge."

His entire face lit up. "It was so great to grow up here. I rode my dirt bikes off those small cliffs over there...." He pointed out some cliffs which appeared to be fairly steep. Damn! "... and my uncle would let me drive the tractor from the age of eleven. Oh, and when I was seven, I swung from ropes in the barn," he pointed with a flourish, "and my uncle accidentally hit me with his truck." He laughed. "It was amazing."

Holy crap! He was hit by a truck! That must have been really painful. But clearly he was fine, so now he had a funny story to tell. I shook my head and thought about how different our childhoods had been. I had lived in a sheltered bubble compared to my adventurous husband. I shook my head and regarded him with wonder.

Louis seemed so happy that my heart swelled. I can do this. I HAVE to do this! I have to make a good impression on everyone for his sake. How I was going to do this was still a mystery to me, but I *had* to try.

Eventually, we pulled up to a rocky clearing next to a large house. Louis' dad was standing by his car waiting for us, smiling while petting a large German shepherd. As I got out of the car, I remembered how much I liked Michel and what a great time I had trying to communicate with him over Skype. Of course, I couldn't understand a lot of what he said, but he seemed like a genuinely happy person. He made Louis laugh harder than I had ever seen him laugh and he had a deep, rich voice and a contagious laugh. You couldn't help but feel good around him.

As I approached Michel to say hello (I had caught only a glimpse of him at the airport), I heard a sudden commotion. I stopped in my tracks and turned to see the source of the noise. Suddenly, I was hit by a wall of fur.

You heard me. A WALL OF FUR. I should really say, a YELPING wall of fur. I soon found myself on the ground covered in muddy dogs. There were so many, I couldn't discern how many or what kind of dogs they were. Louis had told me his parents had dogs, but I thought he meant two or three. This was an ARMY of dogs.

After the umpteenth paw in the face, I felt Louis' grip under my arm. He pulled me up to a standing position with a furious expression on his face. Once I assured him I was fine, he started yelling at his mother in French. I sincerely doubted she heard a word he was saying since she was running around chasing the dogs with a broom. She was also yelling, but her focus appeared to be the dogs.

It was at that moment I noticed Louis' father holding onto the car for dear life as he laughed his ass off. If I weren't the one knocked on my ass by SEVEN dogs (I counted! There were five miniature poodles, one mutt and the aforementioned German Shepard), I probably would have laughed too. The one thought which made me smile in the midst of the fur-laden chaos was this: even though they didn't speak the same language, Michel and my dad were going to get along really well. They both thoroughly enjoyed watching people in horrendously comical situations. The more embarrassment, the better.

Once I had been freed from the gigantic dog pile, we entered the house and I was reminded of my urgent need to pee. Since Louis had gone back outside to grab the bags, I asked his mother in halting French where the bathroom was. She was about to show me when the dog posse started acting up again. What the hell? Was I exuding some kind of pheromone which drove French dogs insane? Eau du crazy American woman? She gestured down the hall and ran after the dogs with the broom. I walked down the hall and started trying doors. The first led to a storage room piled to the ceiling with food and water. A fallout shelter? The thought of Louis' mom as a doomsday cult member surprised me. I would have to ask about that later.

I tried the next door and found a bedroom decorated entirely in pink. It would have been an absolute dream for me to inhabit this room at the age of seven. Well, Louis' mother does have a desire to stay young... Please, let it be the next door. Ah hah! I found it. I entered the room and closed the door. I saw a sink, a bathtub and a toilet (also all pink), but something just didn't seem right. The toilet was much too small. It was also too low to the ground. Not to mention the complete lack of water. Hmmm.....I knew I was missing something, but my poor sleep deprived brain couldn't figure out what it was. I only knew peeing in the teeny pink toilet was not a good idea. I decided to find Louis instead.

I opened the door and stepped into the hallway to find him coming towards me. I can only imagine the look I must have given him. It had to be a mix of pain, frustration and incredulity. He took in my expression and started to laugh. Then his father came down the hall, assessed the situation and joined in the laughter.

I glared at Louis with annoyance. My bladder was about to explode. "What's so funny?"

He leaned on his father for support as tears fell down his face. "You are looking for the toilet, right?"

I cocked my head to the side. "Yes, I am. Why is this so funny?"

Louis took my hand and led me back down the hallway. His whole body was shaking with mirth. What kind of *faux pas* had I committed now?

Louis cleared his throat. He led me to a door further down the hall from the bathroom I had just been in. I stared at him with confusion and opened the door. Inside was a toilet. A lovely pink toilet and nothing else.

I glanced back at Louis. "Is this why you were smiling? Does the toilet need privacy from the bathtub and the sink?"

Louis laughed even harder. "This is called a water closet. In most parts of Europe, the toilet is separated from the rest of the bathroom. It allows for...more efficient usage."

After stifling an eye roll, I leaned in close to him and whispered, "This would've been a good thing to tip me off about BEFORE we got here."

And with that comment, Louis dissolved into another fit of uncontrollable giggles. He clapped his father on the back and led him away so I could take care of business.

I sighed as I entered the water closet and closed the door. This country was going to take some getting used to.

Chapter Twenty

After a quick dinner with his parents, Louis and I settled in for the night. I was grateful to have him all to myself. I snuggled into him and fell asleep in a matter of minutes. When I woke in the morning, it was still dark outside. I felt around for my cell phone to check the time and was shocked to find it was already eight in the morning. (I love technology! The clock had set itself to the local time.) Why the heck was it so dark if it was eight in the morning? As I was pondering this question, I felt stirring beside me. Louis turned on a small bedside lamp and the room was filled with a soft glow.

"Good morning, *mon coeur*. How did you sleep?" He reached out and pulled me towards him.

I found my favorite spot on his chest. "I feel so much better. I didn't realize how exhausted I was."

He laughed. "Not surprising for my family. They really tire you out."

I swatted his chest. "That's not what I meant! I went over twenty-four hours without substantial sleep." His family certainly added to my fatigue, but I wasn't going to admit it.   Trying to understand thirty French people speaking at top speed would have been tiring for anyone - especially with reduced brain functioning from lack of sleep.

Louis ran his hands through my hair gently.   "You handled it really well, Syd.   I know it was a lot for you."

I turned my head towards him. "I'd do anything for you, Bluey."

He stroked my cheek tenderly.   "You have no idea how much that means to me."

"I think I have a very good idea of how much it means, *Monsieur* Durand.   Although, I have another very good idea…"   I reached up and pulled him on top of me.   It had been far too long since I had given my husband a proper kiss.

Just as things were starting to heat up, the door burst open.   Startled, we both looked up to find Louis' mother bustling around the room.   She was speaking rapidly in French and didn't appear to notice she had interrupted a very intimate moment.

Louis sighed. "And here we go…"   He kissed me on the nose, turned away from me and began to yell at his mother.

As you know, my French is not so great and when people yell over each other, their words become completely intertwined.   It was damn near impossible to catch an inkling of what was going on. (Let's not forget the thick southern accents.)   I simply sat in the bed, nestled safely under the covers until it was over.

In the process of the heated discussion, Simone ripped open the curtains, opened the window and pushed out a wooden shutter which had been covering the window.   The room was suddenly flooded with sunlight, which was not flattering for any of the parties in the room, but it did solve the mystery of darkness.

Ten minutes later, Louis raised his voice even louder and pointed vigorously at the door.   His mother sniffled, stepped through the door and closed it with a loud slam.

I threw my hands in the air.   "What the fuck happened?"

He let out a deep breath. "My mother has no boundaries."

My eyes moved cautiously between Louis and the closed door. "OK...but is it necessary for you two to *yell* at each other?"

He sat down on the edge of the bed. "Unfortunately, my mother doesn't understand anything you say nicely. I am sorry you had to see such a display on your first morning here."

I tried to wrap my mind around yelling as a regular form of communication with your mother. There had been a lot of yelling between them over the phone, but I thought this was due to the stress of the wedding planning. It appeared this may not be the case.

I rubbed my temples and returned my gaze to him. I was still confused. "What happened? Why did she come into the room without knocking?"

He seemed surprised by my question. "Did you not hear what I *just* said about boundaries? Or the lack of them?"

I rolled my eyes. "Yes, I heard that part, but didn't she have a reason to come in?"

"She is eager to get started on the discussion of this week's activities."

What now? Please don't tell me there's some last minute event where I have to balance on tight rope. I have to draw the line somewhere!

I sighed. "Discussion? Isn't everything already planned? Like down to the last detail?"

He chuckled. "Yes, you are correct. Everything is already planned, including several contingency plans. My mother wants to go over the schedule with us. AGAIN."

I massaged my temples again. I honestly have no idea what I was trying to accomplish by this action. I don't think it's possible to rub the tension out of your head, but it wasn't going to stop me from trying.

I took a deep breath in an attempt to calm my nerves. "Well, if it makes her happy." I paused. "Can we talk to her again about knocking? We could have been in the middle of something a little more...serious."

Louis began to get dressed. "It wouldn't do any good. She 'forgets' things too easily." He made air quotes with his hands. "I will lock the door from now on."

I felt a knot forming in the pit of my stomach. Boundaries were very important to me. When I had my episodes of anxiety, I needed a little space in order to get myself under control again. His mother's tactics were in direct opposition to my needs. This was really not a good start to the visit. I felt like I was under a mountain of pressure already. How the hell was I going to make it through this with her invading every aspect of our lives?

My heart rate began to escalate. I had to do something quickly to calm myself down. There was no way I could tell Louis about my concerns. This trip was far too important to him. I would merely have to grin and bear...well, everything. Going forward, we would only travel to see his family once a year. The rest of the time would be spent in my country, with my language and my comforts. I needed to get a grip. I was an incredibly lucky woman and I would do well to remember that. Even though there was a good chance his mother would be the death of me. An extremely good chance. OK, so it was really a done deal.

I took another deep breath and got out of bed. I followed Louis' example and got dressed, assuming his parents were waiting for us to have breakfast. I had taken a quick bath last night (his parents were old school and didn't have a shower), but I still felt the travel grime on my skin. Further bathing would have to wait until later.

As I was putting on my shoes, Louis told me he was going to check in with his parents. I nodded and grabbed my watch off of the nightstand. I put it on quickly, opened the door and was immediately met with his mother's smiling face. I nearly jumped out of my skin.

"Simone!" I smiled like a complete lunatic.

She grinned back at me, handed me a wicker basket with a cloth in it and promptly ushered me outside. Never mind my urgent need to use the bathroom or the stubborn rumbling in my stomach. I exhaled slowly and counted to ten. *Relax*, Sydney. Once I had a modicum of control, a very important question occurred to me. Where could we possibly be going at eight-thirty in the morning? With wicker baskets no less? (No, that's not considered to be a second question. It's simply an essential extension of the first.)

As the myriad of possible scenarios raced through my mind, I noticed she was leading me around the back of the house. I also noticed she was dressed in sweats, old shoes and had a kerchief on her head. This was not the way his mother normally dressed. Something was off.

I let out a sigh of relief as I caught sight of an enormous vegetable garden. There were endless rows of lettuce, tomato plants, pumpkins, grapes and eggplant. It was amazing! Well, it was to me. I couldn't grow anything. All my houseplants died shortly after I brought them home. To my great disappointment, I hadn't inherited my mother's gift for gardening. I grinned, knowing Simone and my mom were going to have some serious bonding material. It was easy to see them spending hours out here together, soaking up the sunshine.

Suddenly, Simone pulled me away from the beautiful garden and into a side building. What were they growing in here? A flash of feathers accompanied by rapid clucking and flying poop answered that question fairly quickly. One of the chickens had jumped up in my face and pooped down the front of my shirt. Apparently they don't like strangers. Simone laughed so hard, I worried for her safety. She kept saying, "chicken shit" in French. Sadly, the profane words are the ones I understand the best and we all know I'll NEVER forget the word for chicken. EVER.

I grinned at her and followed her back to the house. I knew this story would be told over and over at every event we attended this week. In fact, I wouldn't be surprised in the least if this incident made it into Louis' father's wedding toast.

We entered the living room of his parents' house to find Louis and his father drinking coffee and watching the morning news. His mother immediately pointed to me and launched into the story. Louis and his father laughed until they had tears streaming down their faces. As I stood there watching them, I reminded myself what an amazing wife I was. Not every woman would put up with this kind of shit. Pun absolutely intended.

Eventually, Louis came over to me and put his hand on my shoulder. "Syd, I am so sorry." He paused to catch his breath. "Are you alright?"

I smiled indulgently at him. "Bluey, I desperately have to pee, I'm ravenously hungry, I need coffee and I'm covered in chicken shit. What do you think?"

Unfortunately for me, this only made him laugh harder. Well, at least I would have a good story for my dad. This kind of thing is right up his alley. He's always telling me how funny I am. And it's usually during moments like these. Moments of humiliation. Louis and my dad are alike in the most *annoying* ways.

I shook my head and quickly found the water closet. Following this necessary errand, I went to our bedroom in search of clean clothes. I gathered a new outfit and my toiletries from my suitcase and set off for the bathroom. After a long bath, I felt infinitely better. I put on my favorite jeans, a soft blue t-shirt and a pair of work boots. (My sneakers were currently covered in chicken shit.) Thankfully, Louis had warned me the farm was not a place to wear nice shoes, so I made sure to bring two pairs of shoes which were "outdoor friendly." Meaning they could take a beating.

The heels I brought were for formal events only. Parties at his parent's home would be held on the terrace, which would prevent my shoes from being ruined, with the exception of the wedding reception. It would be impossible to avoid dirt completely at the reception, but as far as I was concerned, a woman had an obligation to wear beautiful shoes with her wedding dress. (Yes, even if it was the third...wait, I mean the second wedding. I know, I know! I have to keep up.) No matter what I did, my wedding shoes were going to be trashed.

Feeling somewhat human, I joined breakfast already in progress. I gave the requisite three kisses to each of Louis' parents, kissed Louis on the lips and sat down to eat. I was delighted to find someone had made a trip to the local bakery. There were a dozen pastries along with a few baguettes, jambon (cured meat) and a huge slab of butter. Yum. Simone handed me a cup of coffee and pointed out the cream and sugar. This day just got a lot better.

Louis and his parents engaged in pleasant conversation while I ate everything in sight. It was AWESOME. The coffee took a little getting used to, but once I doused it with cream and sugar, it tasted fine. Louis shook his head at me in disgust. He had always told me how weak American coffee was and wanted to share his love of REAL coffee with me. In all fairness, I did try it his way, but it nearly set my head on fire, so I decided to embrace being an American and throw some fat and calories at it. Works every time! (Besides, the French add butter to EVERYTHING. There was no need for Louis to be so superior about the coffee.)

After I had indulged as much as I possibly could, I sat back and sighed with satisfaction. Louis looked at me and grinned.

"You are pretty content, aren't you, *mon coeur*?"

I rested my head on his shoulder. "I am, Bluey. I've found the key to happiness in France. Who knew?"

He kissed the top of my head. "Are you ready to hear the agenda for the week?"

I giggled. "Why do you have to harsh my mellow so soon?"

He rolled his eyes at me. "You are *such* a dork."

I raised my head and beamed at him. "I know! And you still married me. Sucks for you!"

He picked up a piece of paper which had been written on every which way. There was not a bit of blank space anywhere on the paper. Crap.

Louis looked at me. "Here we go. Our first three days are free; we only have dinners to attend in the evenings. Starting Monday, you will be attending two events during the day with my mother and then my dad and I will join you both for dinner outings in the evening. Your family will arrive on Thursday, so you only have an event in the morning, which thankfully I will be participating in as well. All the formal wedding events begin on Friday, ending with the wedding on Sunday." He paused to draw breath. "I will translate the schedule for you so you can refer back to it. I will put the times you are supposed to be there on the schedule, but my mother is always late, so don't expect to leave on time, OK?"

I held his gaze, trying to keep my face in a calm mask. "OK." I couldn't believe how many iterations this precious wedding activity schedule had gone through over the past few months. What had started out as two days of formal grilling and/or hazing (henceforth to be known as "grazing") of one *Madame* Sydney Durand by the French clan and two days of pre-wedding activity with my family had morphed into three days of informal grazing, four days of formal grazing and the very same two days with my family.

"Keep in mind, when I said our first three days are free, it means we don't have to go anywhere. I have no doubt several family members will be stopping by to visit. The bonus is they always bring food." He tapped me on the nose. "You will get to try all of my favorites."

I nodded, reaching for his hand. "Of course; they haven't seen you in a while. They must've really missed you."

He leaned in and kissed me. "I missed them too."

I put my arms around him. "It must be hard for you to live so far away from them." I suddenly felt very guilty for taking him away from his family. "Are you sure you're happy in the U.S.?"

He held my face in his hands. "I am happier with you than anyone deserves to be, *mon coeur.*"

I leaned my forehead against his and sighed. "*I* don't deserve *you.*"

He laughed. "It's only been a little over a year, Syd. You have no idea what you have gotten yourself into yet."

I glanced up to find Louis' parents watching us while having a discussion of their own. Inserting their own dialogue, perhaps? That was going to be me over the next few days, as I was the lone English speaker in a large crowd of Frenchies.

Suddenly, the phone rang and Simone leapt up to get it. Louis had told me often how his mother could stay on the phone with her friends for hours discussing all of the local gossip. I relished the idea of witnessing this practice firsthand. I was hoping he would translate for me. With no TV shows available which I could understand, I needed a soap opera. Preferably one I wasn't starring in.

Simone answered the phone with an emphatic, "Allô?" and took off talking at warp speed. It would be a wonder if anyone could understand her. I turned to Louis in amazement to find him with an extremely angry look on his face. What had happened in the span of thirty seconds to piss him off so much?

Louis pushed back from the table and left the room in a huff. After a quick glance at his father (who was unsuccessfully squashing a chuckle), I scurried after him. I definitely wasn't going to need any TV on this visit. It seemed Louis' family had enough drama for a lifetime. I was kind of scared since I was part of it now, but I would have to think about that later.

"Bluey! Wait!" I called after him.

Louis stopped when he heard my voice, but the expression of pure rage was still very much on his face.

"What happened? Why are you so upset?" He was really starting to worry me. Where had all of the happiness gone?

"She...." He attempted to slow his breathing. "She invited the priest for lunch today."

Oh shit. I didn't see that coming. He was angry enough about the priest attending the wedding. This was not good. His mother was asking for trouble. Was she purposely trying to create drama? Or did she simply do whatever she wanted without regard for anyone else's feelings? Honestly, either possibility was equally petrifying.

"Um...why would she invite him?" I asked carefully.

"Because she always does whatever the hell she wants to. The man is such an asshole. I get angry just seeing his face."

I touched his arm. "I'm really sorry, Louis. What can I do?"

He closed his eyes and took a moment to collect himself. Then he smiled tentatively at me. "You can come with me into town. We will spend the morning there and have lunch at my uncle's bistro."

"I'll do whatever you want, Bluey. But...what about your mom?"

"She knew exactly what she was doing when she asked him. I told her I wouldn't see him other than at the wedding and I meant it. She will have to deal with our absence."

I kissed him tenderly on the lips. "Let's go."

He exhaled what seemed like an extreme amount of tension. "I will go grab your purse and let them know we are going. Please, wait for me in the car."

"Are you sure?" I didn't want him to face the music alone. Not that I could say anything, but maybe his mother wouldn't cause as much of a scene if I were there. Then again, maybe not...

"Yes, I am. I don't want you to witness another battle. One is enough for one morning. You are still a novice." He grinned.

I pulled him into my arms. "I love you."

"I love you, too." He buried his head in my hair. After a long moment, he pulled out of the hug and squeezed my hand. "You are my sanity, Sydney Durand."

After nodding his head for emphasis, he kissed my hand and walked towards the house. I shook my head as I watched him go. That poor bastard was in big trouble if I were the source of his sanity. But I was ecstatic to find our marriage in a good place. We would face the challenges of this trip *together*. And it appeared there would be many…

Chapter Twenty-One

The next three days passed in a blur. During that time, no fewer than fifty people came to Louis' parents' home to visit the prodigal son and his questionable bride. I use the word questionable because this is how I would qualify the looks I received from a good portion of our visitors. I was scrutinized, probed and generally picked over from every possible angle. Many of our guests took ridiculous advantage of my lack of knowledge of the language and openly mocked me to my face.

No, I'm not being paranoid. I have enough of a French vocabulary to understand when people are being rude. The words dumb, unattractive and uncultured are fairly easy to understand. I must say, my fan club was very careful to only make these types of comments when Louis was out of earshot. It seems they were well aware of both the depth of his feelings for me and his swift delivery of retaliation. Personally, I hoped the assholes got what they had coming to them. I also hoped I had a front row seat.

The only good thing I can say is none of these words were uttered by Louis' relatives. Every one of his aunts, uncles and cousins treated me with the utmost kindness. I communicated as well as I could with them by the hilarious combination of my pocket French dictionary and good old-fashioned pantomiming. Though I had a wonderful time getting to know them, by the end of the third day, I had severely aggravated my carpal tunnel syndrome. I would have to find a new form of communication. Maybe it was time to bust out the smoke signals?

Though the first few days had been riddled with stress, there were certainly good things about being in France. The best thing? Say it with me: the FOOD. My absolute favorite part of the day was our trip to the local bakery. The entire experience was pure bliss. From the first heavenly scent to the last morsel consumed, I experienced nothing but joy. There was no judgment, no fear and no chance of disappointing anyone. There was only a myriad of mouthwatering options, and I had every intention of trying them all. Since freshness is of the utmost importance when it comes to pastries, Louis and I ventured to the bakery in the morning, thereby ensuring a magnificent start to the day.

In direct contrast to my stress-free trips to the bakery were my cooking sessions with Louis' mother. Because she had scheduled a minimum two events per day starting Monday, our time together in the kitchen had to take place during our first few days in France. But there was no reason to feel stressed. Nooo! No reason at all. I mean, it's not like I had trouble understanding his mother's southern accent or her prodigious use of slang! And, it's not like she spoke a million miles a minute or fully expected me to be fluent in French! And it certainly wasn't the case that she has a very different idea of personal space than I do when it comes to a freshly slaughtered chicken!

Breathe, Sydney, breathe. My apologies for the outburst. As you can imagine, I was quite on edge during my French cooking lessons. I'm happy to say, I wasn't expected to pluck a chicken, as Louis had so dangerously joked with me about before our departure. However, I'm quite sorry to say I *did* have to endure the odor of burning feathers throughout a two hour lesson on making cream puffs. The cream puffs were amazing. Consuming them while breathing in charred plumage was…um…a bit…unpleasant.

Beginning Monday morning, we were roused at seven am by loud knocking and a lot of yelling. (Louis not only had locked the bedroom door but also had hidden his mother's key.) I felt an instant sense of foreboding when it dawned on me that I would be separated from Louis for the majority of the next three days. His mother was taking me to a variety of women-only events and Louis was accompanying his father to the corresponding men-only events. As I thought about what was coming my way, I began to literally quake in my boots. Well, they were bunny slippers, but this doesn't mean I was any less scared!

Louis and I were allowed a short breakfast together and were promptly whisked away to our respective events. While I attended his aunt's garden party and viewed every flower known to man, he went to a shooting range. Later that afternoon, while I desperately tried to remember the rules of bridge, Louis raced motorcycles with his childhood friends. Over dinner (to which Simone had conservatively added ONLY eight family friends), Louis reveled in his adventurous day as I tried to steel myself for the next round.

Our second day of gender specific events was no better than the first. The morning held a lecture and lunch with his mother's church group for me and hunting deer for Louis. My afternoon was composed of a particularly lively session of ballroom dancing, while Louis spent his afternoon on the docks with his uncles drinking beer and eating oysters. You will be happy to know, although I fell down far more often than I care to admit, I didn't sustain any real injuries, other than my pride.

On our third day, we were finally allowed to cross gender lines for our daytime activities, yet somehow Louis and I were still separated. My morning consisted of hanging out with Louis' Uncle Remi's fishing club. I was taught how to set up and cast a fishing pole as well as how to descale and *gut* a fish. Though there were several moments during the disemboweling process when I thought I would hurl, the worst moment came when I finished. Due to the absence of an apron, my clothes were coated in extremely fragrant fish parts. Since we didn't have time to go back to the house before our next event, I was forced to accept a spare ensemble my mother-in-law kept in her car for emergencies.

I'm not quite sure what kind of emergency would necessitate a bright orange jumpsuit with fuchsia sequin accents, but then again, there really was no other choice. Coupled with the fact that Simone is a good eight inches shorter than I am and you can easily picture one of my most unfortunate ensembles EVER. I resembled a seventies Vegas showgirl who tried to modernize with capris…

Even more unfortunate for me was our afternoon activity of…*hunting*. A bright orange jumpsuit is rather less than ideal as a form of camouflage while hunting. Following the round of raucous laughter at my impractical attire, I was given Uncle Luc's spare hunting jacket. Once everyone, and I do mean EVERYONE, had taken photos of my latest fashion exploration, I was informed we would be hunting hares. That was it! It was time for me to take a moment.

You know how most kids have a favorite stuffed animal growing up? It's often a bear, but may also be a dog or a tiger or maybe even a damn dinosaur. I had a stuffed RABBIT. Her name was Cinnamon and she held a very important place in my life as a child. In fact, she currently resides in the back of my closet because I can't seem to part with her. So, please tell me, how am I supposed to shoot one of her closest relatives???

After a number of deep breathing exercises, I returned to the hunt and proceeded to spend the entire afternoon "missing" clean shots at a number of hares. Louis' uncles smiled and shook their heads, probably thinking I was just another city slicker who never learned how to shoot.

Though a number of furry little creatures lost their lives that day, I was happy to know I hadn't been involved in any way.

Upon our return to the house late in the afternoon, we found Louis and his dad sitting on the terrace relaxing. They were talking animatedly and burst into fits of laughter often. As we approached, the smile instantly faded from Louis' face. Michel, however, took one look at me and laughed so hard that he doubled over to catch his breath.

Louis jumped up quickly and came over to me. "*Mon coeur*, what happened to you?" I could see the corners of his mouth twitching. He appeared to be struggling between his concern for my current mental state and his desire to join in his father's appreciation for my, um, exotic appearance.

I sighed. "I learned how to gut a fish."

One look at his face told me it wouldn't be long before the laughter won out. I couldn't blame him. I must be quite a sight. Besides the stellar outfit choice, my hair was beyond windblown, I was covered in dirt and I still had traces of fish guts in awkward places.

I rolled my eyes. "Go ahead."

He cackled like a complete idiot. He was so far gone, he couldn't even speak.

"I'm so glad to be the source of your amusement." I patted him on the back. "I'm now going to take the longest bath in human history. Feel free to attend tonight's event without me."

Without a backward glance, I stalked into the house and began removing my dirt, fish and humiliation soaked garments. As I gathered clean clothes for this evening, I thought about the events of the week thus far. It made perfect sense to me why Louis and I had been separated for the uber girly events of the past two days, but I failed to understand why he was not included in fishing and hunting. I can already hear you telling me I'm being unreasonable, but I have a sneaking suspicion his mother purposely excluded him from these events to see how I would fare on my own. (Seriously, he spent the day with his FEMALE cousins at the beach. That activity has *my* name written all over it!) I choose to consider today to be part of the unworthy American hazing process.

After a very, very long bath, I felt somewhat better. Once I had put myself back together, I ventured outside to find Louis and his father still relaxing on the terrace. There was no sign of his mother anywhere.

I regarded him quizzically. "Where's your mother?"

Louis thought about how to respond. "She, um, elected to attend tonight's event in the town square by herself."

I sat down next to him. "She went to the town square event? The one where she was planning to introduce me to every single person in the town?" That was tonight? Oh shit.

I felt all the blood drain from my face. This was a *really* big deal to his mother. And we weren't there. By now, you're well acquainted with his mother's…excitability. I felt dizzy imagining the swift retaliation I would be met with for this. (This tendency runs in the family.)

Louis put his hand on my shoulder. "Syd?"

I stared at him with terror in my eyes. "She's going to kill me. Not figuratively, Bluey. I'm talking literally. She is LITERALLY going to kill me."

I got up and started to pace around the terrace. The usual look of jocularity on Michel's face was replaced by confusion. It was clear even he was starting to doubt my mental stability. And he was definitely the most easygoing of the bunch.

As my mind raced through possible ways to make up for this huge gaffe, I heard Louis and his dad speaking quietly. I mean, what could I possibly do after embarrassing her in front of the entire town? She had been looking forward to showing me off as Louis' new bride for quite some time and I completely wimped out because of some fish entrails and a few dead bunnies. I wracked my brain for a way to make her happy, but at this point, even killing a chicken with my bare hands wasn't going to be enough. What the hell was I going to do?

At that moment, Michel put his hand on my shoulder. I turned to him with tears in my eyes, while he gazed at me sympathetically and began to speak in French. I was in such a manic state, I couldn't focus enough to understand any of his words. I smiled at him warmly, squeezed his hand and looked to Louis for an explanation.

He laughed. "My father is worried about you, *mon coeur*. He said you are much too sensitive and you cannot worry about every thought his crazy wife has."

I felt a small smile pulling at my lips. Did he just call HIS wife crazy?

Louis grinned at me. "He said the reception in the town square was far too much pressure to put on you, especially since my mother has put you through the wringer since the moment you arrived. He is impressed with how well you have done so far."

Slowly, the tension began to dissipate from my shoulders. Louis' father took my hand and led me back to the table. He gestured to the chair and poured me a glass of wine.

I gratefully accepted the wine. *"Merci beaucoup, Michel."* The ruby liquid went down with ease.

Louis chuckled. "One more thing, Syd."

I sighed contentedly as I felt the wine warm my stomach. "What's that?"

"My dad suggests from now on, you travel with a change of clothes." He paused. "He doesn't want you to look like a deranged muppet ever again."

Oh my God! I had totally forgotten about Michel's love of *Le Muppet Show*.

Thankfully, I hadn't taken another sip of wine, since it would have come out of my nose. And no matter how good a wine is, it won't give you the desired flavor if you imbibe it (or in this case expel it) through the wrong orifice.

The three of us laughed so hard, we had red, tearstained faces. I was fairly certain I resembled a matted troll, but I didn't care one bit. I hadn't felt this relaxed and happy at any point thus far on our trip.

Louis and I spent the next hour listening to stories of his father's youth. Louis had heard every one of them a dozen times, but Michel had a great time retelling them for my benefit. He would relay the information with great animation and then sit back and enjoy my prudish reaction to his bawdy tales, once Louis had translated for me. Apparently, Michel was quite a ladies man in his youth and had a very…adventurous sex life. There were many tales of public, um, turns of affection which sometimes ended up involving the police.

By the end of our conversation, I felt infinitely better and I happily realized Michel reminded me of someone I was very close to. My father was often the one to pull me out of a dose of insanity with a crazy tale, though his tales usually involved profanity, not profane acts. Either way, Teddy Bennett and Michel Durand were going to be fast friends. Language barrier be damned!

Following two glasses of wine and some bread with cheese, I excused myself to call Kate. She and her family were leaving for France this evening and I promised to check in with her before she left. I was thankful the nine hour time difference gave me the opportunity to speak to my sister before she boarded the plane. Her voice had immense healing power which I sorely needed.

Kate picked up on the first ring, leading me to believe she had been waiting for my call.

"Where have you been?" She had most definitely been waiting.

"Sorry, Kate. It was a rough day." I sighed.

"What happened? Are you OK?" She was in overdrive. Clearly she was freaking out; convinced she would forget something of vital importance for Sam. I kept reminding her that France wasn't a third world country. They happen to have a plethora of very well stocked stores.

"I'm fine, Kate. I...I...had to fish and hunt today."

I heard her breath catch. "Come again?"

I should just tell her. She could use a good laugh. I took a deep breath. "Louis' mother had me get all dressed up so I could fish, gut said fish and then hunt. Only I had to change my clothes after gutting the fish because there were fish parts everywhere and the only thing available was a bright orange pant suit with fuchsia sequins which was about eight inches too short. I looked like a deranged muppet!" Thank you, Michel. "And then I had to hunt Thumper!"

There was silence at the other end of the line. Had I lost her?

"Kate? Are you there?"

She cleared her throat. "You can't possibly be serious."

"Oh, but I *am*. And I've only described the occurrences of ONE day."

Kate whistled. "Wow. I thought you were being your usual crazy self, but it sounds like Simone might just have it in for you."

"You think?" I was incredulous. Being *my crazy self*? You can't make this shit up!

"Calm down, Syd. I'm sure she's not really out to get you." As if! "She only...wants to be sure you're willing to go the distance for her son."

"OK, so it's like she's planned a series of challenges for me to work through in order to prove my worthiness to be Louis' wife?" Is she fucking kidding me? I was already married to him!

"That's what it sounds like to me." She sighed. "Grin and bear it, sweetie. We'll be there to help tomorrow."

I put my hand against my forehead. "I hope I can make it until then."

Kate scoffed. "Relax. Both Maya and Dad will be there before we arrive and neither of them will let anyone give you any shit. Relative of Louis' or not. They will no longer have you at a disadvantage." Oooh! Listen to my sister curse for real! She's getting all riled up and forgetting her impeccable manners.

I laughed. "The Americans are coming to town."

She giggled. "You know it, baby!"

I closed my eyes. "I love you, Kate."

"Keep your chin up, Syd. And know how much we love you."

"Have a safe flight. Kiss Sam for me, OK?"

"Will do. See you tomorrow!"

I hung up the phone with a smile lingering on my face. I was so relieved my family was coming tomorrow. That may sound terrible, because technically Louis' family was my family now too, but I didn't feel connected to them yet. I was delighted to meet so many of the people who were important to Louis, but the whole experience was extremely intimidating. We had notable cultural differences, a massive language barrier and an opposing level of comfort with certain outdoor activities. (Louis always joked with me how he came from a family of rednecks, but it turns out there was a degree of truth to his statement.)

Having spent very little time with Louis only increased the amount of pressure I felt to impress every person I met. I simply needed to get over myself because, honestly, there is no way to impress people when you don't speak the language. You're automatically designated as being stupid *because* you don't speak the language. Their inability to speak English was irrelevant in this regard.

But more than anything else, I couldn't shake the feeling that my mother-in-law's motives were not entirely genuine. There was a distinct possibility she planned on doing more than just hazing me. Perhaps she was hoping to orchestrate my exit...

Chapter Twenty-Two

At last, the day of my family's arrival has come! It was now Thursday and I had barely managed to survive one week without them. I was thrilled to truly have someone on my side. I know, I know, Louis is on my side, but he's been far too busy to notice all the madness which has been taking place. As far as he was concerned, his family and friends were simply doing their best to get to know me. He had no idea what had been going on behind the scenes.

And I'm sorry to say, neither have you. I kept a few, um, minor incidents from you. It's not a big deal; I just didn't want you to worry. Let's face it, I don't exactly inspire much confidence in being able to handle difficult situations. Then add on not speaking the language, not knowing the local culture or customs, being the target of intense scrutiny and not having my wonderful husband with me as a security measure and you have a recipe for disaster.

I was prepared for being judged as an American: the Ugly American, the Entitled American, the Unworthy American, etc. I was prepared to miss the majority of the content of discussions. I was prepared to feel lost, uncultured and spastic. I was even prepared for the massive amount of insecurity I would feel upon encountering Louis' entourage of gorgeous ex-girlfriends. What I was not prepared for was their OPEN HOSTILITY for me.

During our few days in France, the Durand household was filled to the brim with guests eager to catch up with Louis and to meet his blushing bride. (That description became far too real far too fast.) Included in this sizeable group of visitors were four of Louis' ex-girlfriends. I was decidedly nervous about meeting them considering their link to Louis' past as well as their current status as close friends of my mother-in-law's.

Each of the four were very flirtatious with Louis and touched him far more than was necessary. I was determined to keep my cool and not give any of them the satisfaction of seeing me behave in a jealous manner. Poor Louis appeared to be very uncomfortable and would often excuse himself to the safety of his father's company on the terrace.

This is when the action shifted into high gear. Once Louis had been removed from earshot, the derisive comments would begin. First, the fake smiles the "ex-pack" (as I like to call them) had on their faces vanished. I was then given vengeful glares as they slowly picked apart my appearance. They commented on my hair, my makeup, my dress, my shoes, you name it. (I had a very good grasp on the French vocabulary words for wardrobe items. I would be spending a night in Paris after all. I had some shopping to do!) Each comment was followed by a round of hysterical laughter and a good deal of pointing and in some cases touching. It was really becoming unbearable.

After three days of verbal assaults, the pack decided to dial up the punishment. During Louis' Aunt Jacqueline's garden party, one of them purposely spilled a drink down the front of my dress. (I'll never refer to them by name, since I refuse to learn them out of spite.) The only good thing which came out of it was we had to leave early since Simone had already used her "emergency" outfit following an unfortunate marmalade incident. Wait a minute…now that I think about it, I'm pretty sure the marmalade was meant for me. I was standing right next to her at the time and I bent over to pick up an earring which had fallen on the floor. Poor Simone was merely collateral damage!

Later during bridge club, each one of them came up to me and proceeded to give me air kisses. Let me clarify that every person I had met in France had offered three kisses in greeting. Actual kisses which made contact with my cheek. Louis had informed me air kisses were considered to be rude. After this lovely new development I wondered if they were trying to preserve their precious lipstick, trying to send a nasty message to me or simply didn't want to be tainted in any way by the Ugly American.

The pack also decided it would be fun to "accidentally" call me by something other than my name. They settled on what sounded like "Simpie." OK. What were they going for here? Simpering? Simpleton? Because you know for damn sure they wanted me to get the message, so it had to be a reference in the English language. After I fought the urge to throttle them with my bare hands, I took consolation in this: these horrible women were pissed that the amazing Louis Durand had married an unworthy American. And you know what? They can suck it.

Apparently my punishment was far from over. During the lunch at his mother's church the next day, I happened upon the ex-pack having yet another anti-Sydney discussion. Big surprise, since I was their favorite subject. But this time they went too fucking far. They had the nerve to call me FAT. Jesus fucking Christ! I wear a size four! SIZE FOUR! While it's true I would be considered fat by modeling standards, this is a small town in the south of France. Were they now worshipping heroin chic? What the fuck?

I really wanted to tell them where they could shove their *foie gras*….but not only would this have gotten me into heaps of trouble with my mother-in-law, but also I had no idea how to say it. See? It's a GOOD thing I don't have a firm grasp of the French language. It took every ounce of control I had *not* to hurl every French obscenity I knew at them. And the list was rather long thanks to my father-in-law...

I kept trying to remind myself these women were just jealous that Louis was MY husband and he was fully embracing his new life. Meanwhile, they were still stuck in their small town looking for husbands of their own. When you think about it, they seem pretty damn pathetic, right? Unfortunately for me, this brilliant idea was fairly hard to keep in mind when I was surrounded by the vipers and my knight in shining armor was nowhere in sight.

No matter how hard I tried to fight it, I could feel all of my old insecurities coming to the surface. I honestly thought they had been put to bed once I married Louis; that I had been able to exorcize all my demons. With the mountain of abuse I had been taking, I found myself sliding back into bad habits. Despite the discomfort I was feeling, I wasn't going to share the antics of the ex-pack with him. He was happier than I had seen him in a long time and I wasn't going to ruin it.

You've now been caught up on the treachery I've been dealing with, and can easily understand why I was so excited to have my posse with me. If nothing else, it would be easier to ignore all the horrid comments, since I would be able to partake in actual conversations.

I emerged from the bedroom that morning to find Louis discussing wedding plans with his mother. Perhaps "discussing" isn't exactly the right word. It would seem Louis was told by his Aunt Seraphine that his mother had planned fourteen courses for the wedding banquet. Since his mom was asleep by the time we returned from dinner with his friends, he had to wait until this morning to go ballistic.

Let me give you the play-by-play. He tells her she's just showing off. She screams back he's her only son and she's proud of him. He tries to add something and she cuts across him that all these AMERICANS are coming and since his REAL wedding already took place, he should thank her for being so gracious about it and let her do whatever she wants. He then tells her she didn't behave in anything resembling a gracious manner and she starts to cry. Wow. I understood most of the conversation! My French is getting pretty good!

While I was excited I had absorbed more of the language than I had originally thought, I was eager to escape the yelling. I walked out of the house in an attempt to find a quiet, drama-free zone. I needed a few moments to collect myself before the onslaught of the ex-pack. Simone was hosting a welcome lunch for out-of-town guests, but my family wouldn't arrive until later in the afternoon. If I could just make it a few more hours...

I sat down on the terrace and laid my head on the table. The cool stone felt wonderful on my face. It was probably filthy, but I simply didn't care.

"This is a pathetic sight."

My head snapped up. Holy crap! Was that ENGLISH?

I frantically scanned the terrace for the source of the snarky comment. It couldn't be...she wasn't due until this evening...

"Maya!" I jumped up and hurled myself at her before I remembered this would be way too much affection for her after such a long trip.

"Jesus, Syd. Are you alright?"

I held her for another minute hoping her sassy attitude would help to steel my nerves.

She pulled out of the hug and examined me. "What've they done to you?"

I sighed. "It doesn't matter. You're here now. How did you get here so early?"

She completely ignored my question and narrowed her eyes at me. "Are those bitches still picking on you?"

Yes, I told her about the ex-pack and their exploits. I *had* to share it with someone! Kate would have been far too worried, my mom would have been horrified and Zoe would have started planning retaliation techniques immediately. And I'm afraid I would have been more than tempted to execute these techniques. Maya was the only one who would be able to give me the pep talk I needed to survive *without* supplying ideas on how to get revenge. She didn't trust I could implement any sort of plan properly. But now that she was here, she might choose to implement a few herself. I found myself grinning at the thought. Maya was smart enough not to get caught.

I inspected my shoes. "They called me fat."

For a moment, Maya was speechless, which is an extremely rare occurrence. She then exhaled loudly, closed her eyes for a moment and clenched her hands into fists.

She opened her eyes, smoothed her skirt and exhaled again, very slowly. "Have you told Louis?"

I glanced up at her. "No."

She didn't look pleased. "Why not?"

I pushed the hair out of my face. "He's incredibly happy here. I didn't want to ruin it with my insecurities."

Maya snorted. "It doesn't sound like they're insecurities, Syd. It sounds like these...hicks...are being purposefully heinous to you."

She had a point. "OK, fine. You're right. But he doesn't need to know about it."

"Thank God his taste has improved." She wrinkled her nose and tried to finger comb my hair into some kind of order. "Though your hair needs some serious help."

I touched my long locks self-consciously. "The water here doesn't agree with my hair. None of the products I brought have been able to tame it."

"Don't worry, Syd, I brought some industrial strength hair products." Maya thought for a moment. Then she began to grin like the Grinch who stole Christmas. "In fact, maybe the members of the ex-pack might like to sample some..." Uh oh.

I grabbed both her hands. "Listen, Maya, I'm all for giving these horrible women what they have coming to them, but please, please, please don't embarrass Louis or his mother in any way."

She shook her head. "Syd! You worry too much."

Louis came out of the house, grinning from ear to ear. "Maya! How did you get here so early?"

She batted her eyelashes at him. "I missed you guys so much, I flew in a day early."

He raised his eyebrows. "So what have you been up to since yesterday?"

She winked at both of us. "Wouldn't you like to know?"

Louis gave Maya a big hug while I dissolved into laughter. It felt really good to have someone looking out for me.

Three hours later, Maya and I were sitting on the terrace waiting for the welcome lunch to begin. She brought me a few new dresses since I had lost a number of garments to both wildlife residue and ex-pack pranks. I had been happily installed in a plum wrap dress with a generous neckline and a moderately short skirt. Maya had even supplied matching strappy sandals and beautiful chandelier earrings. I looked amazing, if I do say so myself.

As the guests arrived, I introduced them to my fellow American and watched in awe as she charmed the pants off everyone. It seemed no matter what language people speak, they were not immune to her charisma.

It was easy to see the ex-pack didn't like the look of her. Maya was in a word, flawless. She chose a simple black strapless dress with a long flowing skirt. She added layers of sparkly necklaces, simple dangly earrings and the most beautiful shoes I had ever seen. They were made of a black shimmery fabric, had open toes, an intricate pattern of straps and sported the highest heels in existence.

I watched as they surveyed her with the usual expressions of disdain. The only problem they faced was while they were able to find numerous faults with me, there were no faults to find with her. Her hair was cut in the latest style from French Vogue, her makeup was impeccable, as usual, and her petite frame and beautiful skin sealed the deal in making her the most beautiful woman at the party. I chuckled to myself when I saw them eyeing her shoes with envy.

That afternoon was the best of the trip by FAR. Maya started out the event with a bang by monopolizing all the best looking men. The stares the members of the ex-pack gave her were vicious! And every few minutes she would look over at them and smile. It was awesome!

However, it seemed they weren't finished with me quite yet. Shortly before dessert was served, I had an extremely close shave with my least favorite member of the pack. The ring leader (let's call her Big Hair) tried to corner me at the edge of the terrace. She held a dangerously full glass of red wine and a wicked expression on her face. It would seem their favorite target was still one Madame Sydney Durand.

Just before the moment of impact, Maya literally came out of nowhere and inserted herself between us. She then nudged Big Hair at the perfect angle to both dump the wine down the front of her WHITE dress and knock her into the bushes. It was absolutely brilliant!

I furtively peeked around to see if anyone had witnessed the fray. It appeared Big Hair had purposely chosen to corner me in this spot since there was very little foot traffic. That definitely turned out to bite her in the ass. There were no witnesses. Serves her right!

Maya whirled around to face me. "They don't give up! Are you alright?"

I smiled cautiously at her. "I'm fine. Thank you for rescuing me." I glanced around one last time to make sure no one had been paying attention. "I just wanted to make sure we didn't get caught."

Maya's eyes were wide. "Sydney Durand! Will you please stop worrying about what people think?

That…SKANK was about to ruin your dress. And you're the freakin' guest of honor!"

"I know, but…"

There were no buts as far as she was concerned. "You act like being an American is something you have to apologize for. What kind of bullshit is that? Embrace it!" She walked over to me and began poking me in the chest. "You show these snotty French people, no one messes with you. We are PROUD Americans. They should be so lucky to have you in their family! And if I see one more slight towards you while I'm here, they'll be truly sorry."

"Maya! You know it's not Louis' family; they've all been wonderful. It's his exes and…some of his old friends…and some of the other people who live in the town…" What else could I really say?

She smirked. "Listen, Syd, YOU can certainly continue to project a ladylike image. They know you're trying to make a good impression on everyone and won't fight back, but I don't give a crap what anyone thinks of me. I love you like a sister and no one messes with you. NO ONE."

I believed her. At that moment I was infinitely glad she was on my side. Maya was much more than a formidable enemy. She had the capacity to make your life a living hell. The ex-pack had better watch their backs…

Once the rest of the pack got wind of Big Hair's ill-fated incident with a bush and a glass of wine, they decided to call it a day. The mass exodus of the pack confused poor Simone, but Maya and I were thrilled to see them go. We settled on the terrace with a bottle of wine from one of the Durand vineyards and enjoyed the beautiful view.

By the time we finished the bottle, the party had died down and my mood had vastly improved. Suddenly a thought occurred to me.

"Hey, where's Devon?"

She smirked. "Around."

Hmm. "Why isn't he here with you?" He was invited after all.

She shook her head. "I'm working, hon! He can't be here to distract me."

I really hoped she was joking. "Maya!"

She held her hand up. "Relax. He'll be here for the wedding." She paused. "Now, there's one thing I forgot to tell you about the pack."

I raised my eyebrows. "Did I miss something?"

She looked at me and started shaking with laughter.

I closed my eyes. "Maya, what did you *do?*"

She cleared her throat. "I *may* have given Scary Eyes a container of industrial strength hair gel, which *may* contain a small amount of crazy glue."

My eyes snapped open and my hands flew to my mouth. "Shut up!"

Maya grinned back at me.

Wait a second. "If you gave it to her, what would make you think she'd use it? The whole pack knows about what happened to Big Hair."

Maya giggled. "*I* didn't give it to her."

OK. "Then who did?"

"Monique has your back, Syd."

Holy shit! She got Monique involved?

Maya quickly assessed my thought process and intervened. "Syd! Don't worry! She's a really smart cookie. She figured out what was going on and wanted to help put them in their place."

I couldn't process it all. "But…how?"

"My Spanish is pretty good, Syd."

I cocked my head to the side. "And you just…asked her to give Scary Eyes the tainted hair product?"

"Where do you think I got the glue?" She winked at me.

As the reality of Maya's words sunk in, Louis came out to the terrace.

He beamed. "How are my girls?"

"Great!" Maya and I said in unison.

Louis came up behind me and put his arms around my shoulders. "I'm glad you have Maya to keep you company.

I know this week has been a little lonely for you." He frowned. "I don't think those outside my family have been too friendly."

I winked at Maya. The less Louis knew, the better. I believed there to be an excellent chance the ex-pack was finally going to leave me alone. On the off chance they decided to give it one more try, as of tomorrow's event, they would have the rest of the cavalry to deal with. And that didn't paint a pretty picture. If there was one thing Americans knew how to do, it was fight.

Chapter Twenty-Three

Though the afternoon activity involving the takedown of the ex-pack made the day seem pretty full, we still had a dinner event that evening. While this event in particular would be far less stressful since half of the guests were related to me, this didn't stop me from drinking a very large amount of wine in preparation. I had been balancing on a precipice for the last week and was enjoying being on solid ground.

It's possible Maya and I went a bit overboard with the second bottle of wine (there may have been a few demonstrations of dance moves that we hadn't performed since our freshman year), but it was too late to turn back now. The resurrection of our ancient moves sparked a discussion of some truly disastrous experiences we had been through as eager young college students. Following Maya's recollection of one of our more embarrassing party mishaps, which involved a rogue blender, I heard my dad's voice break through our raucous laughter.

"Duck, have you been drinking?" Oh shit. I was nearly twenty-nine years old, yet I still had some explaining to do.

Maya leapt to my defense. "Mr. Bennett, you have no idea how much this girl needed to drink. SOME people were being very rude…"

I greatly appreciated her efforts to explain my behavior to my father, but it probably would have been more effective had she not teetered drunkenly on her extremely high heels.

My father glanced back and forth between us and smiled. "You girls are really cute, but I worry about your mental functioning."

I carefully got up from the table, swayed slightly and went over to greet my parents. I hugged each of them for a long moment and offered them seats at the table.

"How was your trip?" I thought about how awful it must have been for them to endure two flights, one layover and one long car ride. Neither one of them likes to fly and large crowds make my mom nervous.

My mom beamed at me. "Fine, sweetheart. We're so happy to see you!"

My dad rolled his eyes. "Fine, my ass! The food was awful, the planes were too crowded and at no point on the trip was I offered any chocolate." He punctuated his indignation by banging his fist on the table.

My mom smacked him in the stomach. "Stop complaining! You should've been very comfortable since you lifted the armrest between our seats and took over part of mine!"

I laughed. "Up to your old tricks again, old man?"

My father gave me his most innocent smile. I sighed with contentment. I had really missed my parents.

I was about to ask my mom if she would like a "nice cup of tea" (her favorite thing in the world), when I saw Zoe and Charlie walking towards us from the driveway. I was so excited, I jumped up and ran over to them. Probably not the best idea given the wine had gone to my head and I was wearing high-heeled sandals, but the good news is I didn't fall flat on my face. Or my ass. Things were looking up!

"Sydie!" Charlie opened his arms to me.

I almost knocked him over with the force of my hug and quickly pulled Zoe in to join us. I was so happy, I almost cried.

Zoe started to laugh. "You really missed us, didn't you?"

I pulled out of the hug and beamed at them. "I really did."

"Oy!" It seemed my father was in need of something.

I brought my gaze to meet his. "Yes, Dad?" Then I noticed Simone had just come out of the house and was smiling at all of us.

I walked over and introduced her as best I could to all those she had previously "met" over Skype. Video chats never do people justice, so I think it took a minute for everyone to look familiar to her.

I turned to Simone. *"S'il vous plait, Simone, où est Louis?"*

Charlie grinned. "Nice French, Syd."

I rolled my eyes. I knew my French was awful and he was mocking me, but I wasn't giving up!

She said something which sounded like she would go get him and went back inside the house.

The moment Louis came out of the house, I heard a sound I had missed for over a week: the happy gurgles of my perfect niece. I whipped around to see Kate and Nick approaching with my little angel in tow. I was filled with so much joy, I felt tears form in my eyes. Now that my family was here, I genuinely felt like I could breathe.

I walked over to Kate and Nick and hugged them soundly. "You three are a sight for sore eyes."

Kate beamed at me. "We're happy to see you too, sweetie." She paused. "How have things been here?"

I grinned broadly. "Great!"

Nick laughed. "Wine will do that for you, Syd."

I shook my head. "The wine was simply a celebration of freedom."

Nick seemed confused.

I offered an explanation. "The removal of the ex-pack."

Kate clapped her hand over her mouth. "What did Maya *do?*"

Nick was about to ask a question when Kate smacked him in the stomach.

I chuckled. "She put them in their place."

Kate started to bounce up and down. "I need details!" She kissed Sam on the head, handed her to Nick and linked her arm through mine. "Don't hold out on me, Syd. I want to hear exactly what happened to those horrible women."

Charlie turned to Louis. "Do I want to know what they're talking about?"

Louis shook his head. "I do not even want to know what they are talking about." He then slapped my brother on the back. "Let us grab your bags and put them in the remaining guest room before my mother forgets you are staying there and fills it with more unnecessary wedding paraphernalia."

While Louis and Charlie dealt with luggage, Kate and I joined my mom and dad, Zoe, Maya, Nick and Sam at the table on the terrace.

Kate gave my dad a kiss on the cheek. "How's the hotel, Dad?"

My dad is far too high maintenance to be a guest in anyone's home. He requires professionals to deal with his needs. Suffice it to say the cleaning staff is always given an extremely generous tip. By my mother.

He caressed her cheek. "It's great! You're going to love it."

Kate had insisted on staying in the local hotel, despite the ample room in the house. She was deathly afraid Sam's nocturnal activities would cause too much difficulty for a family which was under a great deal of pressure from hosting such an important wedding. (In other words, she was afraid of pissing Simone off.) Apparently, the mass of out-of-town wedding guests who were also staying in the hotel didn't worry Kate in the least.

For the next hour, my family sat on the terrace and got to know Simone and Michel. Zoe and Kate tried out their

French, while Nick and Charlie took a page out of my book with a dictionary and hand gestures. I sat contentedly catching up with Sam, soaking up her sweetness in an attempt to heal the damage done to me over the last week.

As the sun set, Louis' aunts, uncles and cousins started to arrive. There were endless rounds of introductions and awkward attempts at the triple-kiss greeting, but in the end, everyone was smiling and laughing. It warmed my heart to see our family members getting to know each other. (Or at least making a concerted effort to understand each other.)

Due to my heightened nerves concerning the introduction of our two families, I had neglected to ask Louis about the details of tonight's dinner. It would seem Simone was using this event as a warm up for the wedding banquet, which as you no doubt remember, would contain fourteen courses. As the food continued to appear, I looked to my left and began to watch my father, who had no qualms whatsoever about unbuttoning his pants at the first sign of discomfort. And with a meal of this size, there would definitely be a good amount of discomfort. Not that it would stop him from eating...

I saw my mother lean over and whisper in his ear. My dad simply shook his head and helped himself to more sautéed mushrooms. I watched as my mother surreptitiously tucked his napkin over the top of his pants in case he decided to unbutton them without her detection. I guess she's become a pro at handling him after all these years. I said a silent prayer that my father kept the napkin in place following the unbuttoning process. I then breathed a small sigh of relief and returned my attention to the rest of the table. We certainly were an interesting mix of people.

Kate was having an animated conversation with Monique (because, of course, my perfect sister is fluent in Spanish). I believe Charlie, Nick and Louis' uncles were talking about motorcycles since they appeared to be miming putting on helmets and twisting throttles. My mother and Simone were no doubt discussing gardening or some kind of craft project, while passing a French/English dictionary between them. Maya was talking about God knows what with two of Louis' cousins and the remainder of Louis' aunts and cousins were fussing over Sam. It was an amazing sight to take in. We were a family. One big, loud, pantomiming, dictionary-toting family.

I smiled to myself and looked up to find Louis grinning at me. Since we had finished our main course and had a few minutes before the salad course (followed by the cheese course, the first dessert course and then the final dessert course), Louis came over and walked me to the edge of the terrace for a private moment.

He slipped his arms around my waist. "How are you feeling, *mon coeur*?"

I breathed in his heavenly scent. "I'm so relieved."

He chuckled. "To have your family here?"

I tapped his nose. "Yes, and to know our families are able to get along."

He kissed me tenderly. "And here I thought you were enjoying your victory over…what do you call them? The ex-pack?"

What? He knows about them? Maya!!! Wait…Kate? No, definitely Maya.

Louis laughed as he watched me go through different theories in my mind. "Syd, relax, Maya filled me in."

I was going to have to kill her. I had told her QUITE CLEARLY not to get him involved. I exhaled loudly. "I'm so sorry, Bluey. I didn't want you to worry."

He put his finger under my chin and brought my gaze to his. "I dated those women a long time ago. I was very young and there really weren't many options in such a small town. I feel terrible that they treated you in such a way. Why didn't you tell me?"

I sighed. "Your mother seemed to be so close to them and I didn't want to be a tattletale. I considered it to be part of the hazing process."

Louis cackled. "The hazing process? You think you are being hazed?"

"It sure feels like it."

He pulled me back into the safety of his arms. "Oh, Syd, I am so sorry. I didn't think about it from your perspective. I guess you have been asked to do a lot."

I sighed. "Why do you think I made a reference to a performing seal?"

He cracked a smile. "Your family did not put me through this extent of testing. You are a better man than I am, Sydney."

"You can say that again." Maya grinned.

I pointed my finger at her. "YOU suck!"

She surveyed me without emotion. "Really, Syd, there's no need to be so crass."

I walked over to her. "There's every need for it. Why did you tell him?"

She had the audacity to look bored with my outrage. "Louis had the right to know how you were being treated right under his nose. And once you stop being such a dumbass, you'll realize I did exactly what I needed to do to take care of you."

The pieces were slowly falling into place. I turned back to Louis. "YOU sent Monique to help Maya."

He raised his eyebrows at me. "Why would I do such a thing?"

I grinned. "Because you wanted to help bring down those heinous bitches without getting caught by your mother."

He kissed me on the forehead. "I always knew you were a smart girl."

Suddenly we heard Louis' mom calling him to come help bring another table out to the terrace. Apparently a few more cousins were coming for dessert.

Louis started to walk away, but he turned back to add a quick comment. "By the way, Maya, that was a nice move you pulled on Brigitte."

She smiled at him mischievously. "Who?"

He coughed. "Big Hair." Hiding smirks, they exchanged a subtle high five and Louis left to help his mother.

Maya took my hand. "I really had your best interest at heart, Syd."

I was about to agree with her, when Kate materialized and decided to add her two cents.

Kate scoffed. "When has she EVER had your best interest at heart? Need I bring up the lime green dress?"

Maya scowled at her. "I seem to remember you getting quite a laugh out of that one, O Perfect Sister."

Before a cat fight broke out, I put my arms around them. "I love you both so much." I looked them each in the eyes. "I really, really, *really* missed you."

"We know." They said in unison.

I loved them with all my heart, but they were often far too smug for my taste. I decided to distract them with another topic.

I gestured towards the dinner table. "So what have I missed?"

Kate sighed. "Well, Dad has opened his pants. Then he accidentally started a burping contest with Michel." Kate was being kind; I doubted it was anything other than intentional.

Maya chimed in. "And Louis' uncles are judging."

I slapped my hand to my forehead. The farting contest wouldn't be far behind. "So Dad is making a great impression on my new French family." Sweet! After all the work I've done to try to improve their opinion of Americans, my dad sends it right back down the toilet.

Maya whacked me in the back of the head. "Will you relax, Syd? Look at them!" She pointed towards the table filled with men. It would seem the women felt the need to escape all of the belching since they were nowhere in sight.

I begrudgingly peered at my father. He was laughing so hard, his face was bright red. Charlie, Nick and Louis' male family members were all boisterously laughing as well. It didn't appear that anyone was upset or embarrassed; they were all simply having a good time. I smiled the tiniest of smiles and desperately hoped they had moved on from the burping contest. To something which didn't involve gas…or any other bodily function. (You never know with my dad!)

Kate put her arm around me. "Syd, everyone's having fun. This visit is going to be a success. Just you wait."

Zoe wandered out from the house to find us all watching the menfolk. "What's going on, ladies?"

Maya snorted. "We're enjoying the view."

Zoe shook her head and very wisely changed the subject. "You won't believe what's going on in the kitchen! Simone does NOT do anything halfway. You *have* to see what she's bringing out for dessert."

Five minutes later, the largest chocolate mousse I've ever laid eyes on emerged from the Durand home. It took four women to carry it and two additional women to help settle it onto the already heavily laden table. It was a very good thing the table was made of stone.

After an hour of eating, the entire family had only been able to consume about a third of the massive mousse. I had no idea where Simone was going to put the leftovers and had no desire to think about it given how packed her THREE refrigerators were. (She literally had enough food to feed an army.) Yesterday, I observed her retrieve an item she needed from the back of one of the shelves and watched in fascination as she fit every item back in exactly the right place so the door would close. It was like an edible game of Tetris.

In the end, I think the first evening our families spent together turned out well. Sam was the most popular American visitor by far. There wasn't a heart she wasn't capable of capturing. This little girl had SKILLS! Maya was a close second. While all the Frenchies found her charming, Louis' sixteen year old second cousin, Felix, was completely taken with her. He followed her around for most of the evening, fetching whatever her heart desired and gazing at her longingly. The poor kid was going to be bitterly disappointed once Devon came on the scene.

I was delighted the evening was such a resounding success. With the start of the official wedding events tomorrow, I felt a small sense of unease that our hard won bubble of happiness would be burst by outsiders. We would have to wait and see if our newfound bond would be able to sustain the onslaught of *les visiteurs*, *le vin* and *voila* – the mother of all meals, the French wedding banquet.

Chapter Twenty-Four

The official start to the pre-wedding events for the Durand-Bennett party begins today! Are you ready? Good, because I'm not sure I am. Even though last night's welcome dinner was definitely a success, I woke up this morning with renewed nerves. Today would bring a vast amount of extended family, friends as well as foes posing as friends. I wasn't sure how much stamina I had left when it came to nefarious schemes and backhanded comments. However, I could take solace in knowing I was no longer on my own in the battle.

It seems with the start of the official events, Simone had reverted us back to our gender specific daytime activities. The women would begin the day with a tour of the town, followed by a choir concert at the church, followed by a picnic on the lawn of the church and would end the afternoon with a lengthy session of ballroom dancing in the church's lesson room. The men, on the other hand, would spend the morning touring the town as well (but apparently the men's version), followed by lunch at Louis' Uncle Remi's bistro and would spend the afternoon hunting on the family's property. I just hoped none of my relatives got shot. Or shot anyone for that matter. I had no idea the last time any of the men in my family had handled guns.

The evening would take us to Louis' Aunt Jacqueline's house for dinner. Invitations had been limited to immediate family and out-of-town guests, so I was guessing a total of around fifty people at dinner. In comparison to a number of other dinners we attended during the last week, fifty people felt rather intimate. I might get to join in a conversation this time!

I found myself a little nervous as I got ready that morning. Louis had left at the crack of dawn to help his father and uncles go through all the guns in the family arsenal. They had spent pockets of time over the last week cleaning the guns, but they wanted to give each one a final check before they were used this afternoon. The last thing they wanted was for one of their visiting American relatives to meet with an unfortunate accident. Even if it was as a result of their own stupidity.

A few minutes later, I went out to the terrace to find breakfast in full swing. My entire family was at the table with Simone and her sisters, Jacqueline and Seraphine. I hung back for a moment, just to soak it all in. Neither Louis nor I were present and they seemed to be doing fine on their own. Sure, there was the usual preponderance of dictionaries and makeshift sign language, but everyone was smiling.

My dad was the first to notice I was lurking in the doorway. "Duck! Come and eat! You're going to need your strength if you have any prayer of not injuring yourself before your wedding. Ballroom dancing is not exactly your forte!"

My mom swiftly excused herself from a conversation with Simone and Seraphine and scowled at my father. "Don't listen to your father, sweetheart. You'll be fine."

My father looked at me doubtfully. His superior attitude was palpable. I reminded myself I had to be on my best behavior in front of Louis' family. I was fairly certain any physical expression of sarcasm (such as smacking him in the back of the head), might be perceived as a sign of disrespect and land me back in the entitled American category. Fine. There are other ways to get my point across.

I kissed him on the cheek and smiled sweetly. "Please make sure that you come back from your adventure with all your limbs still intact."

I grinned at the Durand-Bennett party, said a blanket "*Bonjour*" and sat down next to Charlie. As I began to gather pastries for breakfast (perhaps there was something to my father's theory of proper sustenance), I leaned over and whispered to my brother.

"When was the last time he fired a gun?"

Charlie paused. "The Korean War?"

I slapped my hand to my forehead. "Please tell me you're joking."

He shrugged his shoulders. "I'm honestly not sure. I think he used to go target shooting with his old army buddies in the eighties…"

I sighed. "So we have no confirmation he's shot any kind of firearm in more recent past? Like within the last ten years?"

Charlie shook his head. "I checked with Mom, but she isn't sure either. He doesn't always tell her what he's up to. She thinks he's enjoying making her wonder about his safety today."

I regarded Charlie grimly. "I guess we'll have to cross our fingers and hope for the best." I paused. I was about to ask Charlie if he would keep his eyes open for danger when he beat me to the punch.

"I'll do the best that I can, Syd. I'm going to need a refresher course in shooting myself."

I put my arms around Charlie and squeezed. "Please, be careful."

I returned to my breakfast preparation and thought about the possibility of outcomes from today's event. 1) My dad, Charlie and Nick could all come back unharmed. 2) One of them could accidentally get shot. 3) Two of them could accidentally getting shot. 4) All three of them could end up getting shot. 5) Each of them could end up accidentally shooting one of Louis' relatives, a member of their own family or themselves. OK, I can't think about this anymore.

Kate sat down next to me. "No one is going to get shot, Syd."

I nodded with as much confidence as I could muster. "If you say so."

She smiled. "C'mon, you know I'm always right. Besides Louis promised me he would look out for them. There's no need to worry."

She did have two very good points. She was always right, as annoying as that fact was. And you couldn't find a better bodyguard than Louis. I closed my eyes and recognized I was going to have to let it go. It's not like I could go with them and try to run interference for their recklessness.

I opened my eyes and sighed. It was time to get going. I kissed Kate on the forehead, stood up and made my way towards the house. Still munching on a croissant, I lamented how I had enough to worry about on my own today. And it started with the tour of the town. A tour on which I would be quizzed by my mother-in-law. No pressure or anything.

As I was trying to decide whether this morning's tour or this afternoon's ballroom dancing session would be the more humiliating experience, Maya came up to me with a huge grin on her face.

"You're enjoying this far too much, my friend." I paused. "And I use the term 'friend' very loosely. Real friends wouldn't be this excited to witness the certain shame of their loved ones."

She scoffed. "Get a grip, Syd. There will be no shame today."

I regarded her with disdain. "Really? You're banking on my ability to a) UNDERSTAND my mother-in-law's questions realizing there is both slang and southern twang at work, b) know the ANSWERS to her questions and c) relay the answers using BOTH the correct vocabulary words AND corresponding articles as well as mastering a passable regional accent?"

Maya pursed her lips. "Admittedly, this morning's activity will be a bit challenging." While she tried to figure out how to put a positive spin on the situation, another one of my cheerleaders joined the conversation.

Zoe laughed. "Like this afternoon is going to be any better."

I closed my eyes and tried to...what? Center myself? Harness my chi? Find God? I honestly have no idea. I only wanted a moment in which I didn't have to look at the smug faces of those who supposedly loved me.

I opened my eyes again and gave them each my best attempt at a withering stare. "I hate you both." I then turned on my heel and left as they exploded into giggles. A tad dramatic, indeed, but I had been looking forward to a little encouragement, perhaps even a little sympathy with the arrival of my family. Instead, these two appeared to be enjoying a front row seat to my endless discomfort.

I silently hoped my mom and Kate would refrain from mocking me. I was so close to the end of this three ring circus, I could taste it. Only three more days of being on display. You can do this, Sydney! Three more days!

Mercifully, I was able to stumble through the morning tour of *Le Caylar* without embarrassing myself. Well, I think I did. I wasn't able to understand everything Simone said, but no one burst out laughing at any point so I considered it a win. I received a number of bewildered looks following some of my answers, but no one laughed!

Once the dust settled from the morning tour, it dawned on me that I hadn't seen a member of the ex-pack since yesterday afternoon. Had they gotten bored with me? Or were they simply not ready for another dose of humiliation since the rest of the American posse had now joined the party? I may never know. And I'm happy to say I couldn't care less. I had more important things to focus on – like the lunch break I was going to have before this afternoon's obstacle of ballroom dancing.

Following the graciously short choir concert, we were served a lovely "picnic" on the front lawn of the church. Simone had really outdone herself this time. She had set up dozens of tables which were beautifully decorated with linen tablecloths, fresh flowers and delicate china and crystal. She had also included all my favorite foods. There was a plethora of fresh bread and pastries, eggplant spread, a variety of salamis, olive tapenade, an assortment of mild cheeses and pate and a gigantic amount of CHOCOLATE.

I thanked her profusely and wondered if deep down, she really did like me. Mind you, she had never done anything overtly rude to me, I just got the feeling she would have been happier if her son had married a French woman and lived down the street. While it was a bit naïve on her part to believe Louis would have been happy to stay in such a small town, it was certainly a reasonable expectation that her daughter-in-law would speak French. I suddenly felt very guilty for not putting more effort into my studies. The very least I could do after stealing her son was to be able to communicate with her in her own language. French lessons would be put back at the top of my list as soon as we returned to the US. Perhaps as soon as our Monterey wedding is over would be a better idea...

I wish I could say the afternoon went even remotely well. I knew going in, I wouldn't be successful at ballroom dancing, given my decidedly klutzy nature as well as my less than stellar performance at last week's ballroom dancing activity. I believe Simone thought I was still jetlagged last week. Louis is far too much of a gentleman to tell his mother that his wife is…um…athletically challenged. My complete lack of rhythm coupled with eating far too much delicious food at the picnic didn't set me up for success. I had a sinking feeling, despite my best efforts, Simone was going to be sorely disappointed.

Once we finished lunch, all I could think about were the men in my family handling guns. Old school, hard core firearms. Some of Louis' uncles have even experimented with creating their own ammunition. I speculated on the odds they would bring said ammunition with them for this special event or if they would decide to be more conservative and go with the store bought kind. I sincerely hoped for option two as ammunition manufactured by professionals probably had a better chance of functioning properly.

Complicating matters further was with all Louis' male relatives currently hunting on the Durand property, the men available to dance with seemed like complete strangers to me. The sad part was I had no doubt met a good portion of them during the last week, but my mind was on overload trying to remember the people I was related to as *Madame* Durand. I had no option but to boldly soldier on and fervently hope I didn't fall on my ass. Or my face. Or anything else important.

I wasn't helping the odds in any way by stalking my mother-in-law. I was convinced if anyone were in mortal danger, she would receive a call on her cell phone. I therefore guided each one of my partners in her direction for the duration of the afternoon. I understood it was most unladylike to LEAD, but I was out of my mind with worry. Besides, despite all my hard work this week to convince them otherwise, the majority of the townsfolk still thought I was odd. Why not use it to my advantage?

So I spent the next few hours watching Simone like a hawk, whilst, quite frankly, annoying the crap out of my dance partners. I led them all over the dance floor in hot pursuit of my target and spent almost the entirety of each dance staring in her direction instead of smiling and attempting to make small talk. Probably not one of my best decisions, but honestly, when was I going to see any of these men again? I mean, other than the events of the next two days? I KNOW, I'm a real prize.

Simone took a total of eight calls over the course of three hours, but they all seemed to be gossipy in nature. I wondered who in the world she could be talking to considering that all her friends were in attendance of this event. I suppose it's possible she has friends who were not able to travel from a distance to be here. *Or* there was the distinct possibility she was gossiping with either her husband or her brother, who were on the hunt with my family members. Hmmm. Well, I'm sure she wouldn't be laughing if anyone were truly in danger...

By the time we made it to dinner, I was dead on my feet. When we were reunited, I hugged my father, Charlie and Nick tightly and nearly wept with relief. (I wasn't worried about my husband in the least. He had been around guns all his life.) My father just laughed, patted my cheek and told me I worry too much. He could be as smug as he wanted. It didn't bother me in the least. They'd all come back unharmed and I could breathe properly for the first time in a few hours.

After a couple glasses of wine, I felt much better. Our happy family shared a wonderful meal, courtesy of Aunt Jacqueline, who is an amazing chef. Everyone was in high spirits and I felt the tension ease from my body. Tomorrow we would be going to Uncle Luc's vineyard. No guns involved. No weapons of any kind. The odds of anyone suffering bodily harm were extremely remote.

At the end of the meal, the traditional setup fell into place. The men went outside to digest and shoot the breeze and the women headed to the kitchen to clean up. Admittedly, it was rather sexist, but when in Rome! Maya, of course, bucked tradition and joined the men outside for relaxation time. Always a welcome addition to any party, she was able to make her rebellious behavior delightful to her audience.

While the men enjoyed a bit of leisure time following the arduous task of eating, my mom, Zoe, Kate and I joined the assembly line of dish washing in the kitchen. Everyone was happily chatting away, when all the sudden there were gunshots outside. Well, I thought there were, but no one else in the kitchen seemed to be disturbed.

Was I so tired from my afternoon of intense worrying that I was having auditory hallucinations? It was entirely possible. I have a very active imagination. I glanced at Kate to find her furrowing her brow. Shit. There was no way she was sharing in my hallucination. I ran to the window to find out what was going on, taking care not to drop the plate I was in the process of drying.

Apparently, the afternoon of shooting wasn't enough for our testosterone fueled party. Some genius had brought out a few guns and had GIVEN ONE TO MY FATHER. As if he had not tempted fate enough today. I felt all the color drain from my face as I met my mother's eyes. She attempted to appear perfectly calm, but I could see she was panicking as much as I was. She tactfully excused herself to "go to the bathroom" and made a quick detour outside.

Zoe had quickly assessed something frightening was going on and joined Kate and I at the window. The three of us stood there barely breathing, absently drying our plates as we watched my mother approach Charlie. They had an animated conversation which ended with Charlie shrugging his shoulders and rolling his eyes. That couldn't be good.

A few minutes later, my mother returned to the kitchen with a fake smile plastered on her face. Kate, Zoe and I deposited our dried plates in the pile and made our way over to her. We stood in front of her expectantly, hoping she had something positive to tell us.

She shook her head. "Sorry, girls. Teddy won't give up the gun."

The four of us stood there for a moment, staring at each other in disbelief.

Kate cleared her throat. "Did Charlie say how things went this afternoon?" Clearly she was hoping we had all been delusional and my dad had retained the knowledge (and the necessary physical abilities) for handling firearms safely.

My mom sighed. "Charlie said it was touch and go during the afternoon hunt. Dad really gave him a good scare…well, a *few* good scares." She wrung her hands. "Girls, I'm not sure how well he can handle weapons anymore…"

As the gunfire continued, all four of us turned back towards the window to make sure my dad hadn't blown a hole in anything (or anyone). Unexpectedly, Monique emerged into the fray carrying a foreign object. She carefully approached my father and began speaking to him, holding up the item for his inspection. (Was that a bowl of chocolate mousse?) My father grinned and promptly turned his gun over to Charlie.

We breathed a collective sigh of relief following my dad's relinquishing of the weapon. Thank God! He had not shot himself or anyone else. (Now we only had to worry he would accidentally put himself in the path of someone else's line of fire, but those odds were infinitely lower.) We turned our attention back to the window and watched Monique steer my father towards a small table located safely outside the shooting range, which was laden with coffee and desserts. I grinned uncontrollably. She's a genius! The only thing that could draw my father's attention away from such a manly activity was his need to fill his stomach with delicious treats.

Upon Monique's return to the kitchen, the four of us thanked her profusely. I was so happy with her plan to save my father from himself, I hugged her! (A *faux pas* indeed, but it was totally worth it!) She had found a solution none of us had considered. It was so simple, yet it hadn't occurred to any of us. We had every intention of keeping this brilliant strategy in our arsenal. Pun horrifically intended.

Chapter Twenty-Five

With the arrival of Saturday, I was both comforted and petrified. On one hand, I felt a great sense of ease that all weapon related activities were over. On the other hand, I had only one more day before my greatest performance of the entire trip. You may remember, my mother-in-law asked me to recite a fairly complicated French poem, from MEMORY, as part of our wedding ceremony. I had been working on this for the entire trip since Louis chose to spring this particular task on me after we had already boarded the plane for France. My husband is an incredibly sneaky man.

As you know, I've had LOADS of spare time in which to study my lines. It's not like I've had anything else I needed to do, like meet each and every one of my new French relatives, learn their names, their children's names, what they all do for a living and attempt to carry on a somewhat intelligent conversation with them. And it's not like I had a list of activities I was expected to perform for my new mother-in-law as well as her brother and sisters and brothers-in-law. OK, Syd, calm down. I'm aware sarcasm isn't an attractive trait in a lady, but after all the bullshit I've been put through, I needed to have a little tantrum. You can grant me that, right?

Now, let's go back to this ridiculous poem. It's two pages long and is chock-full of pronunciation pitfalls. I was doing my absolute best to memorize the words and remember how to pronounce them properly, but the harder I tried, the more hopeless it felt. One wrong twist of the tongue and you can completely change the meaning of a word. I suppose it doesn't really matter anyway, since even if I manage to remember this monstrous poem, my accent is so bad, people probably won't be able to understand me anyway.

The funniest part of this whole exercise is I have no idea *what* I have been asked to say. Louis has been so busy with his groom activities, he never had time to translate it for me. Though I have a somewhat passable French vocabulary, the majority of the words make no sense to me. This request from Simone could be the single most embarrassing thing she has asked me to do thus far. Instead of focusing on the astronomical level of humiliation this would likely result in, I kept reminding myself this was the LAST task in my long series of labors for my new French family. Unfortunately for me, it was also the most public and the most likely to be filmed. (You *know* one of Louis' cousins will post it on YouTube. At least it would get a lot of hits…)

On the bright side, today's activities should be fun. Uncle Luc has graciously offered a tour of his vineyard complete with a wine tasting session and lunch. Color me excited! There were dozens of wines just waiting to be savored and Luc has told me I may take home as many bottles as I like. Sweet!

I know what you're thinking. I, too, have been concerned about my capacity for alcohol since that unfortunate incident on our flight to New York last year. You know, the time I brought Louis home to meet my parents for the first time? I was so nervous I drank way too much on the plane and kind of, well, passed out on the plane and woke up in the airport infirmary? Come on, you remember! We laughed about it, right? Yeah…I wish I could forget it myself.

In light of memories such as those, I've promised myself not to drink too much today. Tomorrow's wedding is fraught with potential disasters as it is; I can't add a wicked hangover to the mix. Even at my best, I always have the great potential for embarrassment. I'm just talented that way, I guess. Ahem. You have your marching orders, Sydney. Do *not* drink more than two glasses of wine (In total, of course. Those little tasting amounts don't count as full glasses.) Absolutely no more than two glasses…

Fast forward to three hours later. Everyone in my family has imbibed too much except for myself and Kate. I've only had one glass of wine, thank you very much. I think my mom is in the worst shape, but the rest of them aren't too far behind. Louis and his father have spent much of their time watching my parents in their drunken states, laughing themselves silly while my mom fights a massive case of the giggles and my dad slurs his way through his favorite "a rabbi walks into a bar" joke. I have no idea to whom he was telling this joke, since the only people in the vicinity were Louis' aunts and had they understood what he was saying they would have turned bright pink.

I smiled, watching my family enjoying themselves (and being the outrageous Americans in my stead) and decided to take a moment to walk around the vineyard in search of a little quiet. Two minutes into my walk, I noticed a beautiful flower I thought Maya would enjoy painting. (She is a woman of many talents.) Since I had left my camera on the terrace, I took out my phone to capture the image.

Wait a minute. I have cell service here? I haven't had service for the duration of our trip. There's one cell tower in *Le Caylar* and it's at the opposite end of the town. Not that it really mattered, since we had been running from one event to another and now nearly everyone I communicated with on a regular basis was here.

I scrolled through my missed calls list and found eight from the same number. Not good. I didn't recognize the number, but there were three messages left from the person who had it, the last of which was yesterday. I accessed my voicemail and listened to the first message. I felt my heart stop. This can't be happening. Oh my God. I can't breathe. I can't breathe. I can't breathe!!! OK, get a grip, Sydney! You have to do something quick.

I sprinted back to the main house where lunch was in full swing. A quick assessment of the scene told me my mom was completely useless due to her inebriated state and Kate and Zoe were busy "handling" her. Nick was taking care of Sam and this kind of thing was not Charlie's forte. WHERE was Maya? This was a fucking emergency!

I eventually located Maya, relaxing with a glass of wine while admiring the beautiful view of Luc's vineyard. I raced over to her, grabbed the glass out of her hand and slammed it down on the table.

She stared at me angrily. "What the hell is wrong with you?"

I was shaking from head to toe. "I need…I need…"

Her face instantly morphed into sincere concern. "Syd, calm down. Just breathe."

Tears immediately filled my eyes, while I tried to follow Maya's advice. It took another five minutes of coaching from Maya, but I was finally able to form a coherent sentence.

"I'm sorry, Maya. I randomly found I had cell service while I was walking around the vineyard and there were a bunch of messages…" Shit! Keep it together, Syd.

Maya rubbed my back. "OK, what did the messages say?"

I bit my lip. "Um…well, it seems our photographer, Gretchen, has broken her leg. She won't be able to make our wedding."

Maya nodded. "Not ideal, but we can fix it. Did she leave you contact information for anyone who can cover for her?"

I exhaled slowly. "She left me a few numbers, but she hadn't been able to confirm whether or not any of them were available. And who knows how much they charge?" Jesus Christ! The wedding is four weeks away! Where the fuck am I going to find a wedding photographer we can afford within that time frame? Who doesn't suck? Because let's face it, anyone who can take a decent picture was booked MONTHS ago.

I held my head in my hands and felt the tears rush down my face. I can't believe this is happening. I had come *so* close to completing my French mission and had been looking forward to the reward of my beautiful Monterey wedding. The wedding I had been dreaming about for so long. And now I had no idea what kind of photographs I would have to remember it by. Why was this happening? Why?!?

I felt a hand on my shoulder and suddenly found Simone's face filled with concern. I did my best to explain to her what had happened while Maya pantomimed taking pictures in the background. She must have thought we were a bunch of lunatics. But what else is new?

Once we had given the explanation our best effort, Simone took off in search of Louis who was currently touring the property with his uncle.

I turned to Maya. "We need to get back to the house. Our best bet is to get on the computer and start calling photographers. It will have to involve a lot of begging…"

Maya took my hand. "Syd, I think the best thing to do right now is to sit down and have some lunch. When is the last time you ate?"

I glared at her. "Who can think of food at a time like this?"

She smiled tentatively. "My friend, Sydney, can ALWAYS think about food. Besides. It's six am in

California. No one will be there to answer your calls for another three hours."

I thought it over. She had a good point. I would be able to work much more effectively once I had some food in my stomach. Preferably of the chocolate variety.

I nodded. "OK. Let's eat."

She laughed. "There's my girl."

We arrived back at the luncheon to find none other than Nigel and Grace sitting with Charlie and Zoe. I ran over to Pip and nearly squeezed the life out of him.

He laughed happily. "So happy to see you too, Syd."

Grace giggled. "Not as happy as he has been to see all this lovely food."

I smiled at her and hugged her much more gently. "You have *no* idea how happy I am to see you two."

In the midst of all the pre-wedding activities, I had completely forgotten Nigel and Grace were coming. They'd jumped at the opportunity not only to make a side visit to his family in England, but also to enjoy the experience of a French wedding. Before their own, that is. I surmised much of Nigel's reasoning had something to do with Simone's reputation for copious amounts of rich food.

Nigel tucked in to a large plate of meats and cheeses. "So, Sydney, you gorgeous girl, how has your trip been thus far?"

Zoe and Maya exchanged glances and tried not to laugh.

I smiled weakly at Nigel. "Well, Pip, it's been... eventful."

Maya smirked. "You can say that again."

Grace regarded me sympathetically. "Are you alright?"

I sighed. "I was." I shook my head. "I just found out the photographer fell through for our Monterey wedding."

Zoe and Charlie gasped.

I focused my gaze on them. "No kidding."

Charlie coughed. "What happened to her?"

I rubbed my temples. "She fell through her roof and broke her leg."

Nigel nearly choked. "What was she doing on her roof? And how did she fall through it?"

Grace whacked him in the back of the head. "Of course we're concerned for another human being's safety, but THAT is your question at a time like this?"

Zoe bit her lip. It was clear she was desperately trying not to laugh. But when you think about it, the whole situation was kind of comical.

I closed my eyes and began to shake with laughter. Pretty soon all six of us had tears of mirth running down our faces.

"*Mon coeur*? Are you OK?" Louis' face registered a great deal of concern, not to mention confusion, with the situation in front of him. "My mother told me you were very upset by a phone call you received. Something about the wedding?"

I wiped the tears from my eyes. "I'm sorry, Bluey. I found cell reception in the vineyard and discovered we lost our wedding photographer."

Maya giggled. "You mean she fell through."

I bit my lip. "Yes, that's true. She fell through."

The entire group dissolved into laughter with the exception of my poor husband. In desperation, he turned to my brother for some sort of explanation.

"Ah, Charlie, would you please translate?"

Charlie collected himself. "Your photographer fell through her roof and broke her leg. She won't be able to cover your wedding."

Louis nodded grimly. "Did she refer us to anyone else?"

Zoe piped up. "That would be a BIG no."

As the pieces fell into place, Louis began to understand the root of my hysteria. He glanced at his watch and came to the same conclusion Maya and I had thirty minutes earlier.

"OK, *mon coeur*, I will take you back to the house in an hour and we will get to work."

I jumped up and threw my arms around him. "Thank you, Bluey." I loved this man so much. He was going to help me fix this colossal disaster. And then everything would be OK.

Nigel's voice cut through our tender moment. "You know, Syd, I have a friend who is a photographer."

Six pairs of eyes focused on him with interest.

Grace snapped her fingers. "Edward!"

Nigel grinned at her. "Precisely." He came over to me. "Ed just started his own business and is eagerly looking for work."

I caught my breath. Could that be a glimmer of hope?

Grace joined her husband next to me. "Syd, I have seen Ed's work. It is really beautiful. He would be brilliant for your wedding!"

I smiled ever so slightly. "But the question remains, is he available the day in question?"

Nigel took out his phone. "Hmm…no service. Syd, will you please show me the area where you discovered your bad news? Maybe we can change your luck."

I grabbed Nigel's arm and speed walked him to the necessary spot. Since it was nearly seven in the morning in California, on a Saturday no less, he sent both a text and an email to Ed attaching a photo of my pleading face for good measure.

Nigel put his arm around me as we headed back to the party. "Don't worry, Syd, this is all going to work out."

"I really hope so. Thank you so much for your help, Pip. I don't know what I would have done without you."

We arrived back at the luncheon to find an exasperated looking Kate. Nick handed her a glass of wine along with plenty of assurance that one glass was completely fine given she had just nursed Sam. It really looked like she needed it. What in the world had my mother done to her?

I put my hand on her shoulder. "What happened, Kate?"

Her nostrils flared. "I was trying to keep our mother from making an ass out of herself."

Uh oh. "Does this mean you weren't successful?"

She rolled her eyes. "Not in the least. She danced barefoot all around the vineyard, singing her favorite Eurythmics song."

I stifled a giggle. Mom really did love *Sweet Dreams*. She said it was a perfect example of what harmony should sound like. It seemed a little ironic her rendition of it caused such discord with her daughter.

Kate clenched her hands into fists. "Then she tried to get all Louis' aunts and cousins to start a conga line. They must've thought she was crazy!"

I bit down hard on my lip as I pictured that scenario. I was so close to laughing, I was in physical pain. Apparently this was patently obvious to my poor sister.

She narrowed her eyes at me. "It's not funny, Syd."

I nodded and tried to appear serious. A rogue giggle came out and I quickly rearranged my features into what I hoped was an expression of empathy.

Kate glared at me. "NOT funny!" I guess I hadn't been successful.

I watched my sister as she took a long gulp of wine. "Please forgive me. We no longer have a photographer for our wedding. I may be a *little* punchy."

Kate put down her wine glass with far too much force, inadvertently splashing wine on the tablecloth. "What???"

I absently massaged my neck. "She broke her leg."

Kate's mouth fell open. "That's it? Did she find you someone else? Your wedding is *four* weeks away!!!"

Tell me something I don't know, Kate. "She has to stay off her feet for another month. And no, she didn't find us a replacement."

Worry washed over her features. "I'm sorry, Syd. That's really awful."

A voice addressed us from behind. "Do not despair, ladies."

Kate turned around and beamed. "Pip! When did you get here?"

Nigel gave Kate a hug. "A little over an hour ago." He patted his belly. "I've been enjoying the wonders of French cooking."

I studied him hopefully. "Did you hear from Ed?" Was this guy that much of an early riser? I mean, it was seven-thirty in the morning for him.

He nodded triumphantly. "He will be happy to be your photographer."

I threw my arms up in the air and squealed. Kate and I jumped up at the same moment and hugged Nigel.

"You saved the day, Pip!" I beamed. "Thank you so much."

Nigel held up his hands. "But wait, it gets better."

Kate and I looked at each other. Better than saving my ass four weeks before my wedding? I couldn't wait to hear this.

We stared at him expectantly.

"Ed said if you let him use some of your wedding photos on his website and provide a glowing reference for him, he will do the event for free."

I started jumping up and down with excitement. "Are you serious?"

"Indeed, I am. He loved the photo I sent of you and said you will make a magnificent bride. He believes a photo of you in a wedding gown will help him book *oodles* of weddings."

Kate grabbed Nigel and hugged him. "Pip! You're amazing!"

Hot damn. A disastrous situation has suddenly become an amazing one – in the span of ninety minutes! I marveled at the outcome my friend with the sunniest disposition on earth was able to attain. Maybe happiness really was a super power.

I sighed with relief. "Pip, how will I ever be able to repay you for this?"

"It is all part of the job, fair maiden." He winked at me. "But I did have some rather delicious chocolate this morning. Perhaps you can procure me a stash to bring home?"

I laughed, coming to the conclusion that many useful things could be accomplished by supplying men with their favorite treats. Yesterday, Monique had been able to get my dad to lay down his firearm for a chocolate mousse. This theory had some interesting possibilities. Maybe if I prepared Louis his favorite omelet, he would be able to get me out of the poetry reading tomorrow.

No, eggs weren't enough. Frog legs? Escargot? Tripe? In addition to having no idea where to purchase any of these items, I would most likely hurl during any type of preparation. Hurling would *not* have the desired effect. It was going to take a miracle to get me out of this situation. And I think I just used up my miracle in the form of Ed, wedding photographer extraordinaire. Top Ten YouTube videos, here I come…

Chapter Twenty-Six

We have arrived at the home stretch! It is now T-minus fifteen hours until the wedding. Everyone has survived all necessary pre-wedding events relatively unscathed. (Have I mentioned how relieved I am about the absence of gunshot wounds?) Our journey has at long last led us to Saturday evening and the rehearsal dinner was about to begin.

Unfortunately for me, the arrival of the rehearsal dinner meant it was time for me to do something I had been dreading since the moment I had discovered its existence. For this evening's event, I was obligated to don the atrocious dress my mother-in-law had purchased for me several months ago. You must remember my vivid description. I mean, I can't imagine how anyone could possibly forget such a noteworthy ensemble. It's the kind of image that will be etched in your mind. Forever. With no way to remove it.

Deep breath, Sydney. I need a moment to collect myself. OK, in case you've somehow forgotten, Simone had purchased a gold sequined halter mini dress, with red satin roses on the straps and red satin ruffles along the bottom of the skirt. Of course, she also had to purchase four inch red satin stilettos with matching red satin roses on the toes.

I just…I can't think about my horrific ensemble right now, so let us deviate to another topic: our final hurdle, the grandest wedding *Le Caylar* had seen in some time. Was everything ready for the French wedding of the year? Undoubtedly. There was no question in my mind, Simone had enough "emergency" provisions for another two hundred people. Because you never knew when a large tourist group might get lost and wander into your private event. And really, what else would there be to do, as a person who inhabits a small town, but to invite them to stay and partake in the festivities?

Was I mentally ready for the last act to our French drama? I honestly couldn't tell you. I had done the best I could to memorize the poem Simone had her heart set on. I had spent hours wondering what her motive had been in asking me to do such a thing. She had to have known this would cause me an undue amount of stress. Had she purposely asked me to do this to make my life harder? Was she punishing me for taking her son away from her? Did it really matter what her motivation was at this point? I simply had to make it through the next twenty-four hours and I would be able to relax. Or some approximation of it. Maybe. The point is I wouldn't have to jump through any more hoops. I would finally be free!

A most welcome distraction for that evening came in the form of Devon. His arrival caused quite a stir amongst the ladies. It didn't seem to matter what age; every one of them was completely taken with him. He is, after all, one of the most gorgeous men anyone has ever set eyes on AND he is fluent in French. He may not have had the inside track on the regional accent or the appropriate slang, but it didn't make a bit of difference. He had to beat those women off with a stick.

If there were a stick to be had, Maya would have done the beating herself. As the festivities began, I watched with great delight as she became progressively more annoyed. I imagined this was the first time in their relationship when his attention had been so severely monopolized elsewhere. Unfortunately for Maya, one of Devon's trademark attributes was his impeccable manners. There was no way he would insult his hostess, or any member of her family, by not giving them his full attention. For once in her life, Maya had to get her own drinks. Does it make me a bad person that I found this to be completely hysterical?

I was filling my dad in on Maya's impending temper tantrum, when I was momentarily distracted by a bizarre turn of events. I glanced over at Louis' father to find him distraught. This was rather alarming, since Michel was *always* in a good mood. What had happened? Oh my God, was he upset about the wedding tomorrow? Did he want to talk Louis out of marrying me?

Wait a minute. We're already married, so that couldn't be it. Wow. I think I'm actually losing it this time. How could I have forgotten I'm already MARRIED to Louis? I've been married to him for over seven months. It's *possible* the extreme amount of stress I've been under for the past week and a half has taken its toll on my already fragile mental state. I had better find Louis and tell him it's time he committed me to a nice, cozy insane asylum.

All jokes aside, I was really worried about Michel. My dad and I had been watching him for ten minutes now, but his expression didn't improve. He had always been kind to me (to the point of telling me not to worry about HIS crazy wife); I *had* to do something to help him. I excused myself from my dad's company and immediately sought out Louis to discover the cause of Michel's unease.

After ten minutes of fruitless searching, I eventually located my wayward husband inside the house, ostensibly fixing his mother's computer.

"Bluey! There you are. I've been all over the place looking for you. Why are you in the house?"

He sighed. "My mother has insisted I fix whatever she has done to her ancient computer right away."

I raised my eyebrows. "Really? At the start of the rehearsal dinner? For your own wedding?"

He rolled his eyes. "Yes and yes. For some reason, she neglected to tell me about this issue for over a week! She has now decided it must be fixed as soon as possible because there is a video on the hard drive which she *has* to have for the wedding reception." He looked like he wanted to strangle her.

I laughed. "Are you sure you want to help with this task? I mean, has she told you what the content of the video is?"

He froze. "It couldn't be..."

I walked over to him and put my hands on his shoulders. "What does she have on you?"

He shook his head. "Years ago she made this montage of all my Thai boxing fights. It is too much." He frowned. "I bet this is what she wants." He turned off the computer and took my hand.

I rubbed his back. "Is it really *that* bad?"

One look from him told me it was indeed that bad.

As we walked out the front door, I poked him in the side. "I thought you were proud of your career as a Thai boxer."

"I am. It was an amazing time in my life, but it is over now and I do not feel the need to parade my victory videos in front of every person I know."

I squeezed his hand. "She's *really* proud of you."

He stopped and turned to me. "Yes, she is very proud, but I sometimes feel her focus is more on showing off."

I grinned at him. "Who wouldn't? I show you off at every opportunity!"

He kissed me tenderly. "I love you, *mon coeur*."

I put my arms around him and kissed him deeply. It had been quite some time since Louis and I had had some proper alone time. Since we arrived in France, Simone had every minute so tightly-booked that we barely had time to breathe. I was really looking forward to our night in Paris, when it would just be the two of us in our beautiful hotel room in the George V...

Suddenly, I remembered why I had come looking for Louis in the first place. It took every ounce of my strength, but I pulled out of our incredibly sensual kiss. Louis began to protest, but I smacked him playfully on the chest.

"I'm sorry, Bluey, but I need to talk to you about something important."

He started caressing my hips. "Really? Would you like to discuss this somewhere a little more private? You look so *sexy* in that dress." He tried to push me back towards the house.

I laughed. "Louis Durand! Get a hold of yourself!" I wasn't even going to address his absurd comment about how I looked in this ridiculous dress. Sexy was not even a remote possibility. Even the most gorgeous supermodel would look awful in this dress. The things I had to go through for this man!

He grinned. "I am not sure this is the best setting for me to 'get a hold of myself', *mon coeur*." He took my hand. "Perhaps you might help me..."

Clearly my husband had needs to be met, but now was not the time. I had to snap him back to reality.

I took my hand back and pointed a finger forcefully at his chest. "I need your help with something."

He opened his mouth to say something – no doubt some type of double entendre – but I immediately put my hand up. He could see I meant business.

I gazed at him with my sad brown eyes. "Bluey, something is wrong with your dad. I'm really worried. Do you know what happened?"

Louis sighed. "He is upset about Poupette."

I had no idea how to respond to that. Who or what was Poupette?

Louis sensed my confusion and clarified. "The little black poodle. She is my dad's favorite."

I nodded in recognition. I hadn't been successful in remembering the names of all SEVEN of Simone and Michel's dogs. I'm shocked I didn't remember the name Poupette since there are a ton of jokes which can be made from this name if you happened to be an uncouth American. (And of course, I'm NOT. But I do know a few…) My heart went out to Michel; Poupette was his constant companion.

I cleared my throat. "What happened to her?"

Louis shrugged. "No one knows. She has been missing since this morning."

I knitted my brows. Michel had seemed fine earlier in the day. Perhaps reality had set in and he realized she wasn't coming back on her own?

I wondered how much had been done to find her so far. "Where was the last place she was seen?"

"Out by the chicken coop. My dad had gone down to check out a broken hinge. He didn't realize she was not with him until he sat down at the breakfast table. He spent the morning looking for her, but had no luck." He sighed. "He has been in a funk since lunch."

"I'll bet he has." Michel must be beside himself by now. No wonder he looks so distraught.

Louis smiled at me. "Syd, what are you concocting in that brain of yours?"

I chewed on my lip. "I have a plan. Do you have any flashlights?"

Thirty minutes later, I had a team of three and a bunch of supplies. I had managed to rope in Charlie and Nigel, while Louis insisted Monique come with us as our guide. Louis' job was to distract his mother so she didn't realize her daughter-in-law was missing. Thankfully, the toasts wouldn't take place until the end of the meal, so we had around ninety minutes to work with.

As we were about to set off on our search, I recognized we were missing one crucial member. It took me all of two minutes to locate her sulking by the makeshift bar on the terrace.

I tapped Maya on the shoulder. "I need you, my friend."

She scoffed. "At least someone does." She stared bitterly in Devon's direction. He was surrounded by no less than ten panting women. Obviously, Maya was going to have to pry him away from his throngs of admirers at the end of the night. She seemed like she very much wanted to kill someone - quite possibly me since I was standing right in front of her. I decided we needed to get going on our quest *tout de suite*.

"What do you need, Syd?" She swayed a little in her five inch heels. Evidently, she had been drowning her sorrows in a few cocktails.

I used my hands to steady her. "Maybe you should sit down."

Maya smacked my hands away and smoothed her dress. "I'm fine. Now, how can I help?"

I surveyed her doubtfully. It seemed like she was in more of a position to need help rather than to give it. But Maya was one of the most stubborn people I knew, so I had better just fill her in.

"Well, Maya, Poupette has gone missing…"

She immediately interrupted me. "You want me to help you look for a piece of poop? Are you fucking crazy?"

About twenty people peered towards us in an attempt to locate the source of the commotion.

I grabbed Maya by the shoulder, turned her around and walked her to the side of the house where the rest of the search party was waiting.

"Jesus Christ, Maya! There's no need to make a scene!" I gathered my hair in my hands. "We're looking for Michel's favorite dog, POUPETTE."

Maya was about to protest when her brain processed the content of my last statement.

Charlie joined in. "You know, Maya, the little black dog with all the spunk?"

Nigel chuckled and appraised Maya. "She reminds me a bit of you!" In response to Maya's withering stare, Nigel began to backpedal. "Well, you know, Poupette is petite and dark and very…um…spunky like Charlie said, which is really rather a good thing…"

Maya thought it over for a moment. "OK, I'll help you." Then she turned to Nigel. "But, Pip, if you ever compare me to a dog again, there will be serious consequences."

Nigel gulped. "Will never happen again. I promise."

Maya took Monique's arm. It appeared the two of them would be leading us on our expedition. I checked my watch. We had seventy-five minutes until toast time. I crossed my fingers and hoped we would make it. I couldn't stand to see Michel looking so heartbroken. We had to find that dog!

Thirty minutes later, we were no closer to our endgame. We were all a little worse for the wear though; some of us a bit worse than others. As careful as I was, I managed to break one of my godforsaken heels in a soft patch of dirt. It would seem Monique possesses the same MacGyver genes as Louis, and she had me fixed up in about two minutes with a stick of gum. Perhaps French gum contains a tiny amount of actual adhesive? I swear, my heel was as good as new! Maya walked face first into a fence, catching the hem of her dress and tearing an absurdly large hole. Charlie bruised his knee by accidentally slamming it into a large boulder. (Our flashlights, like us, weren't very bright.) But the worst off was Nigel who fell face first into a huge patch of mud. Yuck.

Despite our extensive search, there were no clues as to Poupette's current location. There weren't even signs of any kind of disturbance. What could have happened to her? She would never have left Michel's side voluntarily. He gave her all the food she wanted as well as an unlimited supply of affection. There was definitely something despicable at work here.

Did someone have a vendetta against Michel? It seemed like an absurd thought, given his extremely good natured demeanor. What could he have done to upset anyone? This mystery could take days to unravel. We had exactly forty-five minutes.

I looked at Monique helplessly. She cocked her head to the side and took off running. She must have had some kind of breakthrough! Maybe we would be able to save the day after all!

A quick jog took us to the barn. As a quick aside, let me recommend NEVER running in four inch stilettos. Even if your life is in danger. It's incredibly painful and the potential for injury is astronomical. Should you be running for your life, you may very well have better odds disabling your attacker with your razor-sharp heels.

Monique darted inside with the rest of us in hot pursuit. Once we arrived inside the barn, I yanked my skirt down in a most unladylike display. After our sprint, it had ridden up to about two inches below my ass and I had no desire to let it go any further. It was bad enough the halter top of the dress had come loose earlier in the evening and I almost flashed the entire Durand family.

Thank God I didn't give them fodder for a "Girls Gone Wild" joke. I don't think I could have lived through that kind of embarrassment. Wearing this dress in public was about as much as I could handle. Given the dozens of photos Maya had already taken (including the close call of breast exposure), this dress would serve to embarrass me for years to come. Even after I burned it.

Maya studied me quizzically. "Did you need to adjust your lady parts?"

I rolled my eyes at her. "No, sweetie. I didn't want to EXPOSE my lady parts."

Nigel laughed nervously as he turned bright red. (I could still see his blush under the layer of mud he was unable to wipe from his face.) I sometimes forgot what a proper Englishman he was. How did he fall in with such a group of vulgarians?

Charlie put his hand on my shoulder. "I hate to interrupt you two…um, ladies, but I think Monique found something."

The four of us turned our attention to where Monique was standing. She knelt down next to an exceptionally pregnant pig. Admittedly, it's hard to distinguish a pregnant pig from a regular pig given their rather large girth. But over the past week and a half, I've had quite an education on the subject of farm animals: how to birth them, feed them, slaughter them and cook them. Just thinking about it makes me shudder. I will never be the same again.

I shook my head to clear the images. "Does anyone know what's going on?"

Nigel pursed his newly brown lips. "I think Monique said Poupette and the pig had some type of friendship and she thought Poupette had come out to the barn to settle in with the mama pig until the babies came."

That was both the sweetest and the most bizarre thing I had heard in a long time. If it was what Monique had actually said. I held my head in my hands. What do we do now?

Zoe abruptly burst into the barn. "Where have you guys been? Simone is on the warpath! She needs her blushing bride so the toasts can begin!"

Hang on, Simone was AHEAD of schedule? What the hell was going on? Rats!!! We were out of time and we were no closer to finding Poupette. There was nothing more I could do tonight; I would have to start fresh in the morning. As it was, I would need to duck out extremely early to escape Simone and the hours of preparation she thought she was going to subject me to, courtesy of her team of beauticians. I travel with my own team, thank you very much. (Kate and Maya, the unstoppable duo.) Besides, I was truly frightened of what I would end up looking like if I fell into the clutches of this group of woefully out-of-style women. Ducking out early would kill two birds with one stone. Definitely had to do that.

Charlie very kindly offered me his arm to escort me back to the party. My feet were throbbing from my precipitously high heels. I laughed gleefully when I decided to burn the shoes right along with the dress once this preposterous night was over. Although, it might make more sense to conduct such a ritual in the safety of the United States, far from Simone's tenacious clutches...

Chapter Twenty-Seven

The remainder of the rehearsal dinner was relatively uneventful. Thought that's not to say it was free of humiliation. Maya drank herself into a stupor and then screamed at Devon in a jealous rage. I, of course, have it all on video. (The torn dress gives it a certain tragic quality…) Judge all you want, but I needed some kind of bargaining chip for the barrage of photos she took of me in my, uh, rather unique ensemble. They could end up on Facebook, Twitter, Google, maybe even a billboard! I had to do something.

Besides, I didn't escape the evening unscathed. I was fortunate enough to be the subject of not only my father's toast, but also a good portion of Michel's toast. Because Louis translated his father's toast into English and my father's into French, I had the great pleasure of being embarrassed in two languages. As though wearing the dress of a maniacal strumpet weren't enough.

On a much happier note, once the rehearsal dinner had concluded, Louis and I found the opportunity for some alone time. I'm afraid our zeal didn't allow for much sleep, but the amazing sex did wonders for restoring my spirit. Since I had decided to get up at the crack of dawn to continue my search for Michel's canine companion, I knew I was going to be an absolute zombie for our wedding day.

After all the work I had done to get into Simone's good graces, I was fairly close to sending it all down the toilet. Skipping out on her beauty regimen was a given because a) I had already said no thank you three times and she refused to listen and b) I wasn't going to allow photographic evidence of myself with blue eye shadow and a bouffant for all eternity. But operating on so little sleep pretty much guaranteed I would mess up Simone's chosen poem SEVERELY. Even at the top of my game, the end result would have been iffy at best. I did feel a little bad about purposely contributing to her embarrassment, but now is not the time for dwelling. It's time to get back to the search.

Zoe had graciously offered to help me comb the countryside for Poupette at an ungodly hour of the morning. Since everyone in my family knows I have virtually no sense of direction, my guess was Zoe lost last night's round of roshambo. No one in the Bennett family wanted to see Simone freak out due to her missing daughter-in-law (who would probably have ended up in a ditch somewhere on her own), so they opted to send an escort. Louis was the obvious choice, but we needed him to run interference with his mother once she noticed I wasn't available for her petrifying team of beauticians.

Zoe met me in front of the house at five in the morning. I was so exhausted, my eyes were in constant pain. I wasn't exactly sure how I was going to find Poupette if I couldn't see, but luckily for me, Zoe had the eyes of a hawk. After three hours of skirting the Durand property, we had to admit defeat. The wedding was starting in three hours and I had to give Kate and Maya some time to work with; quality hair and makeup takes time, my friend. Not to mention, I needed a good twenty minutes in the shower to clean off all the grime from the morning. (I *may* have fallen into a mud puddle, or two, due to the stellar combination of my tired eyes and natural klutziness.)

As Zoe and I walked up the driveway, we came upon Michel walking in circles in front of the house, absently blowing his nose into his handkerchief. He seemed so bereft, it nearly broke my heart. Was all hope really lost? Where in the world could this dog be? Was she being held for ransom? At this point, I was willing to entertain almost any theory since she was nowhere to be found.

I was so distracted by Michel's appearance, I almost didn't see Kate running at me like a lunatic.

"Syd!" She hissed. "Simone is looking everywhere for you. Get in the car!"

I hesitated. "But…"

She grabbed me and shoved me towards her rental car. "All your stuff is in the trunk. Get in and hide in the back seat. Now!"

I quickly did as she asked. Zoe threw one of Sam's blankets over me for good measure. I held my breath and waited for Kate to get in the car. Then I noticed something moving on the seat next to me. What the fuck? Did some kind of animal sneak into the car? As the panic rose in my throat, I heard a small moan.

Wait a minute. I know that voice. "Maya?" My voice was barely above a whisper.

She coughed. "Is that you, Syd?"

Duh. "Yes, it's me. What are you doing hiding in the back of Kate's car?"

"I could ask you the same question!" She snapped.

Jesus Christ, Maya! Now is not the time for this. "Shhh! Keep your voice down!"

"You started it!"

I could easily picture the gigantic pout on her face right now. I had a sneaking suspicion things had not gone well with Devon last night. She was going to be in a right foul mood this morning. Given my severe lack of sleep and desolation over not finding Poupette, it would be a miracle if I didn't kill her.

A couple of minutes later, Kate got into the car. She spoke so quietly as she turned to put on her seatbelt, I had to strain to hear her. "Shut the hell up, you two!" I peeked around my blanket to see her smiling and waving. Simone must be waiting to resume her search for me until Kate left. I had the good sense to keep quiet until I was told the coast was clear. I had been through far too much to get caught now.

Five minutes later, we arrived at the hotel. Kate wrenched open the door and yanked off my blanket disguise. I gratefully removed myself from the pretzel shape I had twisted into and got out of the car. I turned to help Maya and nearly jumped out of my skin.

You remember my grand aspiration, absurd as it may be, to be perfect? Well, Maya IS perfect. Or, more precisely, she always LOOKS perfect. But the woman who got out of the car after I did was about as far from perfect as you could get. Her hair was a rat's nest, her makeup was smeared literally all over her face, her dress was horribly wrinkled (not to mention the huge gaping hole from last night), her stockings were torn and her shoes…well, they were completely caked in mud.

I turned to Kate. "Where did you find her?"

Kate exhaled loudly. "Uh…passed out on the hood of my car." She paused. "This morning."

My eyes must have bugged out of my head. "What? How? When? But…I…"

Maya put her hand on my shoulder. "Don't worry, Syd, I'm fine."

I stared at her in complete confusion. "You don't look fine. Not anywhere near an approximation of fine." I rubbed my head, which had started to throb. "What happened to you?"

She sighed. "I got pissed at Devon for ignoring me, yelled at him in front of everyone and then tramped off into the woods by myself."

The corners of my mouth twitched. "I remember the yelling. But, how did you end up passed out on the hood of Kate's car?"

She cocked her head to one side. "No idea."

Kate shook her head ruefully. "It might have something to do with the THREE empty bottles of wine I found next to the car."

I shook my head. "But you walked all the way from Louis' parent's house?" Granted it was only two miles, but, Maya had been quite drunk and she was wearing FIVE inch heels. In that state of mind, who knows what could've happened to her? She's lucky she didn't break an ankle walking over uneven terrain, completely wasted, in those damn shoes - exquisitely beautiful as they may be.

Maya was exasperated. "Syd, I have no idea. And it doesn't matter anyway…"

I hugged her gently. "Thank God you're in one piece. Are you alright?"

Her eyes filled with tears. "I don't know."

Kate cleared her throat. "I hate to interrupt you guys, but the wedding is in two and half hours. We *have* to get started right away."

I nodded and took Maya's hand. "It's all going to be OK. I promise."

She shrugged her shoulders and followed me into the hotel.

Once we crossed the threshold, Kate became a drill sergeant. She promptly sent Maya back to her room to shower and told her to come back to our room in no more than forty minutes. She threatened to send my mother, who was miraculously waiting in Kate's room, after her if she were even a minute late.

My mom observed Kate with horror after Maya left. "Was that really necessary? The poor girl is struggling. Besides, I'm sure Devon can help to put her right."

I turned to Kate quickly. "Did you call Devon when you found her?"

Kate shook her head. "Didn't need to. He was the one who called me."

My sleep-addled brain simply couldn't process her statement. "I don't get it."

She laughed. "Syd, he followed her from the party. He knew she was too angry and too drunk to deal with him rationally, but he wanted to make sure she was safe. Once she made it to the hotel, at SIX in the morning, he called me to come and get her."

My mom whistled. "Wow. He really knows how to handle her."

Kate winked at us. "No doubt. He's definitely a keeper."

⌒⌒

Two hours later, I was a beautiful bride. I had managed to scrub all the grime off my body and was only left with a few small scratches, courtesy of some rather unfriendly thorn bushes. Kate had worked her magic and wrestled my hair into her signature French twist. I closed my eyes and thought of the last time she had done this for me. The night I proposed to my dear, sweet Louis. I marveled at how much had happened since that day just over a year ago.

There were moments of pure joy and moments of overwhelming sadness. There were moments when I thought I wanted to kill him and moments when I thought he wanted to kill me. Our first year together wasn't easy by any stretch of the imagination and I had questioned my impulsive decision to marry him repeatedly.

But somehow, we had managed to work through all the bullshit and come through the experience stronger than we were before. We had years of fighting ahead of us, but I wasn't worried. I knew we would always make up afterwards. We were definitively not a marriage which would end in divorce. Thank you very much for your odds, Mr. Mark Darcy.

"Hello! Earth to Syd!" Kate was waving her hand in front of my face.

I blushed. "I'm sorry. I was thinking about the last time you…"

She interrupted me, smiling broadly. "Put your hair in a French twist. I know. But you have to get it together, bride. It's time to go."

All the sudden, I felt sick to my stomach. Was I really going to do this? How did the poem start again? Why did I agree to this? I'm completely insane! Whoa, Sydney. Just breathe. Everything will be fine.

Kate took my hand. "Syd, *relax*."

I nodded. "Right, relax…" Like that was so easy! No one else was going to be up there in front of five freakin' hundred people making a complete ASS out of herself!!!

Kate pulled me to my feet and turned me toward the full length mirror in her room. "Look at her."

Are we playing this game again? Who am I looking at? We're the only two people in this room!

She shook her head at me when I stared back at her in confusion. "Look at YOURSELF in the mirror, Syd."

I followed her instructions obediently. I saw a woman in a beautiful ivory satin gown, with delicate straps, a low sweeping neckline and a long flowing skirt. Her hair was perfect, as was her shimmery, understated makeup. She had glossy crimson lips and wore delicate diamond earrings. She was breathtaking.

I smiled. "OK, Kate, I see what you're getting at. At least I'll look amazing when I embarrass the hell out of myself."

She giggled. "You're going to be fine. Now let's get going before Simone sends a hunting party after us…"

My mother burst into the room carrying a ball of tulle - also known as my niece, Sam. She looked adorable in her puffy, pink dress and the sight of her perfect little face set my soul at ease.

My mom seemed completely harried, but once her eyes settled on her two girls, she broke out into an elated smile. Kate was gorgeous in her crimson strapless satin dress. The dress hugged her in all the right places and the skirt was fairly short. This was another of Simone's choices, but for once, I heartily agreed. My sister looked hot! I couldn't wait to see Zoe and Maya in their matching dresses.

"Girls! You both look beautiful, but we have to go!" My mom grabbed Sam's diaper bag and motioned us out the door.

As we ran out to the parking lot (I had wisely decided not to put my heels on until we arrived back at the house), we passed Maya and Devon in the hall. Maya seemed exhausted, but much more like herself. She was drop dead gorgeous and smiling! I was grateful to Devon for putting her back in a good mood for today's astronomically important event. I smiled at both of them as I headed toward the final countdown...

The wedding ceremony Simone had planned was beautiful. While I mentally prepared myself for the walk down the aisle, I said a silent prayer the ceremony would be everything she wanted it to be. I was about to take my father's arm, when I discovered something was missing. Where was my bouquet? I frantically searched the immediate area, but there were no flowers to be found. I can't walk down the aisle like this! Flowers are one of Simone's favorite things in the entire world!

As I began to shake, Simone surprised me in a most unexpected way. She approached quietly and handed me a bouquet of red roses mixed with purple irises. I caught my breath and looked up at her in shock. Simone had wanted orange gladiola and birds of paradise. I had readily conceded to her on this as I had on most issues, but she seemed to be sending me a message by giving me my favorite flowers at the last minute. I was speechless. Did this mean she accepted me? Did I actually pass the test? Was I finally deemed to be good enough for her son? I searched her face for these answers, but she just smiled, squeezed my hand and hurriedly returned to her place in the procession. I stared after her in amazement.

Once my dad poked me in the ribs a couple times, I came back to reality and stumbled down the aisle with him to the beautiful outdoor dais Michel had built. He had created handsome designs in the wood, which Simone had accented with yards of tulle and purple irises. As we were married for the second time, Louis and I stood under a wooden archway, also of Michel's creation, and were pronounced man and wife by Uncle Remi. (Monique had worked her magic with an online ordination!)

I'm delighted to say I made it through Simone's poem without stuttering OR swearing. As to the exact wording, pronunciation and accent, I couldn't tell you how well I did, but honestly neither could anyone else in the vicinity. As I carefully made my way through the poem, Simone began to cry. The further I progressed in the poem, the louder she wailed and with such emotion, I worried for her state of mind. I'm still not certain if she displayed this level of emotion to cover the sound of my horrible accent and/or mispronunciation or if she were really *that* moved by my performance.

The silver lining of the whole ordeal is should anyone post a video of the ceremony on YouTube, you would simply see my mouth moving (and I did look pretty damn good) and would hear nothing but Simone wailing in the background. From my point of view, this wasn't the worst thing in the world. For once, I wasn't the one who was the center of embarrassment. Imagine that?

Even better than this silver lining was Louis' radiant happiness following the ceremony. He looked so dapper in his beautifully cut gray suit (with a pink tie at the absolute insistence of his mother), I felt like a giddy young bride as he helped me into the wagon. It turned out to be rather fun riding around the town in the back of this old-fashioned vehicle. Someone had placed soft blankets over the hay bales and Louis kept a firm hold on me the entire time, so I wouldn't go bouncing out the back. And the smile on his face as he waved to his friends and family members (and gestured to his hot wife) was priceless. I haven't felt this happy in a very, very long time.

Oh, and I haven't even mentioned the best part! I found Poupette! Once we finished our tour of the town and the wagon turned onto the Durand property, I saw a flash of black disappear behind a cluster of rocks. Despite Louis' protests, I insisted on getting out to investigate. I took off my four inch cream satin heels (Simone insists four inches to be the minimum heel height for a respectable French woman), hiked up my skirt and took off after the tuft of black fur in the distance. Louis, in turn, took off after me.

It took us a good twenty minutes, but we managed to capture Poupette. Once she determined who we were, she covered us in doggy kisses and happily jumped in the back of the wagon. Uncle Luc laughed heartily as he drove us back to the house. Louis and I were a little, ahem, worse for the wear following our wild dog chase.

Upon our return, we found a large crowd waiting in front of the Durand home, all eager to start the wedding reception. There was a collective gasp once Louis helped me out of the wagon. I quickly surveyed our appearances, hoping we weren't the source of the shock. A cursory glance gave me the answer to that burning question. *No such luck.*

Louis' hair was tousled, his suit was wrinkled, he was covered in a coating of dust and his shoes were caked in mud. My hair had stayed perfectly in place (Kate is a rock stat!), but the bodice of my dress was covered in muddy paw prints, the hem of my skirt was coated in mud and my stockings were ruined.

Before anyone had the chance to make a comment, Michel burst into laughter. Poupette had leapt into his arms and was smothering him with kisses. The entire wedding party was so moved by this reunion, Louis and I had a moment to breathe.

Louis put his arm around me. "You are crazy, *mon coeur*."

I smiled up at him. "For taking off after a dog and ruining my dress? Or for ensuring your mother will hate me for the rest of my life?"

He laughed. "She will no doubt be pretty pissed. But it does not matter, Syd. What you did for my dad was…just…so YOU."

I kissed his nose. "Is that a good thing?"

As he was about to answer, my father approached us. "Good-O, Duck! I love what you've done with your dress."

I blushed. "Flattery will get you nowhere, Dad."

He kissed my forehead. "You're a firecracker, Syd. The Durand family is lucky to have you. Right, Louis?"

Louis shook my dad's hand. "We are indeed, Mr. Bennett."

My dad grinned at us. "You two have made it through quite a lot in the last year. I'm impressed you stuck it out. And as you know, Duck, I'm not impressed easily."

Louis and I grinned at each other. We had absolutely been through a lot and had lived to tell about it. I had no doubt we were about to add to our already impressive repertoire of tales with our impending French wedding reception.

I gently wiped the tears from my eyes. "Thanks, Dad."

Louis cleared his throat. "Thank you, Mr. Bennett. That means a lot to us both."

My dad grinned. "You're welcome." Then he turned to me. "Now, Duck, I believe all your hard work in France has earned you a bottle or two of wine. You may as well make this a night to remember. Plus, I need some new stories for my buddies at the senior center.   Last year's drunken airplane episode has gotten old…"

I really love my dad.

Chapter Twenty-Eight

The Durand-Bennett wedding was one of the wildest scenes *Le Caylar* had seen in some time. And it was going to be perfect, if Simone had anything to do with it. (She was a woman after my own heart.) To that end, once she had gotten over her initial shock of Louis' and my appearance, she moved into damage control mode. There was no way we were going to kick off her coveted reception in our current disheveled states. She had Louis change into a backup gray suit and covered my mud laden bodice with a rather complicated wrap of a beautiful pale gold scarf.

I had thought my skirt was a lost cause, but Simone whipped out a roll of three inch wide gold sparkly ribbon and went to town with a needle and thread. I couldn't believe it! Within five minutes, she had bedazzled my skirt into submission! When she steered me towards a mirror, I was in complete shock. The dress looked completely different than the one I had chosen, but it was just as beautiful. Maybe I needed to have a little more faith in my mother-in-law and her accessorizing prowess.

After I thanked Simone profusely for her remarkable design work and Maya worked her usual magic with my makeup, Louis escorted me to the wedding reception in his parent's backyard. Backyard is a bit misleading of a term considering the family owns over nine hundred acres of land, but it is an apt description nonetheless. There were tables of guests as far as the eye could see, punctuated with three dance floors, two bands, a choir and endless buffets of delicious food. Simone had outfitted the entire setting with twinkly white lights and more flowers than I had ever seen in my life. Given that it was now three in the afternoon and it didn't get dark here until after nine at this time of year, the presence of the twinkly lights led me to believe this party was going to carry on for a long period of time. It was clear this reception was going to be *legendary*.

The cocktail hour was indeed a sight to be seen. A few of Louis' old buddies from his bartending days in college agreed to take shifts the bar, mixing drinks and putting on crowd-pleasing shows a la Tom Cruise in *Cocktail*. There were lights, flames and choreographed dance moves. The few moments I caught were highly entertaining and oddly enough, somewhat erotic. After viewing a couple of exchanges involving a "volunteer" from the surrounding audience, I understood why Louis enjoyed being a bartender so much in his younger days. The women quite literally fell into your lap...

Any of my past drinking stories were put to rest collectively by my family. It would appear all those, except for Nick, who was in charge of Sam, felt it was their duty to show Louis' family that the Americans could keep up with the French. They were so woefully wrong. The hangovers they were going to experience tomorrow would be EPIC. I didn't think my father would be physically able to mix his hangover remedy, even if he were able to find the ingredients.

Let me set the scene for you. I think you'll enjoy this almost as much as I did. (Payback is a bitch, yo!) Louis took Charlie and Zoe along with him to the Get 27 table. Get 27 (pronounced "jet") is a particularly potent French liquor which tastes like mint with a strong aftertaste of ....lighter fluid? Jet fuel? (Ha!) It's also bright green. I would liken it to gasoline-flavored mouthwash. Louis once told me, the advantage of this type of alcohol was if you overdid it and hurled, your breath would be minty fresh. I was fairly certain both Charlie and Zoe were going to share this experience at some point in the evening.

My mother and Kate joined Louis' aunts at a table with a selection of wine from Uncle Luc's vineyard. My mother conducted herself in a similar fashion to the wine tasting earlier in the week. It was too bad that instead of taking care of her as she did then, Kate elected to drink right along with my mother. The two of them became sloppy drunk before the entrees arrived and ended up doing the tango. With each other. (Don't ask.) It was a good thing Kate had planned ahead and pumped some breast milk for Sam. She didn't need to learn about the wonders of hangovers at such a tender young age. There would be plenty of time for such things in her teenage years.

I've saved the absolute best for last - my father. He made the grave error of joining Louis' uncles at the Pastis table. My father LOVES the taste of Pastis. Since this is the "flavor of the South" (of France, that is), all men who grew up there learned at an early age how to handle this particular alcohol. Sadly, my father had not. Since the rest of my family was drunk with a capital "D", Nick had his hands full with Sam and I was performing the last of my wedding responsibilities, he was left to his own devices. It was not pretty.

After the wedding cake had been served, I found him under a table clutching a bottle of Pastis in one hand and a plate of cheese in the other. He was, of course, singing as he has a tendency to do when intoxicated, but instead of his go-to choice of old army marching songs, he was singing... well...a rather explicit Prince song. I have no words to describe what it's like to hear your father sing the lyrics to *Get Off*, so we'll just skip that part. Since I had exposed him to Prince in the first place, I felt it necessary to redirect his song choice as quickly as possible. After several false starts, I was able to coax him into a rousing rendition of *New York, New York*. A much better choice, but he's probably headed for YouTube's Top Ten videos as well.

Amidst my family's massive drunken episode, Louis and I made rounds to tables upon tables of guests, picking up food and cocktails as we went. This task took FOUR HOURS. (With a few short bathroom and checking-on-drunk-family-members breaks squeezed in between.) And that was having speed round conversations with each group of table inhabitants.

I guess this makes sense considering there were over four hundred people in attendance. Phew! I was lucky enough to smile and nod for the most part; Louis really had to do all the heavy lifting. His voice was a bit hoarse by the time we were through, but the grin on his face was everlasting. I think our marriage felt more real to him once he had shared the pomp and circumstance with his all his French peeps.

Louis pulled me aside towards the end of the evening to tell me, many of his family members had been impressed by my "balls." Intrigued by his statement, I asked him to elaborate. He smiled as he informed me, not only did he receive consensus I had rightfully earned my place in the family by the level of commitment I had shown since my arrival, but also, his relatives wanted to congratulate me personally on my "Americaness."

Apparently, my crazed rescue of Poupette without regard to the fate of my wedding gown was viewed as reckless though well-intentioned – the epitome of the American way. I laughed as I ascertained my new French relatives didn't consider all American traits to be undesirable. It seems having "balls" is a good thing here as well. As long as it's used in small doses...

I received more pats on the back that night than I care to admit. It was rather painful in a dress with an open back, but in the end it was worth it. I had broken through the barrier and was now a RESPECTED, card carrying member of the Durand family, even if I couldn't completely understand them. But I knew I would get there one day. And I looked forward to it with relish.

I felt an immense sense of relief as the evening came to a close. Over the last week and a half, I had cleared every single one of the hurdles which had been put in front of me. There had been MANY; they had all felt ridiculously high and I had repeatedly thought I wouldn't make it. Whenever I had felt these doubts, I simply thought about everything Louis and I had been through and knew if I could get through all the uncertainty, pain and self-doubt of the past few months, I could get through anything. We Durand women are extremely resilient, you know.

The cherry on top of the evening? As the last family members were leaving the wedding, we were able to solve the mystery of Poupette's disappearance. Monique approached us with an air of triumph, holding a bottle of champagne and three glasses. She grinned as she told us the dog-napper turned out to be an old girlfriend of Michel's. Marie had traveled three hundred miles for the wedding and was bitterly disappointed when Michel wouldn't betray Simone for her. So, as her supreme act of vengeance she stole his favorite dog. (The bond between a French man and his dog is ironclad.) Poor Poupette had been trapped in Marie's mother's cellar overnight.

You may be wondering how Monique was able to come to this brilliant conclusion. I sure was. It would seem Monique observed Poupette to have a negative reaction to Marie during the reception. (Because, of course, all seven dogs were in attendance of our wedding reception.) It didn't take long for her to pry the truth out of Marie using a little empathy and a whole lotta wine. Forget the tourist trade, I think Monique has a career as a detective in her future.

⌒

The next morning was a true sight to be seen around the breakfast table. Every member of my family, save Nick and Sam, looked to be a sickly shade of green. Very little food was consumed and there was a propensity of head clutching and moaning. I decided it would be rather unladylike to behave in a smug manner, as they had often behaved towards me during one of my classic hangovers, and offered them each a glass of Simone's hangover remedy. I have not a clue what was in it, other than a small amount of Get 27 (hair of the dog that bit you, my friend). The distinctive odor and tinge of green made it unmistakable.

Thankfully none of the Bennett family drunkards had to board a plane until the following day. Everyone had taken advantage of their trip to France as a jumping off point for further European travels. My parents were on their way to both Germany and Norway. My father was planning on looking up a few long lost cousins in Munich and my mom was very much looking forward to a visit with her close friend in Norway. Nick, Kate and Sam were off to merry old England and Charlie and Zoe had planned a romantic trip to Italy. And, of course, Louis and I would leave tomorrow morning for our one night in Paris. The anticipation was killing me!

After helping Simone with the dishes, I ventured out to the terrace to find the broken shells of my family. Kate was sitting in front of a large pile of crackers which she appeared to be sharing with both Zoe and Sam. My mom had regained some of her color and was having a pleasant chat with Nigel, Grace and Devon. Charlie and my dad were sitting stoically in silence staring at some unknown item on the horizon and Louis was keeping Nick company as the only other non-hung over person present. Maya, it seemed, was missing.

I smiled at the collective group and approached my father. "Are you alright, Dad?"

He didn't respond. Uh oh. Is he in some kind of trance? Both Charlie and I tapped him on the shoulder and he slowly came to life.

He peered up at me. "Duck. What's the good word?"

I put my hand over his. "I'm fine, Dad. How are you?"

He coughed. "A little worse for the wear since last night."

Charlie laughed. "No kidding. I feel like I've been run over by a truck."

I winced. "Did Simone's hangover remedy help at all?" I really hoped it had some kind of positive effect. It both looked *and* smelled disastrous. Why else would you drink such a nasty concoction?

My dad pursed his lips. "Couldn't tell you. I still feel like a bomb went off in my brain."

I began to cackle uncontrollably.

Charlie rolled his eyes at me. "Laugh all you want, Sydie. It won't be long before you're on the other side of this equation."

My laughing subsided. "Don't I know it, my brother! I'm happy to be where I am for the moment."

My dad carefully got up from the table. "I have some business to attend to."

Charlie sighed as my dad walked towards the house. "I hope no one needs to use the bathroom for a while…"

I cleared my throat. "Hey, have you seen Maya?"

Charlie shook his head. "Not since last night."

Maya had made quite the spectacle of herself during the wedding reception. Thankfully it wasn't for drunken shouting this time. She and Devon had taken salsa lessons shortly before we left for France and the two of them had wowed the four hundred plus guests with a scorching performance. Honestly, simply seeing the two of them side by side was an experience in itself, since they were both

obscenely attractive. But watching their obscenely attractive
bodies move in such a manner was…indescribable.

I kissed Charlie on the top of his head. "I'm going to
check in with Devon."

Charlie nodded and resumed his staring straight ahead.
It was almost like he was seasick. Ugh.

A quick conversation with Devon alerted me to Maya's
location. I had to ask him to repeat himself since I thought
he said she was in the garden. OK. Maya doesn't do dirt.
Especially dirt which may or may not contain some type of
animal excrement. You know how much her shoes cost!

A few minutes later I was looking upon a most bizarre
sight. My good friend Maya, a well-known nature hater, was
gazing dreamily at Simone's enormous flower garden with
the most ridiculous grin on her face. My mind raced in
different directions all at once. Was she still drunk from last
night? Had she not slept? Was she on drugs? What the hell
was wrong with her?

I gasped. It couldn't be. I ran over to Maya and
grabbed her left hand. Staring back at me was the largest,
most perfect diamond I've ever seen.

"Holy shit, Maya!" I giggled gleefully and scooped her
into my arms.

Her entire being was light. I had never, in the nearly
twelve years I had known her, seen her this happy. From
everything you've heard, you must be shocked. I mean,
Maya is pretty much a sourpuss at heart. A loveable
sourpuss, but a sourpuss nonetheless.

I put her down carefully and she grinned at me with
tears in her eyes. "I'm getting married, Syd!"

I jumped up and down. "I know! I'm so excited!"
Suddenly I stopped jumping. I pulled her over to a large
rock and sat down on it. "Wait! Tell me everything."

She joined me on the rock, laughing all the way. This
new, HAPPY Maya was freaking me out a little. But in a
good way. It was just going to take some getting used to.

"So, when we finished dancing, he went to get us drinks."

I nodded. "Before or after cake?"

"I don't know." She paused. "Does it matter?"

I shook my head. "Only trying to discern when it happened."

She rolled her eyes. "You have to focus on the important details, Syd!"

I shushed her. "Then get on with it!"

She smirked. "So he came back with two glasses of champagne, found a remote table for us to sit at and popped the question."

I was shocked. "Just like that?" No preamble? No, I'm such a lucky man to have met such an amazing woman like you, blah, blah, blah…(We all enjoy those blahs, don't we?)

Maya nodded. "Just like that." She put her ring in front of my face for emphasis. Yes, Maya, I know a ring like that (and a man like Devon for that matter) does not need unnecessary preamble.

I grinned like an idiot at her. "I'm so happy for you!"

She clapped twice quickly. "There's no time for happiness, Matron of Honor. We have a lot of work to do. Why do you think I'm out in this garden? There are flowers to be selected, color schemes, table linens, invitations…"

Suddenly my head started to spin. Holy crap! Matron of honor! I still have one more wedding of my OWN to go in less than four weeks. And this is the one I had been looking forward to the most. This is MY day. Something was going to have to be done to head off the monster. Delicately, of course.

I hugged her. "Matron of honor! I'm thrilled, Maya. Thank you for asking me."

She pulled out of the hug and grabbed my shoulders. "I have a bunch of bridal magazines in my hotel room we can look at after breakfast. Oh, and when we get back, we have to start looking at venues…"

I laughed. "Maya, one step at a time. Have you called your parents? Devon's parents?"

She waved at me dismissively. "Of course, we called last night. Now about the flowers, I was thinking…"

I put my hand up. "Now it's time to tell your *extended* family. Or did you make those calls last night too?"

She shook her head. I couldn't imagine how no one in my family would notice a rock of that size (it had to be at least three carats) on her hand, but then again, they were all really drunk.

I linked my arm through hers. "OK then. Let's go tell them."

She began to protest. "But we have so many decisions to make."

I stopped and put my hands on her shoulders. "Maya, you've been engaged for less than twenty-four hours. Enjoy what's happened! Savor it! Once the planning kicks in, the whole things starts to feel like work."

She nodded begrudgingly.

I glared at her pointedly. "And let me remind you, we still have one more Durand-Bennett wedding to go. And this is the wedding *I* have wanted since I was a little girl. I swear, if you stress me out in the next four weeks fussing over your wedding which is a year away, I WILL kill you. And then poor Devon will be heartbroken. Understood?"

She had the good grace to appear shocked. "Sorry, Syd. I guess the girly girl in me finally clawed her way out."

I chuckled. "I'm happy to meet her, but tell her to come back in a month, OK?"

She took my hand and smiled. "Will do."

As Maya and I walked back towards the terrace, I thought about all the planning she had ahead of her. The excitement and the thrill of planning the perfect day to marry the perfect man. Of knowing you were going to have a perfect life together. Personally, I couldn't wait for the planning to be over and the actual living of the perfect life to begin. I took a deep breath. Louis and I had made it through two weddings relatively unharmed despite a myriad of challenges. We had almost made it to the wedding of my dreams. What could possibly go wrong now?

Damn it, Sydney Durand! You know better than that! Your father told you NEVER to ask that question. What the fuck were you thinking? God only knows what kind of heinous acts are going to befall you now. Just know you brought this on yourself...

Chapter Twenty-Nine

I can't believe it. I have actually cursed myself. After everything I've been through, *I* was the key to my own undoing. Why did I have to ask what could go wrong? What would possess me to do such a ludicrous thing? I'm going to blame lack of logical reasoning as a result of my complete mental exhaustion. Pulling off a week and a half long feat of wedding labors took every ounce of energy I had. There was simply nothing left to power my battered brain.

Because of the enormous amount of commotion on the day of our departure, I didn't have time to think about my reckless question from the previous day. Louis and I were embroiled in the turmoil of packing, saying heartfelt good-byes to every member of his family and of course, making sure the American branch of the family made it to their various flights. Though our trip had been an amazing (and terrifying) experience, I was mind-numbingly tired and all I could think about was the king-size bed waiting for us at the George V. Unfortunately for my poor husband, I had sleep, not sex, at the forefront of my mind.

On our flight to Paris that afternoon, the doubt started to creep into my consciousness. As I flipped through my trashy magazines, I tried to shake off my feeling of paranoia. I mean, what did I have to worry about? It wasn't possible to *cause* bad things to happen simply by thinking they couldn't happen, right? Seriously, who really believes in superstition? Crazy people, right? Exactly! Only crazy people. Sydney Bennett was crazy. Sydney Durand is most definitely not. Sydney Durand is logical. She is intelligent. She will *not* be swayed by such nonsense.

With my irrational thoughts temporarily at bay, Louis and I spent the next day and a half in heaven. We did nothing but eat, drink and relax. (*After* we repeatedly assured his mother we had arrived safely in Paris. A *ninety* minute flight away…) Louis treated me like a queen. It was AWESOME! As soon as we arrived at the hotel, he drew me a bubble bath and ordered room service.

Once he had scrubbed me clean, he fed me a delectable selection of pastries and then settled me into the softest bed I have ever slept in for a wonderful nap. Then he took me out shopping on the *Avenue des Champs-Élysées* where he bought me a beautiful dress and a number of elegant accessories. We then had a late dinner (which by European standards is eleven pm) and returned to our hotel for champagne and the best sex I have had in my entire life.

The next day was filled with more shopping, eating and touring of the most magnificent French landmarks. We spent the morning at the *Louvre*, had lunch at the top of the *Le Tour Eiffel* and spent our afternoon browsing in the *Galleries Lafayette*. Louis insisted I try pastries and chocolates on nearly every street we walked, so by the time we boarded the plane for San Francisco that evening I was fairly certain I was going to explode. I was so exhausted from all the walking (and all the *eating*), I fell asleep on the flight. This had to be a good sign; I NEVER fell asleep on airplanes. Maybe my luck was changing. Maybe everything was going to be fine! Maybe I had finally broken the cycle of insanity!

Maybe I was on crack. Three weeks have passed since we arrived home from Paris, which means we are now three days from my dream wedding. Work has been completely crazy for both Louis and me, so we haven't seen much of each other. I have been furiously planning for next year's department budget, organizing open enrollment and educating the employee population on our new dental plan. Louis has been dropped into the deep end of the pool at his new job and is now spearheading a major overhaul of the company's most valuable database. So, you know, no pressure or anything.

But it's not these banal work issues which have made my blood run cold whenever I think of my asinine query as to what could possibly go wrong in the remaining three weeks before our wedding. It's the fact that these wedding plans simply KEEP GOING WRONG. It was bad enough the photographer fell through (it never gets old) while we were in France, but problems kept cropping up. It's like I was playing a giant game of whack-a-mole. As soon as one issue had been resolved, another one popped up in its place.

I may not make it to my perfect wedding! I *may* have to be carried off in a lovely white straightjacket. I can see it now; I'll be clutching patches of tulle and ribbon as I giggle maniacally about seating charts...

Shall I fill you in on the details? You might need this information for my commitment hearing. Are you ready? Here we go. During our first week back, which was three weeks before the wedding, I received a call from the Monterey Plaza Hotel regarding our menu choices for the reception. Apparently, there was some kind of issue with one of the hotel's suppliers and many of the items we had chosen were no longer available. In fact, all but THREE of the items were no longer available. In light of Louis' packed schedule, I roped Maya into going with me to sort out this mess, claiming she needed training for her own impending bridal responsibilities. It only took us EIGHT hours to accomplish our task, since Maya was far more focused on what she would like to eat at her own wedding than on what I might end up shoving down her throat at mine.

With my nerves frayed slightly from such a *lovely* experience, I focused on relaxing and stupidly told myself the worst was over. I should've known by that point, I had seriously angered the wedding gods by being so bold and careless with my ponderings. There was a lot more fun coming my way before Louis and I made our third and final trip down the aisle.

During our second week back, which was now two weeks before our wedding, I received a regretful phone call from our florist. There had apparently been some kind of freak storm in…some foreign country…the details escape me…and I now had to choose almost *all* new flowers. The good news was she would still be able to get the vibrant purple orchids which were integral to the overall look of the wedding, since my colors were pink and purple.

Yes, I said PINK and PURPLE, not blush and aubergine or whatever stupid ass name some wedding planner would want to give these colors. It almost broke my heart, but I wouldn't be able to have the pale pink roses I had dreamt of being the cornerstone of my bridal bouquet for pretty much as long as I could remember. I would have to settle for pale pink tulips. It really wasn't so bad. (OK, so it was in my mind, but what choice did I have? The show must go on.)

During our third week back, with one week to go to our wedding, we had our immigration interview. Did I neglect to tell you we found out about this the week before we left for France? Louis and I had to venture to the San Jose Field Office of the USCIS (United States Citizenship & Immigration Services) to justify our relationship. How would we do this? By answering trivial questions, like, what color is his toothbrush? What side of the bed does she sleep on? What is his favorite color? What does she like to eat for breakfast? We also had to bring a collection of photos of the two of us with each other's family members as well as the two of us celebrating important occasions together.

I should have done this preparation before we left for France, but well, I kind of lost my mind with all the stress. Since I had spent the last two weeks trying to keep our wedding from falling off the rails, I had put off the daunting task of piecing together our greatest hits in a photo album. (I may not have mentioned it before - I take A LOT of photos. It's a nasty habit I picked up from my mother.) Because of this rash decision, I spent the entire night before our interview culling through photos and putting them in an album in chronological order. I also felt the need to add colorful accents and cute words, as though I were being evaluated on my ability to scrapbook. I had truly lost my mind! What can I tell you? It really wasn't that far of a gap to bridge.

So, there I found myself, less than a week away from our wedding, completely freaking out for our immigration interview. Since I hadn't slept, I had overcompensated by drinking WAY too much coffee. No matter what I did, my appearance was haggard and I had developed this nasty habit of twitching uncontrollably. The immigration officer was probably going to think I was strung out on drugs. And that our marriage was a sham. And then after all our hard work, Louis would be deported. I really should have gotten some sleep. I seem to have misplaced my ability to use logic and reason. If you find it, please let me know.

Once we finished our interview, I felt certain I had ruined everything. I was definitely a little, um, hyper from all the caffeine, which made me far too eager to answer his questions. I often cut Louis off and was terrified I had given the impression I didn't trust him to give the correct answers. If I were this guy, I would totally think Louis and I had some kind of financial arrangement for obtaining a green card. What had I done?

When we arrived back at the apartment, I did my best to relax. Louis had taken the day off from work for the interview, but he raced to his laptop as soon as we got back home. He really wanted to make sure his project got off the ground as soon as possible. While he toiled away, I absently flipped through the channels. This wasn't helping me; I simply couldn't concentrate. I tried reading a book, surfing the internet and looking through my recipe books, but nothing could take my mind of my perceived colossal blunder with our interview.

I closed my eyes and tried to isolate the source of my discomfort. After a few moments of reflection, I discovered I was *angry*. I mean really fucking pissed off. The last year had been filled with stress, whether through joyous or challenging events. I felt cheated because I had convinced myself, when I came back from France, I would be able to relax for the last few weeks before our final wedding. But no, I've had issue after issue and have consequently been traumatized within an inch of my life. What the fuck?!?

This wedding is *everything* to me. It may seem stupid, but this is the wedding I've wanted for as long as I can remember. Why can't it just go off without a hitch? Why can't I just enjoy the fruits of my labor? And I'm not only talking about planning the wedding. I'm talking about enjoying the wonderful man I married. The man I've searched for, for a *very* long time. Seriously, do you remember the succession of men I dated before he came along? It was a complete DISASTER.

I jumped about ten feet in the air when I heard Louis' voice.

"*Mon coeur?* Are you alright?" His face was full of concern. How did he know I was completely freaking out? Could he see it in my face that I had ruined our lives?

As I peered up at him, I caught sight of myself in the mirror in the dining room. Holy shit! I hadn't noticed my entire body was shaking and I had tears pouring down my face. I looked like crap.

I put my head in my hands and began to sob. "No," I told him in-between hiccups.

He came over and put his arms around me. "What is the matter? Are you worried about our interview?"

I wrung my hands. "I completely messed it up."

He pulled me to my feet. "Stop putting so much pressure on yourself. Everything is going to be fine."

I exhaled slowly. "I wish I were as confident as you. I behaved like a complete idiot."

He put his finger under my chin and brought my gaze up to his. "You just need some sleep, Syd."

At the mention of sleep, I dissolved in his arms. I was tired of feeling exhausted. When would I be able to relax?

Louis picked me up and carried me into the bedroom. He helped me into my favorite comfy pajamas and put me to bed. I was so worn-out, I fell asleep before he even left the room.

I woke up a few hours later to find a peanut butter and jelly sandwich waiting for me on my nightstand. Louis remembered this as one of my favorite comfort foods. I smiled and glanced at the clock. I had been asleep for five hours. As soon as I sat up, I was ravenous. I ate my sandwich in about five bites (I'm such a lady!) and brought the plate into the kitchen.

Louis looked up from his laptop, when I put my plate into the dishwasher. "How are you feeling, *mon coeur?*"

I came up behind him and put my arms around his neck, resting my chin on his shoulder. "Much better. Thank you for my sandwich."

"You are welcome. Though I do not know how you Americans can eat peanut butter. It is disgusting." He wrinkled his nose.

I laughed. "Peanut butter is disgusting, but you enjoy eating sheep's *brain*." Simply saying the words "sheep's brain" made me shiver involuntarily.

He looked at me with a straight face. "But of course. Where is the confusion? Sheep's brain is delicious."

I grimaced. "We will have to agree to disagree on this one."

Louis pulled me into his lap. "So, how do you feel about an outing?"

I regarded him skeptically. "What kind of outing?" I had the distinct feeling my husband had some kind of plan for cheering me up. This wasn't necessarily a good thing since we had *very* different ideas of what constituted a good time.

He grinned. "You will just have to trust me."

I pursed my lips. "OK, let's say I decide to trust you. What do I need to wear for this outing?"

He winked at me. "Jeans and a t-shirt will be fine, Syd."

I examined his face for a moment. There were no clues as to what he had up his sleeve. As I got up to return to the bedroom, I pointed a finger towards him. "Remember, I'm in a delicate state, Bluey. Do *not* mess with me."

He held up his hands in mock protest. "I wouldn't dream of it, *mon coeur.*"

⌒

An hour later, I was standing outside Louis' favorite motorcycle gear shop, since I had absolutely no intention of setting foot inside. My senseless husband just informed me that he's brought me here to outfit me in full motorcycle regalia. He actually thinks I'll get onto his death trap *voluntarily*. It may seem odd, but at that moment, I thought he was crazier than I was. What an accomplishment!

It took Louis thirty minutes, but he did eventually talk me into entering the shop. I mean, it couldn't hurt to *look*, right? I had always wanted those cute motorcycle boots. This would be the perfect place to buy an authentic pair. Oooh, and I bet they have a nice collection of biker jackets too. That could be fun…

It took another two hours, but Louis eventually convinced me to purchase not only a pair of motorcycle boots and a motorcycle racing jacket with internal safety padding, but also a helmet and a pair of riding gloves. Louis loved riding his motorcycle, but he was an absolute stickler for safety. As we left the store, I couldn't believe what I had done. Was I truly going to get on this thing?

We arrived back at our apartment and for the next hour, I sat next to Louis on the curb in front of our complex, staring at his motorcycle. Louis didn't say anything, he just patiently answered my questions as they came up. He went through all the dials and levers on the motorcycle with me four times and didn't show any sign of exasperation.

I was scared shitless, but I decided to get on the bike anyway. Louis checked my helmet, jacket and gloves multiple times and then gave me a few last minute tips. He told me the wind was going to feel pretty strong and it would be a good idea for me to position my head behind his shoulder for my first few times out to avoid hurting my neck. The first *few* times? A little cocky are we? He was assuming I would become an adrenaline junkie like he was. I was just hoping I wouldn't die. Though it would serve me right if I did, for being so reckless and killing myself before my dream wedding.

The ride was so…exhilarating! I absolutely loved it. That's not to say I wasn't deathly afraid at first, but I pushed back the fear. (I held onto Louis with an iron grip; he's lucky his jacket has padding too.) I was DONE with feeling afraid and stressed…and tired! I was fed up with thinking about all the minutia that isn't important. Out here, on this bike, all you have to think about is the moment. You're only existing in *this* particular point in time. And it feels amazing!

When I shared my feelings with Louis, he was as giddy as I've ever seen him. I wasn't sure if he were happier about discovering I shared his love of motorcycles – at least to some degree - or discovering he had been able to bring me out of the latest bout of the crazies. Either way, we had found a moment of precious joy.

The next morning, we received a call from our immigration officer. I, of course, was convinced they had the building surrounded and was quickly scanning the apartment for exit options. Louis squeezed my hand and reminded me we would deal with whatever happened together. A moment later, we were informed Louis was cleared for a green card. Our officer, Bob, told us he could tell we were the real deal from the moment we walked in the room. He then commented dryly that no one other than a couple in love would go through the trouble of three weddings in three *different* locations to satisfy all their family members. When you put it that way, Bob, it does sound completely insane.

I allowed myself to breathe for about five seconds before I entered panic mode once more. We were now three days away from our third and final wedding, which meant only one thing. The Frenchies were coming to town...

Chapter Thirty

Taking our trip to France to meet Louis' family was one of the most unique and educational experiences of my life. Having the French contingency come to America was a whole other animal. Simone and Michel were the first to arrive, two short days before the wedding. Thankfully, all the details were in place for our final foray into wedded bliss. (My game of whack-a-mole was over and I honestly wasn't sure who won.) Louis and I would be able to spend a little time showing his family the wonders of San Francisco, since we had both taken off work until the following Tuesday, when the Frenchies would return home. Unfortunately, we no longer had a honeymoon in our immediate future because Louis couldn't take any more time off from work.

You will be thrilled to know Louis' parents were staying in our apartment, at Simone's insistence. My gallant husband tried repeatedly to convince her they should stay in a hotel for their OWN comfort, but she wouldn't be swayed. I was convinced she wanted to get in one last episode of hazing, but the actual reasoning turned out to be far more basic. Simone is simply nosy.

I'm sure you remember the lack of boundaries she showed in her own home during our recent visit. I quickly discovered she applies the same standards to other people's homes. Upon her arrival, she searched through every one of our kitchen cabinets. I had stupidly thought since we had a major bonding moment during our trip to France, she would somehow leave me alone. Alas, her curiosity (and fierce determination that she knows best) wouldn't be contained.

Therefore, I bit my tongue while she rearranged my dishes, making clucking noises and glancing my way every few minutes. When she started towards our bedroom, I turned to Louis with a murderous look on my face. This was where I drew the line. She wouldn't touch a thing in my closet. I could easily see her sorting through my underwear and deeming it unworthy. There HAD to be a limit to her invasiveness.

Louis quickly redirected his mother to the living room couch and put on one of her favorite French movies. He had very cleverly stocked up on DVDs his parents would enjoy in order to give us some breathing room. He had also signed us up for a couple of French TV channels in case the movies didn't do the trick. (The man is a genius!)

We planned to take them to a number of tourist attractions in San Francisco, but we were going to have to spend some time in the apartment and his mother wasn't able to sit still very easily. It suddenly dawned on me that maybe I wasn't going to be able to relax during these last two days before the wedding. Maybe I was actually going to have the nervous breakdown I keep talking about. Or maybe I was just going to kill my mother in law...

Michel, on the other hand, was a very pleasant houseguest. All he required was a bottomless platter of chocolate chip cookies, a TV with French programming and a comfortable bed for naps. Louis and I had prepared all these items for him and he was content to sit with us and talk, smiling as he ate his cookies. His rich voice and infectious laugh set me at ease. I sat back in wonder at the stark contrast between Louis' parents. Though I guess it's merely the pleasure of a mother-in-law to drive her daughter-in-law completely berserk. Unfortunately for me, she only had one daughter-in-law to torture. And I couldn't even find security knowing we lived so far from her reach. Not even an ocean AND a continent could keep Simone from her task.

That afternoon, we took Louis' parents to Pier 39, Alcatraz and Ghirardelli Square. Since we were doing a lot of walking, I wore casual clothes and my favorite converse. Simone wore a suit and four inch heels. Before we left, I pulled Louis aside and asked him if his mom had more comfortable shoes to wear since I envisioned her with major blisters at the end of our activities. He simply shook his head and told me she would only wear heels outside the house. ("She is French, after all," he mused.) I sighed, realizing this would be another area where I would fall short. There was no way in hell I was going to traipse all over the city in heels. Americans may appear to be loud, fat and stupid to most Europeans, but we're also comfortable.

The next day, Uncles Remi and Luc, Aunts Seraphine and Jacqueline and cousins, Monique and Sophie arrived. Thankfully, this gave me some breathing room since Simone had much to gossip about with her sisters. (No doubt she led with the poor quality of my kitchen organization. Thank God she had no stories to tell about my unmentionables.) A little more breathing room was coming my way very soon due to our imminent departure for Monterey. Tonight was our rehearsal dinner (Third and final, baby!) and tomorrow was the big day. In a few hours, we would all be resting comfortably in our OWN hotel rooms. Which had locks on the doors. And lovely little chains too.

Louis and I had rented a minivan to transport our posse of Frenchies down to Monterey, so after a quick lunch we loaded everyone in and started our road trip. The amount of luggage was mind boggling, but thankfully my parents had arrived last night and had also rented a minivan to handle our overflow baggage. I had given my parents the astronomical responsibility of transporting my wedding gown to the hotel. It scared the crap out of me to be separated from it, but there was simply no way to fit it in our van without it getting crushed. I made my father promise he would do everything in his power to protect it. He was about to make some sort of sarcastic comment when the look of gravity on my face silenced him. Even my father could see I would *not* be trifled with so close to the final wedding.

A few hours later we were all happily installed in our hotel rooms. Louis and I were given the bridal suite on the top floor of the hotel. The view was breathtaking and the suite was more luxurious than any I had seen before. And to make things even better, all our family members had been given rooms two floors below us. Ahhh. Sweet relief.

After Louis and I had a relaxing bubble bath together, we got dressed and took the elevator down to the second floor to check on our families. The rehearsal dinner was due to start in one hour and we wanted to make sure everyone was going to be on time. Louis headed down one corridor to check on his family and I headed down another to check on mine. It was then that the comedy began.

First I knocked on my parents' door. My mom answered the door in a fluffy white bathrobe.

I giggled. "Nice outfit, Mom! Is that what you're wearing tonight?"

She pulled me into the room. "Syd! Look at you! You look beautiful!"

I did look pretty nice, if I did say so myself. I had chosen a strapless pale pink dress, with a fitted bodice and flowing mid length skirt complete with a lace overlay. I wore my hair in loose waves, applied simple shimmery makeup and capped off the ensemble with silver strappy sandals.

I hugged her gently. "Thanks, Mom. And thanks for all your help."

She put her hand on the side of my face. "Your special day is finally here."

I smiled. "Almost. And don't make me cry! Maya will know…" You know how she feels about fixing makeup she's already applied to perfection.

My mom bustled over to the dresser and picked up a necklace and a pair of earrings. "Let's get out you outfitted with diamonds, Syd."

Kate and I had always had the privilege of borrowing our mother's diamond pendant and earrings for special occasions. Who wouldn't feel special wearing these beautiful pieces of jewelry? My mom had generously cleared me to wear them for tonight's dinner and tomorrow's big day. It was the final touch every girl wanted.

After she had adjusted the necklace and earrings, she stepped back to admire me. "Even better! And I didn't think that was possible."

Suddenly, the bathroom door opened. "Duck! You look stunning!"

I had to stifle a laugh. There was my dad, fresh from the shower, wearing nothing but a towel and a huge grin. I went over and carefully gave him a kiss on the cheek. He was still fairly wet and I had no intention of damaging my dress.

I grinned at him. "I love you, Dad."

"And I love you, Duck." He tapped my nose. "Now, unless you want to see more of your father than you ever have, I suggest you exit the room."

"That is a sight I could *never* extract from my brain." I walked to the door and waved to them. "See you in forty-five minutes. Don't be late!"

I closed the door to my parents' room and wondered who I should pop in on next. While I pondered my choices, three doors opened simultaneously and three heads popped out. I laughed when I saw Kate, Zoe and Maya all staring at me.

"Hi, girls!" I beamed.

The three of them burst into the hallway, each talking at the same time.

Kate squealed with delight. "You look amazing! That dress is perfect for you!"

Zoe whistled. "Nice choice!"

Maya kept her voice calm. "You look really hot, Syd."

I laughed. "Thank you! You all look pretty hot yourselves." Kate was wearing a gray short sleeved scoop neck dress with a knee length skirt, Zoe was wearing a black sleeveless sheath dress with a beautifully embroidered skirt and Maya was wearing an emerald green halter dress with both bedazzled neck and hemline.

I took a deep breath. "I can't believe we're here."

Zoe smiled. "It's been a long road."

Maya snickered. "And rather short as well, since you knew Louis for about five minutes before you married him the first time."

I smacked Maya in the butt and then pulled the three of them into a group hug. "I don't care if this sounds cheesy. You three are...well, you mean the world to me. Thank you for getting me here in one piece."

Kate stroked my hair as tears formed in her eyes. "I'd do anything for you, Syd. You know that."

I nodded, unable to speak.

Maya smirked at me. "You would, wait, you WILL do the same for me. So, make sure you bring your A game, bitch."

Zoe laughed. "Thank you, Maya, for such a heartfelt statement." She tapped her watch. "We'd better get the men moving."

After one last hug for each of them, I took off in search of Louis. He wasn't hard to find; all I had to do was follow the yelling. I went as fast as I could in my rather high sandals, which ended up being a bizarre kind of gallop, and found Louis in the doorway of his parent's hotel room.

"Bluey! What's going on?" I stopped to catch my breath.

The look on his face was not pleasant. "My mother is not ready yet."

I regarded him with my poker face. "OK. When will she be ready?" At that point, I felt only a mild irritation at this news, so I had to be the one to stay in control.

He shook his head. "I have no idea."

I put my hand on his arm. "Don't worry. The dinner won't start for another thirty minutes. You and I will head over to the restaurant with my family to greet the out of town guests. Your family can meet us there when she's ready." The restaurant was only two blocks down the street, so it would be easy for them to get there.

He still seemed uneasy. "I don't know, *mon coeur...*"

Plan B. "Do you want me to ask Charlie to wait for them? Or Devon?"

He sighed. "Devon would be great."

I kissed him on the nose. "I'll go ask him. Be right back." I suspected Maya wouldn't be thrilled Devon's fluency in French had once again landed him with an important responsibility for Louis' family. Given that he was the only American fluent in French attending the rehearsal dinner, I had a bad feeling she would be feeling resentful once again. It was a good thing there wouldn't be an open bar. None of us wanted a repeat of that fateful night in France. And I really didn't want my wedding makeup artist in such a damaged state on the long sought after BIG DAY. I might end up looking like a clown.

Luckily, Maya was supportive of my request and happily hooked her arm in mine as we walked to the rehearsal dinner. Louis had threatened his mother with disinviting her to the wedding tomorrow if she didn't arrive at the restaurant within thirty minutes. He had to have known he had made a completely empty threat, since he knew very well that a) she would arrive at the restaurant in her own good time and b) wild horses couldn't keep her away from tomorrow's event. She was fascinated at the prospect of a "lavish" American wedding and looked forward to her position as the mother of the groom. All eyes, after all, would be on her.

The rehearsal dinner went off without a hitch. (Say it with me, WAHOO!) Simone arrived only an hour late and seemed happy to make an entrance on the arm of the gorgeous Devon. The rest of Louis' family had grown tired of waiting for her and left her under Devon's careful watch. Ever the gentleman, he performed his duty without complaint. Upon his arrival, Louis told him gratefully that we would forever be in his debt for handling his mother so well. I turned to see the glint in Maya's eye as she imagined how she would collect on this debt.

The evening was filled with meaningful toasts from many of our family members and friends. I was completely overcome with emotion as I surveyed the room. So many of my favorite people had traveled here to share this wondrous event with me. I was flooded with memories while I studied each of their faces and remembered with fondness (and some embarrassment, quite frankly) the experiences we had shared. I had grown into the Sydney Durand I am today based in large part on the amazing people right in front of me.

By the end of the evening, our guests were all happily acquainted and perhaps a little tipsy. OK, maybe slightly drunk would be a better description. Thankfully, my family had been conservative with the alcohol this evening, thereby removing the opportunity for colorful stories being told about them the next day. I think the hangovers they'd had the day after our French wedding still lingered rather vividly in their minds. If they did manage a repeat of their drunken episodes at tomorrow's wedding, they would be fortunate enough to have access to all the necessary ingredients for my dad's tarlike hangover remedy.

During the last fifteen minutes of dinner, our fathers decided they would make their toasts. Michel began and told a loving history of Louis' life (as translated by Louis, so you had to wonder a *little* about the actual content of his speech). The lack of bawdy jokes coupled with the laughter from the French posse following certain portions of his speech, led me to believe Louis had censored the good material. I felt a pang of jealousy as I knew I wouldn't have this option once my father got hold of the microphone. Steeling myself for the worst, I drained the remainder of my glass of champagne and flagged down the waiter for another one.

At the conclusion of Michel's toast, my father stood up and smiled at the crowd. He cleared his throat and we were off and running.

"I've been lucky enough for the past twenty-one years to be the father of this incredible young woman. She has surprised me again and again with her intelligence, her tenacity and her endless capacity for empathy. I've watched her stumble through the wonders of dating and have had to tolerate a long procession of men who were simply not good enough for her. Imagine my surprise when she brought home a Frenchman, of all people, and told us she was going to marry him! She didn't even give us time to talk her out of it!"

The room erupted into raucous laughter, with the French posse laughing the hardest of all following Louis' translation.

He paused and gazed at me with tenderness. "I didn't think you would ever find a man who'd be good enough for you, Duck. But you're a most determined young woman. Not only did you find him, but you were brave enough to grab him right away and not let go. And you didn't give a crap what anyone thought about it. You made me so proud, my little Duck."

He kissed me on the cheek and hugged me. "I love you."

I nodded, my eyes swimming with tears.

My dad then raised his glass to the room. "May Duck and Louis have a long and happy life together."

Everyone applauded and took a long sip of their drinks.

As the commotion died down, my dad turned to Louis, microphone still in hand. "And my previous conditions still apply. If you cause her any pain, I'll break your kneecaps." He then patted Louis lightly on the cheek and hugged him.

Those who had paid attention to my dad's last comment burst out laughing. The remainder looked around in confusion. I shook my head and sincerely hoped Louis wouldn't translate the last tidbit for his family. I wasn't sure if they would find my father's declaration funny or not. Americans already had a reputation for violence; he certainly didn't need to reinforce it.

As Louis and I said goodnight to our guests, I was filled with hope for tomorrow. I was so close to the wedding of my dreams. (Well, I hoped I was. I wasn't sure I could take any other last minute glitches. Keep your fingers crossed for me.) I was giddy at the prospect of donning my beautiful gown and walking down the aisle towards my incredible husband. It may have been the champagne mixed with the high I felt from my dad's sentimental toast, but I felt so happy I thought my heart was going to burst. Kate and I walked back to the hotel, hand in hand, singing, *I'm Getting Married in the Morning.* (*My Fair Lady*? Come on! It's both a Broadway show AND an incredible movie starring Audrey Hepburn!) A sure sign I was deliriously happy, since my singing voice is atrocious.

I almost forgot to tell you! An unforeseen bonus to tonight's festivities was my mom telling me about a mix up with my aunt's airline tickets. Somehow, not only had she managed to miss the rehearsal dinner, but she would also barely make the ceremony. I was thrilled at this turn of events, since my aunt's favorite sport is to give me a hard time. (I'm not sure what great sin I've committed to make her hate me as she does, but she's never said a nice thing either to or about me.)

Wait a minute. My mom is the one who made the reservations for her. There's no way my mom would have made such a mistake. Unless, she was giving me one last gift before the wedding. Not having to set eyes on my aunt until the ceremony was over. Thank you, Mom. Now all I had to worry about was whatever Simone had in store for me...

Chapter Thirty-One

Do you remember when I said I had made it to the wedding of my dreams? Yes, of course you do, since that was just last night. Well, this was an incredibly stupid thing for me to say. One would think, after all the craziness I've been through in the past year, the past month, the past week (take your pick), I would finally catch a break. One would think I would be able to leisurely enjoy the last few hours before my wedding with my closest friends and family. One would think I would be allowed a little peace and quiet FOR ONCE. No, no and no.

Deep breath, Sydney. Clearly, I have some explaining to do. OK, I don't know if you remember this, but shortly before I met Louis, I had this crazy dream about my imaginary wedding and all sorts of ridiculous things went wrong. My wedding dress was misplaced, the flowers were ruined and my bridesmaids dropped out of the ceremony like flies. I couldn't help but remember this dream since one event which took place on my actual wedding day was eerily similar. Perhaps similar is not strong enough of a word. It was the EXACT same thing that happened in my crazy dream. The worst possible thing that could happen to any woman on her wedding day. You guessed it! My wedding gown was, in fact, missing.

I had assumed my parents had kept it with them following their transport of this precious cargo to the hotel and I would retrieve it from my mom's care the morning of the wedding. The rehearsal dinner had been all consuming and I hadn't even thought to ask my mother what she had done with my gown. Then, the morning of my wedding, the one I had been waiting a lifetime for, I called my mom to ask her if I could come pick up my dress.

The other end of the phone was silent. That was odd. I *had* heard my mother say hello, hadn't I?

I cleared my throat. "Mom? Are you there?"

She stammered. "Um, Sydney, have you checked your closet?"

I was confused. "Why would it be in MY closet? Don't you have it?"

I heard my mom whispering furiously in the background. What was she up to?

She coughed in an exaggerated fashion. "OK, honey, I don't want you to panic, but..."

You have to be fucking kidding me. Has everyone missed out on the most basic Sydney-handling instructions??? The FIRST and ONLY thing I'm going to do when someone tells me not to panic, is PANIC. And do you want to know why? Because whenever someone tells you not to panic, it's DEFINITELY time to panic!!!

I took a deep breath. "Why shouldn't I panic?" My voice was strangely calm.

My mom's voice; however, was shaky. "Well...when we got here yesterday...I, um, asked the concierge to deliver your dress to your room. I thought it would make you happy to see it sitting there when you arrived."

I knew the dress was not in the closet in the bedroom since I had unpacked last night. There had been plenty of room for all our pre and post-wedding ensembles. A pit started to form in the depths of my stomach. I was getting married in seven hours and I didn't have a wedding dress. I DIDN'T HAVE A WEDDING DRESS!!! I had no idea what I was going to do. It's not like I had a backup dress. I mean, who could possibly be prepared for this kind of scenario? As the anxiety overwhelmed me, my whole body began to shake.

"Syd? Are you there?" My mom's voice was becoming hysterical. "Is it possible there's another closet in your room? It is a suite, right?"

I jumped to my feet, dropped the phone and ran to the living room, only tripping four times on the way. (I *am* a klutz, after all. A klutz in panic mode is a disaster waiting to happen.) There were two other closets. Could it be? I ran over to the first one and wrenched open the door to find…an ironing board. I held my breath and opened the other closet door to find…extra blankets. Awesome! Maybe I could fashion them into a makeshift wedding dress. Maya could bedazzle them or maybe we could sew some fresh flowers onto them…oh my God! I've just lost my mind. Right here, right in front of your very eyes.

I couldn't even imagine not getting married in my beautiful dress. You remember it, don't you? I've certainly described it to you often enough. But let me remind you of the absolute perfection I had chosen. The white satin fitted bodice had spaghetti straps and was intricately beaded in the most beautiful floral patterns. The white tulle skirt was floor length with a hint of a train. Because of the multiple layers of tulle, the skirt was very full and small patterns of beadwork had been woven into the design. It was breathtaking and it fit me perfectly. Best of all, I felt like a princess, as every woman should on her wedding day.

When the reality of my missing dress ultimately hit me, I collapsed on the floor in a heap and began to sob.

Louis had just gotten out of the shower and came running into the room, a towel flapping around his waist.

"*Mon coeur?* What is the matter?"

I kept sobbing, "My dress..."

He was baffled. "What about your dress?"

I pointed back to the bedroom. He looked between me and the door to the bedroom and walked over to the door cautiously. I then heard him pick up the phone from the floor, ascertain my mom was on the other end and speak to her for a few minutes.

When he returned to the living room, he was dressed in a t-shirt and jeans. He knelt next to me and began to rub my back.

"Syd, it is going to be OK."

I stared at him in disbelief. "How?"

He sighed. "We will find your dress. Do not worry."

That was it. "Are you serious? Don't worry? DON'T WORRY?"

He put his hand on my shoulder. "*Mon coeur...*"

I shook my head and got up. "This is BULLSHIT. After everything we've gone through. After everything it took to make it to this day."

I began to pace the room as Louis stared after me. He must've thought I had finally lost it. Wait, I *had* lost it, hadn't I? I don't think I can tell you for sure. But, please, what woman wouldn't lose it in this situation? Crazy or not? No DRESS on your wedding day? There's no sane way to deal with this kind of crisis.

I took a deep breath and tried to slow down my thought process. Yeah, good luck with that, Syd. I held my head in my hands. "This can't be happening. I can't think of any way out of this mess."

Louis ventured into the conversation I was having with myself. "Your mom has every employee of this hotel looking for your dress at this very moment. We will send our family members out to look too if necessary."

Our families. Abruptly a very disturbing thought occurred to me. I snapped my head back to him. "You know, if it weren't for your mother and her four fucking suitcases, we could've been able to fit my dress in the van with us and I wouldn't be in this situation!!!"

At last, I had someone to hold responsible for this atrocity. And it felt good! Right now, I didn't really care if it were entirely her fault or not. Louis certainly could have told her she couldn't bring all four bags with her, but he chose not to. He hadn't wanted to engage in *that* battle. His decision had just bit him in the ass. Hard.

Louis studied me, weighing his options of how to respond to this statement. He knew there was a great amount of truth to what I had said, but probably wanted to protect his mother from my wrath.

He opened his mouth to speak. I held up my hand to silence him. "Do NOT even think of defending her right now."

He sighed. "Syd, we will find the dress."

My eyes widened in mock surprise. "Really? Well, if you're sure, then there's no reason to be worried." Is he kidding me? Patronizing me like that? Acting like it's no big deal that my dress is GONE?

Suddenly, the pent up rage I had against his mother burst. I was absolutely livid at the thought of all the hoops I had jumped through for her. I thought of all the costume changes, the endless parade of visitors I was pranced around in front of and most of all, the number of humiliating performances she required me to give. I began to seethe with anger as I thought of the various times she had laughed heartily at my expense. And now, because of her selfish need to have every possible clothing option available to her for a TWO DAY trip, I didn't have my wedding dress. Something *had* to be done.

I hadn't noticed it, but my hands were balled into fists and I was shaking with fury from head to toe. I met Louis' gaze and found he was looking at me with an expression of pure panic on his face. This is highly unusual for someone as calm as my husband, but I believe it was clear to him, his mother should fear for her safety at this moment in time.

I started for the door and Louis instantly pulled me into his arms. "Syd, please calm down."

I made a futile attempt to escape, flailing my arms uselessly against his iron grip. "I'm *perfectly* calm. I just need to *talk* to your mother."

Suddenly, there was a knock at the door. Louis released his grip and sprinted over to it. If his mother were on the other side of it, he would need to remove her from my sight *tout de suite.* Thankfully for all parties involved, he opened the door to find Zoe and Maya bearing gifts. Zoe had a pint of Ben & Jerry's Chocolate Therapy and Maya had a bottle of tequila and three tumblers. (Apparently shot glasses were too small for this type of occasion.) What an interesting pair they made. It was easily enough to distract me, if only for a moment.

Zoe came over to me and pulled me into her arms. "Listen, sweetie. I know this sucks. I know you're scared and pissed and…outraged. But I promise you, it *will* be OK." She had that right. I was pretty damn outraged. At the hotel. At my crazy mother-in-law. At the world. But what good would it do me? It wasn't going to make my dress reappear.

I sighed and squeezed her tight. "Thank you. I really want to believe you, but…"

Maya rubbed my back. "Syd, I guarantee you, the hotel staff will find your dress." I would later discover she threatened to have her extensive and well-traveled network ensure this hotel paid for their extreme carelessness in losing one of their bride's gowns.

I turned to Maya. "I wish I had your confidence."

She smirked. "Of course you do."

I gazed miserably back at her. "What if you're wrong?" Now, if Kate had told me my dress would turn up, I would *have* to believe her, because as we know, she's always right. But Kate was nowhere to be found. She was most likely leading the dress recovery expedition. If it were in the hotel, she would find it.

Maya rolled her eyes at me. "When has *that* ever happened?"

Zoe rolled her eyes at Maya. "Plenty of times." Then she turned to me. "Instead of reliving all those fun stories, let's talk about a backup plan."

Maya shot daggers at her.

Zoe didn't even flinch. "Just in case we need it."

Maya scoffed. "You won't need it, but if for some really bizarre reason, your dress is not found, we can modify your rehearsal dinner dress into a wedding dress."

I gawked at her. "Pink? I'm going to get married in a PINK dress?" Simone would LOVE that. Maybe she was behind this whole thing. Maybe she didn't like my dress and plans to force me to wear one of her choosing. OK, MAYBE your overly stimulated brain is carrying your delusions a little too far. Get it together, Syd.

Zoe laughed. "You would've loved the idea as a little girl."

I threw my hands up in the air. "I was seven years old! I really liked pink!"

Maya cleared her throat. "Sydney. Relax."

I gave her a murderous look. She knew how I felt about being told to relax. Especially in a situation like this! Who could possibly relax now? I eyed Maya, focusing on the bottle of tequila in her hand. I bet a little liquor would help me relax.

I held out my hands and she gave me the bottle and one of the glasses. After sitting down at the table and pouring myself a generous shot, I turned to Maya.

"So, how exactly, would you modify my dress from last night?"

She brightened. "Well, there's this, um, costume shop up the street."

I closed my eyes and exhaled slowly. I then opened my eyes, downed my generous shot in one grossly unladylike gulp and returned my attention to Maya.

I grimaced from the aftershock of the tequila. "Please, go on."

She faltered slightly. "There's an ivory lace gown in the window. The bodice is absolutely hideous…"

Zoe imparted a meaningful look at Maya, making it very clear that her last comment was not helping and she needed to get to the point.

Maya exhaled quickly. "The skirt of the gown is made of this really delicate lace. It's floor length and must have tons of layers of crinoline underneath because it is a pretty full skirt. We could hack off the hideous bodice and attach the skirt to your existing dress, using the pink lace skirt as an overlay to cover the Frankenstein job we'll have to do to piece it together."

I pondered her idea for a second. Zoe jumped in for the final sell.

"And remember, I brought my veil as your something borrowed. The color is somewhere in-between your white dress and antique ivory, so it should blend nicely."

The ticking clock signaled it was eleven in the morning, leaving us six measly hours until the wedding. I looked back at Maya, tears forming in my eyes.

"OK," I whispered.

Maya leapt into action. "I'm going to go to the costume shop now and work my magic." She was gone before I could even say good-bye.

Zoe sat down at the table next to me. "Do you need anything?"

I nodded, taking a moment to formulate my thought. "Will you help me kill my mother-in-law?"

Zoe cackled. I smiled weakly and poured myself another shot.

She squeezed my hand gently. "That's the last one you get, my friend. This day will be more than enough to handle completely sober."

For the next hour, I paced the room, desperately wondering what garment I would be wearing to the wedding ceremony today. The hotel still hadn't located my dress and there had been no word from Maya as to the status of the dress with the hideous bodice. It was five hours until the wedding and the stress was becoming more than I could handle. Zoe insisted on staying with me until we had a game plan in place. Since Louis was out scouring the hotel for my dress, I think she was worried I might target his mother if left alone with my thoughts for too long. And she was absolutely right…

At noon there was a knock at the door to our suite. Zoe and I looked at each other in confusion. Who could *that* be? We hadn't ordered room service and any person we knew would have called the room first to gage my mental state. They wouldn't have been daring enough to walk right in to the lion's den.

I cautiously walked over to the door and peered through the peephole. Whoever was had knocked was pretty damn short, since I could only see a tuft of blond hair. As I wondered who it could be, I heard a very distinctive, "Allô?"

I froze. It was Simone. She was on the other side of the door. She was purposely putting herself in my path. How was I going to keep from killing her? Well, OK, not actually killing her, but I was pretty sure I wanted to wring her neck!

I stared at Zoe helplessly. "It's Simone! *Why* is she here?"

She seemed as confused as I did. "Open the door and find out." She paused. "And be nice."

Be nice? Really? I sighed. Fine, I would do my best to be NICE. As I reached for the doorknob, I realized my hands were shaking even more than before. Was it the rage charging through my veins? The outrage? The indignation? Whatever you label it, I was still fucking pissed off at her.

I opened the door and tried to smile. I don't think I was very successful due to the look of unease on her face. She smiled tentatively and offered me a white garment bag.

I found myself suddenly unable to breathe. What was in the bag? I had worn so many dresses of her choosing in France and I hated every single one of them. She and I were at completely opposite ends of the spectrum in terms of our preferred style and I had accepted that. I had endured being her Barbie doll for the sake of her family and friends, but I had no intention of doing so here. On MY turf. On MY big day. Especially not when she had been involved with the disappearance of my dress.

Zoe helped me into a chair. "Syd, breathe. It's just a garment bag."

I started laughing. *Just* a garment bag! She had never been on the receiving end of one of these things. She had *no* idea of the endless possibilities of *just* a garment bag.

The giggles fizzled out when I discovered Simone starting at me as though I were crazy. Well, in truth, I was crazy, but I shouldn't let her see that. A girl had to maintain some privacy and, um, some sense of decorum. I cleared my throat, thanked Simone for the dress (I was assuming it was a dress and not a pantsuit or kulats or God knows what else…) and took the garment bag from her. I then laid the bag on the couch, swallowed my fear and unzipped it. The contents shocked me more than I can say.

She had found my dress. SIMONE had found my dress! It had somehow ended up in a completely different bag than the one I had packed it in before I gave it to my parents, but I wasn't going to dwell on details.

I breathed a sigh of relief and sank to the floor in complete exhaustion. I glanced from Simone to Zoe with an absurdly large grin as tears of joy spilled from my eyes.

Just then Louis burst into the room. He took in the whole scene with a bewildered air.

Zoe approached him carefully. "Your mom found the dress."

Louis slapped his hand to his head and laughed. "Of course she did."

Right behind Louis was one of the hotel managers. His name was Bernard and he had a particularly superior manner. I had instantly hated him when he met with us yesterday to discuss a few last minute wedding items.

Bernard sighed expressively. "You see, I told you there was nothing to worry about, Mr. Durand. It turns out the dress had been placed in a storage closet overnight. We're sorry for the...*inconvenience*, but as you can see, we had it cleaned and it looks as good as new."

Louis instinctively came up behind me, ostensibly to hold his blushing bride in his arms. I knew better. Louis was there to make sure I didn't rip Bernard's arms off. Since my physical options were off the table now, I had no choice but to inform Bernard, the smug bastard, I would make it my life's work to ensure he was UNBELIEVABLY sorry. The jackass had the audacity to roll his eyes at me, smirk at Louis and saunter out of the room.

Once Bernard had escaped to another part of the hotel, Louis released me from his hold. I turned towards him to find him speaking rapidly with his mother. After a few minutes, I became impatient.

I tapped Louis on the shoulder. "How did she find it?"

He grinned at me. "She banged down every door in this hotel until she located it."

I was speechless. I had spent the last few hours hating his mother with every fiber of my being. Suddenly I found myself experiencing a very different emotion. I was... grateful. It felt pretty strange to go through such a drastic change in the span of five minutes. But, that was one of the delights of having Simone Durand in your life. You never knew what kind of emotions she would incite.

I approached her tentatively. *"Merci beaucoup*, Simone."

She smiled at me as the tears continued to run down my face. Zoe and Louis watched while she pulled me to her arms and stroked my hair. *"Ma cherie, ça va. Calme-toi."*

I giggled when I discerned she was telling me to calm down. The irony of her statement was priceless considering her role in this morning's wild goose chase. I had to give her the fact that she had ultimately righted the wrong, no matter who the true culprit was. Simone may have been the reason why the gown could not stay under my watchful eye, but my parents were foolish enough to hand it over to the hotel staff, who were then inept enough to misplace it.

While Simone continued to fuss over me, Louis called our families to let them know the dress had been found. Everyone rejoiced that today wouldn't be the day I was committed to an insane asylum. (Although, there's a really nice place right down the street.) Instead, today would be the day Sydney Durand would marry the man of her dreams. For the third time. Are you ready? Because I sure am.

Chapter Thirty-Two

The moment we've all been waiting for has arrived. The wedding ceremony is about to begin. The guests have all arrived, the flowers are in place, everyone is dressed in their wedding finery and best of all, the bride is wearing her gorgeous wedding gown. But before I would be able to walk down the aisle, the wedding gods had one final joke for me to withstand.

As I was preparing to leave my suite on the fourth floor of the hotel and take the elevator down to the terrace where Louis and I were getting married, the power went out. The hotel staff brought numerous glow sticks (Because who needs flashlights?) to light the SERVICE stairwell as Kate, Maya and Zoe helped me and my big, beautiful and rather poofy, dress down the stairs. I almost tripped what seemed like a thousand times, but I made it through unscathed! I have never been so happy to see sunlight.

Fortunately, the power returned so music was playing when Louis and his parents entered the ceremony. Unfortunately, the power went out AGAIN as I came to the top of the stairs with my mother. I was only able to bite back the long list of curse words which ran through my mind because I had just let out a massive string of profanity down the glow stick-lit service stairwell. That was enough for a lifetime. Or, at the very least, enough for one day.

My father looked up at me from the bottom of the stairs, probably hoping I would crack, utter something insanely inappropriate and he would get a good laugh. He was out of luck in this instance. I was going to hold it together if it KILLED me.

A few minutes later, the opening bars of Canon in D drifted over the terrace and my mother and I started slowly down the stairs. As we made our descent, I said a silent prayer that the power would stay on long enough for me to make it to Louis. I didn't think I would be able to stifle foul language through another disaster and I had absolutely no desire to express such vulgarity in front of our guests. Once we reached the bottom of the staircase, my father offered me his arm and the three of us began our journey up the aisle. I let out a sigh of pure happiness. Finally.

With each step I took, I became more aware of the beauty before me. The terrace afforded a breathtaking view of the sun-dappled water surrounded by the stunning coastline. Gorgeous orchids and tulips were artfully arranged with yards of tulle and silk around the circumference of the terrace as well as up the aisle, culminating in an exquisite wedding arch. It was magnificent.

A nudge from my father reminded me I had to keep moving. I smiled as I took in the faces of the most important people in my life, but my heart stopped when my eyes settled on Louis. I was prepared for my husband's gorgeous appearance, but I wasn't prepared for the look of awe on his face when he saw me. This wasn't our first trip down the aisle, after all. Here I was *again*, coming towards him in a beautiful white dress.

But somehow, it was different this time. We had made it through some harrowing times together in our eight months of marriage. We had skipped over the honeymoon period and fallen right into the hard times. It hadn't been pretty, but we had fought through valiantly and had proved to ourselves (and to our naysayers) we had what it took to make our marriage work. And we did all this while still getting to know each other. THAT is quite an amazing feat.

With this last trip down the aisle, Louis and I were solidifying the pact we had made to each other over and over again. We would be together through the good and the bad, the happy and sad…how embarrassing! I'm about to start singing an Al Green song. Let me spare you that horror and make my point in a different manner. As I walked down the aisle towards Louis, we exchanged a look of triumph. We had done it! And anyone who didn't believe we could, could just suck it. That's right! I said, "Suck it!" Coming out on top after eight months of hell gives a lady the right to say such a thing. Deal with it.

Now, let's return to the ceremony already in progress. As you may remember, my incredible boss (and friend), Vivian, had agreed to "officiate" our ceremony. Since Louis and I were already married, she suggested using the time to share the details of our rather *unusual* story with our guests. Vivian crafted a brilliant tale of our courtship, which she had witnessed firsthand and regaled our audience with vivid accounts of the early days, adding in her extensive inside information for fun. At the conclusion of the ceremony, she gave us the book in which she recorded our story, a memento which I will cherish for the rest of my life.

Louis and I then raced back down the aisle in an attempt to run away from the plethora of bird seed being pelted at us. (It was important to me to be kind to the seagulls, but bird seed was surprisingly sharp when thrown with such force.) While shielding my eyes with my bouquet, I took a quick glance behind us to ensure the world's cutest flower girl was close behind (and safe from the hailstorm of birdseed). Though she hadn't been able to walk down the aisle, she very nearly upstaged the bride from the safety of her mother's arms as she clutched her basket of rose petals. She was truly a vision in pink satin and tulle.

After a quick champagne toast with our families at the top of the stairs, Louis and I returned to the terrace to take a myriad of wedding photos. We smiled in various groups and formations, while our guests enjoyed cocktail hour. (We would have been done much faster if our photographer hadn't had to take extra photos to compensate for my annoying tendency to blink in response to any sort of flash.) If it weren't for Pip, who snuck me all of his favorite foods, I would have entered our wedding reception with nothing but champagne in my stomach. I think we can all imagine what a disaster that would have been! And I have come way too far to ruin my dream wedding for something as stupid as not being able to eat.

How do I begin to describe our reception? It was …magical. Let me set the scene for you. Come on, take a deep breath and picture it with me. We had selected a ballroom with an entire wall of windows overlooking the water. The dozen circular tables were covered with white linen tablecloths, vases of orchids and tea light candles. The dim lighting coupled with the white twinkly lights throughout the room gave the space a soft, glimmering quality. And the view of the sun setting was a spectacular beginning to our long awaited party.

Shortly after we were introduced as man and wife, for the THIRD and final time, Louis and I made rounds to the tables of guests. Once Kate and Zoe figured out how to bustle my dress, I was able to move fairly freely. I even regained the ability to walk unassisted!

With each table we went to, I was able to sneak more food. I hit up my friends, relatives and even relative strangers - a few of Louis' new coworkers. (What better way to get to know someone than to share food?) After covering half of the tables in the room, I convinced Louis to return to our table for a quick dinner. About halfway through my meal, I realized I would have to stop if I had any hope of eating wedding cake. And really, what would you rather eat?

The hotel had made a chocolate wedding cake with dark chocolate filling infused with Kahlua. I had very generously conceded to have only one layer of this delectable combination so Louis could have two layers of his Grand Marnier soaked sponge cake with raspberry filling. For those of you who know me well, this was a VERY big deal. Cake is one of my favorite things in the world. In light of this fact, I had already paid one of the waiters to send three pieces of the chocolate cake to our suite, since Louis and I would be feeding each other his cake for the photos. (This was a very calculated decision on my part: if he was dumb enough to smear it on my face, the golden cake would be far less obvious on film.)

Once dinner had been cleared, Louis and I had our first dance. We reprised the song from our first wedding, since the meaning was just as poignant now as it had been then. As we danced to Etta James singing "At Last", I thought about how at our first wedding, I had been overwhelmed with joy that I had found a man who seemed to love me as much as I loved him. Before Louis, I had been convinced I would be alone forever (perhaps a bit dramatic, but true nonetheless). But this time, I knew without a doubt, we were meant to be together for the rest of our lives.

Many couples had trouble making it through the first year of marriage with little in the way roadblocks, yet Louis and I had bulldozed our way through years' worth of problems in eight short months. We were scarred without a doubt, but we had survived and we were ready to fight another day. The impact of this accomplishment hit me as he looked deeply into my eyes. I gazed into his achingly beautiful blue eyes and felt completely content. At last.

Once our dance concluded, Louis kissed my hand tenderly and graciously gave me over to my father. My father smiled at me and then grimaced as Stevie Wonder's "Isn't She Lovely" started to play. I thought it was a beautiful song choice, but my father doesn't understand anything outside of classical music. Or possibly opera. (At least during his sober moments…)

"Duck! Why do you have to play such noise during our dance?"

I was about to answer when he spontaneously dipped me. My dad is surprisingly spry for a man who is built like Santa Claus.

I grinned. "You know you love it, old man."

He winked at me and twirled me around the floor. "So, is the third time the charm, Duck?"

I laughed. "I think so, Dad. I think we can finally relax."

My dad chuckled. "Unless you're dumb enough to get pregnant."

My eyes widened in shock. "Bite your tongue! That's not even *remotely* funny." Seriously, my heart started hammering in my chest at the mere thought of being pregnant right now.

My dad continued to laugh. "You're so impressionable, Duck. You really need to learn to relax."

For the second time that evening, I bit back a very long stream of profanity. In this case though, I wasn't worried about decorum. I simply didn't want to give my father the satisfaction of knowing he had pushed me to utter his favorite catchphrase.

When our dance was over, I kissed my father on the cheek and chose a good vantage point to watch Louis' dance with his mother. As they began to sway to "What a Wonderful World", I thought about the adventure my life had become upon the arrival of Simone Durand. She looks innocent enough, but that's simply her genius disguise. She is crafty, tenacious and extremely passionate. She's someone you definitely want to have on your side, not go up against in battle. I chuckled to myself, knowing even though I had learned to love and appreciate her, I would be battling her in one manner or another for a very long time.

Following these heartfelt dances with our parents, Louis and I headed over to the cake. As we were handed the ceremonial knife, I pleaded with him not to smear cake and/or frosting all over my face. A second later, Maya seemed to melt out of the shadows to give Louis a meaningful look. My interpretation of that look is this: "Ruin the masterpiece I've created on your wife's face and I *will* hurt you. Beyond recognition." That last part came from her newfound status as bride to be. I didn't think it was possible for her to become any bitchier, but clearly I was mistaken.

Whether it was due to Maya's influence or his good heart, Louis didn't smear my face with frosting. After he carefully fed me a bite of cake, he leaned in and whispered he would have frosting sent to our room for later in the evening so he could smear it anywhere he desired. I blushed a very deep shade of red and felt a pleasant tingling sensation from my head to my toes. With all the stress from the last few weeks, our time in the bedroom had been limited. Thank God tonight would be different.

Once I had returned my thoughts to a more chaste nature, it was time to face something I had been dreading for a good portion of the evening. I had purposely bucked wedding reception tradition and scheduled the toasts for the absolute end of the evening, banking on the fact that many people would be too tipsy to remember the contents of the toasts. Please! You know my father is going to embarrass me! The less of the content people can remember, the better. Even if it would be recorded for posterity. I could at least control who would be able to get their hands on a copy of such a recording.

As I was about to hand my father the microphone, along with a very strict warning not to say anything inappropriate, which he would quickly disregard, we accidentally discovered our family was going to expand once more. (No, I didn't take a pregnancy test in the hotel bathroom.) When offered champagne, Zoe inadvertently told us she couldn't drink because of the baby. We all starting screaming and jumping around like lunatics while Zoe blushed profusely. Unfortunately, the microphone had already been turned on for my dad's toast and the ENTIRE room heard the news. After accepting the profuse amount of congratulations, the shocked couple scurried off for a moment alone. Zoe was only five weeks pregnant, but clearly needed to inform her parents quickly due to the slip.

My father cleared his throat and waited for the room to quiet down. He smiled at our guests and took my hand, while Louis held my other hand.

"Lyn and I are honored to have many members of the Durand family with us this evening. We thank you for making the trip." He paused. "We're also thrilled to have so many dear friends of ours and of our darling Duck's here with us. I'm sure you were all as surprised as we were when you found out that our cautious daughter decided to marry a Frenchman after knowing him for a month!"

Raucous laughter broke out. Way to exaggerate, Dad. OK, so it was only a slight exaggeration, since I had known Louis for SIX weeks when we got engaged, but it was still an exaggeration! I took great satisfaction in rolling my eyes at him.

"I'm sure you were also as surprised as we were when it was clear that these two not only loved each other, but they would never give up on each other. They went through a shit-storm in their first few months of marriage and it would've been easier to just walk away." He regarded each of us warmly. "But these two held on, worked through all of it and came out even stronger than before. And they did it with grace, humility and a little bit of alcohol." The room erupted into laughter once more.

My dad banged a knife on the side of his glass to regain the attention of the room. "And I'd just like to say on behalf of my family, we've never been more grateful that Sydney chose this moment to throw caution to the wind. Not only did she find her perfect match in every way, but she gave

her family an incredible new addition." He turned to me.
"Thank you, Duck."

Well done, old man. My dad was such a master at setting
up a smoke screen of sarcasm and sneaking in a heartfelt
moment. He really was a softie at heart.

My dad held his champagne glass in the air.
"Congratulations to Duck and Louis!"

The room broke out into applause. I threw my arms
around my father and squeezed him tight. "I'm so lucky to
have you, Daddy."

He sighed. "I know. Make sure you don't forget it."

My dad cleared his throat. "And now I believe my son-
in-law would like to make a toast to his beautiful bride."

I turned to Louis with a quizzical look in my eyes. This
wasn't part of the plan. He winked at me and took the
microphone from my father.

"Thank you, Ted, for such a beautiful toast. It means
very much to both me and Syd." He smiled genuinely at my
father and then turned to me. "I would like to propose a
toast to my amazing wife, Sydney."

My heart began to beat very quickly as I imagined what
he was going to say. Even though he had known me for a
rather short period of time, he had PLENTY of stories in
his arsenal which many members of our audience hadn't
heard. I exhaled slowly and hoped he hadn't decided to take
my father's place with an embarrassing toast. Of course, he
probably wouldn't see it as embarrassing, but simply good
humor. Oh shit…

He must have seen from the look on my face how
worried I was, so he squeezed my hand. He then turned to
our curious audience.

"Just over fourteen months ago, I met this incredible
woman. She disarmed me from the first moment I met her.
Never in my life had I come across such honesty,
such…vulnerability and warmth. Sydney is the kindest,
funniest, most intelligent woman I have ever met. And

from the moment I touched her hand, I knew I wanted her to be my wife."

There was a collective gasp from the audience.

Louis grinned and said, "And not because I wanted a green card." The room quickly exploded with laughter. Apparently that joke never gets old.

Once the noise died down, Louis took my hand and looked at me tenderly. "I love everything about this woman, right down to her quirks and her rather odd sense of humor. All of it makes her the extraordinary person that she is. A person who stood by her new husband through a long series of difficulties. Through his behaving like, a jackass, quite frankly…"

Laughter flared up throughout the tables once more. My dad gave Louis a nod of approval for working profanity into his wedding toast. He firmly believes a few judiciously placed curse words add emphasis to any point worth making.

Louis chuckled and turned to me once more. "Despite everything we went through, you never gave up on me. You supported me through everything. I am truly the luckiest man in the world, to have married the love of my life. I will be forever yours, *mon coeur*."

For a moment, I simply stared into Louis' eyes as our onlookers applauded. I was absolutely speechless. As my eyes filled with tears of joy, I put my hands on either side of his face, kissed him gently and said, "I will be forever yours, Bluey."

The rest of the evening passed in a blur. Due to the momentous occasion, I allowed myself a couple more glasses of champagne…OK, maybe three glasses, but what kind of trouble could I possibly get into now? (Don't answer that! I know I should NEVER have asked the question! Damn it!)

As Louis and I shared the last dance of the evening, I perused the remaining guests in the ballroom. My college friends were outside on the terrace with a few bottles of champagne, no doubt reliving the craziness of our youth. (I *may* tell you the stories one day, but we have definitely discussed enough turmoil for now.) Nigel and Grace were chatting up a storm with Monique and Sophie as Maya and Devon were twirling around the dance floor. Simone was practicing dance steps from her childhood with her sisters as their husbands observed fondly. Kate and Nick were still trying to capture a photo of Sam in her adorable flower girl dress while Zoe and Charlie snuggled quietly in the corner.

Then my eyes settled on something I hadn't seen in a very long time. It would seem both of my parents were positively giddy about becoming grandparents again so soon and consequently had a bit too much to drink in celebration. My father was pulling out all his dance moves from the fifties, which unfortunately including a lot of twisting and hand jiving. (I'm not entirely sure the entirety of those gestures were authentic dance moves.) My mother's face was as red as the tomatoes she grew in her garden and she was talking far too loudly to anyone who would listen about her next grandchild.

Suddenly, the thought occurred to me *I* wasn't the one getting drunk and doing embarrassing things, yet again. I giggled at my mom's brilliance in requiring my father to wear suspenders to this wedding. No one needed a repeat of his pants dropping episode from our first wedding. (With the force of his dance moves, it would have been a distinct possibility.) After that occurrence, it had taken me a full five minutes to recover from my laughing fit. My father; however, had not been amused.

As the song came to an end, Louis took my hands in his. "Are you happy, *mon coeur?*"

I regarded the motley group of people who had become our collective family and smiled.

"Without a doubt, Bluey."

Epilogue

I can't believe we've finally reached the end of our wedding extravaganza! Louis and I had pulled off three weddings over the course of eight months across two continents involving literally HUNDREDS of people. We had brought our families together to share in the joy, the laughter and of course, a decent amount of embarrassment (to the great delight of both my father and father-in-law). In the end, we had all grown closer together, expanded our cultural palate and made great strides in our pantomiming skills. What language barrier?

After all the activity and emotional turmoil of the last year, I was ready for a period of calm. Wait a minute. Period. When was the last time I had my period? I frantically started looking through my calendar even though I already knew I wouldn't find the familiar "P" notation. Yes, I mark a big, fat letter "P" in my calendar on the first day of my period each month. Laugh all you want! Though, I hardly think this is the time.

Oh my God! This is totally my fault! I shouldn't have made the joke about taking a pregnancy test during the reception at our last wedding.

OK, Sydney, slow down. Take a deep breath.

I couldn't possibly be pregnant. Could I? No. Absolutely not. It was just the stress of the wedding. I mean the WEDDINGS. Plural. Twice the weddings, twice the stress. And stress can absolutely delay your period. It's a well-known fact. It is! Feel free to look it up.

Phew. That was a close one. I'm so relieved!

Shit. Could I really be pregnant? No, no, no, no, no. NO! It simply isn't possible.

I'm going to kill my father.

Author's Note

Thank you so much for reading *French Toast*! If Sydney wormed her way into your heart, or perhaps tickled your funny bone just a little, I would be grateful if you took a few moments to write a review of your reading experience. Amazon or Goodreads; take your pick! Your time, effort and thoughtful words are greatly appreciated! Who knows? You may even wrangle a few unsuspecting folks into giving Sydney's brand of humor a try!

Acknowledgments

I once read that writing the second book is even harder than writing the first. I found this to be absolutely true! I would not have been able to finish Sydney's second adventure without the help of my wonderful family and friends.

To my outstanding husband, Sebastien, who is not only the inspiration for Louis Durand, but also the anchor in my life. Thank you for loving and encouraging me through the journey of the sequel. You never stop inspiring me!

To my beautiful boys, Ryan and Xander, for reminding me what is important in life and for making me smile when no one else can. I love you both deeply.

To my sister, Megan, for being an incredible source of sanity and comfort. I am continually amazed at the amount of faith you have in me. Thank you for once again being an insightful editor, a gifted cover designer and the best friend a girl could ever have.

To my sister-in-law, Jen, for eagerly jumping aboard for another round of editing. I cannot thank you enough for your perspective, your reassurance and your humor. I am truly grateful for your presence in my life.

To my brother, Colin, for being the most honest and kind-hearted person I know. Thank you so much for your love and guidance.

To my brother-in-law, Josh, for the endless encouragement and validation. Thank you for helping me to keep my sense of humor intact!

To my nieces, Sabrina and Skyler, and my nephew, Jackson, for devouring my first book with relish. Thank you for your undying interest and enthusiastic support. I am so lucky to be related to each of you.

To my nephew, Evan, for being such a bright spot in my life. I have a great appreciation for your unique view of the world!

To my wonderful friend, Cathy, for rounding out my trio of editors. Thank you for diving into my family and bringing me the viewpoint of the objective outsider. I am thrilled with your collaboration and touched that you understand and adore Sydney as much as I do.

To my amazing friends, Erica and Jenean, for agreeing to be my beta readers at the last minute. Thank you so much for the last minute polishing you gave to Sydney and her crazy family!

And to all of you who read *French Twist,* for following Sydney on her lengthy journey to happiness. Thank you for appreciating her, quirks and all, along with the wonderful personalities she shares her life with. I hope you will continue to follow her story in the upcoming *French Fry.*

About the Author

Glynis never expected in her wildest dreams to be a writer. After thirteen years in the Human Resources Industry, she decided to stay at home with her two amazing sons. Ever in search of a project, she was inspired to write the story of how she met and married her wonderfully romantic French husband, Sebastien, in six short months. The end result became her first novel, French Twist. As this was just the beginning of their epic love story, Glynis continued to chronicle their adventures in the sequel, French Toast, and is currently working on the third and final installment in the series, French Fry.

When she is not writing, she is trying to keep the peace amongst the three men and two cats in her life, finding missing body parts (Lego pieces are small!), supervising a myriad of homework assignments and keeping a tenuous hold on her sanity by consuming whatever chocolate is in the vicinity.

Connect with Glynis Astie

Blog: www.glynisastie.com

Twitter: https://twitter.com/GlynisAstie

Pinterest: http://www.pinterest.com/glynisastie/

Facebook:
https://www.facebook.com/glynisastieauthor

Also by Glynis Astie

French Twist

French Twist

Sydney Bennett had spent her life in pursuit of perfection. She planned, weighed her options and made careful choices based on calculated outcomes. Through all of her efforts, she had come pretty close to perfection, if she didn't say so herself. She had fled the cold winters in New York for sunny California, found a job that she loved and lived in the same town as her sister, and best friend, Kate. The one area of perfection that had always eluded her was her love life. No matter how hard she tried, she always ended up with a broken heart. After a particularly traumatic breakup, Sydney vowed that she was done with love.

Just as Sydney threw herself into her new plan to forget about men, a handsome Frenchman tossed all of her intentions out the window as he swept her off of her feet. Louis Durand had lived a life filled with excitement and adventure. He was impetuous, intelligent and incredibly charming. So naturally, he scared Sydney half to death. From the moment they met, Louis and Sydney's romance progressed at warp speed. Sydney did her best not to run, but her deep rooted relationship anxiety threatened to provide an easy exit. When Louis mentioned marriage before Sydney even knew his favorite color, she was more than tempted to reach for her running shoes. Will she be able to put her fears aside to follow her heart? The one thing that Sydney will learn is that sometimes perfection comes with a twist...

"It was easy to root for Sydney because she was so darn likeable and her insecurities felt authentic...She made me laugh, she made me cringe with embarrassment and her relationships with her family made me cry (in a good way)."

-Meredith Schorr, author of *Blogger Girl* and *How Do You Know?*

"Based on real life events, French Twist is a beautiful love story that really makes you believe that love at first sight is possible...I look forward to reading more by this talented author!"

-Hilary Grossman, author of *Dangled Carat*

"Sydney Bennett is a mix of artlessness and anxieties with layers of zany...It's light, fun, written with humour and happiness and all of that jumps off the page."

-Cathy Ryan, Between the Lines Book Blog

"I really found the writing of the author refreshing and lively...I found the book quite entertaining... I cannot wait to start with book two."

-Lynelle Clark, Aspired Writer Book Blog

"I thought this book was completely charming, fun, and romantic...You will get wrapped up in the story and swept away by the romance of it all."

Steph, Steph the Bookworm Book Blog

Made in the USA
Middletown, DE
16 April 2015